SilveR dew

suzi davis

central
avenue
publishing
2011

To my boys.

Slugs, snails and puppy-dogs' tails,
and all the love in the world.

silver dew

Chapter One – Running from the Past

Drip. Drip. Drip.

The icy raindrops fell heavily, splattering against my skull and dripping from my drenched hair. I clenched my teeth together tightly, desperately fighting the chills that trembled throughout my body. I pushed the sensations aside in an attempt to detach my mind from my physical self, to withdraw deeper into the quiet depths of my soul. I searched and strained with every last extension of myself for that safe place within, trying to find that intangible sanctuary of focus and power.

The wind rose higher, howling in my ears like the painful screams of a child. The rain pounded down on me relentlessly. It soaked through my clothes and into my skin, drowning me. My whole body began to tremble and vibrate with chills as with each passing second, I became more aware of the world I was so feebly trying to ignore. I had closed my eyes in an attempt to shut it all out but my lack of vision was only intensifying the sensations around me. Raindrops steadily trickled down my neck, sliding down my spine in an ominous chill.

It was all too much. I was miserable, I was afraid, I was exhausted, frozen, and wet. A dampness had set into my bones of which I was sure I'd never truly rid myself. This was torture and there was no reason why it should continue. I had the power to end it – so why didn't I? My necklace was glowing faintly against my chest, its quiet warmth the only comfort this moment had to offer. Its heat increased with my emotions, and as I became more aware of my miserable surroundings, fiery frustration flickered around my heart.

My eyes snapped open.

I found myself staring directly into his intense, gray-blue eyes. He sat so closely that I could have reached out and touched him – but I didn't dare. The smirk that had once pulled up the corners of his lips had now completely disappeared. There was nothing to lighten the overwhelming strength of his steady, ancient gaze. I immediately recognized my own powerful frustration, magnified and reflected back at me ten-fold in his mysterious eyes. His lips pressed together, his eyes narrowed dangerously, accusingly as they darkened to an intense, thunderous gray that bordered on the edge of black. I fought the instinct to shrink back from him.

I determinedly refused to look away. I would not back down - I would not cower before him. The air in the small space between us seemed to crackle with the intensity of our emotions, the vivid focus of our wills. The only sounds were those of the wind stirring the branches over our heads and the steadily falling drops of rain. Our eyes were locked together, unwavering, unblinking.

Drip, drip, drip.

A fat, icy raindrop hit me square on the head. Fresh, freezing rivulets ran down my neck dispersing the meager, lingering warmth under my clothes.

"Enough," I quietly announced. It was an effort not to yell. My whole body began to tremble with violent waves of shivers as my concentration completely fell apart.

Sebastian blinked at the sound of my voice. The fire in his eyes cooled but didn't dissipate entirely. He sighed in frustration.

"This is hard for me too, Gracelynn," he reminded me gently. My eyes tightened into a glare. He sat, quite comfortably, with his back against the tall pine we were sheltering beneath – that *he* was sheltering beneath. I was soaked to the core by the surprisingly heavy summer rains. He was bone dry, miraculously having chosen the only spot in this whole, vast forest that was protected from the driving sheets of rain. "I hate to see you suffer," he murmured in reaction to the accusation in my eyes. He was obviously amused by my irritation; his eyes sparkled, a smile twitched at the corners of his mouth; a dimple was hinted at in his smooth cheek.

"Obviously, this is what *you* want," I retorted but there was only a weary acceptance to my bitter words. I knew why he was doing it, we both did. I spoke my next thought out loud. "But it's not working. I don't think I could possibly want to be dry anymore than I do right now but I still can't make it happen." My words were laden with defeat. I lowered my gaze in shame, hating myself for letting him down, for not being as strong as he expected. For weeks now, Sebastian had been trying to teach me to control and focus my recently rediscovered "magic". But no matter how hard I tried, the only control I could manage was fleeting and weak. The only time my wants were fulfilled by the supposed magic I possessed was when I acted instinctively, without thinking, and when my emotions were strong enough to overpower my rational control. When I was calm and focused, and actually wanted to control my ability, it just wouldn't work even though Sebastian insisted it should.

The stress, frustration and fear of the past few weeks weighed heavily on my shoulders. On top of my most recent failure, it was enough to bring sparkling tears to my eyes. I tried to swallow the miserable sob rising in my chest.

The icy, cold raindrops abruptly stopped hitting me though the sounds of the raging storm continued. I glanced up in surprise to see that the wind had somehow stirred the branches above to form an impossibly effective shield between myself and the storm. Even the wind felt more distant now as the air around me had instantly stilled and already felt warmer than it should. I felt no satisfaction or triumph, for I knew it hadn't been me. I wiped the tears from my eyes and looked back to Sebastian just in time to see his lips move in a silent curse.

He met my questioning eyes with an exasperated sigh. "I want to motivate you, Gracelynn. We both know how important it is for you to learn to control your ability but I just can't seem to push you hard enough. I hadn't meant to let you off so easily." He muttered another curse under his breath, shaking his head.

"That was easy?" I began shivering again as soon as I spoke, the initial comfort of being sheltered from the rain wearing off as I remained chilled in sodden, freezing clothes.

In one smooth, fluid gesture, Sebastian shifted his body towards mine and removed his jacket. He twirled it out and over my shoulders, wrapping me up in it tightly. He did so without hesitation, with no thought for himself. His jacket seemed to have soaked up all the warmth from his body and it instantly soothed and comforted me. I relaxed slightly, pulling it in closer to me and enjoying the sense of warmth and safety. I knew it would be fleeting, just another illusion, a lie I pretended to believe.

"Thank you," I told him quietly. He smiled back at me, all his love for me bright and clear in his eyes. It was impossible not to react to that look. I felt my heart swell and lift within me, my expression softening and a small smile forming despite my misery.

"You're welcome. I know I should push you harder but it's so difficult, Gracelynn. As soon as I see you in pain, all I want is…" As his words trailed off, a strange look came over his face. Not one of frustration or defeat, as I had expected, but one of sudden speculation.

"I'm sorry, Sebastian. Really, it's my fault. I shouldn't-"

My words were drowned out by a sudden gust of howling, icy wind. I hugged Sebastian's warm jacket tighter against my body. The branches above us swayed and bent, submitting to the wind's invisible force. Amazingly, not a single drop touched me, even with the new angle at which the rain fell. Sebastian though, was suddenly getting soaked.

"Sebastian? What…?"

He grinned back at me, the heavily-falling rain instantly flattening his messy, dark hair and dripping from his nose and chin. My features settled into a disapproving frown as I realized what he was up to.

"Stop it. You're going to freeze," I scolded, my irritation adding a slight edge to my typically gentle voice. I started to remove his jacket, fully intending upon giving it back to him but he just grinned at me and shook his head.

"Keep it. It won't make a difference anyway – I *want* to get wet. I want to be cold. I want to do whatever it takes to motivate you, even if that means freezing to death."

I clenched my teeth together tightly. My amber necklace flared against my skin, a steady warmth slowly spreading out from it and across my chest.

"Stop it," I repeated, the beginnings of my anger clear in my voice.

Sebastian's grin deepened, a dimple appeared in his cheek. "I'll drown myself in the rain if that's what it takes to help you," he replied, teasingly. We both knew he was only half-joking.

I watched as the rain soaked into his dark, gray hoodie and his black jeans. The whole time I was quite comfortable - almost warm, my hair and clothes drying quickly while I was completely and impossibly protected from the summer storm. He continued to smile at me in a charming and incredibly irritating way, despite his obvious shivers.

My amber necklace flared even hotter, the heat of it spreading throughout my torso and up my throat to where it smoldered in my eyes.

"Stop it — *now*." My words were firm and commanding, a forgotten strength within them. Sebastian's eyebrows lifted slightly at the tone of my voice. The rain seemed to lighten around him for a second but then it suddenly increased, down-pouring like never before. His smug grin returned.

"You can't beat me like that, Gracelynn," he teased. His smile wavered though as he began to shiver even harder. "Focus. All you have to do is want for me to be dry."

"I do!" I argued in frustration, the power behind my words fading. "I want you to be dry but it doesn't make a difference! I can't do it."

"Focus!" His dark eyes flashed as he spoke, his smile abruptly gone. I couldn't remember him ever having spoken this harshly to me before. "You're not giving it everything you've got."

"I *am*."

The amber pendant burned against my skin, the heat erupting throughout my entire body. I squeezed my eyes shut as tightly as possible, straining with all my might, with all my will to "want" Sebastian to be dry. I began to tremble from the effort.

"Focus," Sebastian repeated. His voice sounded far away now. "Focus on what you want."

I placed a hand over my chest, pressing the teardrop shape of my amber pendant firmly against my skin. I let the world slip away, all the sounds, all the sights, all the miserable sensations. There was nothing left but me and Sebastian, and all that mattered was what I wanted...

"*I want for us to be dry*." The fire from my necklace exploded up my throat and escaped my lips on those whispered words. Complete and total silence settled around us, the sounds of the storm instantly severed from the air.

"Gracelynn?" Sebastian's voice broke through the sudden quiet. The uncertainty behind his words made my eyes pop open in surprise. He was staring at me wide-eyed, his blatant shock obvious.

I tipped my head back and saw bright, blue sky peeking out between the branches of the tall pines above us. The rain had stopped and there were no clouds to be seen. The only evidence of the storm that had been raging moments before was the muddy, needle-strewn ground and the sparkling drops of rain that still dripped from the branches and clung to the ferns around us. The forest was quiet and still, at peace.

I grinned triumphantly, my heart soaring victoriously as the sun warmed me through. I had done it! My joy was short-lived.

"Gracelynn, how did you do that?" Sebastian demanded as he scrambled to his feet. He dropped onto his knees before me in the mud, his hands squeezing my upper arms firmly, his eyes earnest and seemingly afraid as he searched mine for answers. I frowned in confusion, not understanding his sudden intensity or the question. "That shouldn't have been possible," he whispered when I didn't respond. His words hung heavily in the air between us.

I noticed his clothes were dry already, as were mine. I lightly ran my fingers through his soft, black hair – not a trace of dampness to be found.

"I just… wanted us to be dry," I tried to explain. I shifted uncomfortably beneath his steady gaze. "I didn't *exactly* mean for the storm to disappear but I don't understand why you're so upset. You did the same thing once." He obviously didn't know what I was referring to, his eyes squinting slightly as he tried to remember. "In the garden shed, the first day we kissed. That random storm that came out of nowhere and ended so abruptly," I reminded him.

His eyes brightened with understanding and then clouded once more.

"I didn't want that storm to happen, Gracelynn," he denied. "I did want to kiss you - I couldn't help but want it so badly that the opportunity was bound to come up but I didn't want that storm to start or to stop the way that it did. It was just one of the strange events that my presence triggers. But this…" He looked around us wide-eyed, his face paling slightly. "To intentionally stop a naturally-occurring storm in its tracks and to make it completely disappear like that… You said it didn't work that way. I don't understand. Why would you deceive me?" His voice faded to a whisper as he desperately searched my eyes, a sudden, confused panic overtaking his features.

I froze, my whole body instantly tensing as I realized it was happening again. My heart began beating too fast as my own panic set in. I struggled to control my emotions, forcing myself to speak slowly and carefully while staring steadily into his frighteningly unfocused eyes.

"I didn't lie to you; I would never lie to you. I'm not her, Sebastian. I'm not Caoilinn."

"What are you saying?" His eyes filled with confusion. He blinked, looking around, disoriented. "I don't understand. Where am I?" His voice was unsteady, his lilting accent more pronounced as it had once been, so long ago. His eyes darted back and forth, his confusion obvious and overwhelming. Fear gripped my soul.

"I'm Gracelynn," I reminded him softly. I gently placed my hands on each of his cheeks and turned his face back so that his eyes would meet mine. "I'm Gracelynn."

I held my breath as he stared back into my eyes, counting the seconds as they slowly crept by. Like a passing storm, his eyes gradually began to clear and refocus. The wispy clouds of the past were blown back to where they belonged – for now at least. He still looked dazed but I could tell he was himself again. My fear slowly subsided.

"Gracelynn," he whispered back to me. He leant forward to lightly kiss my lips, his relief a match for my own. Just the feel of his warm, soft lips against mine even for that brief moment was enough to set my heart pounding, to erase the rest of my fears. "I don't know what happened just then. I apologize. Sometimes I… forget."

"I know," I quickly reassured him. I buried the sudden, heavy guilt that hit me, lowering my eyes to the forest floor in case he might catch a hint of it. Ever since I had made Sebastian remember his past, he had been having these kinds of episodes. The memories that had initially been so clear to him had quickly dissipated into a thick fog so that he now had to search to remember even the simplest of things. He often became confused, frequently calling me Caoilinn or becoming so lost in his own thoughts that I would have to repeat his name several times before he would come back to the present. Since the day he had remembered, the day we had started running, he also had frequent, painful headaches and tossed and turned each night, plagued once again by the nightmares from his past. And it was all my fault.

"It's not your fault," he argued, guessing at my thoughts.

I sighed, feeling miserable once more. "It is. I wish I'd never told you your true name. I don't want you to be… like this. I want you to forget again," I confessed.

"And I want to remember. I never want to forget you or anything else, ever again." He pulled me into his arms and I closed my eyes. For a moment, I relaxed in the warmth of his embrace, the comfort of his body so close to mine. I let myself forget about the fact that I had just made an entire weather system cease to exist because I had "wanted to be dry" or that my boyfriend, the love of my life and my soulmate, had just mistaken me for Caoilinn, a reincarnation of my soul from thousands of years in the past. I didn't even worry about the mud that we were now both kneeling in, that was steadily soaking into my stained and worn, once-perfect designer jeans. In that moment, none of it mattered beyond the fact that we were together and safe, for now. I sighed, feeling almost content for a heartbeat.

"Caoilinn could never have made an entire storm just disappear like that. Instead of fading away, the magic inside of you must have grown stronger with time. It's fermented, like a fine wine," he mused, his warm breath tickling the side of my neck as he spoke.

A thought occurred that I didn't like one bit but I forced myself to say it aloud. I couldn't quite meet Sebastian's eye, so I held myself more tightly against him.

"Or perhaps she did deceive you. What if Caoilinn lied?"

Sebastian slowly pulled away from me, forcing me to meet his gaze. He shook his head in denial as I'd known he would. His brows pulled down into a stubborn frown, his dark eyes smoldered beneath his long, thick lashes. "You shouldn't take something I said in a moment of confusion so seriously. I have faith that you would never deliberately deceive me. My rational mind knows that it's not even a possibility for you to have lied. You didn't lie," he repeated.

"We were talking about Caoilinn, not me," I reminded him gently.

He shrugged, flashing me his most charming grin as his expression lightened and brightened. "Sometimes it's the same thing."

"Perhaps," I hedged.

He laughed softly at my obvious denial, leaning down to sweetly kiss my lips. "I may have been drawn to you because of who you once were, but I love you now because of everything you are today. I love *you* – Gracelynn Stevenson," he declared, smiling down at me affectionately. "Never doubt or forget that."

"I'll try." I smiled back at him playfully. "But it is nice to be reminded."

"I will tell you that I love you for every single day of eternity – I promise," he responded without hesitation. His solemn words were lightened by his teasing grin. Then his lips came down to meet mine in a kiss so sweet and simple, it left me breathless.

I reluctantly broke away from him, my heart thudding wildly in my chest, a rosy flush blossoming over my cheeks. "We should keep going," I reminded him breathlessly.

"I agree," he responded, pulling me closer, a smile brightening his intense eyes.

"You know what I mean," I reproached, attempting to be stern. His smile broadened upon hearing my tone, his eyes laughing at me. "The Others are still close."

The smile abruptly disappeared from his face. He sighed and slowly moved back. "I know. The closer they get... I can almost *sense* them."

My eyes automatically began searching the shadowy forest around us. I knew that if any of the Others were close enough for us to see, we wouldn't be standing there still. It was an instinctual reaction. The moment Sebastian spoke of the danger, I felt almost like I could sense it too - lurking nearby, waiting, watching, driving us further and further east.

"They might have been close enough to see the storm disappear, and if they did, they will know it was you. We may have given them a glimpse of your true strength."

"Maybe they'll be afraid," I suggested - I knew I was. It was starting to really sink in just what I had done and how impossible it should have been.

"Or maybe they'll feel threatened enough to make their move before a fifth joins them," Sebastian warned. "You're right – we shouldn't stay here. Let's put as much distance between ourselves and this place as we can before nightfall."

With that being said, he grabbed my hand and led me forward through the thick forest brush. He was always like that, as soon as he'd chosen a path, he was already on it.

We traveled at a light jog, using deer trails to make our travel easier where we could, skipping over twisted roots and scrambling up and down the rough, rocky terrain as we headed further east. We were traveling through Quetico Provincial Park, along the border between Ontario and the United States. It was a world-renowned destination, known for its back country camping and canoeing. Only, we didn't have a canoe so we spent our days navigating the highlands and avoiding the low-lying bogs while following the riverbanks and lake shore as best we could. Miraculously, and mostly due to Sebastian, we continued to somehow travel eastward without getting too lost. Sebastian expected us to reach the easternmost edge of the park within a few more days and then it would be onward to Thunder Bay, Ontario. Beyond that, I didn't know what, if anything, Sebastian had in store for us.

We had begun our journey from Victoria, British Columbia, traveling on Sebastian's motorcycle. At first we had slept quite comfortably in cabins or motels and eating at restaurants as we made our way along Highway 1 through the provinces and eastward across Canada. I supposed the Others must have thought we had it too easy, and suddenly whenever we tried to go near a city, *something* would always happen to deter us. This was when we started camping on the side of the road and eating gas station foods or stopping at the occasional roadside hut or diner. Apparently we still weren't suffering enough. Nearly a week ago, Sebastian's motorcycle had suddenly stopped running. The gas tank had been full, the engine purring along smoothly one second then rapidly losing power the next. Sebastian had pulled over to the side of the road and the engine came to a stuttering stop, never to start again. That was the first time he had sensed the proximity of the Others as he suddenly knew with a deadly certainty that there were four of them and they were only a few kilometers behind us. We'd had no choice but to run into the wilderness of the nearby Quetico Park. At the time we had feared they were ready to make their final move but it now appeared that they had merely been watching us from as close as they dared, pushing us to see how far we'd go. This felt like it was a game to them, and Sebastian assured me it most likely was; a deadly game that must be played by their rules. We could only hope that I would be able to regain the full potential of my magic before this game came to an end.

Our journey had gone from bad to worse once we were forced to flee on foot. It had been a tough trek through Quetico and our progress had been agonizingly slow. At least we were able to travel light with nothing but the clothes we wore and one small pack on each of our backs. Sebastian was quite a skilled outdoorsman; he built a fire each night with ease, hunted rabbits, birds, squirrels and even chipmunks. He found edible plants and berries, fresh water and always kept us traveling in the right direction.

I might have enjoyed spending so much time outside, having never been allowed to go camping myself, if it weren't for the circumstances. Though some things were unpleasant, the novelty of it all and the fact that I was with Sebastian stopped me from despairing completely, at least for the most part.

Our journey since leaving the West Coast had been both amazing and horrifying. There were some beautiful moments and amazing sights we had seen as we traveled across the country. The towering, majestic peaks of the Rocky Mountains, the low-lying valleys, and flat, never-ending plains of the prairies, the breath-taking, natural magic of aurora borealis, the storms, the sunsets and spending every night in one another's arms. But there was also the constant fear and paranoia. The random and alarming reminders that the Others were close by, that they were following us, herding us towards… something. And there was also the pressure that had been placed upon me to learn to control my magic so that we might hunt down and destroy the Others before they could do the same to us.

It had been over a month ago when it had started, since the day Sebastian had remembered. The day when I had spoken his true name, unheard for hundreds of years. The day when I had unknowingly renewed the Binding between our souls and reawakened the dormant magic within me. The day when all hell broke loose. The day when we had begun the never-ending run for our lives.

As I jogged along beside Sebastian through the woods, my thoughts began to drift back in time to that wonderful and terrifying day when it had all began…

Sebastian grabbed my hand in an urgent grip as we raced out of his bedroom and down the hall in the Jensons' house. It vaguely surprised me when I felt no pain in my arm though the memory of the Binding was fresh enough to still make me wince in anticipation.

He hauled me along behind him without glancing back. I nearly tripped as I scrambled down the stairs after him, trying my best to keep up with his frantic pace. I slammed into his back at the bottom of the stairs where he had come to an unexpected halt. He cocked his head to one side, listening, standing so still he barely breathed. My heart pounded in my ears as I strained to listen, my breathing raspy and unsteady from fear.

That was when I noticed the house was quiet, a deadly silence hanging over everything like a heavy mist. The warmth and familiar sense of comfort that usually filled the Jensons' home had vanished. The quiet creaks and groans of the original wood floors, the sounds of the old beams expanding under the morning sun's warmth, the vibrant hum of life that filled the air — it was all gone. There was nothing but silence.

"Don?" Sebastian called Mr. Jenson's name quietly and apprehensively as he slowly stepped away from the staircase, towing me along protectively behind him. Together we quietly inched around the base of the stairs, my heart in my throat, my hand clammy and limp within Sebastian's warm, firm grip. "Don?"

Sebastian paused again by the kitchen door, his hand squeezing mine more tightly as he reached for the door handle.

Creak.

The unexpected sound of the loose floorboard from the hallway above our heads made us both flinch. The tense silence lasted for a split-second longer and then suddenly heavy footsteps were pounding down the hall above us.

"Run!" Sebastian yelled. His words were completely unnecessary; my heart was already racing, my whole body so tense that I was in motion the instant the first heavy footfall fell.

Sebastian pushed me ahead of him as we raced through the kitchen and out the side door of the Jensons' home. We sprinted around the house, my mind only registering the slightest sense of relief to see that no one was waiting for us in front. He leapt onto his motorcycle, kicking up the stand it rested on and thrusting his only helmet into my hands. Without hesitating once, I slid onto the bike behind him and stuffed the helmet onto my head. It seemed ridiculous to me that I had once been so afraid of riding on his bike when now I couldn't wait for its engine to come roaring to life. Sebastian fired up the engine and accelerated almost simultaneously. I barely had time to wrap my arms tightly around his waist before we lurched forward, the back tire spitting out gravel as we swerved around my car that I'd parked so close to his bike.

"NOOOOO!"

I recognized Walter's howl of rage behind us, much too close for comfort.

I was nearly frozen with fear but somehow I managed to turn my head over my shoulder just enough to glance back towards the Jensons' house as we peeled out onto the quiet, morning street.

The sun was so bright, it made it difficult to discern many details in that one, fleeting glance. But I immediately recognized Walter's dark silhouette as he angrily kicked in the door of my black Austin Mini. It was more than confirmation enough that he was working with the Others and had not just been looking out for my mother's interests as her new confidante. Another figure, who I figured to be male though he was shorter and slighter in build, stood just behind Walter, motionlessly watching us race away. And I just caught a glimpse of a third tall, dark figure rounding the corner of the house before the hedge at end of the driveway blocked them all from my view. A cold shiver ran down my spine as paralyzing fear overwhelmed me.

I hugged Sebastian even tighter and squeezed my eyes shut, wishing the nightmare away. I took several slow, deep breaths through my nose before I regained enough control to speak.

"They're not following," I forced myself to call out between clenched teeth.

I sensed, rather than saw Sebastian's nod of response. He didn't ease up on the throttle one bit, leaning into the next corner at nearly double the speed limit. I felt like I was going to throw up as the bike tipped down, leaning dangerously close to the asphalt before coming out of the curve.

Over the sound of the rushing wind in my ears and the frantic pounding of my heart, I could just make out Sebastian's steady chant that sounded more of a frantic plea: "I want for us to be safe. I want for there to be only four. I want for us to be safe. I want for there to be only four. I want…"

He had told me moments before, five would be enough for the Others to combine their wants and overpower our desire to escape - and to live. I had only seen three but what if there were more still inside the house or in the back yard? What if there were five, or even more? Tears trickled down my cheeks and were whipped away by the wind as I wondered for how much longer we were going to live…

I SHOOK AWAY the memory with a shudder.

"Are you alright?" Sebastian had pulled us to a halt as soon as he felt my hand tremble. He turned to face me, his gray eyes softened with concern.

"I'm fine," I lied. He rolled his eyes at my generic response but thankfully let it go. I hated bringing up the past; nothing good ever seemed to come from it.

Sebastian looked around at the lengthening shadows in the forest, glancing quickly up at the fading blue sky. "It must be getting close to six o'clock by now. Let's find a spot to make camp for the night and then I'll go hunting for dinner."

I nodded my agreement, forcing out a smile as I pushed the frightening memories away.

"You take such good care of me," I teased. Sebastian laughed in response.

"Yes, kidnapping you two weeks before you graduated from high school so that you could run for your life across the country with me was extraordinarily responsible. I'm actually quite impressed with myself; I've turned you into a runaway and a dropout. You're welcome, by the way," he added with another laugh. I was glad to see he was smiling but nonetheless, I continued in a firm but gentle tone.

"You didn't kidnap me – I'm not a child and I *chose* to come with you."

"What choice did you have? If you had stayed…" His smile faded with his words.

"I had already chosen you," I reminded him softly. I held out my right arm, slowly turning it over to indicate the intricate, black design of my tattoo that twisted in and around itself as it wrapped up the full-length of my arm and disappeared beneath my stained t-shirt sleeve. "Before you remembered the Others, before we knew what kind of danger we were in, I had already chosen to be with you." I twiddled with the ancient ring on the fourth finger of my left hand as I spoke, my fingers stroking the twisted metal and rubbing the small, warm amber heart at its center.

Sebastian's eyes followed my movements, a small smile curving his lips as he watched me play with the ring.

"You were so angry when you took my ring back. I half-thought you were doing it to spite me, and half-hoped that you might be motivated by something more."

"It was mostly-spite," I retorted but now with a smile of my own.

Sebastian grinned back at me, pleased by my playfulness. "I'll turn that spite-ring into an engagement-ring yet," he promised with a cheeky sparkle in his eye. "Come on, let's choose a campsite."

Sebastian took my hand, lacing my fingers through his as he slowly continued down the trail. I could already see an open area up ahead that would be as good a spot as any. It would appear that at least some of Sebastian's wants were still being fulfilled.

I followed Sebastian down the trail but once he had turned away,

I let my smile fade. He hadn't been able to hide the strain in his eyes and the forced quality to his laughter that had now left me ill at ease. I knew he must sense the change in the air that had begun not long after the storm had disappeared. There was a strange, expectant sense of gathering catastrophe of which even I was aware. It was a heavy, intangible quality to the air, a mood emphasized by the evening light and eerie silence, unexpected in the forest. I knew, with an undeniable certainty, that something was about to happen. Something had changed.

Chapter Two - Fire

I was surprised when Sebastian left me to set up camp while he hunted. Apparently, he was trying to pretend nothing was wrong – which made me even more certain that something was. The fact that he had left me alone despite whatever new danger we faced bothered me. It meant that whatever had changed, whatever new danger lay ahead for us, it was inevitable. It wouldn't make a difference if he was with me or not, if we were going to die, there was nothing he could do about it. It could only mean one thing – the Others must have been joined by a fifth and they were already close on our tails. The realization was not as horrifying as it should have been. I had known this would eventually happen; in a way, it was almost a relief that it would be over soon… almost. I felt strangely numb with only a faint sense of fear quivering at the edges of my empty calmness.

I tried to keep myself busy while I waited for Sebastian to return, forcing my mind to stay focused on the tasks at hand. I liked to have camp properly set-up and ready for his return, wanting to contribute some small effort to our survival in any way I could.

There were still no clouds in the sky and the air felt warm and calm, sticky even. I didn't bother building a lean-to for the night, even though I had learnt how from Sebastian's expert teachings. Tonight we would sleep under the stars. Because of the earlier, heavy rains the ground was still damp enough that we'd be able to have a fire but we'd need to use the tarpaulin to sleep on.

I set myself to work, using a stick to dig a small fire pit and then gathering several armfuls of firewood, searching underneath the thick brush to find branches and twigs that would be dry enough to burn. The light was beginning to fade in the depths of the woods so I lit the fire without waiting for Sebastian. I was only slightly comforted by its quiet crackling and its gentle glow. The feel of unseen eyes on my back made me shift uneasily as I laid out our bed.

"Just your imagination," I muttered to myself. A bead of sweat slowly trickled down my spine.

I knew Sebastian would be back soon. He was never gone for longer than half an hour – sometimes returning after what felt like just a few minutes with enough food to last us several days. I knew if I stood around, idly waiting for him, my thoughts would head in a dangerous direction so I forced myself not to think about the terrifying dangers that lay ahead of us and instead pushed myself into action. I grabbed our water bottles and began marching towards the sound of a nearby, rushing river. The fire was small and the river was close enough that I felt safe leaving the campsite unattended for a few minutes.

I found a good spot where the river bank wasn't too steep and I began to cautiously make my way down the slope. The river was running low this time of year, and I had to carefully make my way over the uneven surface of rocks and pebbles to reach the water's edge, wary of the slippery stones with only the fading sunlight to guide my way.

It was noisy there, the sounds of the rushing current drowning out all else. It made me feel increasingly nervous, as if anyone could sneak up on me at any moment and I'd never notice. I filled up our water bottles quickly, frequently checking over my shoulder and glancing back to the faint sparkle of embers drifting up between the trees where I'd set up camp. I forced myself to calm down, taking a few quick minutes to wash the sweat and grime off my body that had collected throughout the day. I had gotten used to being outdoors and being dirty, scared and tired. But I tried to wash myself at every opportunity. My long, wavy hair had quickly become a problem and so two weeks ago now I had taken Sebastian's sharp pocket knife and sawed off the length of my ponytail, leaving just enough hair to pull it back from my face with an elastic band. It had felt surprisingly liberating, the weight and heat of my thick hair so easily cut away and thrown aside. I had no idea how I looked without the trademark locks I'd proudly worn all my life and surprisingly, I didn't really care.

The cold river water felt so refreshing against my hot, sweaty skin that I was tempted to throw myself into the river, clothes and all. My body twitched and my muscles trembled from the sudden strong desire. The water seemed to beckon to me, flashes of silver sparkling just below the surface, enticing me to jump in. The shadows were rapidly lengthening and it was hard to tell how deep or how strong the current was away from the river's edge. I reluctantly decided to wait until morning when perhaps Sebastian and I would have time to take a morning swim together. I doubted it though.

I watched curiously as the flickers of silver that I'd seen began to grow in both brightness and multitude. My eyes opened wider in amazement as a school of fresh river trout rapidly swam for the surface, leaping into the air in perfect synchronization so that their silvery scales flashed under the sun's last weak beams before disappearing again into the river's rushing waters. I doubted I'd ever grow used to the strange anomalies that occurred when Sebastian was nearby. I watched the river in wonder for several more seconds, waiting to see if any other fish would perform for me but the waters flowed steady and straight without the slightest sparkle of even one trout's metallic scales.

I sighed as I ran my now cold, wet fingers through my hair, drying my hands and dampening the short, tangled locks that barely brushed my shoulders. Lifting the heavy water bottles, I wearily stood, carefully making my way back to the river's bank and scrabbling up and into the woods. The exertion made me start to sweat again, the clean, refreshed sensation the river had blessed me with quickly becoming a distant memory, just like everything else.

I hurried back through the trees, guided by the light of the fire. I hadn't been gone for long and only had to add a few more sticks and stoke it slightly upon my return. I set to work boiling the river water in Sebastian's collapsible camping pot and then, still not wanting to sit still, I searched the shadows for more dry firewood for the evening.

"Hard at work?" The sudden sound of Sebastian's voice from behind me made me jump. My heart leaped into my throat, my pulse pounded in my ears. I spun around, my hand automatically grasping my necklace for comfort and reassurance.

"Sebastian!" I scolded, my voice still shaking slightly.

He laughed softly. "I'm sorry, Gracelynn. I didn't mean to startle you."

"Well, you did."

He grinned, unable to deny it. Even without the sounds of the crackling fire and nearby rushing river, and with the rapidly fading light, he could still be practically invisible when he chose. When he wanted to be quiet, he was dead silent. I supposed it was why he was such a good hunter. I never helped him hunt. The fact that he could kill a handful of small animals with just a knife in a few short minutes was information enough for me to imagine the process. It was something I definitely didn't need or want to see. Besides, I wasn't silent even when I wanted to be, as Sebastian enjoyed pointing out, and I would scare away the game if I accompanied him. My help would have been more of a hindrance. At least, that was the reason we had agreed upon.

"Rabbit tonight," he announced with another smile. He held out a handful of long, thin sticks to me, the rabbit meat already skinned, chopped and skewered onto the sticks between small chunks of wild mushrooms and some other dark green vegetable. The first night he had hunted, he had brought a whole pheasant back to our campsite, plucking and beheading it in front of me without realizing something was wrong until I darted into the bushes and began throwing up. Since then, I would never recognize the animals he brought back from his little expeditions if he didn't tell me what they were. Our meals were as innocent and unassuming as the meat found at a local grocery store – not that I had ever shopped for meat myself. Eliza, our cook, had handled all our household groceries and meals. How different my life was now from just a few short months ago, I mused to myself. Though to be honest, my life had changed the moment I had first met Sebastian, almost nine months ago now.

We cooked our meal quietly, working together quickly and efficiently. Sebastian occasionally spoke, complimenting me on how well I had set up the camp or thanking me for refilling our water supply but his attempts at conversation quickly melted into silence. The tension between us grew while the rabbit meat sizzled and browned, its appetizing scent woven through the smoke in the air.

"Are you going to tell me?" I eventually asked, not able to stand the silence between us for even a moment longer. I sat up straighter, crossing my legs as I stared across the fire at Sebastian impatiently.

"Tell you what?" he asked innocently. I almost rolled my eyes; Sebastian was many things but he certainly wasn't innocent. He was giving himself away. I fixed him with a hard, unwavering look and waited. He was, at times, just as stubborn as I and he refused to look away or speak, keeping his expression carefully blank and deceivingly calm.

I tapped my fingers impatiently against my knee, realizing I would have to be the first to bend. "The Others have found a fifth," I stated.

He cocked his head to one side. "Why would you think that?"

"I don't think that, I *know* that."

"And why do you think you know that?" he quizzed, his expression still calm as he slowly reached forward to rotate the sticks of meat balanced over the fire.

"Well, I'm not sure exactly… Maybe I just wanted to know and so I do," I suggested with a small shrug. I felt certain I was right about the Others.

His dark eyes briefly met mine, the orange flames of the fire reflected in them. Something in my stomach tightened before he dropped his gaze.

"It doesn't work that way," he muttered but I wondered if we were both thinking the same thing. "But you're partially right. The Others *have* found a fifth but I think they knew where the fifth was all along and now they're leading us right to him – or her, somewhere in southern Ontario, maybe even Quebec…" His voice trailed off as he squinted into the campfire flames. I could tell he was straining to 'sense' the Others.

The rabbit meat was starting to blacken on the edges now, the vegetables shriveling away from the fire's heat. Since Sebastian's attention appeared to be far away, I took over the task of rescuing our dinner, balancing the steaming hot kebabs over some nearby rocks to cool. Sebastian was silent the whole while, staring in a trancelike daze at the fire's dancing flames.

"Sebastian?"

No response, he didn't even blink. The sense of dread weighed down on me heavily, like a rock dropping in my stomach. I swallowed back my sudden nausea.

"Sebastian?" I repeated, speaking slightly louder. I might as well have been trying to get the attention of the twilight sky. I was about to stand up to walk around the fire and shake him (which had worked before when he had fallen into one of these unbreakable trances) when a thought suddenly occurred to me. I took a slow, hesitant breath and then quietly called out, "Seamus?"

Sebastian's eyes snapped to my face, his attention sharp and focused like the point of a dagger at my throat. "Yes?" he answered mildly, obviously unaware that anything had been wrong.

"You… umm… Well, how do you sense the Others? Shouldn't it not 'work that way'?" I decided not to upset him by mentioning what had just happened – what good would it do anyway?

He gave me a strange look before answering, his eyes flickering briefly to where I had moved the sticks of meat from the fire to the rocks. He shook his head slightly as if to clear it before frowning at the fire once more.

"I think that I'm able to sense the Others, not because I want to but because… I can. I just do."

"That doesn't make any sense," I pointed out, almost a little peevishly. His lips curved up into a patient smile.

"I know," he agreed. "But how else can I explain it?" He paused, deliberating. "I think that I can sense the Others because their abilities are all connected to mine, because I gave them their abilities. I think it's something I probably could have always done – if I'd remembered them. The more I become aware of them, the clearer the sensation becomes. And the closer they are, the easier it is to sense them."

"Do you think that they can sense you too then?" I asked, my mind jumping to the next logical conclusion.

Sebastian didn't answer, he didn't have to. His silence said it all.

How would we ever escape them? I didn't speak the question out loud for I knew I wouldn't like the answer. I pushed it aside and asked another question instead.

"If we're getting so close to the fifth, why don't they just go ahead of us and join together now? Why did they bother chasing us if they've known where a fifth was all along?"

Sebastian sighed. He reached over to the cooled kebabs and politely handed me a stick. I didn't take a bite yet, even after our long day of hiking through the woods I was still too close to losing my appetite.

"It's a game, Gracelynn, it's all a game. I remember doing similar things to… others; testing them, observing their reactions, pushing them to see how far they'd go. I fear this is more about you than me," he reluctantly admitted.

My nausea rose up in my throat once more. I had to work hard to swallow it back down. "Why?" I asked, my voice sounding weaker than it should have.

"I'm not exactly sure, I can only guess."

"Please, feel free to speculate."

He smiled but his expression was tight, making his handsome face appear unfamiliar in the flickering firelight.

"They remember me, and they think they know me but they don't know anything about you other than what I had told them of Caoilinn so long ago. I think they want to test your loyalty to me, test the strength of the bond between us, and to test your determination, your strength and the true extent of your ability. They want to know what they're dealing with before they make their final move."

My breath caught in my throat. For several long seconds, I couldn't respond. We just stared into each others' eyes, reading the emotions within them.

"It's hopeless then, isn't it?" I whispered. Without thinking, I took a tiny bite of the juicy rabbit meat – it tasted delicious, like warm, smokey chicken. Despite my mind's objections to eating, my stomach growled hungrily in response.

"There's always hope, there's always an answer," Sebastian wisely reassured me, his expression calm and patient once more. I searched his eyes for further hidden truths but all I saw was his open, honest love - and the wispy smoke that stung my eyes. "Let's eat, we'll need our strength for tomorrow."

"Tomorrow?"

"Yes, it comes right after tonight."

"Ha ha," I replied sarcastically. "What's happening tomorrow that we'll need our strength for?" I restated.

"The sun will rise, I think they day will probably be quite warm and you and I – we'll run. Now that a fifth is definitely ahead of us, I think the Others might finally let us put some distance between ourselves and them."

"But we'll be running straight for the fifth," I objected in confusion.

Sebastian grinned. "That's exactly what they'll think."

I opened my mouth to ask another question but he just shook his head slightly, gesturing to the stick in my hands. "Please, Gracelynn. Try to relax, try to rest, and please eat. I will tell you more tomorrow but for tonight… just trust me," he gently encouraged. The silent plea in his eyes was enough to bring the meat back to my lips. I took a big bite and chewed, digging into my meal in silence though this time it was more peaceful and companionable than the tense quiet of before.

We each ate three of the kebabs, saving four for the following day. I was still hungry after our meal and had to fill my stomach with berries and water before it would stop gnawing on itself. I was hungry all the time now and ate so much more than I was used to. I was definitely burning more calories with all the exertion I pushed my body through each day. My body was also bigger and stronger than before our journey. Gone was the skinny, mildly toned, teenaged-girl from Craigflower Academy. I was still lean but definitely muscled now, my arms and legs strong, my body toned and more powerful than before. It was a satisfying feeling to know that I could propel myself through the woods and over rough terrain day-after-day, to run when I had to and to sleep on the hard-ground at night with only mild discomfort. And to know that I was stronger than most girls my age, that I was in better shape. I had no idea how to fight but I felt like now, if it ever came to that, I could probably handle myself or outrun my pursuer at the very least. Of course, none of that mattered when you were being chased by people who had to merely want you to be dead and you would be.

I sighed.

"Are you tired?" Sebastian asked, his voice tinged with concern. I shook my head, forcing a smile onto my lips.

"Not really. The sun's only just gone down and we have enough firewood to stay up for a while longer - if you'd like," I added. Sebastian smiled in response.

"It is nice to sit by the fire," he agreed. He unfolded his legs and stood up, moving around the fire to my side. I shifted my weight so that I could lean against him as he sat down, my head resting lightly against his shoulder, my muscles relaxing from his proximity while my heart began slowly and steadily picking up in pace.

I closed my eyes and let myself absorb all the sensations the moment had to offer. Sebastian's body radiated warmth and comfort beside me, along with a tantalizing electric energy that tickled through the warm night air. The fire popped and crackled, the quiet sounds of the nocturnal forest creatures slowly awakening reached my ears, alongside the other species who were just settling down. It all blended together with the sound of the river's steady current in the background of my thoughts, its comforting white noise slowly washing away my worries and easing my fears. I took a deep breath in through my nose, trying to inhale all the vivid details of life around me. The air smelt like pine, dirt and smoke, and I could faintly smell our leftover dinner. The light perfume of sweat combined with the appetizing scent that always clung to Sebastian's skin, which made me think of ice and snow and summer rains, drifted to me through the warm air. I breathed it all in and tried to rejoice in the fact that I was alive and I was with Sebastian, and no matter how afraid I should have been, I felt strangely safe and at peace with the world. Though maybe that's how everyone feels right before they die.

"I'm sorry about what I did today," I said quietly as I reopened my eyes. "It's starting to really sink in just how impossible... how inhuman... I'm afraid of what I might be capable of."

He slid his arm around my shoulders and pulled me protectively against his chest. "Don't be afraid. The magic doesn't control you — you control it. You're bound to make mistakes as you try to remember how to focus your ability. I only wish I could remember something useful, something that might help you but Caoilinn's magic was always so different than mine. I never thought to learn about her powers, only my own."

"Why must you always put the blame for everything on yourself?" I pulled back from him slightly as I spoke, my tone colored by affectionate exasperation.

His warm laugh in response made my body glow with pleasure from head to toe. "I apologize. It's an incredibly irritating quality that I must have picked up from someone who I spend far too much time with as it is."

I fought the smile twitching at my lips. "You should be more careful about who you associate yourself with then. I hear it's gotten you into trouble in the past."

For a second I feared I had gone too far. Sebastian blinked in surprise, his expression momentarily freezing in place before he suddenly tipped back his head and laughed. The sound was loud and unexpected, echoing throughout the trees and shadows around us. I initially flinched before becoming caught up in his contagious laughter. His joy was irresistible. These days there weren't enough reasons to laugh.

As our laughter died down and faded away to shared grins, Sebastian met my eye with a powerful fire in his own. "Oh, Gracelynn. What would I ever do without you?" he murmured as he tenderly reached out to remove a small piece of forest debris that had become entangled in my hair.

"You'd forget me soon enough," I teased.

"No. Never again," he denied, his smile fading while the passion in his eyes burned brighter. He slowly reached out to brush my messy hair back from my face, his fingertips lightly grazing my temple as he did so. I automatically flinched back, my whole body tensing suspiciously, my breath catching in my chest as the memory of him once trying to erase my memory flashed behind my eyes.

Sebastian froze. The hurt my involuntary action had caused him briefly flickered in the depths of his eyes before he forced a smile onto his face.

"You won't ever forgive me for trying to make you forget, will you?" There was no hurt or accusation in his voice as he spoke, only a sad kind of curiosity.

"I've forgiven you. It's impossible to stay angry with you – especially when you don't want me to be," I pointed out. "I forgave you almost as soon as I remembered you – remembered *us*. I know where your intentions lay, where your heart was the whole while but… I won't so easily *forget* what you did or that you might try it again one day."

"I'll never make you forget me or anything else, ever again," Sebastian solemnly promised. He linked his fingers through mine as he spoke and raised our clasped hands. His warm, lips began gently brushing over my knuckles, his soft breath raising the hairs on my skin.

I bit my lower lip, not wanting to speak the truth but knowing I had to.

"I wish I could believe you," I whispered.

Sebastian raised his eyes to mine. I was surprised to see the hesitance in them. He lowered our hands and gazed back to the fire, attempting to subtly avoid my eye.

"I couldn't erase your memory again if I wanted to," he reluctantly confessed. I frowned back at him, puzzled. "You don't want to forget me or anything else, ever again – you *really* don't want to. It's like slamming into a brick wall; my attempts have absolutely no effect on you whatsoever so you needn't worry."

"Your *attempts?*"

He didn't even have the courtesy to look ashamed. He shrugged.

"I know how afraid you are, Gracelynn. I know what a nightmare this has been for you. I thought that maybe if you forgot what we were running from you might…" He didn't finish his sentence. My glare effectively silenced him.

I took a long, slow, deep breath, trying to calm myself. "I can't believe you thought the fact that you've been trying to tamper with my memory unsuccessfully would actually make me feel better. Really, Sebastian! How am I supposed to trust you?"

To my extreme annoyance, he laughed. "It should be easy. I lie to myself all the time and have no qualms with my own trustworthiness," he declared with a grin. "But I didn't lie to you," he pointed out when I didn't share in his smile. "I just didn't tell you that I had tried to alter your memory – until now."

"Withholding information and lying aren't that different."

"I disagree. Lying is dishonest, while withholding certain pieces of information can often be considered… prudent."

I raised an eyebrow at him. "Prudent?"

"Yes. For example, you said you didn't want to hear the details of my past-"

"Because it doesn't concern me," I interjected. "What you did before we met, whatever choices you made when you couldn't remember – it doesn't matter. All that matters to me is us. All I care about is the present."

He smiled, a familiar mischievous gleam sparkling in his large, wise eyes. "But I haven't tried to affect your memory lately, that was weeks in the past. And since we're only talking about the present…"

He suddenly leant forward, his face abruptly inches from mine, his eyes intense beneath the fans of dark lashes. He took me by surprise, barely giving me time to catch my breath, my anger abruptly vanishing.

"Presently, I was about to kiss you," he finished, his hands gently pulling me closer as he spoke.

His lips brushed against mine lightly at first, teasing and enticing me with his sweet, playful kisses. Unable to stop myself, I leant in closer, my hand automatically sliding around his strong shoulders and up the back of his neck, my fingers curling into his black, messy hair. It was the sweetest manipulation possible and I didn't even try to resist.

My heart pounded harder, my body came alive as an intense and overwhelming sensation began building in my chest. My lips parted to inhale the sweet, exotic warmth of his breath, the taste of his mouth filling my mind and overwhelming all my senses. Within seconds, all my reason, all of my self-control was long gone and there was nothing but his body and mine, and the undeniable need to be together.

I broke free from his kisses to catch my breath but I couldn't stop touching him. I pulled him tightly against me as he kissed down my neck, his lips rough and tender all at the same time. Fire erupted throughout my body, lingering under my skin and demanding to be satisfied and further fueled by his touch.

"Gracelynn?" His warm breath tickled against my collarbone, sending electric chills all over. Our bodies shifted closer together.

I struggled to find the necessary air to speak. "Yes?" We had slowly moved together to lie down on the thin tarpaulin covered by a soft blanket that was to be our bed by the fire. My excitement and passion flared. He reluctantly pulled back from me, propping himself up on one elbow so he could look directly into my eyes. His hand lingered on my hip, then began to stroke slowly up and down my side as he spoke.

"I think, maybe, we should stop," he quietly announced, the look in his eyes and the feel of his touch completely at odds with the words on his lips.

I immediately shook my head, pulling his face back down to mine. "I don't want to stop." My words were slightly breathless, my voice sounding suddenly much more mature and sexier than I'd expected to be able to pull-off. He made a low noise in his throat as I passionately kissed him that sounded half-groan, half-moan and only further increased my desire. He broke his lips apart from mine again to speak but this time I kept kissing down his throat, my hands sliding under his shirt and up over his firm stomach.

"You wanted to be married first," he reminded me. I hesitated, his words finally breaking through to me.

"I did," I reluctantly conceded, my lips tickling his skin as I spoke. I sighed and nuzzled into his neck, breathing in the warm, heady scent of his skin, my hand still slowly trailing back down his stomach. I smiled triumphantly as his hand tightened on my hip in response, pulling me over almost roughly to lay half on top of him. There was nowhere to look but his beautiful, passion-filled eyes. He stared back at me, looking deeply into my eyes. I could feel his chest rise up and down beneath me with each breath that he took.

"Marry me first," he repeated. I could see just how hard it was for him to stop, to slow things down between us. My sense of reason was slowly and reluctantly returning to me.

"I have two conditions," I told him, kissing his lips as I spoke.

"Anything."

I smiled. "You have to ask me properly and you have to do it soon. I don't want to wait anymore, Sebastian. Life's too short and I know what I want – I want you."

"That's easy; I'm yours. I've always been yours – for as long as I can remember, and for as long as I can't," he added with a small laugh. "And life, for us, can be as long as we want it to be."

I carefully slid off him, leaving just my arm wrapped around his chest. He hugged me tightly against his side and we looked up at the sparkling night sky that peeked out between the tree branches above where we lay. The fire crackled cozily nearby while our pounding hearts slowed and reason fully returned. A blush spread out and over my cheeks that had nothing to do with the hot night air as I recalled how forward I'd been just moments ago.

"I'm sorry," I apologized for the second time that night. "I don't know what came over me." I turned my head against his chest, hiding my blush against his skin.

"It's my fault as much as yours," Sebastian answered. "I think we both may have allowed our momentary 'wants' to overpower one another's better judgment."

My brows pulled down as I gazed up at the night sky above us.

"I just wanted to be together, to forget about everything else…" I realized my mistake as soon as I said it. Sebastian chuckled softly by my side.

"And I let my wants be overpowered by your own."

"You did?" I asked, surprised.

"Yes. Because no matter what I may want in a moment of passion, deep down inside, I know that what I truly want is for you to be happy. And I don't think you'd be happy if you compromised a moral that you've stuck to and defined yourself by for so long."

I didn't answer. I silently considered his words.

"But a part of me must have wanted to forget that responsibility – enough that your magic was able to seduce me so easily," he teased.

"I did not seduce you!" I argued, shocked at his suggestion. He laughed quietly. "If anything, it was the other way around."

"Then I should apologize." Sebastian sat up as he spoke, pulling me up with him. His eyes were bright with excitement, his smile so happy and teasing that I realized just how long it had been since I'd seen him smile like that. "You do need to learn to control your emotions though, Gracelynn. You must always be aware that what you may want in the moment is not necessarily what you want in the grander scheme of things," he reminded me more seriously.

"I know," I agreed. "I'm trying, Sebastian, really I am. This is just all so new and overwhelming – and frightening. I'm trying so hard but I feel like I'm getting nowhere." My happy mood was quickly fading, reality destroying the beautiful magic of our evening together.

"It will all be okay, I promise. You're doing just fine. It will come back to you, you just need more practice," he added with a grin.

He shifted onto his knees as he spoke, reaching down to the edges of his shirt and tugging it up and over his head so that he knelt bare-chested before me in the firelight. I couldn't help but swallow hard. His smooth skin looked bronze under the fire's soft glow, all the perfect angles and contours of his muscles highlighted by the flickering firelight, his stunning physique punctuated by the black lines of the mysterious tattoos that decorated his body.

"More practice?" I repeated uncertainly.

His grin widened. "Sure. We know the answers we're seeking are hidden within my tattoos so perhaps you should spend more time looking at them." His muscles flexed and tightened as he stretched out on the blanket beside me, lying on his chest and resting his cheek on his folded arms. "Go ahead. Let me know if they trigger any memories for you – they sure haven't for me."

I shook my head at his back, biting my lip as I smiled. I slowly climbed onto him, sitting on his lower back so that I could properly examine the large, Celtic cross design that was spread out before me. A million sensations came back to me as my eyes followed the twists and turns, the depth and details of the design overwhelming me. I remembered the first time he had shown me his tattoos, that night he had revealed so many truths to me. I thought about the day he had given me his ring too, out on the middle of the frozen pond beneath the beautiful mural he had painted on the underside of a bridge. I was whisked away on a warm breeze of pleasant memories as I traced the designs of his tattoo with my finger, but nothing further came to me, no memories of a forgotten magic or a life I had lived thousands of years in the past, or hints of the secrets I had hidden for my future self.

"What do these words mean?" I lightly ran a finger over some of the small, twisting text that was woven between the images decorating the cross.

Sebastian didn't answer right away. I leant to the side so that I could properly see his expression. His face was scrunched up, his expression almost pained, the muscles in his neck and jaw strained as he struggled to answer.

"It's so hard to remember," he murmured between clenched teeth. He still didn't open his eyes or relax. "I think…" I could almost feel the mental exertion of him trying to remember, his muscles trembling beneath me. "I think they mean something like… *trust and feel the pattern.*" His expression suddenly relaxed though sweat now beaded upon his brow. "It's a loose translation of an archaic form of the Celtic language."

"Oh. What does it mean though?"

"Your guess is probably better than mine since it's a message meant for you. If only I could remember something more useful but no matter how hard I try, I can't remember anything about the origins of my tattoos other than that they are clues for you, based upon the images from your spell book."

"I wonder why you remembered everything but that?"

Sebastian didn't give me an answer because there really wasn't one. Perhaps one day we'd find out but it was obvious that question was not about to be answered anytime soon. Still, I wanted to know so badly what his tattoos might mean. I wanted to understand why he couldn't remember their origins when he should remember everything now. The only one of his tattoos that he knew anything about was the mark left from the Binding – and that wasn't even really a tattoo, it was just the mark the spell had left behind. And Sebastian hadn't remembered Caoilinn casting the Binding spell until I told him of my dream-memory of it, and then recast it myself.

I admired his tattoo for a while longer, finding no further hints or clues trapped within the dark, detailed designs. My eyes were beginning to sting from both the fire's smoke and the lack of light. A wave of tiredness suddenly swept over me and I let myself slide off Sebastian's back, curling up against his side. I had thought he was already asleep since he had been silent for so long and his breathing was so deep and even. He turned towards me immediately, pulling me into the warmth and safety of his arms and sliding our extra blanket up and over us both. Unable to resist, I lightly ran my fingers through his soft hair, gently brushing it back from his face. My hand froze in shock as I realized there was another, tiny tattoo marking his scalp just above his temple. The twisted, black lines were hair thin and formed a small Celtic knot, no larger than a dime. I stared at it curiously, wondering how I'd never noticed it before. Even though it had been hidden by his hair, I had thought I knew all of his tattoos.

"Have you always had this tattoo?"

Sebastian opened his eyes, looking sleepy and confused. "I wasn't born with any of them, Gracelynn," he mumbled with a half-smile.

"This tattoo on your scalp – why haven't I ever noticed it before? Why didn't you tell me about it?" I pressed. I brushed my fingers through his hair again, straining to make out the details of the tiny, tightly formed design in the fire's flickering light.

Sebastian closed his eyes with a sigh. "I don't know. It's just a small mark – it's never seemed important."

"It's so strange…"

He didn't respond so I started lightly running my fingers through his hair again, trying to discretely inspect the rest of his scalp for more tiny, hidden tattoos. He caught my hand and brought it down away from his hair, brushing his lips against the back of it in a sweet and gentle kiss.

"I love you," he mumbled sleepily. "Now leave my head alone. That's my only other tattoo – I promise."

"I love you too. And fine, I'll stop but promise you'll tell me if you remember any other tattoos that you haven't told me about." My eyes were feeling heavy and were already starting to close. I tried to fight off a yawn. "I hope you sleep well."

"So do I," Sebastian agreed softly. Though he tried to hide it, I could still hear the fear in his voice. I didn't know how he fell asleep each night, knowing that those terrifying dreams and tormenting nightmares would always be waiting for him. I had once been plagued by nightmares and new how truly terrifying it could be. And those were just dreams, a somewhat innocent expression of my inner turmoil by my subconscious mind. What haunted Sebastian was his actual past, nightmares that he had actually lived through and must relive, night after night. I remembered how frightening it had been the one and only time I had remembered part of Caoilinn's life — her death. I recalled the way my mind had slowly fallen backwards through time, sinking deeper into the dark past with each slow and hypnotic breath. And as I remembered, I felt myself sifting deeper through my thoughts than I typically dared to go, the memory blending with the present and mixing into my dreams. As I hovered on the edge of consciousness, I was vaguely aware of the other memories that were hidden in the depths of my soul, lurking in the nearby shadows but I moved past them all, drifting as far back as I could go, straining towards that one life, so long ago, when Sebastian and I had first met…

Chapter Three – Sweet dreams

The outer grounds of the temple were strangely silent today, despite the afternoon's warm sun. The other Priestesses were preparing for the harvest ritual which would take place in a few nights' time when the moon was at her fullest. I would be involved in the ceremony of course – I always was. But I was never asked to join in the preparations. I was rarely invited to join in anything other than to teach and to lend my strength to the important ceremonies. I had studied and been raised to the Sisterhood in the same way as all the others, my knowledge was comparable with any of their own, but my strength and my natural ability was not. I was more powerful than any Priestess or Druid in the land and though I was respected because of it, I was also an outcast and feared, even by my own Sisters.

I was alone wherever I went, set apart and above all others. Even as a child, I had never fit in. I was indulged as most children were but my mother quickly realized that my desires were being met not just by those around me but also by strange twists of fate that brought me what I wanted. My strange and potent ability became most obvious when a dog in our village had puppies and my mother traded for one of them. I adored the little puppy and he never aged a single day, remaining in the state that I desired him. I was too young at the time to understand just what I had done and why it was wrong. My mother had turned me over to the temple as soon as she realized what I could do. She had high hopes that I would find a place for myself there, that I would be a valuable part of the Sisterhood and be accepted and understood in a way that she would never truly be able to. I had only seen a handful of summers when she gave me up to the Sisters. My mother passed away shortly after that, abandoning me to my fate, never learning of my true unhappiness, my inability to belong anywhere or to ever truly be understood.

The other Priestesses didn't trust me. I was too powerful, able to easily and effortlessly twist fate to meet my every need. I was unable to continue aging as once I reached my teenaged years, I no longer wished to grow any older. I didn't want to grow old, to get sick or to die and so I didn't – I couldn't. The only emotions directed towards me were envy and fear. I had no friends in the temple, I had no family anywhere. I had no joy in my life other than to serve the people as my magic and my Gods demanded.

I rarely left the temple. It wasn't because I wasn't allowed, I simply chose not to. I hated the looks of awe and fear that the villagers would give me. I despised the way they wouldn't meet my eye when I spoke to them. I resented them for the way they made me feel – hurt, isolated, inhuman. I blamed them for my mother's rejection, for her abandonment. I convinced myself that I was better than them, that they deserved my disdain and I avoided the nearby villages. Yet even though my face was rarely seen outside the temple walls, my power, beauty and apparent youth were instantly recognized and acknowledged, my reputation preceding me wherever I went.

As I contemplated my past, I wandered closer to the temple gates. I found myself standing before them now, looking down the hill to the small village below. The rich green grass of the surrounding countryside glowed emerald under the bright sun and unfolded like a beautiful tapestry before me. The hills rolled all around, creating a small valley in which the village was located. The temple where I stood was on top of the highest hill, the cliffs and the nearby ocean just visible from where I stood. The lands were vibrant and lush and full of life. My heart felt dead and lifeless in contrast. I feared I was coming too close to wanting this life to be over with. Was I ready to move on to the next? Would I find any love or acceptance there? Would I ever?

I was distracted from my dark thoughts by the movement below me. Just where the path down to the village crested the hill, a young man had appeared, breathing hard and covered in sweat as he jogged up the steep path.

I hesitated as I watched him approach. I knew it would be better to withdraw within the safety of the temple's walls and call one of my

Sisters to assist him. It would be expected of me – one as powerful as I was not typically involved in the villagers' trivial problems and I had no desire to change that. But still… there was something about this boy that made me pause. His dark head was down, his whole body radiating his determination to reach his goal. He was close enough now that I could hear the rhythm of his feet beating against the path. And despite myself, I was curious. I was overwhelmed by the sudden desire to speak to him, to know why he was in such a rush to reach the temple though there was no reason why I should care.

Without any further hesitation, I stepped forward through the temple's gates and walked to meet him on the path.

He glanced up as we neared one another, his gray eyes steadily meeting mine. I couldn't imagine how I looked to him, stepping forward from the temple with my long, white blonde hair and dark robes swirling in the breeze around me. His eyes were bright and sharp, the intelligence and kindness in them obvious in just one glance. He stood before me boldly with his shoulders pushed back, his stance straight and tall. He didn't speak immediately; he looked surprised and was obviously too out-of-breath to form words. I knew he must recognize me but he didn't look afraid or intimidated as I had expected. The look in his eyes was one of steady determination and hesitant wariness. I waited patiently for him to speak, studying him all the while.

"Priestess." He somehow managed to get the word out between ragged breaths. He dropped his gaze as he spoke and made the slightest of bows with his head. He immediately straightened up, his eyes snapping back to my face as he rushed to continue. "Please, I beg your assistance. The Gods have truly favored me today by bringing me before you, for you are the only one who can possibly save my mother."

I should have turned and walked away right then and there. But by the will of the Gods, I didn't. "What ails her?" I calmly asked.

"My mother births a child as we speak but the midwife fears she is too old and the babe too big. She says they are both lost to us." His voice caught as he spoke, the emotion flaring in his eyes. His breathing was slowing and steadying now. I noticed he was trembling slightly despite the hot day and the sweat on his brow.

"The midwife knows more of childbirth than I," I readily admitted. It was true, living in a temple with a group of women sworn to chastity, I had never even witnessed a birth and had only the vaguest idea of what the process was about. "If the midwife has pronounced the situation hopeless, I am sorry to say that it must be so."

"No." His eyes flared once more and flooded with unshed tears. The way he spoke to me so defiantly, so fearlessly, made me reconsider him. "I refuse to accept that. She is my mother, she is dying, she's afraid and in pain, and her babe is dying inside of her. You must help. Please. I beg you. Please." Tears spilled down his cheeks as he spoke, leaving clear trails through the dusty grime that coated his face. His eyes shone with the tears, so bright and sparkling that I was unable to immediately look away. My heart stirred within my chest, the sudden empathy I felt for this young man powerful and unexpected. I knew in that moment that I would not be able to refuse him though I couldn't yet understand why. It had to be the will of the Gods.

"I will come," I agreed. Relief flooded his face, words of gratitude and thanks already forming on his lips. "But I make no promises. Most likely your mother and the babe will both die, but I shall do what I can."

His expression became weary and somber once more at my pronouncement. He nodded his head in agreement. "I appreciate the truth of your words. Thank you."

The young man sounded so genuinely grateful that for a moment, I was at a loss for words. I blinked twice, quickly regaining my composure and wondering over the strange effect this boy was having over me.

"There is little time. Let us make haste." I began marching down the path as I spoke, the young man's long legs and steady stride an even match for my own.

We half-marched, half-ran down the winding path that led us to the village. I asked the boy a few quick questions about his mother as we approached. He had three older sisters who were caring for her alongside the midwife. He was the youngest sibling of the four. Many had been shocked when his mother had conceived another child near sixteen-summers after his own birth. I guessed her age to be close to that of the Head Priestess's – far too old to be bearing children as far as my limited knowledge told me. I could not imagine how I was going to help this poor woman or if it were even possible for me to do so but I had told the boy I would try, and so I would.

Thankfully the boy's family lived at the edge of the village, close to the base of the hill. We passed only a few other villagers as we made our way there, all of whom gasped at the sight of me and hurriedly scurried away. They feared me, they rejected me, they didn't remember that I had once been one of them. My heart wept from the aching loneliness that chewed at its edges and my anger flared, cold and sharp. I pushed all the emotions aside, maintaining the calm, collected composure that was expected for someone of my station.

As we neared the young man's home, the sounds of his mother's agonized moans and cries began to reach my ears. I needed no further direction and marched ahead of him, striding up to the sturdy little hut with its finely woven roof. I pushed the door open without announcing myself, knowing it was not truly necessary. The shocked gasps as I entered the dimly lit room confirmed that I had been recognized.

I took the scene in quickly. Three young women knelt about the mother's bed. They were all quite attractive and had long, dark, nearly black hair and bright blue eyes. The similarity between the sisters and their brother outside was obvious. Their mother looked to be even older than I had expected, streaks of silver twisted throughout her loose dark hair that stuck to her sweaty forehead. She had obviously once been an attractive woman but her face was now worn with exhaustion, her skin pale as death, her beautiful gray eyes clouded with fear and pain. Her swollen belly protruded beneath a coarse blanket, her arms and legs so thin and frail in comparison. I quickly took note of the pile of blood-stained rags nearby and the large dark stain on the dirt floor. I took a quick, steadying breath.

"Your son has brought me to help you." I spoke only to the woman, watching her without displaying any emotion as her eyes tried to focus on my face. "I will do all I can but no matter what you may have heard, there are limits to my powers. I will try to save you."

"And the babe?" she asked, her voice stronger than I had expected, her words carrying a clear confidence just like her son's. "Please, save my baby."

"I will try."

I turned to the daughters then who all immediately dropped their eyes and shrank back from me in fear. I swallowed down my disgust at their reaction.

"Leave us," I quietly instructed. They rushed, almost gratefully, from the small room.

"Who are you?" the woman asked in the silence that followed. She peered at me in disorientation, her eyes now focused on my face, her expression one of confusion and vague recognition. "You are familiar to me."

I was about to answer that I was a Priestess from the temple, one of the most powerful ever known… but then, for some reason, I changed my mind.

"I was born in this village many years ago. My mother's name was Liadan, and my name is Caoilinn." It felt strange to say my given name out loud, so few people had ever heard it. The woman relaxed though and nodded slightly.

"I remember your mother, she was a good woman. I forgot she gave a babe up to the temple. Thank you for coming, Caoilinn."

"It is my duty but I am glad I came," I quietly answered surprised and a little unnerved by the sudden sense of kinship radiating out from the woman towards me.

I began working on the woman as fast and thoroughly as I was able to. I tried everything I could possibly think of, combining my natural skill and ability with my temple training in a way that I had never attempted before. I chanted and prayed, I blessed her, I performed spells and incantations, I drew designs over her body and belly, I strained with all of my power, with the whole essence of my being to save her. But no matter how strongly I wanted for her to survive, it was all to no avail. She was dying.

Eventually I sent for the midwife. I let the boy and his sisters know that we were about to deliver the child and that though it may survive, their mother would not live for long afterwards. It was the woman's choice and they all accepted it. The young man was the only one brave enough to respond; he whispered his thanks through his tears.

It was not long after that I watched the midwife deliver the baby boy. It was the first birth I had ever witnessed and I found myself awed and nearly brought to tears by the beauty of it. I had seen many amazing and miraculous things in my young life but it was all nothing in comparison to this. As I saw the pure joy and love on the mother's face as she took the small, crying babe into her arms, I realized how sheltered my life in the temple had been. My heart tore open even wider as I felt the loss of my own mother, my own family, my life. The pain hit me hard as I seemed to really feel it for the first time. But I had little time to wonder over this miracle of life that I had witnessed, now all of my energy and power had to be focused on the mother.

"I can only hold her here for a little while longer." I forced the words out between my clenched teeth. The mother didn't appear to hear me, completely at peace and captivated by her new baby, held weakly in her arms. The midwife reacted immediately.

"I'll send the girls in to say their goodbyes," she muttered, head down and shoulders hunched as she scuttled around me.

"No," the mother immediately objected in that surprisingly clear and firm voice. "I know I don't have long. Please, ask my Seamus to come."

The midwife nodded in understanding and disappeared outside. Only seconds after the door had closed behind her it burst open again and Seamus, the dark-haired young man who had first brought me to his mother's aid, reappeared. He rushed over to kneel before his mother's bedside, his eyes barely taking in my presence or acknowledging me.

"My sweet Seamus. I want you to meet your brother, Gradaigh Mathuin. You must take Grady from me now for he grows too heavy for my arms to hold any longer. Please ask your sister, Emer, to care for him and raise him alongside her dear Braonan. She has enough milk for two," the woman instructed, the strength behind her words rapidly fading.

Seamus nodded silently, carefully lifting the tiny baby from his mother's arms and cradling him tenderly in his own. I looked away as I saw a single tear trickle down his cheek.

"I love you with my whole heart, Seamus. You're so like your father – patient, strong, so kind. I only wish I had lived long enough to see you happy with a family of your own. I know she'll be quite the woman, the one you eventually do choose," she mused, sounding and appearing almost sleepy now. I could feel my control wavering. No matter how I wanted this woman to live, I could defy the wills of the Gods no longer. Tears of frustration filled my eyes.

"'Tis time for me to go now. Leave us, sweet Caoilinn. I will forever be in gratitude for the gifts you have given me – my babe, this time to say goodbye, this peaceful tranquility absent of pain."

I shook my head in denial, straining to speak while maintaining my flimsy concentration. "I can't… I don't want to give up," I gasped. I was exhausted – both emotionally and physically, and unexpected tears began rolling down my cheeks. I told myself it was because I wasn't used to failure, wasn't used to appearing weak or flawed in front of others. My whole body began to tremble.

"It's alright," Seamus quietly reassured me. He met my gaze with his own tear-filled eyes. His expression was open and honest, accepting and peaceful – not a shred of resentment for my failing to save his mother. "Please, wait outside. It's time."

I slowly nodded. I rose from the small, rickety stool I had been perched on at the foot of his mother's bed, smoothing my robes and attempting to regain my composure. Without looking back, I strode from the room, aware that with each step I took, his mother slipped away from the world of the living a little more. I heard her voice weakly whispering goodbyes into her son's ear and I knew with an unquestionable certainty that she would be dead moments after I stepped out the door.

"She's gone," I told the three young women who waited outside. They gasped and inched away from me, wrapping their arms around one another as they consoled each other's grief. I watched them comfort one another as I stood a few feet away from them, exhausted, drained and alone.

Several minutes later Seamus emerged from the hut with the new babe, Grady, sleeping peacefully in his arms. He walked around me and over to his sisters, murmuring words of reassurance to them all. He carefully passed the innocent babe over to his eldest sister and then kissed each of their cheeks and embraced them. The eldest disappeared, presumably taking the baby back to her home. The other two reentered the tent, tears streaking their cheeks as they avoided my gaze and hurried around me.

Seamus stood facing me, studying me silently, his face without expression. I stared back boldly, reexamining his attractive features. His cheeks, though dirtied, were young and fresh – his youth apparent as he was nearly of an age with myself. His black hair curled down and around his ears, nearly brushing the tops of his shoulders. His eyes were large and a dark, mysterious gray that at times hinted at a hidden blue tint; they were the exact same color as his mother's I realized. His eyes, though dry now, were filled with such unspeakable pain that I felt the uncontrollable urge to say something that might offer him some comfort, however small.

"She was a very strong woman, another would not have lasted as long as she."

Seamus nodded his agreement, his lips pressing together tightly as if he were holding something back.

"I told you that I might not be able to save her. I…" I hesitated, my voice unexpectedly wavering. A sob rose in my chest as I stared into his dark, beautiful eyes – eyes so filled with his loss and agony that I couldn't help but share in his pain. "I tried to save her. Please believe me. I tried so hard… I…" Exhaustion swept over me and I collapsed to my knees. I quietly sobbed, my whole body trembling as I allowed myself to feel all the emotions that I had held back for so many years. In my exhaustion, I allowed myself to be the young, innocent girl of seventeen summers that I normally worked so hard to pretend I was not and I broke down and cried.

And then something truly shocking happened. My tears and sadness were enough that I did not hear or sense his approach until he was already kneeling right by my side. Before I could object or speak at all, Seamus took me into his arms. He held me tightly, the warmth and security of his embrace unfamiliar but so comforting that I was powerless to push him away. I tensed for a moment, so surprised by his closeness, by his boldness and audacity that my tears momentarily ceased. I hadn't been touched by another or experienced this kind of physical closeness in so long… I didn't know what to do.

"It will be fine," he murmured, his words laden with such genuine kindness and reassurance that I was completely disarmed. And so I let him hold me and comfort me and I cried until my tears ran dry. And somehow, on a day when others should be comforting him for his loss, Seamus found himself kneeling on the dirty ground, comforting the most powerful Priestess in all the lands who sniveled and trembled before him.

My tears eventually stopped and I regained control of myself. I reluctantly pulled away from his embrace, only to find myself looking directly into his stunning eyes and for several long heartbeats of time, I was unable to look away.

"I should return to the temple," I quietly announced, dropping my gaze to the dusty ground. The sun hung low on the horizon, my absence would be noticed soon if I did not return.

"I'll send for a horse," Seamus offered. He reached for my hand to help me up in a way that was so natural and easy, it really did seem that he didn't have to think about it.

"No, that's not necessary. I'll walk."

"But you're exhausted."

I didn't reply. It was true but I wasn't about to admit that I didn't know how to ride a horse. I turned my back and began walking away from Seamus, unsure of what else to say, unsure of why I felt like I needed to say something else.

"I'll walk with you then," he stated from behind me and quickly reappeared by my side. I knew I should send him away but I couldn't seem to find the strength.

We made our way back up the hill slowly and in silence. There was so much to think about but I truly was exhausted and had little energy left to think of anything other than placing one foot in front of the other. I even stumbled a couple of times, to which Seamus immediately reached out to steady me. He eventually looped my arm through his so that I might lean upon him more heavily. Once again, I could not find my voice to object – not that he ever asked.

When we neared the temple gates, our pace slowed even more. The reluctance I felt weighing down my heart and slowing my steps apparently (and for some inexplicable reason) affecting Seamus also. His footsteps came to a complete stop, pulling me to a halt with him before the entrance to the temple's grounds where we had met just a few hours ago.

"What you did today… I will be eternally in your debt." His expression was earnest, his eyes full of gratitude and thanks while still shadowed with the pain of his loss.

"It is my duty to serve the Gods and the people," I answered.

He shook his head in objection. "It was more than that."

"It was still not enough." He didn't respond. I started to turn away, feeling tired and sad once more.

"Caoilinn?" he gently called after me. I froze at the sound, surprised that he would call me by my name and not my title but even more shocked by the pleasure it caused for me to hear it said so from his lips. I glanced back over my shoulder, my heart beating strangely. He looked confused himself and spoke hesitantly. "May I… may I come to visit you one day?"

"No," I answered immediately. His expression changed ever-so-slightly. The corners of his mouth turned down, disappointment darkened his eyes. "But perhaps I will come to you," I finished, barely thinking before I spoke.

He smiled, the expression brightening his face and emphasizing his handsome features. I allowed a small, answering smile to grace my face in response.

"Goodbye, Seamus."

I turned and walked away, the smile lingering as my heart beat ever-more quickly. Something was happening to me, something unexpected and new and powerful – and forbidden. Something that I had never thought possible… I had finally connected with another soul. I knew I had found a friend in Seamus and with that friendship, the possibility of love. And I realized in that moment that I wanted his love more than anything else; my whole heart and soul ached for it – for him – and I would do whatever it took, to make him mine…

I AWOKE WITH a start. It was like being plunged into cold water – one moment I was Caoilinn, I was in Ireland, thousands of years in the past, living her life, thinking her thoughts, feeling what she felt – and the next I was back in the present. I was Gracelynn. I was me.

I sat bolt upright, gasping for air as I tried to calm my pounding heart.

"Gracelynn? Are you alright?" Sebastian sat up beside me. The sky above us was starting to brighten, the night stars fading away. The forest was slowly awakening, the birds beginning to chirp and call out their morning songs. The fire had died down to a pile of smoldering embers in the night, leaving Sebastian straining to make out my expression in the low light before dawn.

I tried to calm myself, taking slow and steady breaths as I rubbed the goose bumps from my arms.

"I dreamt I was… I mean, I *remembered* being Caoilinn." He met my pronouncement with stunned silence, tensely waiting for me to continue. "It was the day she first met you. The day your mother…" I looked to him questioningly and watched as the strangest expression crossed over his face, a twisted combination of hope and fear and pain.

"The day my mother died," he eventually confirmed. He squeezed his eyes shut as he strained to remember. "It was both the saddest and the happiest day of my life. I lost my mother but I found you." I felt my jaw drop open.

"So it was real – it was true. It was all true," I gasped. "You were really there. That was your real mother, and your sisters–"

"My sisters!" he repeated excitedly. Even in the dim light I could see his eyes brighten. "I had forgotten I had siblings. I wonder if I have relatives alive in Ireland still? Of course, it would be nearly impossible to hunt them down but still, the idea is intriguing," he mused. "What else did you remember?"

"That was it, really. The dream ended after your mother passed away and you walked with me back to the temple. I wanted to see you again even though I knew I shouldn't. I realized I was falling in love or… that I was about to fall in love."

"You always said the moment you realized you loved me was the first time you had to say 'goodbye'. I'm glad you remembered that day, it was such a sad end to my mother's life but a beautiful new beginning for us." He paused, his arms sliding around me and pulling me against his chest in an embrace that felt identical to how he'd held me in my dream-memory of Caoilinn. The strange familiarity melted the tension from my muscles and soothed my unsteady heart. "Did you remember anything about your magic? Did you remember how you were able to help my mother? What you did?"

"No, not really. That part of the dream was sort of... blurry. I remember chanting and praying and painting designs on her body... but mostly I remember just *wanting* her to survive. I had to focus and I had to strain, but it seemed like that's all I really had to do," I told him disappointedly. It wasn't an amazing or exciting revelation – it was what Sebastian had been telling me all along. I just needed to want something enough to make it happen, I just needed to focus.

"I wonder if examining my tattoos triggered something within your subconscious then. Perhaps you should study the designs every night before you sleep so that you might remember more. It could be the key to understanding your magic." Sebastian waited patiently for my answer, gently stroking my short, tangled hair. The gesture felt so bizarrely familiar, almost identical to the way he had comforted me (or Caoilinn) nearly two thousand years in the past and just moments ago, all at the same time.

"I'm not sure how much more I want to remember," I confessed quietly. "It scares me, Sebastian. *She* scares me."

Sebastian laughed out loud. "That's ridiculous, Gracelynn. How can you be afraid of yourself?"

"I'm not Caoilinn," I stubbornly stated, pulling away from the warmth of his arms.

"No, you're not anymore," he agreed patiently, "but you once were. You don't need to be afraid of what you'll remember, I'm sure it can only help. Caoilinn was very much like you – sweet, caring, passionate, innocent – you have nothing to fear from her."

I didn't answer. I wasn't so certain that I agreed but I couldn't see any benefit from stating so. I couldn't help but remember the intense and possessive way Caoilinn had felt when she looked at Sebastian, when she had decided that she wanted him. I glanced up at the sky that had shifted from a black-blue on one horizon to a bright azure at the other, trying to push my dark thoughts away along with the fading night. Sebastian followed my gaze.

"The sun will be rising soon. Shall we break camp?"

"I couldn't sleep anymore if I wanted to," I agreed. I paused before rising, straining to get a read on the energy that clung to the air around us. I realized, with great relief, that the heavy sense of creeping, impending doom that had hung over us last night had now evaporated like midnight's mist at dawn. "Have the Others moved any closer?"

Sebastian immediately shook his head. "No and I'm almost certain they won't. If we make good time over the next few days we should be able to put some real distance between us – as long as we appear to be charging towards their fifth, of course," he added with a cheeky grin. He held his hand down to me and pulled me to my feet beside him.

"Are you going to tell me about this plan of yours then?" I asked curiously and with a touch of wariness.

"Yes, but let's get moving first. I'm anxious to be on our way."

I quickly tried to examine his expression before he turned away. There was a furrow between his brows that seemed to grow deeper with each passing day and a near-constant strain to his eyes that made me wonder if his headaches ever completely left him. I tried to push aside my concern or at least attempt to hide it from him. I knew that it would only add more stress to his already over-loaded mind if he realized how worried I was. All I could do for now was to want for him to be okay and I definitely did, more than anything. So why wasn't it working?

It took us only a few minutes to break camp. I rolled up the tarpaulin and our blankets together into a tightly packed bedroll that I lashed beneath Sebastian's backpack, then scattered the remaining firewood and carefully packed up our water bottles and supplies. While Sebastian dealt with the remnants of the fire, I jogged a short ways into the woods for some privacy to change into an only slightly-less stained shirt than the one I'd had on. When I returned to camp his pack was already on his back and the small clearing looked exactly as it had when we'd found it. There were no traces of our being there, not that it would stop the Others.

Sebastian handed me my backpack with a smile.

"Are you ready to go for a morning run?"

I groaned in response as I shrugged into my backpack and adjusted the straps so they wouldn't slip off my shoulders. "Just do me a favor, please?" I requested as we were ready to set out.

"Anything," he automatically agreed.

"Want us to get away from them. Want us to be safe. And… want to be able to keep up with me!" I laughed as I leapt around him and began charging through the trees, racing towards the narrow hiking trail that wove alongside the river. I could hear Sebastian laughing behind me – the sound coming closer with every passing second. I was a good runner, fast and strong, but he was better. I knew I'd be spending most of the day chasing after him.

We ran for hours, slowing to a fast-paced march when the terrain became too steep or started to turn boggy, and nearly sprinting when the ground was flat and rocky. It felt like we were flying through the forest at times, the marshes and old-growth trees blurring by, the thin grasses and rocky terrain disappearing behind us as we charged endlessly on. We stopped for lunch close to midday, both starving and tired but not as exhausted or as hungry as we should have been. Either Sebastian's wants were becoming more effective again or perhaps my own wants were starting to influence events too. I somehow doubted it though.

We had emerged from the forest onto the sandy shores of a small lake (small enough that I could see the other side but still too large to easily swim across). The waters were still and peaceful, the glassy surface perfectly reflecting the bright blue sky and the rocky shoreline on the opposite side covered with a thick forest of ancient, towering trees. I let my eyes drink it all in, taking a moment to admire the beautiful natural surroundings as I slowly sat down on the warm, sandy beach.

Sebastian sat beside me, handing me first my water bottle and then proceeding to unpack the leftover meat skewers from the night before. My mouth began to water and my stomach rumbled just at the thought of the delicious food. We ate in companionable silence, gazing out over the beautiful lake before us without another living person or sign of civilization anywhere to be found. The moment was almost perfect.

There was a cool breeze rising up off the lake that at first had been refreshing but was now a bit too chilly for the weakening sun. I dug a sweater out of my backpack while Sebastian loosened one of our blankets from the bedroll bound to his pack and wrapped us both up in it. I relaxed into his shoulder.

"I could almost fall asleep," I sighed happily. It was true. I hadn't felt this peaceful and relaxed in some time now and with my tired legs and full belly, and Sebastian's warm body so close to mine, I was sure I could fall asleep if I let myself blink for too long.

"We'll rest for a bit," Sebastian agreed, "but not long. We need to keep moving."

"I know."

I watched in wonder as the majestic silhouette of an eagle came soaring out over the trees on the far side of the lake and began slowly and gracefully circling over the water, searching for its own lunch.

"What exactly is it that we're moving towards anyway? Besides our own demise," I added sarcastically. Sebastian didn't laugh at my bitter humor.

"We should reach the edge of the park tomorrow. By my calculations, it should only take us a few more days to reach Thunder Bay – a week at the most. And then…" he hesitated, glancing at me uncertainly from the corner of his eye.

"And then?" I demanded, suddenly not liking where this was going.

"And then we find a way to get to Toronto," he concluded. I was about to ask why but then it hit me. I couldn't believe what he was suggesting.

"You want to get my father involved in this? Are you crazy? Sebastian, the Others will guess what we're doing. They won't let him help us, they might even hurt him! No. Absolutely, not. This is far too dangerous. You need to come up with another plan."

"There is no other plan, Gracelynn. This is our only option," Sebastian told me gently but firmly. "We can't outrun the Others much longer, the fifth is too close now. Our only hope is to get to your father before all five are there, in Toronto. The fifth can't influence him on his or her own. You can convince your father to help us before the four Others arrive, I know you can," he insisted.

"No," I argued. "Even if he knew and somehow believed the whole story, what could he do to help? Besides, I'm not certain he'd even want to help us, no matter how convincing I was," I added somewhat sadly.

"We don't have to tell him the whole story or even the whole truth. We just have to tell him enough that he'd be willing to help get us out of the country – and fast."

I stared at Sebastian incredulously. "Oh, sure. That'll be easy. Dad, even though I haven't seen or spoken to you in months now, do you think you can come up with plane tickets, passports, ID and all the correct paperwork so that Sebastian and I can run off overseas together? Oh, not to mention you're going to have to pay for it all and there will probably be people looking for us, and by the way, we need to leave as soon as possible! Yes, I'm sure he'll agree to that no problem," I grumbled sarcastically. To my surprise Sebastian laughed.

"Well, not if you ask him like that. But if you said it in the right way and if we both wanted him to help us…"

"It won't do any good unless *he* wants to help us," I pointed out. "And besides, the Others will be sure to want him *not* to."

"Which won't do any good if he does want to help," Sebastian retorted, a sparkle of blue to his gray eyes as they caught the sunlight within them.

This time it was I who scrunched up my eyes, fighting the dull ache that was beginning to pierce my temples. "But why Sebastian? What's the point? The Others will find out where we fled to easily enough. They'll follow, they'll catch us and they'll win. Why should we involve my father and risk his safety when it won't make a difference in the long-run anyway?"

"Because we won't just be running away from them, we'll be running to a place with answers. We'll be running towards our only hope, to my home, to the key to our past and hopefully, the key to fully reawakening your magic."

I knew the answer immediately. The green rolling hills and ancient countryside hovering on the edge of my conscious mind. "Ireland," I whispered, my words swept away on the cool breeze. A silence settled between us as the circling eagle suddenly dove towards the lake's still surface, its golden talons ready and outstretched, swooping down upon its prey. There was a splash and a flash of silvery scales and then the eagle rose up smoothly, its prize in its claws, triumphant and proud. For a brief moment, I felt empowered.

"Do you really think we'll find answers there?" I asked Sebastian quietly as we watched the eagle fly away with its meal.

His arm tightened around me as he pulled me to his side once more. "We have to."

Chapter Four – Closing In

Sebastian was right - we reached the eastern edge of Quetico Provincial Park the following day. We had miraculously made it through the entire length of the park on foot, without getting lost, without seeing any other people – or rangers, and well-ahead of the Others. The distance we'd covered in the past week or so didn't seem possible. In fact, I was pretty sure that it wasn't possible. I knew it must have something to do with Sebastian (or even possibly myself) but how was it happening? Had the distance been shortened? Or had time slowed down somehow? Or had the actual landscape been altered by our desires so that we could travel the most direct and easiest route possible? My head spun with all the possibilities - or impossibilities. Sebastian had once said that his influence over events was limited by what was possible, but he'd also later admitted that those limits may have been self imposed. It was all so complicated and confusing.

The terrain did not change much once we left the park's border. We were still in a vast and dangerous wilderness crisscrossed by fast-flowing rivers, streams and waterfalls, lakes wide enough to appear to be seas, forests that never seemed to end, swampy bogs and the rocky, grass-strewn landscape of the Canadian shield. The days blended into one another as we traveled. We marched and jogged as far and as fast as we could each day, breaking only for lunch and supper, and to sip water from our packs. The weather held steady for us and each day was hot and warm, even beneath the forest's shade. We camped each night under the stars and spent every evening 'practicing' different ways for me to learn to control my magic – all with limited success.

I slept deeply and soundly each night, and had no more dream-memories of Caoilinn's life. Sometimes as I fell asleep, I could almost sense the memories hovering on the horizon of my thoughts, beckoning silently to me. I was afraid to face those memory-dreams though. I knew that there were answers hidden within them but I also felt certain that I wouldn't like everything I learnt, and so I cowardly shied away from their beckoning call.

My nights might have been completely peaceful and restful if not for Sebastian's fitful sleep. He awoke me several times each night, tossing and turning, sometimes moaning in pain or fear. At other times he would awake with tears already sliding down his cheeks, terrified and ashamed of what he had faced in the nightmares from his past. He stoically refused to speak of these dreams, his expression instantly darkening if I so much as mentioned them. No matter how he pretended to dismiss them, I knew his nightmares haunted him throughout the days too. I couldn't help but be aware that each day he laughed a little less, each smile seemed a little more forced. His lack of sleep combined with his near-constant headaches led to even more periods of confusion and disorientation… it was truly terrifying. I felt like Sebastian was slipping away from me right before my eyes and there was nothing I could do to save him. My fear for him motivated me even more to learn to use my magic. I wanted so badly for the nightmare we were living in to be over, to be safe, for his pain and suffering to end… but it didn't.

Three days after leaving the park we started to see signs of civilization. We crossed a worn dirt road that appeared to have recent tire tracks on it. A few hours later we came across an old hunting cabin and as the day went on, we started to find more man-made trails and tracks. It wasn't long before we found ourselves on another dirt road that eventually turned to pavement. We followed along its side warily, noting the appearance of telephone poles and the sounds of distant traffic and even passing a few long and winding driveways that led off into the depths of the woods. When we stopped for a quick lunch of wild mushrooms, berries and some fish Sebastian had caught and cooked the day before, I reluctantly pulled a thin, long-sleeved shirt from my backpack. Sebastian watched in amusement as I pulled it on overtop of my tank top, covering up the black, twisting design of the tattoo that encircled the length of my arm. It wasn't really necessary; why bother hiding from people who could find us easily and effortlessly if they really wanted to? But it made me feel better. I was still self-conscious about the strange, dark design and was especially aware of the way other people reacted to it. Sebastian left his matching tattoo uncovered, snaking down from beneath his t-shirt sleeve to where it coiled around his wrist and thumb, and twisted into the palm of his hand. Ever since I bore the mark of the Binding too, he seemed almost proud of the odd design.

It wasn't long after lunch that we found ourselves at the side of a main road. The rush and noise of the cars and trucks that passed us was disorienting after nearly two weeks in the peace of the wilderness. I found myself flinching from the sound and speed of each vehicle that passed us by. A bright green sign just close enough for us to read announced the road to be Highway 588. Another sign just below it read Thunder Bay: 70km.

"Well, I guess we're on the right path," I commented in the quiet that followed a big-rig's passing. A swirl of dust and debris hit me in the face as I spoke and I found myself spitting out bits of grit.

"Was there any doubt?" Sebastian teased. He didn't smile though, his voice sounding strangely flat. His eyes didn't sparkle today, they looked as gray and empty as an overcast sky. Worry and nausea settled over me; I tried to push it away.

Sebastian began walking down the side of the highway. I jogged to catch up to his side, tucking the strands of hair that had come loose from my ponytail back behind my ears.

"Are we going to follow the highway now?" I was surprised he'd want to. Over the past few days he'd felt the distance between us and the four Others growing but they could catch up to us easily and quickly once they reached the main road.

"No, I don't think we should walk anymore," he answered. He spun around as he spoke so that he was facing me and continued to slowly walk backwards beside me, a small smile pulling up the corners of his mouth.

"Then what…?"

I didn't get to finish my question. As a vehicle approached from behind me, Sebastian grinned and stuck out his thumb, waving to the driver in a friendly and quite charming manner.

"Sebastian – we are not hitch hiking! It's dangerous and it's illegal," I objected. Sebastian's grin deepened at my words, his cheek dimpling and his eyes laughing at me.

"People hitch rides every day, Gracelynn. Relax. We'll be fine and it's the fastest – not to mention cheapest, way to get to Thunder Bay."

My stomach bubbled nervously as the truck Sebastian had been waving to slowed down and pulled over on the roadside just ahead of us. It was an old, black Chevy with a small cab and a very large and hairy dog sitting on the front seat beside the driver. The driver himself climbed out, a very large man in worn-out jeans and a t-shirt even more stained than my own. His cheeks were bright red either from sunburn or alcohol. I certainly hoped it was just from the sun.

"Where are you youngsters headin'?" he yelled, lighting a cigarette as he waited for us to catch up.

Sebastian started to jog towards him, I had no choice but to follow.

"Thunder Bay," Sebastian called back as he jogged.

"Sebastian, I really don't like this," I objected under my breath but before he could answer the man called out again.

"Well, you're in luck! Headin' that way myself. Not much room in the cab but you're welcome to ride in the back if you don't mind the breeze," the man offered. His voice was gruff but friendly enough. We were close enough now that I could really see his face and there did seem to be a genuine kindness that brightened his hazel eyes. The man looked us over briefly, his eyes lingering on me for slightly longer than Sebastian. I knew I looked very different than I had a few months ago, tanned, athletic and dirty with my short, shaggy hair and torn jeans. But still, I was surprised by the way the man's near-indifference injured my pride and made me automatically smooth my hair and stand up a little straighter.

Sebastian paused at the truck's back bumper, turning towards me in time to catch a quick flash in my eyes. "We don't have to, if you really don't want to," he quietly offered. His expression was hopeful but I knew he'd accept whatever answer I gave. It was so hard to say 'no' to him.

"I guess it's better than walking," I grumbled.

Sebastian grinned. "After you," he said, gesturing elegantly to the truck bed as he spoke. I rolled my eyes but smiled anyway, wondering how he worked his charm so easily.

"Thanks! We really appreciate the ride, sir," Sebastian told the man as he climbed up and into the truck beside me. We both took off our packs and Sebastian immediately began pulling our bedroll apart, using the folded tarpaulin as a seat for us with the truck's cab to lean against and the remaining two blankets ready to protect us from the highway's wind, even though it was a hot and sunny day.

"No problem. Ain't no hair off my back. Just knock on the window if you need anything, otherwise it's straight to Thunder Bay from here. I'll get ya there in under two hours - might need to stop for gas soon but we'll see."

"That sounds perfect. Thanks," Sebastian repeated.

The large man grunted in response, ground out his cigarette beneath his boot and then heaved himself back into the cab, the whole truck shifting with his weight. The big dog that looked like some kind of wolf cross-breed barked at us from the front seat. I winced as the man reached over and smacked it before throwing his indicator on and pulling back out onto the road.

It was a good thing Sebastian had the blankets out and ready because within minutes the wind was whipping at my legs. The wind felt pleasant and warm enough that at first it didn't bother me but that didn't last long. Soon I was wrapped up tight under a blanket and was comfortable enough to doze against Sebastian's side.

I awoke just as we were entering the outskirts of the town of Thunder Bay. It was amazing to see so much traffic and so many buildings when just this morning we had been out in the middle of nowhere still. I was surprised the noise of the traffic hadn't woken me sooner but it was actually the sound of Sebastian's voice yelling through the small slider window to our driver that I woke up to.

"We're going on to Toronto from here — we've got friends who live there," I heard Sebastian lie.

"Well, you can't hitch all the way to Toronto from here, it'd be a whole night and day of driving and that's if you found a ride for the whole way," the man drawled. I almost had to strain to understand him as he pronounced Toronto more like *Taranna*. "You wanna be dropped off at the bus depot? There's one not too far from here and there's a bus that'll be headin' out to Toronto either tonight or in the mornin'."

"That'd be great. Thank you!" Sebastian called back through the glass. That seemed to end the conversation between the two as the glass slid shut with a snap.

Sebastian turned to me as I sat up, noticing that I was awake.

"We're almost there," he announced with a quick smile.

"I heard," I answered. The speed limit had gone down since we were nearing the city and it was easy to speak over the wind now. I pushed the blanket down so that it only covered my legs, letting the sun's warmth soak into my browned and freckled skin. My mother would have a heart attack if she saw how 'rugged' I'd become, I thought wryly.

"Do you really think we should take a bus?"

Sebastian shrugged. "We might as well try it. I'm surprised we were even able to hitch a ride, to be honest. I thought the Others would be wanting to slow us down more. Maybe we'll be able to catch a bus too."

"Maybe," I agreed somewhat doubtfully. "I've got my wallet still — I should be able to pay for the fees with my credit card at least. How much do you think it'll be?"

"I've no idea," Sebastian replied. "Some prices are steeper than you think," he added ominously, a strange far-away look taking over his expression.

I wasn't certain how to respond, so I didn't. I was relieved when a few minutes later he reached over to link his fingers through mine, squeezing my hand affectionately. My heart glowed with a warmth that matched the sun's golden rays.

We reached the bus depot about twenty minutes later. It was significantly larger and busier than I'd expected but apparently Thunder Bay was quite a large town and this was just one of the three busy bus stations. For someone who'd lived such an indulgent life, I'd spent surprisingly little time exploring my own country. I had been on a year-long exchange in Germany when I was fifteen that I had hoped would be an exciting year abroad but had been just another extension of my sheltered, upper-class life. I'd traveled with my parents on "family" vacations to Hawaii, France, Greece, the Bahamas and even Japan but the only time I'd ever traveled out of British Columbia (and still within Canada) was on a school trip to Ottawa. We had toured the parliament buildings and driven into Quebec City for a day but had explored surprisingly little of the province and I had seen basically nothing else of southern Ontario and Quebec.

The man was smoking another cigarette when he dropped us off at the bus depot, not bothering to get out of the cab this time. We both thanked him heartily enough and Sebastian even reached in to shake his hand through the window, causing the dog to bark again which earned him another hard smack. I was happy to have our hitch-hiking experience behind us, feebly hoping that it would be the last time I'd ever hitch a ride.

We dodged a bus pulling out of the large parking lot as we walked towards the main building. There were several long Greyhound buses parked in front of the long, navy blue building, some unloading passengers and luggage, others looking like they were preparing to embark. Unfortunately, none of the displays on the front of the buses were lit up to announce where they were going or even where they'd come from. I could only hope that one would be heading to Toronto, and soon.

Inside the busy bus station we had to line up behind the other ten or so people already waiting in front of the Departures counter. As "luck" would have it, the line moved quickly and steadily; it was only a matter of minutes before we'd reached the front.

I let Sebastian do all the talking, letting out only the faintest sigh of relief when the woman behind the counter said that there was a bus leaving at 9:10 that night (in just a few short hours) that also just happened to have two seats still available on it. The cost of the last-minute tickets was nearly $300. I made the purchase on my credit card, not caring that my mother and the Others would be able to trace the transaction. Hopefully, by the time anyone realized we were in Toronto, we'd be long gone.

We waited inside the noisy, air-conditioned bus depot under glaring fluorescent lights. It was hard to get comfortable on the hard, plastic chairs. Sebastian was fidgety and unexpectedly anxious the whole while, glancing nervously at the door every time it swung open or closed. I could see the effort he put forth to appear calm and relaxed, joking casually about the different characters we saw and speculating on who they were and where they might be going. It was all an act, the unease and tension clear in Sebastian's troubled eyes.

It was quieter once we boarded the bus, almost two hours later. Most of the passengers immediately settled down, tilting their seats as far back as they could and pulling out books, headphones and even blankets. Some spoke quietly, their voices murmuring back and forth in a low buzz, the details of their words indistinguishable above the bus's idling engine.

We sat together in two empty seats near the front of the bus, Sebastian insisting I take the window seat so I wasn't jostled by people coming down the aisle.

"What's going on?" I asked him in a low voice once we were settled into our seats, our backpacks stuffed under our chairs.

He turned to me with an all-too-innocent expression on his face, denials ready on his lips. Something about my expression made him hesitate. I could almost see the words changing upon his tongue.

"Something's... not quite right," he finally admitted. He frowned as he spoke, the words obviously not accurately expressing whatever it was that he was feeling. He closed his eyes tightly, tipping his head back with a weary sigh. "The fifth is getting closer – and fast. The Others appear to be increasing their pace too. I can sense them all so clearly now, it's almost like they want me to know that they're closing in on us."

I couldn't prevent the soft gasp from escaping my lips as he spoke. An ice cold chill ran down my spine and gripped my heart with sudden fear. Sebastian's eyes flew open, his hands instantly reaching for me.

"It's alright, please don't be afraid," he urged, one warm hand tightly holding mine, the other gently cupping my face. "We're still ahead of them. We'll be in Toronto by six o'clock tomorrow evening and then we'll find your father. It'll all be alright from there." His steady confidence and soothing voice slowly settled over me like a wave of calm. I squeezed his hand back, resting my head against his shoulder as I forced myself to relax.

"I hope you're right."

I wasn't certain if the calmness that had chased away my fears was a result of my own emotions, Sebastian's magic or just exhaustion. Either way, my current lack of fear felt false, like I was somehow lying to myself. I certainly wasn't relaxed enough to fall asleep any-time soon even though my muscles ached wearily from the weeks of travel. Luckily, Sebastian seemed to sense my need for a distraction.

I reopened my eyes as he slowly turned my hand over in his. The bus had just finished boarding and the driver was pulling the doors closed. I took no interest in looking out the window. I didn't care to see the navy blue bus depot disappear or the new sights that Thunder Bay might have to offer. My attention was solely focused on Sebastian and the slow, deliberate shapes he was tracing into the palm of my hand, right over top of the beginning of the black marks from the Binding.

I wasn't certain what he was doing at first. I glanced up at him to see a small but tender smile on his face and a bright sparkle in his eyes that seemed to make the faint tint of blue glow brighter in their gray depths. My heart beat faster with each twisting, tickling stroke of his finger in my hand. I smiled as I realized what he was doing.

"What are you spelling?"

His smile deepened to a playful grin. I turned my body towards him even more, full of curiosity. The rest of the bus and the world seemed to disappear far beyond us as I was completely entranced by the natural magic of Sebastian.

"You should be paying more attention, Gracelynn," he teased.

I snorted softly and indignantly, smiling all the while.

"Do it again?" I asked sweetly, glancing up through my eyelashes at him.

He laughed quietly, shaking his head. "You don't need magic to get what you want."

I smiled back. "Funny. I was just thinking the same thing."

We stared into each other's eyes for a moment, the playful mood between us slipping slightly as we each read the intensity in one another. Sebastian was the first to look away as he slowly began spelling out more letters into the palm of my hand.

I-L-O-V-E-Y-O-U

"I love you too," I whispered.

He smiled and lifted my hand, gently and tenderly kissing the center of my palm before he laid it back on my lap and began writing out more letters.

W-I-L-L-Y-O-U-M-A-R-R-Y-M-E-?

My heart skipped a beat even though I knew he was just teasing me.

"Is that really how you're going to propose?"

He grinned. "Is that really how you're going to answer?"

I paused, briefly contemplating, then picked up his hand and began slowly writing my answer into the palm of his.

N-O.

He laughed out loud, seemingly delighted by my response.

"Are you saying 'no' to the first question or the second?"

"The second," I answered without hesitation.

He slowly linked his fingers through mine. My heart began beating strangely, my breathing became uneven. His eyes darkened and softened, his expression growing more serious and unexpectedly nervous as he watched me. His lips parted slightly, the words hanging on his lips before he finally spoke.

"And your answer to the first question?"

"Are you really asking?" I whispered breathlessly. He had definitely caught me off-guard but in an unexpectedly, wonderful way.

"I shouldn't have to ask," he agreed with a smile. "We've actually been married for over two thousand years but I understand the contract is somewhat void since you don't currently remember it."

"What?" I demanded.

Sebastian looked at me in surprise, obviously not understanding the sudden change in my mood and tone. I sat up a little bit straighter.

"You married Caoilinn?" I tried to keep my voice even. The faint edge of jealousy was nearly undetectable; it made so little sense that I didn't expect Sebastian to notice anyway.

"Yes, of course I did," he admitted, looking confused.

"But that means you're still married to her," I pointed out, a sick feeling growing in my gut. It didn't help at all when Sebastian laughed.

"Gracelynn – she… she died nearly two thousand years ago." The pain that flickered in his eyes disappeared so quickly, I nearly missed it. "And besides, you are Caoilinn," he argued calmly in a carefully hushed voice. My feelings were hurt and my typically mild temper suddenly flared.

"I am *not* her," I snapped. I pulled my hand from his and sharply looked away from him. I knew I was behaving childishly but I couldn't seem to help myself. Of course I knew that he and Caoilinn had a close and intimate relationship but naively, I'd never considered that he might have married her and it bothered me for some reason… but why?

"Why is this upsetting you so much?" He spoke the very same question aloud, his voice patient and concerned. I glared angrily out the window, watching the dull grey buildings and city lights blur by, frustrated and angry because I wasn't certain of the answer myself.

"Because," I paused, searching for the correct words. "Because you committed yourself to her for life – for your life. That means you're still committed to her… so how can you really be committed to me? How can you marry me when you're married to her still? When you still love her?" I finished sadly. My anger was quickly fading and hurt tears quivered in my eyes as I pinpointed the source of my pain.

"But you are her in the same way that she was always you," Sebastian quietly replied. I stubbornly shook my head, still refusing to look his way. "The way I feel about you… This isn't a Caoilinn-thing or a Gracelynn-thing – it's you. The soul of who you are, the core of your being is the same and that's what I love, that's who I can't resist no matter what your name or appearance or age or anything! And that's who I committed myself to."

I blinked away the hurt tears that had begun gathering. I only felt slightly better. My pride was still injured but I could see the silliness of my reaction now.

"Caoilinn and I were not married in the modern sense, anyway. She performed a private ceremony that no one else witnessed but ourselves and the full moon. It was the first step in Binding our souls together, the night when she shared her magic with me and when we committed ourselves – our souls - to one another," he explained. I still didn't really understand. "I wish you could remember. It's hard to believe that I once forgot."

I didn't answer. I knew I'd over-reacted and I felt a torrent of shame as I realized how I'd ruined his proposal. No matter how jokingly he had done it, he had still just asked me to marry him.

"I'm sorry, Sebastian. I… I'm sorry," I repeated lamely. I met his gaze now and his eyes were large and wise, boring down into the depths of mine.

"Don't apologize. I do forget sometimes that you're not her and that you don't remember or know everything that happened between us. I shouldn't have brought it up."

"Let's just forget about it," I suggested, knowing that it would never be so easily done.

"That would have been easy once," he joked. Neither of us laughed. "You should get some rest."

I shook my head, looking out to the bright sky and the world that we were speeding by. "It's early still. I'll sleep when you do."

"I'm not going to sleep tonight," Sebastian unexpectedly announced.

"What? Why not?"

"I don't want to," he answered simply. "The way my nightmares have been lately… I don't think it would be a good idea to sleep on a crowded bus."

"Oh, I see." He was probably right but I didn't like the idea of him staying up all night alone. "I'll stay up with you then," I decided. His response was immediate.

"No, you need to get some sleep."

"And you don't?"

"I don't want it to affect me so it won't for now," Sebastian dismissed. "Stay up with me for now, if you're really not tired, but I want you to eventually get some sleep too – so you know you will," he pointed out.

My eyes narrowed at him and my fingers crept up to my chest

to clench the warm amber of my necklace. "You can only make me sleep if I want to – and I don't. I want to stay awake with you and I don't want it to affect me either," I challenged.

He smiled. "It'll be a good test of your control then. Let's see how you do."

His confidence was extremely aggravating and only served to make me more determined – perhaps that was his intention though.

Sebastian and I stayed awake and talked for hours. I watched as the sun slowly moved lower across the sky, eventually sinking out of sight and leaving its heat smoldering on the horizon in a flare of color. We quietly talked and joked throughout the night, the guilt and tension that had arisen between us disappearing as quickly as it came. I felt surprisingly happy and victorious as I leant against his shoulder and watched the sun rise the following morning. I was exhausted and stiff from sitting in the bus seat all night but I had done it. I was awake and definitely not as tired as I should have been.

"Was it your magic that overpowered mine or your stubbornness?" Sebastian asked me teasingly as we watched the golden rays spread out from the eastern horizon. We were traveling along Highway 17/18 and had just passed through Sault Ste. Marie. We should be in Toronto that evening, in about twelve more hours.

I smiled and kept my voice deliberately light. "I'm not stubborn."

"Of course not," Sebastian agreed grinning. "How about we hop off at the next gas station and buy some breakfast?"

"That sounds like a great plan!" My stomach grumbled delicately in agreement. A gas station breakfast of coffee, doughnuts and cold sandwiches sounded delicious to me.

It was a few more hours before the bus stopped to refuel, giving all the passengers a chance to get off and stretch our legs. Sebastian and I bought a huge bag full of gas station foods – enough so that we would have three full and junk-laden meals that day. Once we were back on the bus, our stomachs full and our coffee cups empty, I did start to feel a little more tired. I reclined my chair slightly and was surprised when Sebastian did the same, pulling one of our dirty and worn blankets from his bag to drape over us (the air-conditioning had started to raise goose bumps on my arms).

I raised my eyebrows at Sebastian. "Going to take a nap?"

"No, but I thought I'd watch you sleep for a while and get some rest vicariously."

"Ha-ha." My sarcasm was ruined by a rather large and long yawn. "I'm just going to rest my eyes," I warned. "You better not let me fall asleep."

"I wouldn't dream of it." I could hear the amusement in Sebastian's voice but could only guess at his smirk as my eyes were already closed. I was rapidly being lulled to sleep by the bus engine's steady hum and Sebastian's nearby warmth.

I really must have been exhausted for I slept deeply for most of the day, missing lunch and supper. It wasn't until the sun had traveled across the vast blue sky that I began to stir and even then, I might not have awakened at all if it weren't for Sebastian's sudden loud moans.

"No… no! I didn't really want… no!" he half-cried, half-yelled, jolting me awake.

I sat up straight, looking around in confusion, my heart beating wildly in my chest. I was confused to see many shocked and curious faces peering over the neighboring seats at me, or rather - at Sebastian. My thoughts were thick and groggy from sleep and it took me a minute to make sense of the situation.

"Sebastian, wake up," I urged, shaking him gently as I spoke.

"No… please…not her!" he moaned even louder, his head tossing feebly.

I shook him harder, worried for what he might call out next. "Wake up!" I insisted, my voice sharp and demanding, a familiar echo of my mother's. I squeezed my amber pendant so tightly in my hand it hurt, focusing all of my strength and will through it. I lowered my voice and spoke slowly and forcefully, in sudden cool control of the situation. "I want you to wake up – now!"

Sebastian's eyes flew open.

I was about to sigh in relief but my breath caught in my chest as I saw his panicked expression.

"What's happening? Where are we?" he demanded in a loud, fearful voice. He started to half-rise out of his seat.

I grabbed his hand and yanked him back down as hard as I could.

"Sebastian, shush! Calm down."

His wide eyes momentarily focused on my face as I spoke, the mysterious depths swirling with confusion.

"Caoilinn? I don't understand - what's going on?" He winced in pain as he spoke, his fingers flying to his temples to press against them.

"Everything okay there, miss?" the bus driver called out. I met his concerned eyes in the mirror over his seat and tried to smile reassuringly.

"We're fine, thanks," I politely responded, throwing him my most charming smile. It didn't work as well as it once had. The driver frowned, still looking concerned and a little suspicious. A lot of eyes were still turned our way.

"Sebastian?" I spoke his name softly, gently placing a hand on his arm. He didn't answer, didn't move, he just continued to clutch at his head in pain. "Seamus?" I repeated, feeling the beginnings of my own panic setting in as a thin trickle of blood ran from his nose and dripped from his upper lip. I grabbed the corner of our blanket and gently touched it to his skin to wipe the blood away. His head snapped up at my touch, his eyes wide once more as he flinched away from me.

"The Others – they're so close. I can sense them! We've got to run, Caoilinn! We have to run! They're going to kill us!" Sebastian began yelling, standing up as he spoke and tugging forcefully on my arms.

Another trickle of blood ran from his other nostril. At almost the same time he abruptly let go of my arms and dropped to his knees in pain, curling up on his side in the middle of the aisle and clutching at his head again.

Two men rushed to help but everyone else remained seated, eyeing Sebastian and me warily. The bus immediately pulled over, the driver angrily turning around.

"What the hell is going on here?" he demanded.

"They look like junkies," someone further back in the bus called out.

"Yeah, I think he might just be tripping out," one of the men who'd come to help Sebastian suggested, glancing at me apologetically as he spoke. The other man looked disgusted and threw his hands up in the air.

"Goddamn coke fiends! They must have been snorting the stuff in the bathroom. Look at that kid's nose." The man nudged Sebastian with his shoe as he spoke, causing him to moan and his eyelids to flutter. His grip on his head did seem to be loosening a bit though and his nose had definitely stopped bleeding.

"We're not drug addicts!" I was completely shocked by the accusation. I'd never done a single drug in my life – I hadn't even taken Tylenol with codeine when my wisdom teeth were removed!

"Sure you're not," the bus driver agreed dryly. All three men shook their heads at us. Sebastian moaned on the floor, his head beginning to toss again and his eyelashes fluttering more regularly. "I thought it was strange you two didn't sleep last night but now I guess I know why. Grab your stuff and get off my bus," the driver challenged, glaring at me. "You can file a complaint with head office if you don't like it but you're not riding with us any further! I should call the cops and have 'em pick you up."

A few people near the back of the bus clapped. I was too shocked to speak. The Others were nearly upon us, our only hope was to get to Toronto before them and now we were getting thrown off the only bus that would take us there… what were we going to do?

Chapter Five – Reunion

"Gracelynn?" Sebastian's voice weakly asked. His eyes were open now and he gazed up at me from the floor. His confusion was clear but it was the kind of confusion you'd expect from someone who had awoken to that scene.

"Help him up and get 'em off," the bus driver instructed the two men standing beside me. They both nodded their agreement and reached down to roughly pull Sebastian up by his arms.

I could sense this was an argument that we weren't about to win, even with Sebastian's power of persuasion. These men absolutely did not want us on the bus – there would be no convincing them to let us stay.

I reached under our seats and pulled out our bags, stuffing our old blanket into the top of Sebastian's with the bag of leftover food we'd bought at the gas station.

"Are you okay?" I asked Sebastian, noticing how he seemed to need the men's support to stand.

He nodded, standing up a little straighter. "I'll be fine."

"Come on then, we're getting off the bus," I told him in a low voice that made my displeasure very clear. For some reason, the men holding onto Sebastian's arms suddenly released him and began moving back towards their seats, refusing to meet my eye.

Sebastian calmly accepted the situation in a way that only he ever could. He paused and took in my expression, nodding slowly as if he understood. He then took his bag from me and gestured for me to go first. The bus was silent, all eyes on us as we exited.

We were deposited on the side of a fairly busy street on what appeared to be the outskirts of Toronto. For a minute we stood there, dazed and overwhelmed by the sudden noise and heat of the day, and the abrupt change in our situation. Sebastian recovered first, grabbing my arm and pulling me along the sidewalk.

"We have to keep moving – the fifth is here and the Others are on their way. They'll be here by morning," Sebastian warned, slipping his arms through the straps of his backpack as he spoke.

"I know."

Sebastian lifted a questioning brow at me. I pulled my pack on and began marching down the sidewalk beside him.

"We both fell asleep and we shouldn't have. The Others must have wanted us to get thrown off the bus to stop us from reaching Toronto. The driver thought you were high on cocaine because of your nosebleed and the way you… well, you sort of freaked out. He said he was going to call the police," I added.

Sebastian used his black t-shirt to wipe the blood from his upper lip and nose, barely pausing in his stride as he did so. His expression was hard to read. I thought he might be angry.

"This way," he instructed, taking the next right turn and getting us off the main road where we'd been dropped off. "We need to find a map or a phone book - or something, and figure out where we are and how far it is to your father's house from here. If we can hitch a ride, we still might make it in time…"

It was our only hope and it wasn't much of one. There were too many "if's" to this plan. It all depended on if we could make it to my father's tonight. And if he agreed to help us. And if he could get us out of the city tomorrow. And if we could stay out of the Others' clutches until then. If, if, if, if. It was the only plan we had though.

We criss-crossed up and down the streets, always on the lookout for someone chasing us and for a sign of where we were and how far it was to where we needed to be.

We eventually confirmed that we were in fact on the outskirts of Toronto. We decided the best course of action would be to find a phone book and look up my father's address, then try to either ride a city bus or catch a cab there. It took us nearly half an hour to find a phone booth – precious time that we didn't have but every time we tried to ask in a store for a phone book we were denied. It was a frustrating and frightening setback; another obvious indication of the Others' proximity.

I leafed through the thick, worn out phone book in the booth we had stopped at, trying to ignore the stains on the pages and the stickiness to the cover. It was a relief to find my father's name and address fairly easily – I hadn't been certain that he'd have his number listed. There was even a map of the different areas in Toronto in the front of the phone book, but when we eventually found my father's address on the map, all of our hopes came crashing down.

"He lives on the other side of the city," I quietly announced. My father and his new wife Dahlia, lived at least fifty kilometers away.

I looked to Sebastian for hope. His face was pale and drawn, faint purplish bags shadowed his large, hollow eyes. "Let's try and catch a bus," he said as he took my hand and led me away. There was no hope in his voice though, only despair and defeat.

We walked slowly after that, our feet dragging with each step as the sun began to set. A few blocks away we found a bus shelter and we sat down together on the bench. I felt like curling up in Sebastian's arms and falling asleep for the rest of my life. It would have been the perfect escape. Sebastian pulled a pack of cigarettes out of his backpack that he must have bought earlier at the gas station. I didn't bother to comment or complain as he lit a cigarette and began quietly smoking, blowing perfectly shaped rings out that knotted together into complicated Celtic knots in the warm night arm. I rested my head on his shoulder despite the occasional trail of cigarette smoke that wafted my way. We watched the traffic whiz by and wanted a bus to come with every fiber of our beings. We waited, and waited.

When I first saw the bus' bright lights coming down the street towards us in the hazy twilight, I thought I might be dreaming. Neither of us dared speak our hope out loud as the bus approached and slowed. Sebastian butted out his cigarette and we stood up together, clasping one another's hands tightly as the bus came to a stop and opened its doors. Hope rose in my chest like a ray of light breaking through a stormy sky.

We had to first wait for the passengers to disembark before we could move forward. All my hopes were destroyed as the driver began shaking his head at us.

"Sorry kids. This is my last stop for the night, I'm off-duty now," the dark-skinned man apologized in a friendly-enough tone. My throat tightened up from frustration and fear. I felt like the world was falling apart around me as I realized, this could very well be the end.

"Please, sir. I have to get to my father's house tonight. I *want* to see him. We have to," I desperately begged, trying to keep my voice from quivering.

The man looked confused, his dark brows pulling down over his eyes. "Sorry, there sweetheart but you'll have to find another way to your dad's place. I'd love to help you out but there's nothing I can do for you – I'm off duty. Good luck."

"Thanks," Sebastian answered politely as the driver slowly closed the doors before us and began to pull away. Sebastian turned his back on the bus and held his arms out to me. I threw myself against his chest, giving in to the panicked despair that threatened to overwhelm me. In the fading light, with my exhausted, bleary eyes I almost missed the sign on the back of the bus. As luck would have it, a driver not wanting to yield angrily honked his horn, catching my attention. The car's headlights lit up the back of the bus that it nearly rear-ended. The sign was perfectly highlighted for me, the car's headlights focused straight onto a photograph of my father. I gasped out loud.

"Sebastian, look!" I cried as I pushed away from him, pointing towards the now retreating bus. Sebastian twisted around just as the car lurched around the bus, obscuring the advertisement on the rear from view.

"What am I supposed to be looking at?" he asked in confusion, squinting after the bus.

"I can't believe it!" I exclaimed excitedly. "There was an advertisement for a law firm – my *father's* law firm. **Stevenson Justice** 'a local lawyer fighting for local rights'," I quoted. Sebastian didn't seem to understand, his expression still doubtful and defeated. "Sebastian, my father always works late – always. If his office is nearby…"

A dim spark of hope lit up Sebastian's expression. He grabbed my hand and we started running down the street, back towards the phone booth we had used earlier.

I cursed myself for not thinking of this sooner. I had just assumed that if my father lived on the other side of town that his business would be there also and it probably was but any hope, not matter how small, was all we had right now and was worth investigating. My hands shook as I turned the pages of the phone book, rapidly searching the yellow pages until I found it, Stevenson Justice, 1420 Elizabeth Street. The street name sounded so familiar, I was sure we'd passed it earlier. The map in the front of the phone book confirmed it. Elizabeth Street was only two blocks away from where we'd been dropped off by the Greyhound bus. If we hadn't started criss-crossing through town incase the police were searching for us, we would have walked right past my father's office. As soon as we realized how close we were, we took off running hand-in-hand, back the way we'd come. I could almost feel the seconds ticking by as the sun sunk below the horizon and a cool evening breeze began sweeping the city streets.

Despite the cooler evening air, we were both sweaty and slick faced when we reached the street-level entrance to my father's small, two story, office building. My father's office appeared to take up the whole first floor and I thought there might be a small apartment on top. I could imagine him spending many nights there, working late to establish a new firm in a new city. I could only hope and fear that I'd find him here still tonight. Butterflies fluttered nervously in my stomach and my palms became sweaty. I took a quick second to run my fingers through my dirty, knotted hair and to wipe the perspiration from my face on the sleeve of my thin, cotton shirt before I boldly reached forward and tapped on the door.

Nothing happened, no one answered. We could see into his office through the tinted glass door and there was obviously no one there, all the lights off and his staff long gone. I refused to give up though. I knocked again and again, eventually pounding on the door with my fists, growling in frustration. Sebastian gently pulled me away.

"I think someone's coming," he quietly announced.

I squinted at the glass, just able to make out the faintest hint of movement before a light flicked on inside. My heart began beating double-time as a shadowy figure approached the misty, glass door and slid the lock aside with a click. The door opened just a few inches.

"I'm sorry, we're closed. You'll have to come back tomorrow," a gentle, female voice told us.

"Dahlia?" I only just managed to call out her name before she closed the door. I watched her hesitate, then push the door open wider. It was her. My father's new wife stood before me, familiar to me only from the few pictures my father had sent me of her and the one or two times I had stopped by his office in Victoria before he'd left my mother and moved to Toronto with his legal secretary. She looked nothing like my mother. For one thing, Dahlia was fifteen years younger and she also smiled a lot more. She was a little chubby but in a cute, rather pleasant way, with short brown hair that curled around her round face in a semi-wild mess. She was short too and though bubbly and cheerful, I remembered she was also very intelligent and could be quite forceful when she wanted to be. She really was a good match for my father.

Dahlia stared at me with her large, brown eyes. She blinked uncertainly, obviously seeing some kind of resemblance in my face but unable to place the familiarity.

"It's me, Grace," I clarified. "Gordon's daughter."

"Grace? Oh my God! It that really you? Is this Sebastian? Oh my God! Come in! Come in!" she ushered us inside, recovering quickly. She couldn't stop staring at us both though as she brought us in and sat us down in the office waiting room, her eyes too wide still and her mouth hanging slightly open.

"Grace – what happened to you? Your mother told us you ran away from home but Sebastian's foster parents told Gordon a completely different story – that you'd gone traveling with Sebastian for the summer and decided to leave early, before graduation. Lucky for you, you had enough credits and work turned in that you would still have earned your diploma. But… what happened? Why are you here and why are… you look so different!" she declared, her tongue babbling away but her eyes sharp and taking in every detail of our appearances.

"I've changed a bit."

"I would never have recognized you!" Dahlia interjected. "I doubt your father will either. What is he going to think of all this?"

"Is he here?" Sebastian chimed in politely. "We need to speak with him as soon as possible."

"No, he's actually been at a meeting for the past few hours but he was going to swing by the office to pick me up before heading home. He should be here in about half an hour's time. But… maybe we should clean you up before he arrives or I swear, you'll give him the shock of his life! And you've got to explain to me what's going on. Where have you been? What are you doing turning up here unannounced at eight o'clock at night?" Dahlia demanded. My head spun from all her questions.

"We've been traveling across Canada," Sebastian neatly cut-in. "We wanted to do it as cheaply as possible and rough-it where we could so we've been camping mostly. We hiked through Quetico Park a few weeks ago and then decided to take a bus out to Toronto to visit with you before our next destination."

"And where is your next destination? The Jensons said you were traveling on your motorbike – where is it? And what is it that you need to talk to Gordon about that's so important?" Dahlia drilled.

"That's between my father and I," I firmly and politely replied. For a second I was worried that Dahlia might be offended by my firm tone but instead, she grinned in response.

"So there is a bit of your father in you after all," she commented, still smiling at me. "Here, let's get you upstairs and into the shower. Sebastian, you don't look too badly but Grace you're a mess! You can fix yourself up while Sebastian tells me the whole story," she suggested. I easily agreed, wanting to be as presentable before my father as possible and knowing that even Dahlia wasn't likely to get much out of Sebastian. He would handle her questions better than I could anyway.

Dahlia led us upstairs to the small apartment overtop of my father's office. There were really only three rooms – a small kitchen/living room, a tiny bedroom with a small, double bed and a little bathroom with a toilet, sink and stand-up shower. The second bedroom in the place had been converted into a storage room for office documents and files. Dahlia set about making tea and chatting with Sebastian while I got myself into the shower.

I was shocked when I saw my reflection in the mirror. I hadn't spent much time looking at my reflection in the past few months other than the glimpses I'd had in rivers and lakes. Even on the bus, I'd only glanced quickly at myself in the small bathroom mirror, knowing I most likely wouldn't be pleased with what I saw and not finding it important enough to look. Now that I found myself in front of a fairly large mirror under the bathroom's bright lights, there was nowhere else to look.

I had cut my hair short enough that it didn't quite reach my shoulders. With the extra weight cut off it, my wavy locks had sprung up into lose and messy curls and I was shocked to see there were actually small pieces of dirt and debris tangled into my hair. My hair was lighter in color than I'd realized too and my chestnut locks had been bleached and highlighted to a light, golden shade from the sun. My face looked much the same as I remembered though my eyebrows were a little thicker (having not been plucked all summer), my nose and cheekbones were dusted with freckles and my eyes appeared slightly smaller than what I was used to with their lack of mascara. My clothes looked disgusting under the bright lights – all the rips and stains obvious and overwhelming. I stripped down in front of the mirror, noting the small scratches, bruises and mosquito bites, and the dusty dirt that appeared to cover me from head to toe.

I showered as quickly as possible, only taking the briefest of moments to enjoy the hot, steamy shower. The water that ran off me was a muddy brown and I almost giggled out loud as I realized half of my "tan" was in fact due to the thin layer of dirt and dust that had coated my skin. I scrubbed my body and my hair clean, tugging conditioner through my tangled locks and enjoying the sweet, floral scent of the soaps and shampoos.

I hurriedly dressed in the clean clothes Dahlia had so thoughtfully gathered for me. They were hers so they fit me quite loosely but I didn't mind. I cinched the cord on the flowing, white peasant skirt as tightly as it would go so it wouldn't slide off my hips. I luxuriated in the feel of the clean and crisp cotton as I combed out my hair and applied a quick sweep of Dahlia's eye shadow to my eyes, not bothering with any other primping as I knew I was quickly running out of time. Besides, I was curious about what Sebastian and Dahlia were discussing and wanted to rejoin them as soon as possible.

I glanced in the mirror one last time to inspect myself before exiting. My curls were damp still but hung somewhat neatly to just below my jaw. I looked clean and fresh, like I'd been on vacation somewhere tropical with my freckles and tanned skin. I looked a lot more presentable anyway and enough like my old self that my father wouldn't be too shocked – I hoped. The thin, mauve tank top Dahlia had provided me with just wouldn't do though. The thick, black tattoo that snaked down and around my whole right arm contrasted drastically with my neat, conservative outfit. I knew my father would have a fit if he saw it – it was difficult enough to look at myself.

"Dahlia?" I called, cracking the bathroom door open only slightly.

"Yes," she immediately answered.

"Do you have another shirt I could borrow? Maybe something with long sleeves? I'm a bit cold in this one," I lied.

"Oh, sure. Just one sec, hun." I heard her bustle away and rummage through the small chest of drawers we'd seen in the little bedroom. I reached through the door with only my hand for the new shirt but was shocked when Dahlia thrust the door open and I was forced to jump backwards. She smiled at me wryly.

"I'm not sure if this one will fool your father though, he's sure to notice that tattoo," Dahlia stated matter-of-factly as she handed me a thin, white, zip-up hoodie. I put it on over my tank top protectively, wanting to hide the Binding mark from her sight. She was right though, the black pattern twisted out beneath the cuff and around my wrist to coil into the center of my palm. "Really, Grace. If you had to get matching tattoos, couldn't you at least have chosen a smaller and more discrete design? You're going to give your father a heart attack."

I didn't laugh because it wasn't really a joke. It might very well be true.

"Thank you for the clothes," I said politely as I stepped out of the bathroom, moving immediately towards Sebastian who sat on the end of a leather couch. He smiled at me reassuringly as I sat down close to his side, leaning into him ever-so-slightly.

"You look paler," Sebastian commented with a grin.

"It happens when you lose a layer of dirt," I answered with a shrug.

"You do look a lot better Grace. Perhaps you'd like to clean yourself up quickly too Sebastian? I expect Gordon will arrive soon but you should have a few more minutes," Dahlia mildly suggested. "I'm afraid there might not be time for you to shower and I don't think it would be a good idea to lend you any of Gordon's clothes – not that they'd fit you anyway."

"I'll just freshen up then. I'll be right back," Sebastian added quietly, patting my leg quickly before standing up. I immediately felt anxious, unsure of what to say to Dahlia and how much (or how little) Sebastian and her had already discussed. I also didn't want my father to arrive in Sebastian's absence; the idea of confronting him alone terrified me even though I knew the task of convincing him to help us would fall mostly upon my shoulders.

"Would you like some water?" Dahlia offered as Sebastian closed the bathroom door. She watched me with her large, kind eyes; eyes that were bright with intelligence and saw much more than one might expect. I knew that no matter how sweet and caring she appeared to be, I needed to watch what I said around her just as closely as I must with my father.

Dahlia handed me a glass of water and then sat down on the small loveseat adjacent to the couch I sat upon. I could feel her eyes studying me so I carefully avoided meeting her eye.

"Does your mother know you're here?" Dahlia suddenly asked.

"No, no one does." I realized after I spoke that it wasn't entirely true – the Others must have realized exactly what we were up to by now.

"Did you want to call her?"

"No, thank you. I'd actually prefer if my mother didn't know that we'd been here," I admitted. Dahlia studied me curiously, twisting one of her wild curls around her finger as she contemplated.

"Sebastian said you weren't planning on staying in Toronto long, perhaps only for the night?"

I didn't answer, not wanting to give anything away.

"He made it sound like you were in some kind of trouble, like you were running from something?"

Again, I didn't comment. My nerves were starting to increase and

I reached up to hold onto my amber pendant, its quiet warmth instantly soothing me.

"Grace… what kind of trouble has this boy gotten you into?" Dahlia asked, lowering her voice. Her eyes flickered to the bathroom door, as if expecting Sebastian to suddenly come barging back out. "You've got to tell me the truth, hun. Has he put you up to asking your father for money? Was it his idea to come here? If you're afraid of him or if you need help–"

"No," I cut in. "It's not like that at all, Dahlia. I love him – I want to be with him and he hasn't gotten me into anything. This is actually all my fault," I admitted, the truth of my words dragging down my heart. It really was my fault. If I hadn't made Sebastian remember his past, if I hadn't performed the Binding spell and in doing so, reawakened the forgotten magic inside of me, none of this would be happening. I couldn't very well tell Dahlia all that though.

"I don't understand what's going on." Dahlia's brown eyes were wide with what I felt to be genuine concern. I could tell she really did want to help, I just wished I could trust her.

The bathroom door swung open and Sebastian stepped out into the room. He looked amazing – I shouldn't have been surprised. He'd brushed his black hair back from his face and it shone as if it had been freshly washed. His hands and face were clean, and he'd traded the shirt he'd been wearing for a "fresh" one from his bag that was impossibly white and wrinkle-free. He met my eyes with a smile and I instantly relaxed. My renewed calm lasted for only a heartbeat though as we all heard the sounds of the office door downstairs being unlocked.

"Gordon must be here." Dahlia quickly rose, looking quite anxious herself. "I'll go and greet him, and let him know that you're here." She quickly disappeared around the corner and down the stairs. Sebastian came and sat by my side. He took my hand (the one that wasn't nervously clasping my pendant) and linked his fingers through mine. His grip was warm and firm and reassuring.

"It'll be alright," he murmured. We could both hear my father's voice rumbling downstairs now and Dahlia's soft soprano, tinkling in response. My heart began picking up in pace, my throat and lips becoming far too dry. "Just want for him to believe us. Want him to help us."

"It won't work," I whispered back. I could hear heavy footsteps on the stairs now.

"He'll want to help you, Gracelynn. It's going to work. I know you can do this. Just focus – you've got to really want this."

"I do," I assured him, my throat too tight for my voice to come out any louder than a whisper even if I'd wanted it to as my father entered the room.

The last time I'd seen my father in person, he'd been furious with me. He had kicked me out of my home for dating Sebastian and "tarnishing" our family's reputation, and he had practically disowned me. We'd spoken on the phone many times since then and though neither of us had ever apologized, I felt like we'd come to a mutual understanding. I wasn't sure how our relationship stood now though. When Sebastian had erased my memories last Spring, I had gone back to being the "perfect daughter" and since my father wasn't around anymore, that had meant catering to my mother's needs. She had banned me from speaking to my father, so I'd only stayed in contact with him through the occasional email sent quickly from a school computer. And I hadn't contacted anyone in my family at all in the past month and a half since my memory had been returned and we'd be running from the Others. I could understand why my mother would say I'd run away from home – it would certainly appear that way to her.

My father looked momentarily stunned to see me even though I was certain Dahlia had told him I was waiting upstairs. His eyes rapidly scanned me over, taking in my shorter, messier hair and tanned skin. I smiled nervously and for a second, he almost smiled back. Then his eyes fell upon Sebastian's hand linked together with mine on my lap. His eyes immediately moved to the tiny curl of the black tattoo peaking out beneath my shirt sleeve and the heavy amber ring nestled so innocently on the fourth finger of my left hand. I felt like cursing under my breath as I could almost see the thoughts flashing through my father's mind. I could guess at the conclusion he was coming to. His color was already starting to change, a scarlet flush rapidly spreading across his round cheeks. I knew I had to do something to take control of the situation – fast, so I did the only thing I could think of.

"Daddy!" I cried out, forcing a broad grin to stretch across my face. I quickly dropped Sebastian's hand and jumped up from the couch, skipping across the room and joyfully throwing myself into my father's arms. In that moment, I wanted so badly for my father to just love me, to be happy to see me and to give me one of those big bear hugs that I remembered from my childhood. I felt him hesitate, sensed his momentary stunned surprise and then the next thing I knew, his big, strong arms were wrapping around me, squeezing me tightly against his round belly. A sob began rising on a strong wave of emotion within my chest. "I missed you Daddy," I whispered against the smooth fabric of his dark blue suit. I smiled as I realized he smelt like brandy and cologne, the scent surprisingly nostalgic.

My father loosened his grip on me and awkwardly patted my head.

"Hi, sweetheart. I missed you too, Gracie," he answered, gruffly. I thought I heard Dahlia sniff away a tear behind him.

I took a small step back and looked up at my father. His color had returned to normal – just the slight red flush to his cheeks that was always present. I could see the emotion sparkling in his eyes but with each passing second, his expression grew sterner, the lines in his face deepening and his joy at seeing me fading.

"Dad, I'm sorry to just drop in on you like this but we really need your help," I began, speaking softly and uncertainly. I tried to remain focused, I tried hard to want for him to help us but it was difficult to concentrate with so many conflicting emotions grappling around inside of me.

My father frowned, narrowing his eyes suspiciously at Sebastian who now stood slightly behind me.

"Why don't we all sit down," Dahlia suggested. She gently placed her hand on my father's arm and he reluctantly moved towards a large leather recliner in the corner of the room that I had assumed would be his chair. Dahlia moved into the kitchen and began making my father a drink while I resumed my seat beside Sebastian, keeping a carefully calculated distance between us this time. My father's eyes were on me the whole while, his expression stern.

"Good evening, Mr. Stevenson," Sebastian greeted him in a polite and respectful tone. My father fixed him with a hard stare, not immediately answering. The tension in the room grew.

"What kind of trouble have you gotten my little girl into?" my father eventually demanded, sitting up a little straighter as he spoke. He could be quite an intimidating man with his broad shoulders, the hard angles of his features and his sharp, hazel eyes. It was impressive that Sebastian didn't shrink from his glare.

"We need your help, Dad," I repeated, redirecting my father's attention onto me. I forced myself not to drop my eyes, to meet his hard, unwavering stare. I decided just to launch into it, grasping my necklace tightly in my hand for strength as I spoke. "We need to get out of the country as soon as we can – tonight if possible. There are people following us, *very* dangerous people. The less you know the better. I wish we didn't have to involve you at all but you're the only one who could possibly help us get away…"

My father didn't speak, he just continued to stare at me, his face completely expressionless. I focused my thoughts, my emotions, my desires – I focused with everything I had to want him to help us. I silently pleaded with him in my mind. I begged him with all my heart but still, he didn't answer, didn't respond.

"Here you go, dear." Dahlia stepped between my father and I to hand him his drink, breaking the tense moment between us and offering me just a few moments to recover and refocus. I glanced to Sebastian who gave me a quick, encouraging nod. It was all up to me, I had to do this. My father really was our only hope.

Dahlia sat down on the loveseat near Sebastian and I, and we all waited in silence for my father's response.

"What exactly are you asking me for, Grace?" my father demanded, his voice harsher and gruffer than I'd hoped. But still, at least he was speaking.

"I'm asking for your help. I want you to help us – I need you to. We need travel documents, identification and passports. We need to be booked on the next flight to Ireland. And we need it done as soon as possible." There was no way to make my request sound reasonable. My expectations sounded ridiculous as I spoke them out loud but I tried to sound confident nonetheless. I tried to believe that my father would want to help us, that he would find a way.

"And what makes you think I can accomplish all of this, if I had the inclination?" My father fixed me with another hard stare, he appeared not to even be blinking. The small apartment was becoming increasingly warm with the number of bodies packed inside and a small bead of sweat began forming on my forehead. I resisted the urge to brush it away, focusing all of my attention on the task at hand.

"You can do it. You have the power and connections to make it happen. You can do anything you want to," I added, hoping I didn't sound as desperate as I felt.

Silence settled over the room once more. My eyes were locked with my father's as we battled wills, each stubbornly refusing to be the first to look away. Neither Sebastian nor Dahlia tried to speak or intrude upon our conversation; they both recognized that this was between my father and I, and they remained quiet bystanders.

"I could help you, if I wanted to," my father eventually agreed. "But I don't."

His proclamation pierced my heart with pain from both his rejection and my own fear. I could feel my panic rapidly rising along with the hurt inside of me.

"Please… Dad, I wish I could explain but I can't. I really, really need your help…" I begged.

"No." His answer was firm, his expression hard and cold. "If you really are in some kind of trouble, I can only assume that you've brought it on yourself by the poor choices you have made." He looked to Sebastian as he spoke. My amber necklace began to faintly throb against my chest along with the pain in my heart.

"I'll take you to the police if you want and you can tell them your story. I'll even provide a place for you – and you alone – to stay while you're in Toronto but that is as much help as I can possibly offer you, Grace." The volume of his voice was increasing as he spoke along with the color in his cheeks. I could feel my control on the situation rapidly slipping away like sand through my fingers. "I will absolutely not be taken in by some ridiculous scheme that you have let this scoundrel come up with! How can you possibly expect me to blindly commit myself to help you escape the country and commit identity and documentation fraud for who knows what reason? What the hell is really going on here?"

"Now, now, let's all just calm down for a minute," Dahlia interjected. "You know your doctor warned you not to get worked up like this."

"I will not calm down!" my father thundered, his face bright red, his hazel eyes flashing. "I haven't seen or heard from my daughter in months and then she shows up, uninvited and unannounced, looking and sounding like some crazed vagabond with this... this... *scumbag* so clearly manipulating her!" He gestured furiously at Sebastian as he spoke, a disgusted expression on his face.

I was shocked to my core. I stared at him numbly, an expression of hurt disbelief frozen on my face. Somehow, I had never anticipated that the situation might go this badly even though I had partially feared it might. To hear my father refuse my honest pleas for help, to listen to him insult us and accuse Sebastian of manipulating me – and that he would believe I could be ignorant enough to allow myself to ever be manipulated... I felt my own temper rising, the furious heat of it a match for my blazing necklace. My anger burnt away the numb shock that had initially seized me within its grip and words flew from my lips without thought.

"How dare you!" I cried, suddenly as outraged as he. "I came to you because I needed you, because you're the only one who can possibly help us – who can save us! All I want is your help and this is how you treat me?"

"No, you don't! You want my money, you want my connections – you're just like your mother! What the hell were you thinking, coming here like this?" my father yelled, rising to his feet. I jumped up right along with him, his last comments a slap in the face. I could feel myself trembling with rage.

"I just wanted you to help us," I growled.

"The only way I'll be helping you is out the door! Now get the hell out of here before I call the cops!" my father bellowed right into my face.

I didn't waver for a second, I was far too angry to ever back down and with my anger, a strange, calm control had settled over me. I squeezed my necklace even tighter as it burned red hot into my hand. I focused myself and my will like never before, my eyes burning into my father's.

"I want you to help us," I told him quietly and firmly, my voice a subtle threat.

"No," my father answered, his voice just as dangerous. I took a step closer to him, ignoring Sebastian's sudden hand on my arm. I hadn't even noticed him stand.

"Grace," Sebastian cautioned. I barely heard him speak, letting the rest of the world slip away so that there was nothing but my father and myself, and what I wanted.

"Please," I spat out between clenched teeth. The fire from my necklace was burning into my chest, rushing out from my heart and flaring from my eyes with each word I spoke. "I need you to help us. I *want* you to want to help us."

"N–" my father's voice seemed to stick in his throat. I watched in amazement and numb horror as his hard, steely gaze suddenly softened. His eyes unfocused and glazed over as they started to roll back into his head.

"Dad!" I cried, snapping out of my furious, trance-like state.

"Gordon!" Dahlia yelled as my father suddenly slumped backwards, unconscious and unmoving. I stared at him in horror. What had I done?

Chapter Six - Taking Flight

I watched in horror as my father's legs buckled and he dropped backwards into his chair, the recliner creaking and groaning from the sudden impact. Sweat covered his pale, gray skin and his lips were strangely colorless. The surge of anger and power that had swelled through my body and mind moments before was abruptly extinguished. A new panic set in.

"Oh, God, he's had a heart attack! Oh my, God!" Dahlia cried, frantically running for the phone.

"Wait!" Sebastian instructed her, his voice firm and commanding. Dahlia froze in her tracks. "I think he just fainted. He's already starting to come around."

Dahlia rushed back to my father's side and we all watched as his color quickly returned and his shallow breathing resumed to a more normal pace. My father's eyelids flew open and he stared into each of our faces in confusion, his eyes darting back and forth between us.

"What... what just happened to me?" he demanded. His eyes focused on my face. "Grace? Is that you? What are you doing here?"

I paused, unsure of how to answer but no one else volunteered to speak for me.

"I, umm... Sebastian and I were in Toronto. We came to ask you for some help, remember?" I prompted uncertainly.

"But we don't need to talk about that now," Dahlia dismissed, giving me a stern look. To all of our surprise though my father shook his head, brushing Dahlia's fluttering hands aside and sitting up a bit straighter.

"That's right - I remember. I was just a little... confused for a moment. Of course, I remember. The passports, the plane tickets... I'll have it all taken care of by morning."

We all gaped at him, shocked and stunned into silence. For once,

Sebastian was just as speechless as I.

"Hunny, I think you need to go to the hospital. You collapsed – you might have had a heart attack or a stroke, and now you're not making any sense," Dahlia fretted, the furrow above her smoothly arched brows deepening by the second.

"Nonsense!" my father declared, standing up and shaking off her hands when she tried to support him. "I feel fine. I just got a little hot-headed there for a moment. I'm not sure what came over me but of course I'll help you Gracie. I can't say I understand what's really going on but if you need my help, I'll give it to you and I don't need or want to know any more than that."

I blinked, still stunned. I struggled to regain the ability to speak.

"Um… thanks, Dad. I really, really, really appreciate your change of heart. I wouldn't ask you for help if there were another way…"

"Of course not. I know that, dear. Now if you'll excuse me, I have quite a few phone calls to make. If you want to be on the next flight to Ireland, I'm going to have to call in some favors and wake up a few important people, but we'll get you on the very next plane," my father gruffly assured me. He gave my shoulder a heavy pat as he walked past me and even gave Sebastian a grudging nod before going into the small bedroom at the rear of the apartment, cell phone in hand and fingers already dialing.

Dahlia stared at us wide-eyed for a moment before hurrying into the bedroom after him and quickly closing the door.

Sebastian sat down heavily on the couch, his fingers pressed against his temples. I dropped down beside him and we both silently contemplated our thoughts, Sebastian slowly massaging circles into his brow.

"What just happened?" I eventually asked him, feeling strangely calm – almost numb. At first I didn't think he was going to answer me. He just shook his head and pushed his fingers harder against his skull. I tried to wait patiently for his response but it was difficult when I could feel the seconds ticking away against us. He suddenly began speaking, his voice soft and barley audible, his eyes tightly closed still.

"It's not possible to force someone to do or feel something against their natural will. Your magic shouldn't be strong enough - you told me so yourself."

A cold chill rippled down my spine, my heart brittled by its frost.

"But… you think I did," I stated, my voice flat and emotionless. I knew we had to both face the truth, there was no avoiding it this time. "He didn't want to help us, but I made him. I forced my father to do what I wanted, didn't I?" My voice shook a little at the end, the guilt and fear quickly threatening to overwhelm me. I desperately tried to push it aside but tears already stung my eyes.

Sebastian looked at me then, the pain in my voice reflected in the intensity of his eyes.

"No, you didn't – you couldn't have forced him to help us if a part of him didn't really want to. You would never have wanted to force him against his will," he quickly reassured me, his doubt vanishing. He brushed the loose curls back from my face and studied me cautiously, my own sadness and pain now burning in the dark depths of his eyes. "There has to be an explanation, Gracelynn. Maybe your father had conflicting wants and you just helped tip the balance. Or maybe the proximity of the Others and their wants influenced what went on here," he suggested. He leant forward to sweetly kiss my lips. My eyes slowly cleared, my heart wanting so badly to believe his words. He kissed me again slowly, gently and my heart beat faster. His lips lingered on mine and I leant into him. I desperately needed him to help me forget what I may or may not have just done. I needed him to love me, regardless, and to remind me of who I really was.

"Ahem," Dahlia cleared her throat nosily as she reentered the room.

We broke apart, my cheeks dusted with embarrassment. Sebastian was as calm and collected as ever, merely smiling in amusement at the interruption or perhaps at my guilty blush.

"I think Gordon's going to be up most of the night on the phone. He's adamant that he get you on a morning flight, direct to Ireland. I think he believes your lives really do depend on it," she added, eyeing us both strangely as she came to sit down.

"They do," Sebastian answered solemnly. He stared back at her unflinchingly. It was no surprise when Dahlia was the first to look away.

"I don't know why, but I'm starting to believe you too. This is all just so bizarre!" she declared with a shake of her head, her messy curls bouncing off her cheekbones.

"Tell me about it," I quietly agreed. Sebastian smiled and squeezed my hand. "I'm so sorry to put you and Dad through this Dahlia. I hope to make it up to you one day."

"He's your father, Grace. No matter what he said before, he really does want to help you now and he won't have it any other way." A fresh wave of guilt hit me, causing me to drop my eyes in shame. Sebastian gave my hand another gentle squeeze. "You two might as well try and get some rest while you can. I'll get you some blankets and you can lie down on the couches – separate couches, mind you." Dahlia's small mouth twitched into a near smile.

"Of course," Sebastian agreed. I wondered if he meant it.

Dahlia went back to the bedroom for some blankets. I heard her soft voice briefly murmuring in response to my father's hearty bass as he was apparently between phone calls. It looked like she was fighting a smile as she came back out.

"Here are some blankets for you. You'll have to use the cushions as pillows I'm afraid. Sebastian, Gordon would like a word with you. Grace, why don't you help me to make up the beds while the men have their chat?"

Oh no, I thought, my stomach dropping. Sebastian smiled reassuringly at me though, looking totally unsurprised. He stepped around Dahlia with a calm and confident smile, much to Dahlia's obvious disappointment.

"I'll be back shortly," he told me with a quick and cheeky wink before he bravely stepped into the bedroom, the door closing quietly behind him.

I wanted to eavesdrop and listen at the door but I knew I couldn't with Dahlia still present. She started chatting away, perhaps trying to set me at ease but really she only added to my discomfort as I had no chance of overhearing anything now.

When we finished turning the couches into two makeshift beds, we each sat down upon one and Dahlia flicked on the TV. My eyes kept wandering to the kitchen clock. It was nearly fifteen minutes later that Sebastian finally emerged, his face a little pale, his expression slightly worn but overall, he appeared to be well-enough. I hadn't heard any shouting so it obviously couldn't have been that bad… I hoped.

Dahlia quickly said good night and went back into the bedroom, my father's loud voice clearly audible once more as he grumbled into his cell phone – he certainly didn't seem too pleased. Sebastian kicked off his shoes and lay down on the couch, pulling one of the fleecy blankets over him. I sighed in exasperation as he closed his eyes.

"You're really going to pretend to sleep?"

He smiled in response but didn't open his eyes.

"What did my father want to talk to you about?"

He shrugged. "Oh, the usual. He wanted to know what my intentions were, if I would be able to keep you safe while we're overseas and he wanted to make sure I understood that if I ever put you in harm's way again he would rip me to pieces with his own hands."

"Oh, that's all?" I replied, my tone coolly nonchalant as I curled up under my own blanket on the loveseat.

Sebastian chuckled, his eyes finally opening. "I believe him too — he's one of the most determined people I've ever had the pleasure of encountering. It looks like we'll be out of the country tomorrow morning. It's going to be close but I think we're going to make it. Your father really does have connections everywhere; he's already booked us on a 7am flight and he's just working out the details of our documents now. We're going to make it to Ireland at least twenty-four hours before the Others do, maybe even more."

My heart sank. I'd been so focused on the goal of getting to Ireland, I'd almost forgotten that the Others would just as easily follow and chase us there. "Will we ever be able to stop running?" I asked him quietly.

"Yes," he answered without hesitation. "We'll find the answers we're looking for in Ireland, I know we will. You'll regain full control and use of your magic, and then we'll find a way to stop the Others. They'll never be a threat to us again."

It sounded so easy. All I had to do was master my ability and find a way to take away the magic that the Others had possessed for hundreds, if not thousands, of years. Deep down I knew that it would never be that simple. I feared that there really might not be a happy ending for us but I didn't dare to speak the thought out loud, knowing my pessimism would only upset Sebastian.

I turned the TV off and closed my eyes, listening to the soft and steady rhythm of Sebastian's breathing and the surprisingly comforting sound of my father's deep and muffled voice through the wall.

"Good night," I sighed sleepily, surprised by how heavy my eyelids suddenly felt. All of the stress and emotion of the past few days, not to mention the physical exertion of trying to outrun the Others, was taking its toll.

I barely heard Sebastian's mumbled response as I tumbled into sleepy darkness.

"G'night… Caoilinn… my love."

We were woken at four am by my father himself. He announced that all the arrangements had been made and it was time to go. He would take us to pick up our travel documents on the way to the airport and then we would board a 7am flight to Manchester in the United Kingdom. We would stop there for a brief one hour cross over before continuing on to Belfast City Airport in Northern Ireland, the destination that apparently Sebastian had requested. We would arrive in Ireland about 6:30pm local time that very night.

Before I knew it, all four of us were riding through the relatively quiet early morning streets of Toronto, the tall buildings and bright lights whizzing by us in a blur of shadows and lights.

I had expected we would be picking up our forged documents in a seedier part of town so I was surprised when we approached an expensive, upper-class, residential area. My father brought the car to a stop on the road in front of a large white house where he quickly went up to the front door and exchanged an envelope stuffed full of money for a larger manila envelope that had been tucked beneath the doormat. When he returned to the car, he quickly looked through the envelope's contents before handing it back wordlessly to Sebastian. He smoothly made a broad U-turn and within moments we were headed back in the direction that we had come from.

I stared in wonder at the perfect replicas of my passport and birth certificate (luckily I already had my credit cards and driver's license) that the large envelope contained. Sebastian seemed amused by his own documentation, whispering to me about how my father had somehow come up with his school photo for the doctored ID. We were both tense and nervous though as we approached Toronto's Pearson International Airport. The Others were all close enough now that even I could sense the danger that sparked through the air like an electric shock and no matter how convincing the documents appeared to our eyes, I was afraid that they still might not fool the airport staff and customs officers.

"I don't know how I can begin to thank you for this, Dad. We'll repay you somehow – we'll make it up to you," I assured him as we got out of the car, my meager "luggage" on my back.

"Call me – let me know you're alright," he instructed,. "And once this is all over with, I expect you to come visit us in Toronto, properly, before you begin university, of course." He eyed me somewhat suspiciously as he spoke and I suddenly found myself fighting a smile.

"Of course we will, Daddy." It was easy to let myself become enfolded in one of his mighty bear hugs. I swallowed hard as I realized this might be the last time I'd ever see my father. Fear and sadness threatened to overwhelm me.

"Thank you, Mr. Stevenson. I'll never forget this." Sebastian offered my father his hand. Both mine and Dahlia's eyebrows lifted in surprise as my father accepted it, firmly clasping Sebastian's hand in his own with a grudging respect in his eyes.

"You better not. Take care of my little girl."

Sebastian responded that he would while Dahlia and I quickly hugged goodbye.

My father and Dahlia climbed back into the shiny, dark car. I wanted to stand there and wave goodbye to them but Sebastian was already tugging at my arm, his sudden urgency alarming as he whispered quickly into my ear.

"The fifth's here already. We have to hurry."

Fear shot down my spine. I gave my father's car one last, longing look and then spun around and half-ran into the huge and busy building.

We glanced over our shoulders constantly as we made our way through the massive airport. We checked in for our flight and picked up our boarding passes with no problems other than the comments we received over our lack of luggage. So far, things were definitely going the way we wanted but I couldn't help but wonder how long our luck would last.

"I don't think the fifth has found us yet," Sebastian whispered as we lined up to go through security. "Something you're doing must be working – keep it up," he teased.

"I just really don't want to be found but that's nothing new."

I was feeling cautiously relieved that we'd almost made it to our boarding gate without being discovered but I still glanced over my shoulder at every opportunity, searching the faces of everyone in the nearby crowd and the lineup behind us. I wasn't sure what I expected to see but I had a strange sense of expectancy that I would somehow 'recognize' the fifth member of the Others who had come after us.

We passed through security and into our boarding lounge with no problems or delays. Everything was going quite smoothly, our passports easily accepted as my father had assured us they would be. It was just as we were called by a polite and gentle Irish voice to board our plane when I happened to glance across the expansive room to the boarding lounge across from ours. And that was when I saw him.

My breath caught in my chest, my body was paralyzed by sudden icy fear. For a moment, I was uncertain if I were about to faint or throw up as I watched the slow smirk twist the constantly sneering features of his thin and familiar face.

I didn't need to speak. Sebastian noticed right away that something was wrong with me and quickly followed my gaze. He was immediately moving in front of me, blocking Walter from my view.

"He's alone. He can't hurt us and he won't follow us. I'm certain he's only here to observe," Sebastian calmly informed me, his voice low and steady.

I tried to regain control of myself, tried to calm down but I desperately wanted to flee in fear.

"Don't look at him. Let's just board the plane."

I nodded my agreement, gladly allowing Sebastian to pull me to my feet and protectively shield me under his arm. He angled his body slightly as we crossed the lounge so that he would block me from Walter's view, as if Walter's gaze alone could somehow hurt me.

My hands shook as I gave my boarding pass to the pretty, dark-haired flight attendant. I faintly heard her ask if I was feeling alright and I managed a silent nod in response. Sebastian had to take his arm from my shoulders in order to show his boarding pass. I'm not sure what possessed me to do so, but as he lowered his arm, I automatically turned my head to glance in the very direction he had warned me not to.

Walter stood across the lounge from us still, leaning lazily against one of the large pillars that were spaced throughout the room. His smirk deepened as he caught my eye and he wiggled his fingers in a smug, beckoning wave. I just had time to make out the three, carefully mouthed words he spoke before Sebastian's arm was around me once more. The silent words echoed through my mind like they'd been shouted directly into my ear. *See you soon.*

Sebastian quickly guided me through the gate and down the hallway that led out to the plane. My heart had started beating again and was now pounding in my ears. I really did feel like I might throw up.

"Are you okay?" Sebastian repeated as we found our seats in first class – my father had instantly dismissed the suggestion that we fly coach.

"Yes – no. I don't know." I dropped into my seat, doing up my seatbelt with trembling hands and then tipping back my chair, only to be immediately reminded by a flight attendant that our seats had to remain in their upright position until after the seatbelt sign was turned off.

"Are you sure he won't follow us?" I asked Sebastian after the flight attendant had moved out of earshot.

"Not until four more of the Others are with him," Sebastian responded confidently. I wished I felt so sure.

"What I don't understand is, if Walter was the fifth, then there must have been five of the Others in Victoria the first day we started running. So why did they send him ahead of us? Why did they bother chasing us across the country? What's the point of all this?" I demanded, my fear shifting into frustration.

"I don't know," Sebastian admitted. He reached over the large armrest between our seats for my hand. "There are answers in Ireland. I'm sure of it. We just have to find them."

"But where do we even begin to look? And what exactly are we looking for?"

"The answers are hidden in both of our pasts, and so we're returning to the land and the places where our secrets were buried; where we met, where we fell in love, where I left you last..." His brow furrowed as he spoke. I knew it still caused him pain to think of Caoilinn's death, however briefly.

"I hope you're right."

We sat in silence as the other passengers finished boarding. The flight attendant's words washed over me as she explained the emergency exits and procedures, my thoughts taking me far away. Sebastian was just as still and silent as I, his eyes unfocused, his expression one of faraway concentration. I felt overwhelmed by a hundred different emotions and let myself become lost within a thousand different questions as our plane slowly taxied towards the runway. My eyes closed as the engines became louder and our acceleration began to increase. The force of gravity and resistance pushed me back into my seat as the plane climbed up into the sky and I felt myself falling backwards. Further and further, deeper and deeper I fell, until I was lost within myself and another's past haunted my exhausted and terrified dreams...

I WATCHED HIM silently - not yet ready to announce my presence. I had been surprised to find him here, in this secret place I only ever came to alone. I stood within the shade of a wide oak on the edge of the clearing across which he paced. He should have been able to see me but I didn't want him to, not just yet. Perhaps it was childish of me but I enjoyed taking these moments to observe him. The surge of strong and complicated emotions I felt when I looked at him still surprised me and took my breath away.

Seamus was handsome – there wasn't a woman alive who would reject his tall, strong frame, his dark, mysterious eyes that sparkled when he smiled and his thick, black hair. His appearance alone would never have been enough to attract my attention – it was his heart and soul that I truly loved. His genuine and limitless kindness was a constant surprise to me. His gentle ways, his generous heart, the love and vibrance that radiated from him with every smile and boyish laugh... I was certain there was no other like him and never would there be.

We had met only two moons ago and already I knew that he was somehow caught up in my strange destiny. I felt things when I was with him that I had never felt before – that I had never dared hope I might feel. The love and passion and beauty that he brought to my life, the hope and dreams that he blessed me with – it was near impossible to put to words.

After the first day we had met, I often found myself visiting his sister's home under the pretense of checking on his baby brother. Seamus was always there, waiting for me as if he had known I was coming, and his sister almost always left us alone. We talked easily during these encounters and those conversations were precious and unforgettable. I found myself opening up to him, charmed by his kind and friendly disposition and entranced by his thrilling smiles. I discovered a side to myself that I had never known existed, and I liked it. When I was with him, I wasn't the strange and powerful Priestess who was both respected and feared. I was just Caoilinn, a young woman who had never before known love. And as I learnt more about Seamus, as the look in his eyes deepened and the warmth of his casual touch burned deeper and deeper within me, I found myself not just learning of the possibility of love but falling in love myself.

I sighed and stepped forward into the warm sunlight, the faint breeze lightly blowing my loose hair. Seamus' eyes immediately snapped up to meet mine, not a hint of surprise anywhere in his expression. It often seemed he somehow sensed my presence even when his mind wasn't yet consciously aware of it. The more time we spent together, the harder it was for me to catch him off-guard and the easier it was for him to surprise me. Not that I truly minded.

I considered him curiously, waiting for him to speak. His lips curved up into a half-smile.

"I'm not sure what I'm doing here," he confessed with a small shrug.

Guilt immediately flashed through me. It was a strange sensation and one I'd had limited experience with until lately. "I'm sorry. I didn't realize how badly I wanted to see you. I thought I had more control-,"

"I know I don't." He grinned at my confusion. "I wanted to see you. I followed you to this clearing a few days ago. I left as soon as I had seen where you went but I've been coming here every day since, hoping I might see you again."

"Oh. But why would you do such a thing?" My heart yearned to hear the answer I wanted but I forced my emotions to calm, pushing my own wants and desires aside.

"Because…" he hesitated with the uncertainty of his youth. His eyes suddenly flashed up to meet mine, the love in them so clear and stunning and absolutely undeniable that my heart skipped a beat. "Because I'm in love with you."

I was speechless in a way that only Seamus could have caused. I slowly shook my head as he moved across the clearing towards me, quickly taking my hands up in his before I could voice my objections aloud.

"I love you," he repeated, staring deeply into my eyes. His hands felt warm and rough against my cool, smooth skin. "I want you and only you, forever. There will never be another. Caoilinn, I came here to ask you – to beg you if need be, to be my mate."

I gasped, completely taken by surprise. I was abruptly over-whelmed by the emotions I was feeling, by the confusion of my con-flicting desires. "No… it is forbidden. I could never do that to you. If the Sisterhood even suspected…" My hushed voice began to tremble with fear, not for myself but at the thought of risking his life.

"Hush," he soothed, gathering me in his arms and pulling me against his warm, strong chest before I could object. No one had ever tried to comfort me before Seamus; no one had ever dared suggest I might need to be comforted. He saw all the strength and weakness within me in a way that no one else ever could. He was the source of the weakness within me and yet perhaps he was also my greatest strength.

I gathered my will, preparing to pull away, to deny my heart as I knew I must but his sudden, hesitant, shaky breath shattered my attempted control.

"Don't deny me, please. You'll destroy me if you leave me now."

His fingers slid through my hair, gently tipping my face up towards his but it was I who leant in without thought, inhaling his breath and losing all sense of reason as my lips pressed against his for the first time.

I closed my eyes as I gave in to his desire and to mine. It was a sweet release after fighting it for what had felt like an eternity. I became lost in a world where there was nothing but his warm, strong embrace and his gentle, sweet lips, and a fiery passion that threatened to consume us both. My return to reality was slow and reluctant, beginning with the awareness of a mild scent of lavender in the air and the warmth of the afternoon sun on my skin. My eyelashes fluttered as I reopened my eyes, the world around me instantly brighter, more vibrant and beautiful than ever before. I knew that I would never again see the world with the same eyes.

Seamus' smile was joyous, his eyes flooded with the love that I had often glimpsed through the clouded, grayish-blue haze. I spoke quickly, not wanting to give him false hope.

"I want to be with you, Seamus. But I'm afraid that it might not be what you really and truly want," I hesitantly confessed. It felt so strange to be admitting such a weakness aloud.

"You're all that I want," he assured me. "Unless your magic has deceived me so that I can't trust my own heart," he added with a laugh.

I found myself swallowing hard, fixing him with my piercing, ice-blue stare.

"And what if it has?"

His smile didn't fade for a second. "Then I'm more than happy to be bewitched. I know what I want, Caoilinn. Don't you?"

"I'm not certain you understand what it would mean, to be my mate. We couldn't stay here; we'd only be able to hide what we'd done for so long. Some of the Sisters at the temple are already suspicious. You'd have to leave your family behind you - forever. You'd have to give up everything – your family, your friends, your life, your humanity."

A crease settled between his dark brows. "What do you mean?"

"The mating ceremony would commit us to one another for life, and my life is limitless Seamus." He watched me expressionlessly, his eyes growing more serious and intense by the second. "I'm a year older than you Seamus but I look like I could be years younger. I've stopped aging and I won't ever again – I can't anymore. If you choose to be with me, I'm afraid you wouldn't age either. You would never grow old, you could never die. It truly would be forever."

"I never want to be without you," he answered solemnly. "I understand what that means."

"But for us to join on equal terms, I'd have to grant you the same ability as mine. I can't see how we could be together any other way but that would mean granting you the same blessing and the same curse that I suffer with each and every day, just so that I can be happy, just so that I will no longer have to be alone."

"You're so selfish," he gently teased, "only thinking of yourself. My life, my happiness, my heart and soul is already yours. You speak of our future and our happiness now. I won't live and allow you to be alone - ever. This is what I want too."

"But there will be no going back. Once I give the ability to access the Lost Magic to another, there's no possible way I can take it back," I warned. "Living this way... it's not easy."

"I know. But living without you – it's impossible for me now."

I stared back at him, searching his eyes for the truth, desperately trying to read his soul. That strange shadow of guilt passed over my heart once more.

"I'm afraid it's wrong for me to want this, to want you."

"How can it be wrong? This - us, it is all that is right in the world." I didn't argue so he moved closer to me, gently brushing a loose strand of hair back from my face. "I love you, Caoilinn. Please, will you take me as your mate?"

"I love you," I whispered back, gazing into the eternity of his eyes. "And, yes, I will take you, Seamus – all of you, forever. Forgive me."

MY EYES SNAPPED open as I sat up straight. Disorientation overwhelmed me, my head spun and my mind reeled. I struggled to stand, panicking as I realized something was holding me down, trapping me in this unfamiliar and noisy place. I began clawing at the buckle, my breath coming in shallow pants and abruptly catching in my chest as I realized what I was doing - I was attacking my seatbelt.

"Hush." Sebastian's hand was over mine instantly, undoing my seatbelt with a flick of his fingers. He twisted his body towards mine, his hand reaching for my face. "Calm down, Gracelynn. It's okay, we're safe. We're on the plane – we're just landing in Manchester." His reassuring words were as steady as his eyes.

I took a slow, deep breath and nodded, relaxing against his familiar touch. I looked around me, taking in the dark blue, first-class seats, the bright lights and noisy hum of the plane, and all the passengers, reading, listening to music and talking to their companions as the plane began to slowly circle the airport below. I took another steadying breath as I adjusted myself to it all. It was hard to believe that I'd slept for the entire flight.

"I'm sorry. I… had a bad dream. I was confused for a moment."

"I think we've been spending too much time together," he joked, his twinkling eyes inviting me to laugh. I didn't.

"You asked Caoilinn to be your mate?" I whispered softly. His eyes widened with surprise, his pupils rapidly dilating then shrinking. "Was that like getting married?" A strange surge of emotion twisted my gut as I watched him, confusing and disorienting me once more. I remembered the look in his eye when he had stared at her, when he had confessed his eternal love, and as irrational as it might have been, I was jealous.

"Yes, it was like getting married," he answered cautiously. He studied my face intently as he spoke, obviously confused by the emotions I was trying to hide. "Did you remember the ceremony?" I shook my head and he smiled mysteriously. "You should try and remember - or not," he hastily added upon reading the look in my eyes. His expression became puzzled but I hurried to speak and distract him, annoyed by my own foolishness. I lowered my voice even more.

"She was talking about the 'Lost Magic' and how she could give the ability to access it to others."

A strange expression briefly crossed Sebastian's face as he heard me speak the phrase out loud. He considered for several long seconds, his eyes squinting slightly as he struggled to sort through the millions of memories that crowded his mind.

"She told you that once the ability had been given to someone else, it was impossible to take back," I continued. "Do you remember?"

"Caoilinn thought that was the truth, yes," he slowly agreed. "But there have been other things she thought were true that you have proved are not. She was not as all-knowing as she wanted to seem, she was barely eighteen years old when she died."

"You don't think that she... may have knowingly misled you then?"

"No," he answered firmly. "She always spoke the truth as she thought she knew it."

"Sebastian, I'm not so certain–"

"She would not have lied." His tone was unexpectedly firm, almost angry for a moment. He had never spoken to me with even the slightest edge to his words before and I found myself instantly hurt.

"There must be a way to stop the Others – I'm sure of it," he continued more mildly. "We'll be touching down in just a few minutes and then we'll be boarding our next plane to Ireland within the hour. Once we arrive in Belfast, I figure we'll have at least twelve hours, maybe even twenty-four, before the Others catch up to us. That gives us almost a full day to find the answers we want with our combined ability unimpeded by theirs."

"Twelve hours? Maybe twenty-four?" I quietly echoed. I was surprised. I hadn't spent much time considering what we would do once we got to Ireland or what would happen once the Others caught up to us. Ireland had seemed a magical sanctuary in my mind that once reached, would offer a respite from the stressful race we'd been involved in all summer.

"It'll be enough time," he reassured me but I could sense the hesitance in his projected confidence. I looked more closely at his face and noticed the faint, dark circles beneath his eyes and the weariness that weighed on his handsome features. I realized he was just as exhausted as I, even more so as he allowed himself to sleep so little lately.

"It'll be enough time," I agreed, trying to reassure him too. He smiled tiredly, acknowledging my weak effort. It'll have to be enough time, I thought as we linked our hands together once more and I rested my head against his shoulder. And as the plane slowly circled down and prepared for landing, suddenly I could feel it too. I was overwhelmed by the sudden certainty that there would be answers in Ireland, that they were just waiting for us to find them. Only I wasn't so certain that we would like what we might find.

Chapter Seven – Magic of the Land

Sebastian and I didn't talk much on our next flight over to Ireland. There was a tension between us that should have been eased with our decreasing proximity to the Others, but for some strange reason, it only seemed to get worse. Initially, Sebastian had claimed he didn't want to sleep, afraid that the terror and confusion of his nightmares would confuse his waking mind once more and upset the other passengers (or even worse, an Air Marshall). But, after the first ten minutes of the flight, he wordlessly tipped his chair back and closed his eyes with a sigh, admitting defeat and giving in to what his body and mind truly wanted and needed. Thankfully, he slept deeply and soundly.

I watched Sebastian sleep for a while, studying his worn yet handsome face as I worried about the future, about him and about us. I began to drift in and out of sleep. My dreams were a disturbing combination of imagination and reality, full of doubt, shame and regret. Eventually I gave up my tossing and turning and chose to watch Sebastian once more. He didn't move once, his chest barely rising with each deep and steady breath. He slept like the dead, completely unmoving for nearly the whole one hour flight. It wasn't until I lightly placed my hand on his leg that his eyes popped open.

"We're landing."

He blinked once in response, taking a moment for his eyes to focus properly on my face. I was relieved to see the clarity and the instant recognition within them. He didn't look as troubled either, the familiar sparkle having returned to his eyes.

Sebastian tipped his seat back up and fastened his seatbelt, peering excitedly around me and out the window to the green and vibrant country that could now be glimpsed below.

"Ireland," he breathed, a smile in his voice as he exhaled.

Despite having the window seat, I hadn't really bothered to examine the view during our flight, preferring to watch Sebastian over the golden, sunlit clouds. I turned now and followed his gaze out the window, taking in the expansive country below with a quiet gasp.

I was initially surprised by how flat the land appeared, unused to such an exposed landscape with no mountains in sight. As the plane slowly descended, the gentle ebb and flow of the land became more obvious – the rolling hills, the ocean that sparkled under the early evening sun, the fields and trees, the outlying rural homes and the rooftops of the city itself. I couldn't stop staring at the beautiful, impossibly green countryside that seemed to be rising up to meet us. Everything seemed to glow beneath the sun's golden rays and I could feel the spirit and throbbing energy of this magical land rising up to catch with my breath in my throat. Strangely, it felt almost like I was coming home.

"You are."

I hadn't realized I'd spoken aloud until Sebastian responded. I turned to him, still feeling awed.

"It's beautiful." It was all I could think to say though it didn't come close to describing how I was feeling in that moment.

"It always is," he agreed with a pleased smile. "I've come back to Ireland a few times over the years. It always changes but somehow, it always feels the same."

I nodded my agreement, understanding exactly what he meant.

Minutes later, when the plane touched down, I felt a thrill of excitement run through me. The darker thoughts and doubts that had begun twisting their way through my mind during the flight were banished by that first glimpse of Ireland. I no longer felt afraid, I no longer felt unsure. I knew that we were doing the right thing now, that we were meant to be here. I was certain that Ireland had important secrets to share with us and my heart was ready to hear them.

It was a whole different experience disembarking the plane and navigating our way through customs and security at Belfast City Airport. I felt like I was running towards something exciting and important instead of running away from danger and despair. Sebastian and I kept grinning excitedly at each other, especially when it became apparent that our wants (or at least Sebastian's) were no longer inhibited by the Others'. We didn't have to wait in any lines, always finding ourselves right at the front of each line up and we moved through the airport swiftly, despite the crowds. When I mentioned that I was hungry, we suddenly found ourselves being handed complimentary coupons for a café within the airport that entitled us to free drinks and sandwiches. Still aware of the crunch for time, we took our drinks in to-go cups and packed the delicious-looking sandwiches into Sebastian's backpack. As we were nearing the airport's main doors, we passed an ATM that claimed to work with all International banks. Sebastian smiled confidently as I checked my bank account balance to discover someone (most likely my father) had deposited nearly $5,000. I withdrew several hundred pounds and placed them safely into my wallet, glad to not have to worry about money at least. Everything was falling smoothly into place. I felt another thrill of hope and optimism shiver up my spine and rise into my heart.

"Shall we go shopping? Or should we proceed?" Sebastian teased.

I rolled my eyes at him. "Let's go." I started to march towards the wall of glass doors, my eyes already drinking in the bright sunlight and warm blue sky outside the airport's exit. I suddenly hesitated. "Where are we going? Do you know?"

Sebastian's eyes were full of secrets – and amusement. The intensity in his eyes spoke of promises that made my heart skip a beat.

"It's nearly seven. We only have a few hours left of daylight… did you get enough rest on the plane?" The corner of his mouth pulled up into a mysterious half-smile as he waited for my answer.

"Yes," I cautiously replied.

"Good. I hope you want to stay awake because we won't be sleeping tonight."

"What will we be doing?" My heart fluttered nervously in my chest.

Sebastian suddenly pulled me closer, his gray eyes burning into mine as he smiled. The noise and chaos of the airport faded away and I was aware of nothing beyond his warm embrace and the heart-stopping look in his eyes. I had to struggle to focus, to remind myself of where we were and what we were doing there.

"We have the whole night to explore, to trust in each others' wants…" He gently brushed his fingertips against my cheek, in a gesture that was both tender and thrilling. I laughed softly, trying to lighten the sudden intensity between us that was threatening to steal my breath away.

"And most importantly, for me to learn how to control my ability," I reminded him as I danced a step back. "You're avoiding my question – where are we going?"

Sebastian's smile was full of mischief as he shrugged. "We want to find answers here – so we will."

I froze in my tracks. "That's your big plan?"

"Its brilliance lies in its simplicity."

"Sebastian," I began, only half-trying to keep the exasperation from my voice.

"Just trust me, Gracelynn. Trust yourself."

We began slowly moving towards the large glass doors of the airport's exit, carried along by the crowd. Sebastian stood before me, holding the door open and inviting me to take a leap of faith.

I took a deep breath, sensing that this was an important moment. I tried to focus all of my energy and all of my wants as I boldly stepped forward and through the door.

"Let's go."

I flashed Sebastian a quick smile as I stepped past him, leading the way outside. It felt right to be doing so for after all, even if this was his country, this trip was more about me than him - if it were possible to untwine our lives and hearts enough to make the distinction.

I immediately noticed the difference in the air as we stepped outside. There was a slight dampness to it despite the sun's warmth that carried faint hints of the scents of the land. The air tasted differently too, fresher and fuller than the dry, recirculated air of the plane and airport. The sun, though bright, carried only a lingering warmth to it as it was slowly sliding downwards to the distant horizon. I was glad I'd packed a sweater near the top of my backpack and was about to take it out when a taxi pulled up in front of us. Without thinking or questioning what I was doing, I reached for the back door and hopped inside, Sebastian was right behind me.

"Hi ya? Where to?" the cabbie asked, his strong accent and quick words flowing together so thickly I struggled to understand him.

I shrugged out of my backpack, waiting expectantly for Sebastian to answer. When I glanced at him though he was grinning, smiling just as expectantly at me.

"Well? What'll it be? Where to?" the man demanded somewhat gruffly. I had a sudden sense that he might not like foreigners. I threw Sebastian a dark look for putting the pressure on me like this even though it was I who had jumped into the cab.

"Oh… umm…" I stalled nervously. The man tapped his thick, calloused fingers against the steering wheel impatiently. I couldn't see why he was in such a rush – the meter was already running so really it was to his benefit that I was dawdling.

"Don't ya know where you want t'go?"

His eyes met mine in the mirror and I was surprised by the warmth in their aqua shades, despite his harsh-sounding words.

"No, I don't know," I admitted honestly. Sebastian cocked his head to one side, watching me curiously and silently, that look of expectation still in his eyes. I tried my best to ignore him. "About two thousand years into the past should do," I added a little testily, realizing the ridiculousness of our situation. Where were we going? What did we really expect to find? "Sorry for wasting your time. We'll just wait for another taxi while we figure out–"

"Nah, I know exactly where t'take yous." The driver put the car into gear as he spoke and began pulling away from the curb. "Only one place near Belfast that's old enough for what you're lookin' for. The Giant's Ring's 'bout five thousand years old and a mighty fine sight at sunset to boot. I won't wait for ya while you walk round but if you have a phone, another cab'll come get ya when you're done. Tourists always want t'see The Giant's Ring. Not the first time I've taken a Yank straight there from the airport."

It took me a minute to fully process what he'd just said – or at least I thought I understood what he'd said. I was having a much harder time than I'd expected understanding his accent. What the heck was a Giant's Ring? And had he just called me a Yank?

"I'm Canadian," I corrected as politely as possible.

The man shrugged as he drove us away from the airport and into the city of Belfast.

"Ah, it's all the same, ain't it?"

"Not at all," Sebastian disagreed, speaking up for the first time. "But I reckon ya know that."

I looked at Sebastian, surprised by the sudden change in his voice. His typically light and pleasant accent was suddenly just as heavy and difficult to understand as the cabbie's. For a split second, I'd almost thought he wasn't speaking English.

"Ah! I thought you looked t'be an Irish lad," the driver declared with a pleased grin. "A Northerner too, I'll bet. Been travellin' have ya? Found somethin' you wanted t'bring home to show your folks, then?" He laughed heartily at his own joke, completely ignoring me now that he realized I was the only foreigner in his cab.

"And did your parents teach ya how to speak proper Irish then, lad? Or have you been traveling with your pretty Yank too long to remember?"

I strained to understand what the man was saying as his accent appeared to thicken even more and his rapidly flowing words somehow increased in pace. One word stood out easily enough though.

"I'm Canadian," I repeated, annoyed at how quickly I'd been forgotten. Sebastian laughed, his eyes quickly meeting mine over his smile.

Sebastian and the driver began to banter back and forth, both grinning and laughing and obviously thoroughly enjoying their conversation. I could barely understand a word of it. It actually took me several minutes to realize that they weren't even speaking English anymore though I couldn't honestly say at what point they had switched to Gaelic. It didn't surprise me at all that Sebastian spoke the language with such obvious ease and fluency.

I ignored their chatter and turned my attention to the sights we were passing out the window. I only had a few hours of daylight to enjoy the sights of Ireland and I was determined to absorb as much of it as I could in my limited time. Of course, we might have time in the morning still – if we didn't find the answers we needed tonight, if the Others hadn't caught up to us yet, if we were still alive… I pushed the morbid thoughts away, knowing that if I spent too much time allowing myself to fully realize the depths of our situation, I would become too hopeless and terrified by despair to move forward. And we had to move forward – it was our only choice.

As we drove further away from the airport and into the city of Belfast, I examined everything we passed with great interest. The city itself was an intriguing combination of old Victorian-style buildings and renovated, modern storefronts. Here and there were hints of the damage that the city had suffered during the recent "Troubles" and conflicts between the Catholic nationalists and Protestant unionists. There had been a lot of violence and even bombings in the city, and we still passed the occasional sight of Loyalist graffiti or Protestant flag.

As we traveled down one street, I caught a glimpse of the two giant cranes, nicknamed Samson and Goliath, that loomed high over the city's busy harbor. We traveled away from the ocean and in land through the south-west of the city towards the more residential streets. I gazed out at the small, brick homes we passed in wonder, idly imagining Sebastian and I marrying and moving to Ireland to-gether to live in one of those quaint and cozy-looking houses. As we traveled further west and out of the city, I stared in wonder at the curious murals we passed on the sides of some of the buildings.

I was about to ask Sebastian about them, but just then he caught my eye and gave a quick yet subtle shake of his head before launching into another loud and laughter-filled debate with our driver. The murals must have something to do with "The Troubles" then, I guessed. Sebastian had warned me about the precarious political situation in the city and how even though the worst of the conflict and turmoil had passed, it was still recent enough in everyone's minds that just the smallest spark could ignite another raging fire.

The Giant's Ring turned out to be just outside of the city in a rural part of Ballynahatty. It didn't take long at all for us to drive there, barely thirty minutes. The driver pulled into a parking lot just off the road. The lot was surrounded by surprisingly thick and tall trees, and though it was obvious they thinned ahead, it was impossible to see just exactly what the trees were hiding.

"Out you go then!" the man declared cheerfully, abruptly switching back to English. "Show yer pretty Yank around The Giant's Ring and then get on home. I'm sure yer Mam'll be itchin' to meet 'er.'"

Sebastian and the man shared a grin. Sebastian thanked him heartily and shook his hand before climbing out of the cab. I remained in the backseat, digging through my wallet for the correct amount of fare.

"Nah, nah! Put that away," the man instructed as he saw what I was doing. He shook his head adamantly. "I've already told your lad that I won't be chargin' ya - this time. Welcome to Ireland," he added in a rough voice but with a smile.

"Thank you – that's very generous of you. Thank you very much."

"My pleasure. Now get out."

I grinned back at the man, suddenly liking him a lot more as I put my wallet away and climbed out of the car. As soon as the door closed behind me he pulled away, one hand thrust out the window in a quick wave as he drove back down the straight and narrow street, past the country homes and fields and back towards the city that rose up on the north-eastern skyline.

"So what were you two so busy talking about?" I asked Sebastian curiously. He smiled in his most charming way as he linked his fingers through mine and we slowly started walking towards a path at the edge of the parking lot that led through the tall, gently swaying trees. The path led into the long shadows as the sun had nearly set on the day and a cool, evening breeze was picking up that stirred the branches above us and swept my hair back from my face.

"Just idle chit-chat," Sebastian assured me. "Apparently, I reminded him of one of his sons. He shared some tales of his youngest's debauchery that I wouldn't want to translate. They'd make you blush."

"Oh, please. I'm not that innocent," I objected. Sebastian wisely chose not to answer. The corners of his mouth twitched though as if he were fighting a smile. I felt my cheeks warm – only from annoyance, I assured myself.

"Where are we?" I brusquely changed the subject.

"The Giant's Ring, a mysterious and sacred site that surrounds a five thousand year old henge. And it's also a popular tourist attraction and great place to walk the dog," he added with a grin as a couple were approaching us further down the path with a little Scottish terrier trotting along beside them.

"Have you been here before?"

"Yes, a long, long time ago. I traveled here after… after Caoilinn passed away. It was one of the first places she had wanted to come to after we left the temple but of course, we never made it this far together…" He frowned, the lines in his face deepening with the shadows in his eyes. We fell into silence as we passed the elderly couple and their dog, exchanging polite smiles and nods.

It was cooler in the shade of the trees and I let go of Sebastian's hand to zip up my hoodie; he barely seemed to notice. The woods were thinning ahead and I could now see the green meadow we were approaching, the tall grasses swaying ahead of us and ripples running across the sea of grass like waves in the wind. Leaves and branches crunched beneath my feet and a sudden cool gust of wind whipped my breath away from me and made the tall, old trees above us groan. All I could see was the sea of bright green grass ahead and the flowing dip and roll to the land. A strange sensation was beginning to tingle over my scalp, trickling down my spine and chasing over my skin in a magnetic, electric current. I could feel it in my heart too and in my soul, and I knew that this was a powerful place, the magic of it hung heavily in the very air. I fought the urge to run ahead, to charge out into the large open area we were approaching.

"I feel like I've been here before," I whispered as we emerged from the shade of the trees and out into the fading evening sun. My breathy words were swept away with the wind and out over the knee-high grasses.

Sebastian didn't look at me as he answered. We both stared out at the beautiful sight before us as it filled our vision and overwhelmed us in so many ways.

"Caoilinn told me of this place. She wanted to come here, it was important to her but she never told me why. She described it as if she had been here herself, though I'm not sure if she truly understood the nature of it."

"No," I agreed, the words coming to me without thought. "The magic here is wild, unharnessed. I can feel it in the earth and the air, in the stones. What is it?"

My hair stood on end as I waited for him to answer. The power in the air so undeniable I found myself looking around almost nervously, as if expecting lightning to suddenly strike from the clear and cloudless sky that arched endlessly above us from horizon to horizon.

We stood near the edge of "The Ring" on the brim of a massive bowl in the earth. The steep banks were built up at least 15 meters high all around and sloped down to the flat centre. It formed a huge, perfectly round ring in the earth that looked to be about 200 meters wide. I could see the path led all the way around the ring, there was a solitary man walking opposite us on the far side. Down in the center of the ring, there was a gathering of several large stones, piled up and balanced on top of one another somewhat precariously. Two teenaged boys tossed a ball back and forth just beside the stones, the everyday activity seeming unnatural and out-of-place in this strange, enchanting place.

"The Druids used this place but even Caoilinn didn't know exactly what it was they did here. Even in our time, the stones had already stood for thousands of years. The ring holds centuries of secrets within it."

"But did Caoilinn bury her secrets here?" I wondered aloud.

"I've searched here before, both after her death and several times in the hundreds of years since. If she hid something, it would have been in the tomb but I've never found anything, no matter how badly I wanted to. I wonder though, if perhaps she never meant for me to know all her secrets, perhaps, she only left clues for herself." His eyes focused on the stones at the center of the ring as he spoke. There was a strange edge to his voice that I chose to ignore. Instead, I nodded my agreement.

"Let's walk the perimeter while we wait for the locals to leave," I suggested.

Sebastian took up my hand in answer and together we began walking around the top of the rolling bank. It was strangely peaceful walking there together. I gazed out over the nearby fields, looking as far as I could see and feeling as if I were walking backwards through time into the magical world of the past. I was awed by the massive sky above me and the sacred feel to the earth around me. I was spell-bound by the powerful magic of this place and for a long time, I could do nothing but stare at it all in silent wonder as I watched the sun dip down, sinking lower in the sky.

"It feels like a dream, being here with you," Sebastian commented softly. We paused on the path, turning together to look down into the now-empty ring. The setting sun was falling on the stones at the center at an odd angle that made them seem to glow beneath the surreal light.

"It does," I agreed. "This place is so… intimidating but I feel so peaceful at the same time. It feels right to be here, especially with you by my side."

Sebastian looked at me, his eyes alight with an emotion stronger and brighter than even the fiery, setting sun. For a second I felt certain he would pull me into his arms and kiss me. My whole body suddenly longed for his embrace, my breath swept away from me by the sudden intensity of my desire. Unexpectedly though, he closed his eyes and angled his body away from mine slightly.

"I want you by my side forever. But for that to be possible, we *must* stop the Others. We both need to really focus. You have to remember how to control your magic."

"I know. No pressure but it's all on me," I muttered, feeling slightly annoyed at the way he had ruined the moment between us.

He turned back to me with an amused smile.

"My whole life, my whole existence – it has always been about you. Why should now be any different?"

"Right. No pressure at all."

Sebastian laughed and grabbed my hand, tugging me towards the edge of the bank playfully as his mood instantly lightened.

"Come on, let's see what's waiting for us."

We raced down the steep slope, our steps carried on the wind. It was a rush to charge down the bank and to jog together towards the ancient henge at the center of the ring. With each step, my heart beat a little faster and my legs moved a little slower until I took my last faltering step and came to a stop, standing in awe before the five thousand year-old tomb.

The henge consisted of five large boulders balanced together with a huge capstone on top. There was nothing blocking visitors from approaching the stones or even from climbing on top or underneath them. There was a small, pebbled path worn into the grass around the rocks from the many visitors' circling feet and there were obvious marks both from graffiti and hands and feet from those who had more thoroughly "explored" the site.

The boulders themselves were actually quite smooth in appearance and looked to have an almost unnatural texture. Before I knew what I was doing, I was walking right up and placing my hand on the cool rock, gently stroking the smooth sides and marveling over the energy that seemed to radiate outward from it.

"It's like it's alive," I muttered, mostly to myself as I began to slowly circle the tomb, my hand sliding along feeling each curve and crevice in the stones.

Sebastian didn't comment. He stood back slightly, silently watching me with an ancient and indistinguishable emotion in his eyes.

The sun sank low on the horizon, tinting the sky with a pinkish-orange wash of color. A new magic settled into the air under the strange twilight. Its presence was obvious and undeniable though it was nothing I could harness or focus on specifically. The eastern horizon had faded into a dark, bluish-black, reminiscent of Sebastian's eyes, the stars that began to dot the far sky like echoes of his mischievous sparkles. Night was rapidly approaching and I still had no idea what I was doing.

I crouched down and peered under the capstone and into the small space between the rocks. I shook my head in disappointment, both at the lack of revelations and the traces of graffiti I found on the ancient passage tomb's entrance.

"I don't know what I'm doing," I admitted, suddenly feeling defeated. I blinked back my frustration. "There's something here, I can feel it but I don't know how that's going to help us."

Sebastian watched me with patient and sympathetic eyes.

"It's alright, Gracelynn. I didn't expect it to be easy. Like I said, I've been here many times and I've never found anything but frustration before either."

"Then why are we here?"

Sebastian pressed his lips together, an unreadable expression crossing his face as he debated how to answer. For the first time since we'd arrived in Ireland, a shadow of nervous unease settled in and around my heart.

Just then, a shooting star burst up from the horizon, arcing across the darkening sky in a blaze of pure white light before abruptly blinking out and vanishing from existence. It had been some time since I'd seen such obvious evidence of Sebastian's strange effect on the world and I found myself forgetting for a moment to breathe.

"We both want for you to be able to control your magic. We both want to escape the Others. We both want to be able to decipher the clues hidden within my tattoos and so we will. It's all going to work out – that's all I want and need to know."

I slowly nodded, trying to feel reassured by Sebastian's calm and confident words.

He slowly smiled at me, an idea occurring that sparkled within the depths of his eyes. He shrugged out of his backpack, then suddenly spun and leapt forward, bounding up on to the top capstone in three graceful steps. He crouched down and held out his hand to me.

"Will you join me, my beautiful Yankee girl?"

"Ha-ha," I replied sarcastically. I smiled a little as I let my bag drop down beside his and took his hand, allowing him to help me up onto the rock where we both sat down facing one another cross-legged.

I was surprised by how comfortable a seat the smooth, hard rock made. It still felt as if it were vibrating with life, an energy radiating out from it that trembled throughout my bones and made my amber necklace feel almost as if it were throbbing with a similar energy. I could tell we were sitting at the focal point of the ring's power and magic and I began to feel slightly doubtful and afraid. As always, Sebastian distracted me.

"What are you doing?" I asked as he began sliding his arms out of his thin, cotton shirt.

He pulled the shirt over his head and off before answering, his hair ruffled from the action.

"You'll need to be able to see the designs of my tattoos if you're going to attempt to decipher them," he pointed out. He shivered slightly as he spoke, goose bumps already appearing on his lean, muscled arms as his skin was exposed to the cool evening air.

"You're going to freeze."

"I don't want to freeze so I won't. I don't actually really want to be cold but I thought it might motivate you if I were a little uncomfortable," he added with a cheeky grin. He leant forward and lightly kissed the tip of my nose. "Just try, Caoilinn. I want you to succeed."

Sebastian shifted his body around so that his back was facing me. It was probably best that he missed seeing my expression after calling me by the wrong name. It concerned and scared me when he confused me with Caoilinn – I worried sometimes that he was losing his grip on reality, on the present. But even more than that, it hurt me when he called me by her name. It was a reminder that he still loved her, that he still saw us as one person when we were definitely not. I was not Caoilinn and I didn't want to be her but I was afraid that was exactly what Sebastian might want.

I raked my fingers through my short, curly hair and squeezed my eyes tightly shut. How could I do this? How could I save us and keep Sebastian safe from the Others when I didn't truly want to remember how to use my magic? I didn't want to remember being Caoilinn. I was afraid to control my magic, afraid that I would become Caoilinn again and that I might lose what I thought to be my true self.

Sebastian sat up straighter and glanced over his shoulder at me.

"Gracelynn, are you alright?" he asked, his eyes softened with concern.

"I'm fine," I quickly dismissed, brushing my hair back from my face with my fingers. "I just… I don't know if I can do this. But I'll try."

Sebastian reached back to gently squeeze my hand, his touch warm and familiar, calming my soul.

"You can do it," he quietly encouraged before slowly turning back around.

I wasn't certain that I could but I knew I would have to try. There was no way I could disappoint Sebastian. And so I began studying the designs of the tattoo on his back, tracing the lines and curves with my fingers, committing each tiny and detailed part of the pattern to my memory until I felt like his tattoo had been burnt into the backs of my eyes. And still nothing happened.

"This isn't working," I announced after what felt like hours. The sky was black now, its emptiness filled with millions of pinpoints of flickering, bright white stars.

"Not entirely," Sebastian agreed. He began tugging his shirt back over his head as he turned around. "I stayed reasonably warm the whole time."

"Really?"

"Yes, but that might have been because I became numb after the first half hour or so." He grinned cheekily at me. I tried to narrow my eyes into a glare but found myself smiling and entirely running the effect.

"You're impossible," I complained.

"I won't deny it. Did you want to climb down?"

"We might as well."

Sebastian helped me down from the capstone and then he retrieved our bags. I was surprised when he opened his and began pulling out our blankets and some of our sleeping things, as well as the sandwiches and snacks we'd forgotten to eat.

"What are you doing?"

"It's late. I thought we should eat something and then get some rest. We'll want to be up early if we're going to take advantage of the last few hours of daylight before the Others arrive. And I think we'll probably awake with the sun here," he added, glancing around the large, open landscape, broken only by the gently, rolling hills and small pockets of trees.

"We're going to sleep here?"

"Why not?"

"I don't know." I fumbled for words. "We only have a few hours before the Others catch up to us – shouldn't we be doing something? Didn't you say something about staying up all night?"

"What do you suggest we do?"

"Shouldn't we be searching for more clues or running away or just doing… something?"

"We both want to be safe and we want to stop the Others, so we will. It's all going to work out – it has to."

"But☐"

"This is all we can do, Gracelynn." Sebastian's expression grew more serious. I was once again aware of the heavy weight in his eyes.

It felt like we were sitting around just waiting for our deaths but I knew he was right – what else could we do? I tried my best to have faith in his words but it was a lot more difficult to have faith in myself. I tried to calm the sense of panic creeping down upon me as I took a blanket and spread it out on the ground just a few feet away from the ancient henge.

I felt a bit calmer once I had eaten and was lying curled up against Sebastian's side, a warm blanket tucked up under my chin and another blanket of stars spread out above me as far as I could see. I was tired but not sleepy. I tried to relax in Sebastian's arms but my pulse began to slowly increase, my breath quickening as I became very aware of the sweet smell of his skin and the pounding of his own heart as my ear pressed against his chest. When he suddenly began to speak, it made me jump a little.

"Do you know why I love you?" He turned to look at me as he spoke, his face suddenly inches from mine. My breath caught in my chest, my heart pounding now as his handsome face filled my world and I felt myself becoming lost within his eyes. I found I couldn't speak and when I didn't answer, he slowly broke his eyes from mine, turning to gaze back at the never-ending sky stretched out above us.

"I love you for a million reasons – for every amazing and tiny part of you that makes you, you. I love your passion for life. I love how you're unable to love with anything less than your whole heart. I love how complicated you are, how dependable and how unpredictable you are to me still. I love your quiet strength and your stubborn, strong-will. I love your good-nature. I love how sensitive you are and how good you think you are at hiding it. I love how pure your joy is over the smallest and simplest of things – a sunny day, a smile, a starry, moonlit night…"

I gasped in wonder as each and every one of the stars above us began to swell at his words. The stars glowed and sparkled even brighter as they bathed the night in a magical, silvery light.

Sebastian slowly sat up, pulling me along with him. And despite the absolutely breath-taking starlit sky and the night full of magic and wonders around us, I could look nowhere but at him. His expression was tender but serious, his eyes full of emotions so complex there were no words that existed to describe them. He reached out to take both my hands in his. I was surprised and confused to notice the slight tremble to his touch.

"I love how important family is to you, despite the way your own has treated you. I love how you try to see the good in everyone and how unconditional your love is, once earned." He squeezed my hands tightly as his voice ever-so-slightly trembled. "I know how much your father's approval means to you still, and that's why I waited until I could do this with his permission. So that I could ask you properly, as you requested."

I watched in wonder as he let go of my hands and reached into his jeans pocket. My mind wasn't really processing what he was saying and what he was doing until he pulled out the tiny, shimmering, silver ring.

He held it before me almost uncertainly, his eyes studying every expression on my face.

I stared at the ring in complete shock. It was beautiful. It was a thin, silver band that twisted in and around itself to form a simple yet beautiful Celtic love knot, almost identical in design to the ring that I already wore but this one was smaller, more delicate and definitely more feminine. Several small diamonds were trapped within the twists of the knot, sparkling as brightly as the stars in the heavens above as they appeared to be braided into the ring's intricate twists.

My heart pounded in my chest, my breath caught in my throat, my hands began to tremble as the night wind slowly rose and swelled, stirring my hair and sending shivers down my spine. The ancient magic in the air swirled all around me, rushing through my heart and soul and bringing shimmering tears to my eyes.

I met Sebastian's gaze and a sudden calm settled over me. I could see the thousands of words on his lips, the millions of promises in his eyes as he took a slow, shaky breath and reached for my hand.

"Marry me?"

Those two simple words conveyed a thousand different things. The world hung on my response, the night suddenly silent, the wind still, the stars pausing in their flickering. Sebastian seemed to be holding his breath.

Wordlessly, I slid his heavy, amber ring off my finger and carefully handed it back to him. There was only one possible answer. And as I spoke the word, I felt it carry through the air on an ancient magic, older and quite possibly more powerful than our own. The word reverberated from my lips throughout The Giant's Ring, my solemn vow witnessed by the sky, the earth, the air.

"Yes."

Shooting stars exploded throughout the sky, a sudden warm gust of wind swirled around us and spiraled up to the heavens, catching and intertwining our breaths. And Sebastian's joyful laugh joined my own as he slid the beautiful silver band onto my finger and we tumbled to the ground in each other's arms, the magic of The Giant's Ring and the night itself, alive and flowing through us both.

Chapter Eight – Mistaken

Sebastian and I spent most of the night talking, our discussions ranging from idle to intense. Despite the seriousness of our situation, I felt surprisingly light-hearted, laughing - even giggling, and enjoying myself in a way that I hadn't in a long time. Sebastian appeared more relaxed and happier than I had seen in a while too. It reminded me of the early days of our friendship and it was a happy reminder that I definitely needed.

It was a night of joy and celebration, and a night of passion. At times I became so lost in the ecstasy of his touch that I could barely speak or breathe. I clung to him, never wanting his kisses to end, never wanting to let go. These intoxicating moments stretched into forever, until I remembered a little self-control. It was a strange sensation to have to remind myself that I wanted to wait until after we were married to give myself to him entirely and in the back of my mind, I found myself beginning to question why?

Eventually we fell asleep, tangled in our blankets and each other's arms. We must have both wanted a peaceful rest as Sebastian slept soundly without any of his nightmare disturbances and my dreams were both lucid and calm.

I woke just before dawn, warm and safe, at peace in Sebastian's embrace. The sweet scent of grass hovered in the early morning air as the eastern sky began to lighten. I watched in wonder as the night's stars winked out one by one, enchanted by this magical moment in the calm before dawn. As the sky and day awakened, I admired my engagement ring, hardly believing how perfect and magical a night it had been. I became lost in pleasant, sleepy thoughts as the world around me began to stir – birds called out their happy trills, the sky shifted from midnight blue to a pure and clear azure, and the silvery dew that clung to the blades of grass around us began to slide down towards the awaiting earth. I closed my eyes and sighed happily, smiling as Sebastian's arm gently tightened around my waist.

"Good morning beautiful wife," he whispered sleepily in my ear, his warm, gentle breath tickling my skin.

I giggled, a happy joy bubbling up within me at his words. "Not yet – but soon."

"You're worth waiting forever for."

I turned my head to meet his lips and for a short time, I became lost in oblivion again. I found myself light-headed and breathless when we finally broke apart. We were lying face to face now, staring into each other's eyes. Sebastian gently stroked the side of my face, his touch so careful and thrilling.

"The sun is rising, we should go." It was his suggestion but I could clearly hear and sense his reluctance. A small quiver of fear hit me as I realized that our magical night was over, and I remembered what dangers today might bring. I had somehow managed to thoroughly forget about the Others, because I had wanted to forget I supposed. But now reality was returning like the crack of a whip. I wanted to flinch back from the truth and hide but hiding was obviously no longer an option.

"Where will we go?" I sat up as I spoke and began shaking out and folding the blankets. I felt the definite need to keep my hands busy in an attempt to distract myself from the panic hovering at the edges of my thoughts.

"I don't know," he admitted. He caught my hand and waited until I met his gaze, his eyes steady and calm. "It's going to be okay, Gracelynn, I promise. They don't outnumber us yet, our wants still overpower theirs. There's still time to find the answer."

"Not much time," I pointed out and it was true. I could feel the seconds ticking away now with each fraction of an inch the sun rose higher, its bright warmth and fiery rays cracking the sky open in a blaze of glowing color along the horizon.

"True," he agreed. "Let's get moving then."

We packed up the rest of our things then walked across the ring to the closest path up the outer bank. I wanted to change my clothes and freshen up but it had felt decidedly wrong to do so within the ring's sacred boundaries. Luckily there were public bathrooms set up near the parking lot that we went to use. I dressed in lighter clothes than the day before, sensing that it was going to be hotter. I still chose a thin, long-sleeved t-shirt to accompany my shorts, wanting to hide the tattoo that snaked up and around my arm as much as possible. I pulled my hair up and back into a tight ponytail, quickly scrubbed my teeth with my toothbrush and splashed the remaining water in my water bottle on my face. I felt refreshed but only slightly calmer as I came out of the washroom and rejoined Sebastian. He grinned at me as I approached and pointed towards the far end of the parking lot.

"Look."

A large green tour bus was unexpectedly approaching the parking lot, speeding along the straight and narrow road between the farmers' fields. I couldn't imagine what a tour bus was doing at The Giant's Ring so early in the morning. I jogged after Sebastian as he went to find out.

As soon as the bus stopped, its doors opened and sleepy-looking tourists began slowly coming down the steps. Sebastian greeted the tourists with polite smiles and murmured greetings but it was obvious the driver was his real interest. The minute the tall, thin man began descending, Sebastian launched into a friendly-sounding babble. The driver's greenish-blue eyes darted my way several times as Sebastian spoke and his laughter boomed out over the parking lot, a surprisingly loud sound for such a thin man. They were both grinning like long-lost friends within minutes and the driver finally said something in English as he stepped away from the bus and lit a cigarette.

"Your welcome t'join us. We'll be takin' off again in an hour once this lot's had their fill of the ring at dawn," he told us both, speaking around the cigarette that hung from his lips.

"My thanks, sir," Sebastian held out his hand and shook the other man's hand vigorously. "Would you mind if we wait on the bus? We've seen enough of the ring."

"Sure, sure."

The driver waved us towards the still-open bus door and began slowly walking away, taking long, slow draughts of his smoke.

I followed Sebastian up the steps and onto the cool bus, sliding into one of the front seats beside him.

"What was that all about?"

He grinned at me, cheerfully. "Well, apparently this bus of tourists is on its way north to the coast of Antrim and specifically, The Giant's Causeway. There's room on board and since we're newly engaged, the driver wanted to help us celebrate by offering us a free ride."

"What? Really?" I could hardly believe it was going to be that easy.

"Yes, and since our wants are still controlling our destiny, what we want to find must be further north. It makes sense to go to *Clochan na bhFomharach* - The Giant's Causeway," he translated, when he realized he'd slipped back into Irish. "The rock formations there are millions of years old and virtually unchanged from our time. It's not a sacred place but a place of legends and natural wonder, and it's not too far from where my village and the Sisters' temple once stood."

"Are there any remnants of the temple?" I asked, picking up on his excitement. To my disappointment, he shook his head.

"No, the village and temple were lost many centuries ago – not a trace remains of either," he told me, a touch of sadness to his voice. "The tree that marked Caoilinn's grave is long gone too… it's all been lost to time."

A forlorn silence settled over us both. I wondered at what it would be like for your birth place, your home to slowly vanish and be completely forgotten. In a way, I hoped I would never find out.

"Tell me about The Giant's Causeway," I requested, hoping to distract both Sebastian and myself. He smiled at me in amusement as if he knew exactly what I was trying to do but he answered anyway.

"It's actually a World Heritage Site now," he informed me. "According to local legends, it was built as a bridge to Scotland by the warrior giant *Fionn mac Cumhail*. The stories vary but the general belief is that the Scottish giant *Benandonner* came over the bridge to Ireland and was terrified by *Fionn mac Cumhail*. *Benandonner* fled in terror and in doing so, he ripped up and cracked the bridge – forming the causeway. Really the hexagonal, basalt columns are a product of ancient volcanic activity. It's a beautiful site – the lava plateau was formed right along the ocean with thousands upon thousands of columns of rock and tall, grass covered cliffs that plunge into the waves…"

Sebastian's eyes took on an unfocused, faraway look that told me he was remembering the site and describing it from memory. It was a relief to see him call upon a memory from further into his past without pain or discomfort. He still seemed to become lost within the past though and after several minutes of silence, I eventually had to lightly shake his arm to regain his attention. Still, it could have been much worse – it often had been.

"Sebastian, the driver's coming back." I held my breath nervously as Sebastian's eyes struggled to refocus, a momentary confusion clouding them.

"The driver…? Oh, of course. Yes," he muttered as he blinked his eyes rapidly and gave his head a little shake. He flashed me a quick, reassuring smile but it did little to settle the growing sense of unease in my stomach.

"Alright you two?" the driver asked in a loud and friendly voice as he climbed back aboard the bus. He didn't wait for either of us to respond before continuing. "Some of them are heading back already. Not too impressed with the ring or too damn lazy t'walk about it much. I reckon we'll be headin' out sooner than later. We should make it to The Giant's Causeway within the next coupla' hours. I'm going t'take the coastal route, bit a scenery for the tourists to take in and won't add much time to our trip."

Even as the driver spoke, tourists began climbing back aboard the bus, greeting us with surprised and curious looks but no one asked or questioned why we were there.

"Are you certain this is the right way to go?" I asked Sebastian in a low voice. "Do we really have time to drive up north?"

"Yes and no," he answered with a smile. "It's obviously where we want to go – things couldn't be working out more perfectly. Whether we have time or not… we can only assume the Others haven't arrived yet since our wants are still being accommodated so smoothly. They're bound to be close to getting here and when they do arrive, they'll follow us straight to the causeway. Let's just want to find what we need there before the Others find us."

"You make it all sound so easy," I muttered.

He laughed and raised my hand to his lips, lightly kissing my knuckle just above my ring.

"It's going to be okay, Gracelynn," he reassured me. "It has to be."

I tried to smile back, accepting his arm around my shoulders happily enough and leaning against him. I closed my eyes and waited for the bus to finish boarding, trying desperately to believe that we were riding north to our destiny, and not to our doom.

I couldn't sleep anymore even if I had wanted to, and so I stayed awake for the whole bus ride, staring out the window with unseeing eyes. The sights we passed were beautiful – cities, fields, glens, rolling hills and the occasional church or castle ruin. I couldn't appreciate it though, my mind was so preoccupied with what we were about to do, with who we were certain to face. I couldn't forget Caoilinn's words from my dream; *There will be no going back.* She hadn't thought it possible to take away someone's powers once granted to them, and though I wasn't certain Caoilinn had been entirely forth-coming with Sebastian, I was certain that she believed this. So even if I could find the key to controlling my magic in the next few hours, if there was no way to strip the Others of their powers, then how would it help? This was a puzzle with no solution. We should be fleeing in fear or thinking of ways to beg the Others for mercy… what were we going to do?

While my thoughts became darker and more complex, Sebastian's breathing became slower and deeper and more peaceful. He slept for the entire two hour drive back through Belfast and north along the stunning coastline. Just as we approached our destination, he began to toss and turn, muttering darkly to himself and causing the bus driver to glance in concern at us over his shoulder.

"Sebastian, wake up," I hissed, shaking him roughly. He moaned loudly in response, causing a few of the nearby passengers to glance our way. My mind flashed back to the bus ride into Toronto just days ago, when we had been thrown off the bus. "Wake up," I whispered urgently, right into his ear. "Seamus Coghlan! Wake up!"

His eyes snapped open with a start. I expected and dreaded for him to face the usual confusion upon waking from one of his nightmares. Instead, he roughly grabbed my hand, staring straight and urgently into my eyes with a focus that was both relieving and terrifying all at once.

"The Others, they're here," he pronounced, his eyes wide with horror.

My hand automatically flew to my necklace, squeezing it so tightly it felt almost as if it might cut into my hand.

"Where?" I asked in a surprisingly calm and even voice.

"They've arrived in Ireland and they're close. We don't have much time."

Our roles had strangely been reversed. As the bus slowed down and pulled into the parking lot, it was Sebastian who was panicking and I who was suddenly calm and in control.

"We need to get off the bus."

Sebastian nodded his agreement. I could almost see him drawing strength from my steady tone, a glimmer of fear melting from his eyes. He saw something within me that reassured him, and that in turn, reassured me too.

Almost as soon as I spoke, the bus came to a stop, parking at the side of the large lot along the cliff tops. The driver looked surprised as we both jumped up, barely sparing a minute to thank him as we hurried for the doors.

"Car sick," I explained, knowing it was believable with our pale faces and wide eyes.

"Ah. Glad you made it then! Enjoy some fresh salt air," the driver called after us as we practically leapt off the bus and began jogging across the parking lot.

For a moment I was disoriented. The sun was hot and bright, the salty wind gusting about with a surprisingly chilly blast and the noise of the nearby ocean and crashing waves already filling my ears. The parking lot was nearly full, despite it being barely mid-morning, and many tourists milled about the visitor centre and restaurant at its edge, snapping photos and buying souvenirs. Nearby a small shuttle bus was loading up at the top of a narrow, paved road that led down the cliff and towards the ocean and the causeway below. I looked to Sebastian questioningly, the wind whipping my hair into my face and mouth.

"Shall we climb aboard?" I asked but almost before I'd finished speaking, the shuttle bus closed its doors and began heading down towards the ocean shore with a quick honk of its horn.

"I don't think so. I think we should stick to the cliff-top walk – less crowded and it'll give us a better view."

"Of what?"

"The Giant's Causeway of course," Sebastian answered. We clasped hands and began walking rapidly towards the sign that pronounced the start of the path that wound along the cliff tops, high above the foamy, blue ocean below.

We half-walked, half-jogged along the path, wanting to put as much distance between ourselves and the crowds in the parking lot as possible. The path was wide enough that we could walk side-by-side in most places, a small white, wooden fence erected in areas where the drop-off was more steep. The rocky shoreline rose and fell like most of Ireland seemed to do, heaving with its own rhythm of life. The cliffs jutted out alongside the ocean, covered by an emerald green moss and short, wispy grasses that peeked through the rocky face. The waves crashed below us, splashing up between the columns of the causeway that were so perfectly formed. I was stunned by the appearance of these hexagonal pillars that rose and fell to different heights all along the shoreline, forming a complicated and fascinating pattern from above. The tiled appearance of the rocks and the perfect structure of the columns made it difficult to believe it had been formed naturally without the influence of man or magic.

I began to sweat as we hurried along the path, my backpack weighing heavily on my shoulders and the long-sleeved shirt trapping the heat against my body. The path had changed angles now so that the cliffs actually provided some relief from the wind and the day was heating up steadily. We paused to each have a drink from our water bottles and to wipe the sweat from our faces. Sebastian slipped out of his shirt and looped it into the top of his pants so it swung from his side as he walked. Sweat glistened along the tops of his shoulders and clung in small beads to his back, making the dark lines of his tattoo appear to shimmer and almost sparkle beneath the sun.

"They're very close now," he warned. "Their presence is heavy in the air."

I nodded my agreement. There was something foreboding about this beautiful day, a terrifying sense of doom gathering and strengthening below us with each crash of the waves and blast of the wind.

"I think we're close to what we're looking for. It's just around the corner - we're so close, I know it!" he encouraged, pulling me along even faster.

I didn't answer because I didn't know what to say. I felt much less in control of myself than I had an hour ago, like I was unraveling a bit more with each passing minute. The power of my magic had never felt further out-of-reach to me but I was too afraid to speak these thoughts out loud – too afraid of what it might mean. My only comfort was that Sebastian still had hope and however false I feared it might be, how could I possibly take that away from him?

We rounded a corner in the path, the ocean roaring far beneath us as the cliff plunged straight down towards where the waves crashed into the basalt columns and sprayed the causeway with their slick, salty tears. The wind blasted my face and seemed to suck my breath from my lungs as we found ourselves abruptly thrust into its relentless howl. It was not the wind that made us both freeze in our tracks though, it was the sight of what was waiting for us below.

We stood near the top of a steep and narrow staircase that wound its way down the cliff to the causeway. The shoreline jutted out below, forming a smooth, tiled walkway that lead out a few meters into the ocean. The swirling waters were suddenly eerily calm despite the howling wind that whipped at our clothes. Five dark figures stood out on the peak of the causeway, staring straight up at us as they waited. Even from the height at which we stood, I immediately recognized Walter's thin, sneering face, squinting up against the sun. For a moment I thought I might faint. I grabbed the wooden railing and Sebastian's arm simultaneously, digging my fingernails into both.

Sebastian remained motionless by my side, completely frozen, his muscles rigid and tense. I could tell he was debating whether to run or to fight. I couldn't see a benefit to either. I struggled to regain my balance, reminding myself to breathe and gathering all my inner strength to take control. Somehow I knew it was the only hope we had.

"It was a trap all along." The truth was obvious now but I still felt the need to speak the words aloud. "It wasn't our wants directing us here – it was theirs." My voice sounded flat and hollow in the wind. I watched in disgust as Walter's expression clearly twisted into a mocking smile, almost as if he had heard the words I'd just spoken.

"We don't know that. There still could be answers here. Perhaps if we run, just a bit further–"

"No." My voice was firm and certain. "All they need do is want for us to be dead and we will – instantly. They obviously want us to go to them. *I* don't want to but… I think we should. What other choice do we have?"

Sebastian didn't answer. He continued to stare down at the five Others waiting for us below. His eyes narrowed into a dangerous glare.

"I won't let them hurt you again," he vowed, his voice dark and fierce.

"They won't," I lied. "Let's focus on what we want. Perhaps there's still a way."

Sebastian slowly nodded. We both knew it was hopeless. He squeezed my hand tightly and then slowly stepped in front of me, leading the way down the steep staircase.

"Be careful and stay close to me," he instructed. "If you see any possible chance to escape – take it. Run as fast and as far as you can. I swear I'll find you again."

I didn't answer, I couldn't. I couldn't lie to him for I would never abandon him. No matter what he wanted, it wasn't what I wanted. We would survive this together or we would die together, that was the only way it could be.

I tried to ignore the Others as we made our way down the steep, zig-zagging staircase mounted into the side of the cliff. I couldn't help but notice all of the Others were male and fairly young, except for Walter. The other four appeared to be in their late teens or early twenties. They were all dressed in expensive-looking clothes, all in dark shades despite the heat of the day. They looked like shadows in the sun, voids of light and happiness where only death and despair existed. They were our doom.

Sebastian took my hand again at the bottom of the staircase but walked slightly ahead of me, his stance protective. We moved cautiously out onto the causeway, aware of the slippery stones splashed by the surf. This section was surprisingly level, the columns varying in height only by a few inches and forming a perfect, tiled pathway out to the dark figures who waited by the ocean's edge. They stood before us in a half circle, patiently awaiting our arrival. Sebastian stopped several feet away from them and we waited tensely, examining their strangely youthful and innocent faces.

My heart started to pound in my throat, threatening to choke me with fear. I reached for my necklace a little too roughly. The leather chord it hung upon snapped and so I twisted it tightly around my hand, holding the pendant against my palm where it throbbed and burned in warning. No one looked to me as I moved, all eyes were on Sebastian.

"Seamus, Caoilinn. Welcome," the tall center figure greeted us in a cold and tight voice that carried unnaturally over the sounds of the crashing waves. I was surprised to hear he had no discernible accent – for some reason I'd expected the Others to all be Irish, like Sebastian. The young man who had spoke smiled at me suddenly and there was nothing welcoming about the expression that twisted his handsome face. His black eyes only briefly flickered my way but his gaze narrowed into a glare as he stared down Sebastian. Sebastian didn't speak, he merely shifted so that his body blocked mine a little more. I squeezed his hand tightly, swearing to myself that I would never, ever let him go.

"Do you remember us, Seamus?" a red-haired boy who looked to be about our age asked from the edge of the group. He had a round, freckled face and his expression was surprisingly open and curious. There was something "off" about his eyes though – they were ice blue in color, almost white, and there was nothing boyish or innocent about his chilling gaze.

"Yes, I remember you Charlie," Sebastian answered flatly. "Nathaniel, David, Darius, Walter." He listed their names without emotion, his eyes moving to each expressionless face as he spoke. Walter was the only one who showed any emotion or who paid any attention to me. He sneered the whole while, his beady, black eyes narrowed and gleaming with cruel anticipation.

I desperately tried to want them to stop, to make them all go away and leave us alone. I could feel how futile my attempts were though, like screaming into the wind when your voice is immediately blown back at you despite the strength behind it.

"Why did you bring us here?" Sebastian demanded, speaking to David, the tallest of the five with dark brown hair and nearly black eyes who stood at the group's center. David didn't answer. He gestured to Nathaniel, the shorter and slighter boy to his right, with messy, lighter brown hair.

"You've obviously found Caoilinn and she has apparently regained some use of her magic in this life. Before we decide what to do with you, we need to know exactly how powerful she is and how much control she has," Nathaniel explained in a soft voice with the hint of an English accent. Despite how gentle and polite his tones, there was a strange underlying current to his voice, a subtle threat of power and danger.

"We've been following you since you fled from us in Victoria. Testing you, testing her, testing the strength of your bond and the limits of her control," Charlie added. I flinched as his icy gaze met mine. Sebastian moved another inch in front of me.

"Her power is obviously great." David spoke in a low, regretful voice from the center of the group. I had a definite sense that he was their leader. I squeezed my amber pendent even tighter as Sebastian's whole body tensed.

"She is no threat to you."

"That is for us to decide," David replied, his handsome face blank, his dark eyes deadly. He gave a small nod with his head to Walter.

Walter stepped forward, stopping right before Sebastian. He looked him straight in the eye, the hatred clear in his face.

"I want you to move," he instructed, carefully pronouncing each and every word. Sebastian paled and trembled all over but determinedly stood his ground.

"No," he gasped through his clenched teeth. Walter's eyes widened with disbelief and for a split second I thought he might strike Sebastian. Anger silently and briefly flared in my gut.

"He draws strength from her through the Bond," Darius commented, speaking for the first time in his low and deep voice. He was the burliest of the five with wide shoulders and a strong jaw.

"Move, Seamus!" David snapped tiredly. His voice cracked like a whip through the air, silencing the ocean and the wind for a split second. I felt Sebastian's knees buckle at the sound and before I could react he was already stepping away from me.

"Please, don't do this," he begged as he moved. Tears were filling his eyes. "Please."

"Be silent," David instructed and Sebastian abruptly pressed his lips together and didn't make another sound. Pain, anguish and fear were silently screaming from every inch of him though making me feel even more afraid but not as terrified as perhaps I should have been.

Walter reached for me then and grabbed my shirt sleeve, tearing the fabric in one rough movement and leaving the length of my arm exposed.

"Proof of her ability," Walter declared to the Others victoriously. The black marks left behind from the Binding spell twisted and spiraled up my arm and around my shoulder. Some of the Others looked surprised and uneasy as the black design was revealed. David studied me calmly, his handsome face expressionless still.

"Yes, but we have no clue as to her intent. We have encountered the reincarnate soul of Caoilinn before and she has never once proven to be a threat, avoiding Seamus with ease in exactly the way we have wanted. One would almost think that she didn't want her magic to be reawakened, that she didn't want to be found by her long-lost love," David added cruelly, watching Sebastian's reaction as he spoke.

The shock was clear on Sebastian's face, the denials hanging wordlessly upon his lips. He silently shook his head, a cold fury burning in his eyes.

"You should be happy, Seamus," Charlie commented with a twisted smile. "By keeping you apart for so many years, we also spared her life. Unfortunately, it is unlikely to be so this time."

Sebastian stiffened, glaring at Charlie in a way that did make me afraid, afraid of what he might try to do. I was suddenly glad that the Others were preventing Sebastian's wants from being immediately fulfilled, sensing the dark violence and hatred that was clearly tainting his current wants.

"Caoilinn," David began, his hard, black eyes focusing on mine. I swallowed hard, squeezing my necklace even more tightly in my palm to try to stop my hands from shaking.

"My name is Grace."

David fixed me with a glare that made my knees tremble. He stared right through me, his eyes burning down to my very soul.

"Caoilinn, I need you to answer a few questions for me. I want you to answer truthfully."

"Don't hurt Sebastian, please," I begged, interrupting him once more. I could see I was trying his patience but I didn't care. All that mattered to me was that Sebastian was safe.

"I want you to answer truthfully," he repeated, ignoring my pleas. The intensity of his eyes and voice increased. Sweat beaded upon my brow. "Can you control your magic?"

"No," I answered immediately and automatically, the response springing to my lips before my mind could even process what had been asked of me.

"Are you capable of learning to control your magic?" Nathaniel jumped in, with his surprisingly soft voice.

"No," I repeated, speaking automatically and without thought again.

"Will you master your powers in this life?" Darius demanded.

"No."

They didn't look satisfied; they all glared at me suspiciously and warily still. Walter was visibly fuming, his face full of contempt. Only David appeared calm and collected. "I don't want to master my powers," I added honestly, wanting to convince them of the truth and wanting so badly for there to be even the smallest chance that they would let Sebastian and myself go.

"She lies!" Walter hissed. David dismissed his comment with a slight wave of his hand.

"She can only speak the truth as we want her to. Do not question our abilities, young one," David cautioned. He didn't even glance

Walter's way as he spoke, but Walter still visibly paled, even beneath the sun's unrelenting heat. David turned to face Sebastian. "As long as she is not a threat, she will remain unharmed. But I cannot promise the same for you, old friend. We have a score to settle."

Sebastian visibly relaxed upon hearing David's words, despite the threat of the latter pronouncement.

Darius flexed his muscles threateningly, his expression hard and cold as he stared Sebastian down.

"For the crimes you have committed against The Order, you will be punished. We cannot permit for you to live any longer, especially now that you have been doubly-bound to Caoilinn and her magic has reawakened," Darius slowly pronounced. Somehow the sound of my gasp carried clearly and unnaturally through the air, each and every set of eyes turning to meet mine.

"No," I whispered, panic flooding through my body as I realized I could no longer move.

"I'm sorry, Gracelynn." Sebastian's eyes filled with tears as he spoke. He looked away from me to stare down David, his gray eyes burning with fire. "If any harm ever comes to her, I swear I will find out. I will hunt each of you down and rip apart your souls. I swear it," he repeated, his voice soft yet terrifying.

David nodded amicably, looking almost amused at Sebastian's harsh, half-whispered pronouncement but the others were all visibly unsettled, shifting uneasily as the wind howled around us.

"No," I repeated, my voice a little stronger this time. Once again, the sound of my words somehow cut through the wind and rose above the crash of the waves against the ancient basalt stones. Nathaniel eyed me uncertainly, his gaze flickering back and forth between Sebastian and I.

"Release her now," Sebastian calmly requested, his voice tight and strained. "She doesn't need to see this." He didn't even bother to look my way. I couldn't believe what was happening. I was furious and terrified and sick to my stomach. The wind howled even louder, its intensity seeming to grow with the power of my emotions.

"No, she stays." Walter placed a cold, bony hand on my shoulder, his touch increasing the rigidity of my frozen muscles to the point of near pain.

"She will not be harmed but she must witness what is about to happen to you," Charlie announced with a sickening smile.

"No," Sebastian gasped, the fear returning to his eyes in a sudden flash.

"Her soul needs a reminder of why it is in both your best interests to remain apart, in this and every life to come," David explained patiently. I wanted to scream and cry out loud, to beg for their mercy, to offer myself in place of Sebastian but I suddenly found myself unable to speak. My vocal chords were frozen in place, bound as tightly as the rest of my muscles. My soul screamed in outrage and fury, rising with the powerful, howling wind. "Let's get this over with. Step forward, Seamus," David commanded in a soft and almost seductive voice. Sebastian's face was taut and white as he complied, his movements jerky as he obviously strained to break free from the Others' control.

Walter's hand tightened on my shoulder, his fingers digging into my flesh and bones in a way that should have buckled my knees in pain – if I could have moved. As it was I couldn't even cry out.

I stood there, completely frozen and helpless as I watched Sebastian step forward, his back to me the whole while. We never even had the chance to say goodbye. I should have felt more afraid, I should have felt more heartbroken but as it was, all I could feel was a steadily rising, murderous rage that burned throughout every cell of my body. I began to tremble from the force of it, despite my inability to move. I was angry at Sebastian for giving himself up so easily once he thought that I was safe. I was furious at the Others for not only separating Sebastian and I now but for admittedly keeping us apart for hundreds upon hundreds of years. I was enraged that any of them might hurt him and disgusted that they were forcing me to stand by helplessly, to watch. And I was livid with myself, for not being strong enough or brave enough to take control of my magic and to live up to my destiny.

I could feel the fire burning in my eyes as I glared at Sebastian's back, willing with all my might for him to stop, for him to turn and break free, to run. All the heat and noise and sensations of the world began to slip away from me as my eyes focused and unfocused on the design of the large tattoo on his back. The lines appeared to almost shift and shimmer before me in the heat, a new pattern emerging from the detailed design of which I had never before been aware. The wind howled in my ears and a soft, sweet voice from thousands of years in the past whispered into my ear, *"Trust and feel the pattern."*

The answer was on the tip of my tongue, the power within me flaring into a wild and swirling rage, my necklace burning red hot into the flesh and bones of my hand.

Sebastian suddenly dropped to his knees before the Others, his back arched as he howled in excruciating pain. Walter laughed softly in my ear, obviously thoroughly enjoying not only Sebastian's pain but also my own. Scarlet blood began to trickle from Sebastian's nose and ears as he thrashed against the ground. His eyes briefly met mine, his expression wild with pain while his screams carried on and on. His tormented cry abruptly cut off as blood poured from his mouth. I feared he had bitten off his own tongue as he flipped onto his back and stared straight up into the blinding sun.

The world became red hot again, the terrifying anger burning brightly throughout my body and soul at the sight of Sebastian's ruby-red blood. My eyes fell upon the tattoo on Sebastian's chest, the intricate Celtic knot that lay over his heart. The design shifted and shimmered as I now knew it would and a new pattern emerged and unraveled before me. I knew exactly what to do.

"You should stop now," I warned. My voice was unrecognizable even to me. The deadly calm with which I spoke was both terrifying and commanding. My voice sliced through the air as it never had before, my soft words booming against the jagged cliffs and crashing into the tumultuous waves.

Darius and Walter laughed together cruelly. Charlie and David completely ignored me, only Nathaniel looked concerned.

"She shouldn't be able to—" he began, but he was too late. My lips moved without me ever moving them, my voice spoke without me uttering a sound.

"Five of you may be powerful enough to stop me – but four aren't," I announced in that chilling, deathly voice. I spun around faster than I had ever moved before, than I had ever thought possible. I released all of my fury, all of my power and simultaneously gave up and obtained all of my control as I grabbed Walter by the throat. The fire within me burned hot enough that I wondered how I wasn't consumed by its power myself. I wasn't afraid anymore though and so I took control. I embraced the powerful anger and darkness within me and directed it into the carefully formed lines of the pattern I had just seen. I did it easily and automatically, as if I had a thousand times before. Walter's expression was unexpected, almost comical in its disbelief. The shocked and puzzled expression was only briefly present in his eyes before they glazed over and he crumpled to the ground at my feet. The world was abruptly silent and still.

Chapter Nine – Ghost from the Past

I stared down at Walter's motionless body feeling oddly detached and numb. The world around me was silent still, the wind banished, the waves paused, the silence not one of peace but one of emptiness alike what was inside of me now.

The Others were all frozen, unable to move any part of their bodies except their eyes, just like I had been moments ago. I ignored them all as I glided over to Sebastian's side, kneeling down on top of the hard, rocky columns beside him. I felt like I was moving in a trance as I checked his pulse and listened carefully to his shallow breathing. I even tipped open his jaw, checking his tongue and feeling vaguely relieved to find it was only badly bitten but already rapidly healing. I ripped my remaining shirt sleeve free and dipped it in a salty pool of water on top of one of the columns nearby. He opened his eyes as I began carefully wiping the sticky blood from his face and neck.

"Gracelynn?" His voice was faint and hoarse. He looked up at me in confusion, rapidly trying to take in the scene around us as I helped him to sit up. His eyes focused on Walter's motionless body. "What have you done?" he whispered. I could tell he was shocked and concerned. I hadn't expected him to be watching me so warily, as if I were a danger to even him.

I ignored his question and turned to the four of the Others who stood around us, frozen but still watching and listening.

"Forget us and sleep," I commanded and they collapsed to the hard ground as one, hitting the rocks heavily but without the cracking sound of breaking bone.

I felt my own legs tremble, the last of my strength suddenly threatening to leave me. Once again the world shimmered before my eyes but this time it was from exhaustion. I numbly sat down on the ground as Sebastian stood up and went to check Walter's body.

"He's dead," Sebastian quietly announced. He was staring at me in disbelief, his face pale and drawn. I ignored him, focusing on slowly breathing in and out, letting the sounds and sensations of the world slowly return to me. Sebastian leant over Walter, noticing something upon his chest. He began carefully unbuttoning Walter's shirt, revealing the black twisted knot that had been burnt into his pale skin above his still and silent heart. I barely glanced at it – I had known it would be there. I thought I heard Sebastian gasp.

Sebastian moved to check each of the Others, checking their pulses and the skin over their hearts, just in case. I knew they lived, I knew they bore no marks. I had only knocked them unconscious and blocked some of their memories. It was a relatively simple spell that would leave no marks. Sebastian said something to me but his voice sounded far away. I heard him speak again, confusion and urgency in his tone.

"Gracelynn?"

I frowned at him, puzzled. I knew the name should mean something to me but it sounded strange and unfamiliar. My thoughts swirled dizzily and I teetered on the edge of consciousness as something deep within me stirred. He repeated the strange name and I ignored him still, struggling to figure out what was wrong. Where was I? What was I doing?

"Caoilinn?" he whispered.

"Yes." The word sprang to my lips, my soul speaking without needing or wanting my mind's control.

Sebastian froze, staring at me in shock. I stared back, numbly wondering over the beautiful contrast of his black hair, powder white skin and the dark, scarlet smears of his blood. He spoke in a whisper, his voice rough and smooth at once.

"Caoilinn? Why…? How did you…?"

"My spell book was full of drawings and designs. The pattern for each and every spell I knew was woven into your tattoos," my voice explained. The soft, soprano tones were chillingly numb and in control. "To twist fate, to make something happen that isn't naturally meant to be, you must know the correct design – the correct twist. Grace will remember now."

"But how did you... how are you doing this?"

"Our time is up, my love. Grace will remember and explain."

Sebastian's eyes filled with panic. He rushed forward, grabbing my icy cold, numb hands. "No, don't leave me yet. I..."

"I won't ever leave," Caoilinn's sweet voice softly whispered. "Because I've already gone."

I felt the last of my strength slipping away from me like a dandelion seed tossed up in the wind. My eyes rolled back in my head and the last thing I saw before I lost consciousness was the clear blue sky floating endlessly above me.

I had nightmares. I dreamt of terrifying things. I dreamt of murder – murder that I was pushed to commit and murder that I chose to. I dreamt of violence and a magic so dark and twisted, it left me trembling and screaming in fear. I dreamt of all the terrible and unspeakable things Caoilinn had done in the name of her Sisterhood to discover the patterns for her spells. I dreamt of death and confusion and despair. I dreamt of the look in Walter's eyes when I killed him.

The transition from black dreams to bleak reality was confusing and blurred. I could feel myself stirring in my sleep, fighting the demons that haunted me from thousands of years in the past. I heard myself cry out and then I felt Sebastian's arms around me. I felt his warmth, his steadiness, his firm and solid embrace. The tears came next, the endless tears. And I cried, and I cried, until my tears ran dry and eventually, I opened my eyes.

We were still at The Giant's Causeway but I could tell by the angle of the sun that it was much later in the day, probably mid-afternoon. Sebastian and I were huddled together in the cool shade of a wall of tall, basalt columns. I could see and hear the ocean, I could feel the light current of the wind and I could smell the salt of the sea. There was no one else in sight.

I looked straight up into Sebastian's eyes, clinging to him tightly as I spoke.

"Where are the Others?"

"They've gone," he quietly replied. He paused, examining my expression cautiously. "They began to awaken as soon as you collapsed. I barely had time to get us far enough away to hide – they didn't look for us though. They didn't seem to remember we were here. They took Walter's body with them."

For a second I thought I might throw up, the guilt and terror was so great. I forced the nausea back down though, forced myself to accept and face the truth.

"Walter. I killed him, didn't I? Oh, Sebastian... I wanted to save you so badly. I couldn't stand to see you in pain like that and then... I killed him. I wanted him to die," I whispered, horrified at what I had done. "How could I do that?" And I burst back into tears.

Sebastian rocked me in his arms, gently stroking my hair until my sobs quieted. He tilted my face up, forcing me to meet his solemn and caring eyes. He gently kissed my forehead and then tenderly wiped the tears from my face with his thumbs.

"You did what you had to. You saved us. I'm so sorry you had to do it though, Gracelynn. I know what it's like to have to take some-one else's life," he reminded me with obvious reluctance. "There was no other way..."

"There was." My voice came out so quietly I was surprised Se-bastian even heard. He looked down at me, waiting expectantly. I couldn't meet his eyes. I dropped my gaze to the rough, basalt stones that formed the precise, natural tiles we sat upon. "The Others weren't expecting me to be able to use my ability at all – I could have done anything. I could have just knocked him unconscious, it would have been enough but it wasn't enough for me. I wanted him to die for what he had done to you, for what he was doing to you. I wanted someone to pay for what we've been through," I confessed. I spoke the truth with a chilling coldness that I could no longer blame on Caoilinn – it was all me.

Sebastian didn't respond. He waited quietly and patiently, sensing there was more.

"I will never do it again," I swore, my voice suddenly fierce and impassioned. I sat up straighter as I spoke. "Never. I will never take another's life not even to save my own - not even to save yours. I'm sorry but I can't... I never should have in the first place. And I swear I never, ever will again."

"It's okay," Sebastian comforted. He gently reached for my hand but I pulled away. I knew I didn't deserve his comfort. I was unworthy of his love. "You did what you felt you had to do and you saved me. And I believe that you'll never take another's life again. I don't think you could ever want it enough, not after this," he added quietly. I nodded my agreement, swallowing hard as I tried to push back the dull, numb blackness that was gathering inside of me.

"Do you remember… Caoilinn, speaking through you?" Sebastian asked hesitantly. I blinked back my tears and nodded. Perhaps it was because of my dark mood and angry, bitter thoughts but what immediately jumped to mind was how Sebastian had begged Caoilinn not to leave him.

"She said you would remember everything now," he prompted, distracting me. I nodded reluctantly.

"I remember how to use my magic." Sebastian waited patiently for me to continue, so with a sigh, I did. "The simple spells should be easy. It's a matter of focusing and trusting my instincts, trusting in myself and letting my emotions and wants guide me. I was having a hard time giving in before, releasing my control of my emotions and desires so that I could control my magic… it's a hard thing for me to do but I think I can do it when I need to now. The more complicated spells require designs though."

"The designs in my tattoos?"

"Yes," I agreed. "The more powerful spells, the spells that require altering fate, like taking someone's life or Binding another soul to yours, these require a design that also leaves a physical mark on the person's body and on their soul. The lines of the design represent what was meant to be and how it must be twisted to become what you want it to become. It's complicated. Caoilinn would meditate for days to unravel the correct patterns and designs. She was the only one of the Sisterhood powerful enough to perform these spells but some were able to combine their abilities and they were getting close. She should never have asked you to save that spell book for her – it should have been destroyed."

"Caoilinn never told me any of this. I suppose I didn't need to know since my magic works differently than hers but if there were others in the Sisterhood who could learn to use these spells, then couldn't I have too? Why wouldn't she tell me?" Sebastian looked at me expectantly, the hurt and confusion bright in his beautiful eyes.

"She was afraid to tell you, Sebastian. She was afraid of what you'd think of her if you knew how dangerous and deadly she could be. She feared you'd reject her if you knew of the terrible things she had done." I knew it was the truth as I spoke it, I could feel it right down in my very soul, echoing within the core of my being.

"No," Sebastian denied, slowly shaking his head. "How could she doubt me? She had done nothing that I wouldn't have understood, that I couldn't have forgiven."

"The Sisterhood used her, manipulated her to some extent. They encouraged her to discover the deadliest and most powerful spells. They brought her subjects to test the designs on – animals, criminals, sometimes even the terminally ill who were brought to the temple to be saved. They told her she was serving the people, performing the will of the Gods. She was already starting to question the intentions of the Sisterhood when she met you but she hadn't planned on running away, she had planned on killing herself to escape. You changed all that."

"No. She would never have… she wasn't capable of murder," he objected but I could tell he wasn't trying to convince me but himself.

"Did you think I was?" I asked quietly.

Sebastian didn't answer, he couldn't. He watched me sadly, his eyes full of doubt, denial, betrayal and disappointment. It was breaking my heart. I felt almost as if I had betrayed him myself.

"Sometimes we only see what we want to see. We choose to only believe what our heart wants to be true. The truth was always there, nothing has really changed. The only difference is now you know it."

Sebastian didn't respond. I wanted to cry but the tears wouldn't come. So instead I embraced the huge, gaping cavern of sadness inside my chest that felt like it would split me in two. I let it fill and overwhelm me, the emptiness painful and intense.

"When did you become so philosophical?" Sebastian suddenly asked. His voice was strained, his eyes were weary but there was a gentle, teasing quality to his words that allowed a flicker of hope to spark within the darkness inside of me.

"You're a bad influence on me."

"Obviously," he agreed and he smiled at me in a way that appeared to be only slightly forced. I knew things would eventually be fine between us but I also realized it was going to take some time. By exposing Caoilinn's secrets, I had given him reason to doubt not only her but also me and because of my recent actions, I could only feel that I deserved it.

"We can't stay here. The Others will still be looking for us and eventually they'll return," Sebastian pointed out.

"As soon as they find a fifth, they'll remember. It won't matter anymore that I don't want them to, that I want them to leave us alone. I'm still powerless when they outnumber us. I was only able to stop Walter because they never expected me to be capable of it."

"I don't suppose you remembered how to stop them all?"

"No. I don't think Caoilinn knew how to take away someone else's powers. I'm not sure it's possible, Sebastian. I think our only option, for now, is to run."

"Okay. Where should we go?" He waited expectantly, a small smile on his face that made him look even more like his old self. I relaxed just a little bit more.

"You're asking me?" He waited patiently while I carefully considered. "We need to leave the country again. We should probably avoid the United Kingdom entirely - and North America. I don't know where we should go. We need help, I know that much. I just want someone to point us in the right direction," I admitted with a sigh.

"Hey! Found you!" a man called out, suddenly appearing as he stepped around the wall of basalt columns. He was average height and a little fat, with a large nose and a noticeable bald spot on top of his thinning, gray-brown hair. He looked strangely familiar. I tried not to appear too alarmed at his sudden appearance but I automatically tensed my muscles in preparation to run. "We've been looking all over for you two! The bus is about to leave."

It took a second for me to understand what he meant. I realized why he looked familiar – he had sat near us on the tour bus all the way along the Antrim Coast. Relief washed over me but of course, Sebastian recovered first.

"Oh, thank you! We didn't realize what time it was, sorry. I'm so glad the bus waited." Sebastian helped me to my feet as he spoke.

"What are you doing?" I whispered as we began to follow the man over the uneven, slippery stones.

"You said you wanted someone to point us in the right direction – well apparently we should rejoin our tour group and head back to Belfast. Just keep wanting someone to help us find the right way and they will."

Sebastian flashed me a quick smile before picking up the pace. There was something strange in his eyes when he looked at me, a strain he tried to hide, a glimmer of doubt. My chest ached hollowly and my stomach began to churn as I tried to push back the recent memories. I knew what I had done would haunt me forever as would the terrifying memories of the acts Caoilinn had committed in my dreams. There was no forgiveness for what either of us had done; how could I expect Sebastian to ever look at me the same way again?

It was a quiet drive back to Belfast, even the other tourists falling into a sleepy lull as the bus bumped and jostled along the winding roads. Perhaps it was from the long day out in the wind and sun that I joined in the sleepy silence but I guessed it might have more to do with my headache and desire for peace. At least in the relative silence, I could sink into my gloomy thoughts for a while and punish myself as I felt I deserved.

The bus took us to the hostel in Belfast where most of the tourists were staying. It was a large hostel in a beautiful, historic building with a huge kitchen and large, private rooms. Chance would have it that we were invited to stay and eat with some of the guests and there was also an empty room left available that we paid to stay in for the night. Since there were four bunks to choose from, I chose a different one than Sebastian, assuming he would want to sleep alone. He watched me lie down on the bottom bunk across from his with his ancient, youthful eyes.

"What are you doing?" he asked curiously, a smile pulling at his mouth.

"Going to sleep."

"Obviously. Why are you sleeping over there on your own?"

I rolled over, turning my back to him as I was afraid to face the truth.

"Because I didn't think you'd want me near you after… after what happened today," I confessed, speaking to the wall but in a voice just loud enough for him to hear.

There was silence behind me. My heart sank even deeper, the lonely, empty feeling inside of me growing and threatening to consume me whole. And then suddenly he was there. He slipped into the bed behind me, his warm, safe arms reaching for me and holding me tightly, his lips murmuring reassurances, his fingertips brushing away my tears.

"I always want you near me – always," he whispered into my hair. "There are things I have done too that I regret every moment of every day. I have memories that make me so ashamed, I can barely open my eyes each morning. There are secrets in my past that I fear if you knew, you would leave me in a second… but if it will ease your pain tonight, if it will comfort you now, I will confess to you all my sins."

It was tempting. I had never before asked Sebastian for details of his nightmares for I knew how difficult it was for him to remember. I didn't want him to relieve the horrors from his past just for the sake of my curiosity. But I now understood how truly ashamed, how horrified at himself he might feel and I could never, ever be the cause of anything I knew to cause him pain.

"No," I told him as I rolled over. I wiggled even closer to him, pressing my forehead against his. "I would never leave you – ever. No matter what you have or have not done, it doesn't change a thing. I don't need to know any more of your past than I already do. I will be with you forever. I will be your wife." I sealed my vow with a kiss, pressing my lips against his forcefully, a sudden passionate fire igniting within me.

"I love you," he murmured as I kissed my way along his smooth jaw and down the side of his throat.

"I love you too," I whispered back as he pulled my body against his tightly and his mouth came down to meet mine. He kissed me hard, with a rough, desperate passion that I understood and responded to with every fiber of my being. We were two lost and damaged souls who desperately needed to lose and then find themselves within the other. We were consumed by a frantic passion that stripped away our painful memories and erased all sense of reason, and I never wanted to stop or to return to reality again.

Sebastian slipped out of his shirt and, without thought or hesitation, I slipped out of mine. He held me tightly against his chest, the warmth of his bare skin against mine thrilling me with each ragged breath. His fingers slid down the length of my spine in a slow and tantalizing caress. Shivers erupted throughout my body and I gasped in pleasure. The fire within me was burning into an uncontrollable rage, my cheeks flushing with its heady heat, my head spinning with desire. And even as I burned with this intoxicating, new passion, I still wanted more. I wanted all of Sebastian, every heartbeat, every breath, every part of his being. I wanted all of him, forever. I wanted too much.

"Stop," I gasped as I tore my mouth from his. It was painful to break apart, excruciating even. I tried desperately to catch my breath, to restore reason to my mind.

Sebastian was only inches from my face still and he looked deeply into my eyes, so deeply I could feel his gaze penetrating right down to the core of my soul. His eyes were pools of liquid, dark-blue fire, burning with the heat of our passion and the intense, immeasurable depths of our love.

"Let's get married," I whispered breathlessly. He smiled.

"I think I already asked you that."

"Tomorrow. Marry me tomorrow."

"Are you proposing to me now?" he teased but I could see the excitement sparkling in his eyes, the wild fire melting into bright, glowing embers.

"Yes. One last night to wait and then tomorrow I will be yours forever, in every possible way."

Sebastian grinned and then playfully moaned. He rolled away from me, lifting my shirt up off the floor and handing it to me over his shoulder, his back turned to me still to preserve what was left of my modesty.

"After two thousand years of waiting, why does tomorrow still feel so far away?" he wondered aloud as I sat up and pulled my shirt back on over my head, happy to notice that he still hadn't retrieved his.

"Tomorrow is like a dream, until it becomes today." I snuggled down against his back as I spoke, sliding my arm around him and enjoying the feel of his warm skin.

He sighed happily. "You say the most absurd things."

"Look who's talking."

"Isn't it traditional for the bride and groom to sleep apart on the night before their wedding?" he suddenly asked, his muscles tensing as if he were about to jump out of bed.

"Oh, shut up," I grumbled affectionately, pulling myself even more tightly against his back. He laughed quietly before obliging my request.

My mind began to drift towards warm, sleepy dreams until a thought suddenly occurred, striking through my peaceful mind like a blaze of lightning.

"Did my father really give you permission to marry me?"

"Of course. I asked him the night before we left Toronto," Sebastian responded without hesitation, though his amusement was clear.

"I can't believe he agreed."

"I was surprised myself," he admitted. "I wanted to ask him though. I think he knew I was going to propose to you either way and especially once he saw the ring…"

"He did?"

Sebastian chuckled softly at my surprise.

"He did and he reluctantly gave his blessing, after a few choice words and threats of course. You know, I've never asked anyone for permission to marry their daughter before. It was… well, it was worth it to make you happy."

"Thank you," I whispered, kissing the back of his shoulder. He placed his hand over my arm, twisting his fingers through mine.

"Anything and everything for you. Now sleep so that tomorrow might come sooner."

"It can't come soon enough," I agreed.

We both woke early the next morning and enjoyed the luxury of showers, clean teeth and a complimentary breakfast provided by the hostel. Just as we were finishing our morning meal, our bus driver appeared, speaking loudly to the whole dining area but looking at only us.

"Shuttle's here. Anyone off to the airport this morning?"

Sebastian and I shared a quick look before standing and grabbing our bags. It was a relief to have others guide our way for once and I found it surprisingly easy to trust in my newly-found control.

We bid farewell to our driver at the airport, who never once asked us where we were headed to next. It was a good thing for we both didn't know yet. The answer found us soon enough.

At Sebastian's suggestion, we walked over to the departures board and examined the list of flights on the screen. There were several leaving in the next few minutes that we didn't have a hope of making. My attention was caught by a flight leaving Belfast for Berlin in just under an hour. The print flickered, making the flight number and times attract both of our attention.

"What do you think?" Sebastian asked.

I thought about it for a minute and then shrugged. "It makes sense. I want to be shown the right way and I have friends in Berlin, the exchange family I stayed with three years ago. I know the city and speak the language a bit… we might as well."

"To Berlin then," Sebastian agreed.

I almost expected how easy it was to purchase our tickets and arrange our flight to Berlin. The woman at the EasyJet counter informed us how lucky we were that there were still two seats available. Apparently, the plane was typically full as the flight was only offered twice a week and had actually been discontinued until just a week ago. All these lucky coincidences only served to confirm that we were going the right way, the way that we must go to find the answers we wanted.

We talked and laughed on the plane, enjoying the time together to relax and reconnect during the flight. I was able to push back the disturbing memories of yesterday and look forward to today – to live in the now, as Sebastian liked to say. We teased each other and joked around and talked of only frivolous and silly things. A few hours later, with smiles on both of our faces, we found ourselves sipping coffee on a street patio in Eastern Berlin, miles away from where we'd started the day. It was a comforting feeling, almost like we could escape both of our pasts.

A wave of homesickness washed over me as I glanced down the busy city streets. My smile slowly faded as a lonely, lost feeling began creeping into my soul. I gazed out at the tall, historic-looking buildings that lined the streets and contrasted with the occasional modern building-front spaced in between. Berlin was a beautiful city full of a rich and sad history. The last time I had been here, I'd tried my best to immerse myself in the culture, learning the language as quickly as possibly, trying my best to fit in with the other students at my school. I had never fit in. My parents had made certain that I stayed with the wealthiest family in Berlin and my time with them had been sheltered and disappointing. Just like my own parents, they made certain I never experienced the tourist-side of the city or the real Berlin streets. I was taken to balls and functions and it was all so similar to the life I had left in Canada that I was quickly disillusioned of my time in Germany. I had grown quite close to the young daughter of the family I stayed with but, as so often happens, we lost touch over the years. I hoped to track her down later that afternoon though – she would be nearly sixteen now.

It was nice being here with Sebastian. I was experiencing Berlin in a whole new way already and we'd barely been off the plane for an hour. But it was sad too. I hated running, I hated jumping from country to country, city to city, always looking over our shoulders and never knowing how much we could relax or how long it would be before we could return home. I didn't want any more adventures, I realized. I just wanted to be able to go home and to stay there, with Sebastian.

"What's wrong?" Sebastian asked, reaching for my hand across the table.

"Nothing. I'm just tired."

"You seem upset suddenly," he observed.

I forced a smile and let go of his hand to sip the last of my coffee, carefully avoiding the question. He smiled mischievously.

"I think I know what would cheer you up."

"What's that?" I asked warily.

"Let's get married."

I laughed, my joy returning in a heady rush. He was right, the idea cheered me instantly.

"Okay," I agreed and I took up his hand again with an almost shy smile.

It turned out that Sebastian had just the place in mind. He remembered coming to Germany several hundred years ago and visiting a Protestant Church in Eastern Berlin. It still stood; apparently it was the oldest church still standing in the city though much of it had been restored after the violent World War II bombings. St. Nicholas's Church turned out to be not far from where we'd stopped for coffee and we were directed there quite easily.

My excitement grew as we approached the Nicholas Quarter. The beautifully restored medieval buildings that towered on both sides of the narrow and winding streets added to the picturesque scene of my wedding day. *My wedding day.* I repeated the phrase over and over in my head, my heart beating faster with both nerves and excitement. I vainly wished I were wearing something fancier; I knew Sebastian didn't really care though so why should I? At least I had the clean, white, peasant-style skirt on that had belonged to Dahlia and a thin, long-sleeved turquoise-blue top with a cut and neckline that were both quite flattering..

"There it is," Sebastian pointed to the tall, reddish spires rising up above the buildings at the end of the street we were on. As we rounded the next curve in the road, the church came into full view.

St. Nicholas's Church was a beautiful, old, red brick building. The architecture and design of it reminded me of a medieval castle with its high-arched windows, two tall spires and rounded tower. My heart beat faster at the sight, my pulse raced, my breathing came quick and light as I realized that all my wants were about to be realized and fulfilled.

We walked quickly hand-in-hand, grinning at each other. I felt almost as if I were dreaming. It was hard to believe that in just minutes,

I could be Sebastian's wife. The light blue sky was dotted with clouds overhead, the warm summer sun shone down brightly upon us, the beautiful Berlin streets were picturesque and even the happy tourists and friendly-faced locals that we passed all seemed to share in our joy– it was all so perfect. I smiled back at each welcoming face I saw, feeling unusually confident and proud. A girl with reddish-gold hair immediately stood out to me but it wasn't because of her exotic, wavy hair or her intense, green eyes or even the rougher, slightly-punk way that she dressed, including the low-cut tight black tank top that she wore. It was the recognition in her eyes when she met mine and then the stunned surprise that overtook her expression that made me come to a stumbling halt.

"Gracelynn, what's–" Sebastian didn't have to finish his sentence. He followed my gaze and his words were choked off in his throat. He stiffened by my side, all the color instantly draining from his face.

The day suddenly became darker, colder. The sun slipped behind a cloud.

The girl was one of the Others, there was no doubt about that in my mind. I knew her, I recognized her. I felt connected to her somehow. Her moment of hesitation was over though, the shock of seeing us had passed and she had now settled on a course of action. The determination was clear in her face, even out-numbered she was going to try to make trouble. She was charging straight towards us. I clutched at my necklace in fear, bracing myself for what was about to come.

"Run!" the red-headed girl yelled, fear flashing through her stunning green eyes. "Sebastian - run!"

My own fear was replaced by confusion. I couldn't understand what was happening – was this some kind of trick?

"It's Caoilinn! Sebastian, it's Caoilinn!" she hollered in her thick Irish accent. Her eyes were wide, her face pale as she rushed towards us, towards him. "For the love of God, I want you to run!" she yelled, her voice begging and her eyes pleading as she came flying down the street towards us. She had almost reached us now and I could clearly see there were tears in her eyes. It was then that I realized she was afraid, that she thought she needed to protect Sebastian – from *me*.

The absurdity of it almost made me laugh but at the same time, a strange nauseous feeling began to rise up in my stomach. There was something wrong here, something very wrong.

The girl came to a stop just a few feet before us. At least one of us must have wanted for no one to take notice of the strange scene we were causing as the crowds passed us by completely unaware of anything amiss. I was surprised that Sebastian hadn't moved an inch. He was normally so much more protective of me than this. Perhaps he had realized before I did that the girl wasn't really a threat. I couldn't understand the strange expression on his face.

"You stubborn ass, why don't you run?" the girl demanded, tears of frustration and fear spilling down her lightly freckled cheeks. Her eyes darted to me and she unexpectedly flinched away from my curious and confused gaze. There was something else present in her eyes, something more than just the fear. I felt the connection between us again, a sudden and inexplicable outrage and fury flaring up in my gut as our eyes briefly met. Who was she? "Why won't you run?" she repeated, looking only at Sebastian.

"Because I don't want to." Sebastian finally spoke in a firm but unexpectedly quiet voice. He moved, stepping closer to my side and wrapping his arm tightly around my waist. I couldn't understand why he sounded almost... ashamed.

"What have you done to him?" The girl turned to face me with blazing green eyes. I could see the fear in them still but it was quickly being replaced by her anger. I tried not to feel intimidated but it was suddenly quite hard. Though she was smaller than me, she was obviously tougher, her petite body curved and muscled and the expression in her eye making it quite clear that she would be more than willing to take me on.

"She hasn't done anything except save my life and love me for all that I am unworthy of it." Sebastian answered for me. "Now stop it, Mags. That's enough."

The girl's eyes flashed again. She glared at me and I felt myself shrinking away from the heat of her hatred. I turned towards Sebastian, seeking his reassurance.

"Sebastian?" I spoke his name uncertainly, a thousand questions in my eyes as I waited for him to look at me. "Sebastian, who is she? What's going on?"

He hesitantly met my gaze, his eyes full of shame and regret. I could see the silent plea in them, begging for my forgiveness. My stomach dropped and I swallowed hard. I knew I wasn't going to like what I was about to hear.

"She's one of the Others – the first one to ever join me. We can trust her, I think," he added quietly. "Her name is Magdalene."

"My name is Mags," the girl interrupted, angrily brushing the tears from her face. "Mags Caldwood."

"Caldwood?" I echoed, confused. I looked at Sebastian questioningly but he had dropped his eyes to the ground again. It was the girl who answered me, her voice full of smug, self-satisfied pride as she glared into my eyes. She definitely no longer seemed afraid.

"I'm Sebastian's wife."

Chapter Ten – Nightmare

I stared at Mags dumbly, unable to understand what she was saying. Why would she say that she was Sebastian's wife? And why wasn't he denying it? What kind of trick was this? My mind couldn't comprehend what was going on.

"You *were* my wife," Sebastian quietly corrected. "Once, a very long time ago." He pulled me more tightly against his side but I was barely aware of his warmth. My whole body had gone numb, the bright, romantic, excitement that had been building within me had been severed, snuffed out, completely destroyed by this beautiful, small, red-headed "teen" before us.

"I still am." Mags' green eyes were defiant but her expression was one of intense hurt at Sebastian's rejection. The obvious pain that he was causing her hurt me too – it confirmed their relationship and the strength of her feelings for him even though I was certain they couldn't have seen each other in hundreds of years. It made me feel physically ill nonetheless. "We never divorced."

"We've been separated for three hundred years."

"Because you abandoned me. Because you just got up one day and disappeared, leaving me alone to search for you but never able to find you. I'll enjoy letting you make it up to me," Mags added with a smirk. She glanced at me nervously as she spoke though, almost as if she were worried I might... do what? I was only just regaining the ability to speak.

"She's your wife?" I whispered, the world still spinning dangerously around me.

"She was," Sebastian confirmed. "Gracelynn, I swear I didn't remember her until this very moment. There were glimpses of her face in my memories but I never... I'm so sorry. I thought she was dead."

I took a shaky breath and moved a step away from him so that I might see his face. His skin was still too pale, his dark eyes wide with fear and guilt. I watched his eyes flood with pain as I moved away but I didn't let it stop me.

"So that's how you did it, you crafty old bastard," Mags suddenly commented. The way she spoke shocked me; it wasn't just her coarse language, it was the familiar and affectionate way she cursed Sebastian. She was looking back and forth between us with a wary but speculative expression on her pretty, heart-shaped face. "You wanted to convince yourself I was dead, so you did. I wouldn't ever let you forget me but if you believed I was dead… it was the only way you could leave me. But why?"

"I don't owe you any explanations, Mags, so stop asking." Sebastian's voice was a low, unfriendly growl. I watched the pain flash across Mags' eyes again and I felt my nausea rise.

"Don't be angry at me because she made you forget me!" Mags accused, glaring at me again with her challenging, emerald eyes. "How dare you blame me for Caoilinn's goddamn lies?"

"She didn't make me forget."

"She's the only one who could have. She didn't want you to remember me, so you forgot," the girl insisted.

"I forgot everything, Mags. She's the reason why I can remember your name. If it weren't for Gracelynn, I wouldn't even recognize your face. I'd forgotten it all and she gave me all of my memories back – recently too. Though obviously, I've been having some trouble sorting through it all," Sebastian mumbled, his eyes starting to fall out of focus.

The color drained from Mags' face, her freckles a light dusting across her snow white pallor. Her lips parted to let out a quiet gasp.

"What do you mean all of your memories?" she quietly demanded, her eyes burning with a fiery intensity into Sebastian's. His gaze refocused on her face.

"I meant exactly what I said. She restored all of my memories, right back to the day I was born. I can remember almost all of my life now… well, most of it, sometimes."

"No," she hissed, her eyes widening with fear and horror. She turned to me, acknowledging my presence again as she locked her gaze with mine. A strange sense of *deja-vu* washed over me as she spoke. "What have you done?"

"I…" I fumbled for the right words beneath her heated glare, suddenly feeling awkward and discomposed. "I… Sebastian wanted to remember his past and I wanted him to remember too. I had a dream and I remembered his true name, so I told him–"

"No!" Mags looked outraged. She stepped forward and started to reach for me. Something made her hesitate and she slapped her hand down angrily against her thigh instead. "Don't you effin' understand? You idiot! He can't remember everything, it will kill him! There's not enough room in his mind for all those memories–"

"I know," I cut her off, a quiet strength behind my words that seemed to catch her attention. She took a small, uncertain step back. I felt like she was constantly reevaluating me and I didn't like it.

"It did almost kill me," Sebastian agreed. "Gracelynn saved me by recasting the Binding spell between our souls."

Mags' eyes automatically went to the cuff of my sleeve where the last coil of my tattoo was visible, wrapping around the base of my thumb and curling into the palm of my hand. She looked at the mark with narrowed eyes.

"She'll be the death of you yet." She spoke only to Sebastian again in a low soft voice, turning her body away from me slightly. "I was one of the five who helped to erase your memories of the past. It was the only way to keep you sane. What this girl has done… it would take at least five of us to undo it now and none of the Others would be willing to help us anymore. The memories will destroy your mind, Sebastian. They'll eventually kill you," she finished, her voice hollow, her eyes full of anger and hopeless fear.

I immediately thought of the headaches Sebastian had been suffering, the slow increase in his nightmares, the periods of confusion, the nosebleeds – and I knew she was right. I could see in Sebastian's eyes that he knew it too, that he probably had for some time. I was horrified and overwhelmed with guilt. For a split second, I felt my heart stop beating and my breath abruptly halt as all I wanted was to die right then and there, on the spot. It didn't last longer than that brief second.

Mags met my gaze, fire burning in her eyes. "Why did you do it? How could you do this to him?" she demanded fiercely.

"I asked her to, Mags," Sebastian pointed out, his voice firm yet weary. He turned to me, his eyes urging me to accept his words. "None of this is your fault, Gracelynn. You didn't know."

"It's all my fault."

No one answered, no one argued with me. I didn't want to hear their lies anyway.

"Typical, Caoilinn. Always thinking of yourself and your own wants and never considering anyone or anything else. Never thinking beyond the moment and taking into account the consequences of your impulsive desires," Mags practically spat at me. I glared back at her, squeezing my pendant tightly in my fist for strength as I spoke.

"I am not Caoilinn. My name is Gracelynn." There was a clear warning in my tone. Mags visibly hesitated, her anger cooling slightly.

"I don't give a damn what name you go by - it doesn't change who you are."

"Tell us what you're doing here Mags," Sebastian brusquely demanded.

"Apart from searching for you like I have been every day for the past three hundred or so years?"

"What are you doing here?" Sebastian repeated impatiently.

A smile tugged at the corner of Mags' mouth. "About two months ago now, the Others began to remember you. I'd been keeping tabs on 'em, waiting for the day when it happened. I heard you were in Europe and I knew you'd need my help so I've been working my ass off trying to find you ever since. Every time I tried to leave Berlin, I'd find myself back here again, in St. Nicholas Quarter. I knew I'd find you here eventually, once you wanted my help, so I've been waiting."

Sebastian sighed. "We should go somewhere and talk."

"I agree. Away from Caoilinn – she can't be trusted around you," Mags added, eyeing me suspiciously.

"Gracelynn stays with me."

I didn't object. I let their words swirl around me amongst all the other chaos. The wind began to pick up and drops of rain started to sprinkle from the now-cloudy, gray sky.

"Fine," Mags growled through her clenched teeth, ignoring me once more. "Follow me," she commanded and spun on the heel of her black boots.

Sebastian reached for my hand, his eyes full of shame and regret. Though his expression was dominated by his obvious fear, there was nothing I could do to reassure him. I still couldn't believe this was happening. The reality I lived in and the fragile security it had provided me had been shattered. I felt like I was in shock, too numb to react.

I barely felt the warmth of his hand; I was only partially aware of the desperation in his tight grip. It was several minutes later, as we were approaching the entrance to the subway, when I noticed that he no longer held onto me. I couldn't remember if I had pulled away or if he had simply let go. It didn't really make a difference.

We made a strange trio as we traveled east through the city towards the residential quarter, first on the subway, then on a bus, and finally on foot. Mags completely ignored me. It was as if I didn't even exist to her. She stared constantly at Sebastian, her eyes brimming with love and frustration while silently fuming. Sebastian never once met her gaze, his eyes intent on my face, wordlessly urging me, pleading with me to offer him something. And I stared numbly straight ahead, my eyes unfocused, my emotions and thoughts running wild as I blankly took in the city streets.

I'm not sure how much later it was when we arrived at Mags' apartment. I only had the vaguest impression of how we'd gotten there, images of crowds and line ups and old, gray city streets flickering through my memory. It must have started raining harder since the shoulders of my t-shirt were cold and wet, and my hair hung in damp and twisted ringlets. As soon as I began shivering, Sebastian was instantly by my side. He tugged a thick, hooded sweatshirt from his backpack and wrapped me up in it, pulling me down onto a lumpy, old couch beside him with his arm placed firmly around my shoulder. Memories of the first time we had kissed in a musty, old shed drifted back to me but I forcefully pushed them away. It hurt too much to think about any of that right now. As a distraction, I forced myself to look around and examine our surroundings.

Mags' apartment was small and cluttered. The front door had led us straight into her living room with an attached tiny kitchen area and just one open window providing most of our light. There was stuff everywhere – books, papers, magazines, notebooks, ashtrays, candles and all kinds of curious objects. Every shelf was full, every surface covered, every inch of wall space decorated by strange and exotic oil paintings and abstract, black and white photographs. Despite the apparently unorganized clutter that filled the small place, her apartment was clean; not a speck of dust or dirt to be found. And the small quarters, though cramped, were surprisingly cozy and welcoming, especially after the cold, rain-slicked city streets below us.

I watched as Mags slipped out of her black leather jacket and tossed it over the back of one of the worn and ripped armchairs. She brushed the rain from her wavy reddish-gold hair with her fingers and flicked on a nearby lamp. I forced myself to look at her, to really look at her.

Mags was beautiful, there was no denying it. She was small, petite even, but definitely tough-looking. She was at least four inches shorter than me but her figure was toned and curved like an athlete's. Her face was heart-shaped, her features small and precise – a tiny, pink mouth, a straight, perfect nose and thin, gently-arched brows above her large, intensely green eyes. A scattering of freckles dusted her cheekbones and her hair framed her attractive features in waves of golden fire that fell just past her shoulders. Her ears were full of earrings but otherwise she wore no jewelry. Part of a black tattoo of a dragon peeked out of the back of her right shoulder and I thought I had earlier glimpsed another on the small of her back. She wore a tight black tank-top with a red, lacy bra just visible where the neckline dipped down into her cleavage. A studded belt wrapped around the top of her tight, dark-washed, trendily torn jeans and a pair of heeled black boots added a couple of extra inches to her small stature. As I looked at Mags, I couldn't help but compare her to myself and I saw everything that I wasn't. There was a quirkiness to her, a hint of ancient wisdom and youthful spirit that mirrored Sebastian's own. They looked "right" together, like they belonged together and were connected somehow. As much as I wanted to deny it, the evidence was clear before my eyes.

She threw her keys onto the kitchen counter and then filled up a kettle with water. Once it was set to boil, she marched back into the living room, kicked off her boots and dropped herself into the armchair closest to Sebastian, crossing her legs. I felt him flinch away from her and closer to me. Perhaps it should have been reassuring but it only intensified the nauseous feeling in my gut.

"So where should we start?" she demanded, speaking only to Sebastian.

"The beginning is always a good place."

She arched an eyebrow and smirked at him. "You want to talk about how we met?" Her eyes flashed flirtatiously as she began speaking slowly in Gaelic, her voice a low, sultry purr.

"Stop it," he responded in English, speaking a little too-quickly and firmly. "You mentioned that you and some of the Others erased my memories. Why would you do that?"

She rolled her eyes impatiently at him and shrugged. "Because you wanted us to. You were starting to lose your mind, literally, from the pressure of so many years of memories and experiences. We've all had to "drop" a few memories over the years to hold onto our sanity. Your memories were already starting to fade and be forgotten on their own, the things you no longer wanted to remember were sliding away. You wanted us to help the process along, so we did."

"And how much didn't I want to remember?"

Mags' eyes flashed my way. "Mostly just her."

"No, never," Sebastian automatically denied.

Mags glared at me as he spoke, her eyes narrowing and shimmering from a hint of tears. "You've got him brain-washed all over again, don't you? How do you live with yourself? Wasn't it enough, ruining his life once already?"

"What do you mean?" I was surprised to hear my own voice speak, especially when my words came out in such a fearful, shaky hush.

Mags continued to glare at me, her pretty, little face twisted with contempt.

"You know exactly what I mean." And what really scared me was that I thought I might. I swallowed hard, attempting to bury my shame and anger deep down inside of me where it might never come out and failing miserably.

"Caoilinn used you, Sebastian," Mags continued, turning back to him with impassioned eyes. I listened in mute horror as she spoke aloud all of my worst fears and suspicions. "She manipulated you, she deceived you, she abandoned you to this never-ending, hopeless quest, ensuring that you could never truly be happy without her. She forced you to do what she wanted, always what she wanted and never anything else. She never once stopped to consider your own wants and needs. I helped you to forget her because you wanted to, because you wanted to break free from the chains that she had shackled you with for hundreds of years. And you did forget her, and you were free. We were happy, for a time…"

Silence filled the room except for the steady ticking of a small, mantle clock. I didn't want to believe what I was hearing. I was horrified and terrified right down to my very core that it might be true.

"How can you expect me to believe that? *If* what you're saying is true, and never have I heard anything so far from the truth that I know in my heart, then why would I have left you? Why did I forget everything – not just Caoilinn but all of my life? And why is it so difficult for me to remember so much of my past still?" Sebastian quietly demanded. He shifted uneasily against my side.

"Caoilinn's hooks were in you so deeply, right down to your very soul. After we erased your memories of her, the guilt started to creep back and you started to remember her again in your dreams. The memory of your true name was starting to return to you and if it had, you would have remembered everything. You didn't want to worry me so you tried to hide it but I could see what was happening. You said you wanted to be alone, that you had made a mistake by creating the Others – except for me, of course. At first I thought that was what was wrong with you, so one by one, we erased each of their memories and we left them. We didn't want them to ever find or remember us so they didn't, they couldn't. You couldn't erase my memory even if you'd tried; you could never be strong enough to make me forget you because no matter how much of a stubborn, infuriating, jack-ass you can be, it was something I would never, ever want for myself."

A flash of guilt struck through me, hot and nauseating, demanding I acknowledge my shame. Sebastian had made me forget him once because a part of me had wanted to forget, a part of me had known life would be easier. I could hardly bear to hear anymore; did I really want to hear the truth if it hurt this much?

"I don't know how you forgot all the rest and I don't know why you left me. I simply woke up one morning after we'd erased the last of the Others' memories of you, and you were gone. You had promised that you would never leave me, that you would never try to make me forget you but maybe I had just heard what I wanted to. So tell me why you did it, Sebastian? How could you effin' do that to me, after all we've been through?" she demanded angrily, her voice breaking at the end. A single tear overflowed and trickled down her freckled cheek.

It was an intense moment between the two of them and I certainly didn't want to be there any longer. It was clear to me that I was intruding, that I needed to get away. I wanted to be anywhere else but for some strange reason, I couldn't make a single move to get up. Perhaps really, I just wanted to torture myself. Sebastian held onto me tightly, clutching at me as if I was his only lifeline and I was too weak to push him away. He slowly shook his head, his brow furrowed into a deep frown.

"I can't.... I don't know why I left. I told you, the memories are there but it's sometimes… it's so difficult for me to… I can't remember… ah!" He gasped with pain as he tried to think back in time, his eyes squeezed tightly shut. He began to shake by my side from the effort and from the pain it cost him.

"Stop, don't try! Jesus! It doesn't really matter. All that matters is that I've found you again," Mags rushed to reassure him, looking afraid. It was strange to see the deeply placed fear and concern I felt for Sebastian so perfectly placed in her eyes.

Sebastian's eyes remained tightly closed, his face pale and contorted with pain. I reached up to lightly touch his cheek, his features instantly relaxing at my gentle, hesitant touch.

"Seamus?" I quietly murmured, instinctively sensing it was the only way to draw his mind back to the present. His eyes slowly opened. I watched, sick and afraid as he tried to refocus his vision on my face. "I'm so sorry," I whispered. I swallowed back my nausea and horror as I was faced with proof of the pain and damage I had caused him.

"I'm sorry too, my love," he answered in a hushed and shaky voice. I slid my other hand around to his cheek, lightly cupping his handsome, pale face in my hands. I couldn't believe all the mistakes I had made, all the ways I had unknowingly hurt him.

"Take your goddamn hands off him," Mags suddenly threatened, her voice a low growl. She leant forward in her seat, body tensed as if about to spring forward. I stared back at her in surprise. "Don't let her touch you, Sebastian - ever. It's how she casts her worst spells. It's how she controls you."

I let my hands drop from his face in shock at this accusation. How could she think I would ever hurt Sebastian? And I didn't ever try to control him! I didn't and I never would... would I?

"I'm not afraid of her touch." He carefully took my hand up in his as he spoke. He lightly kissed the beautiful and intricate silver ring that twisted around the fourth finger of my left hand. He looked directly and deeply into my eyes as he spoke, trapping my gaze and making it impossible to look away. "I'm only afraid I may lose her touch forever and then may never know happiness again."

A small spark of hope flickered in my soul. I almost smiled but my fear and sadness were still too great. How could I want him to love me still? How was that fair?

"Why is she wearing that ring?" Mags suddenly demanded. "Oh shit. I think I'm going to throw up. You didn't marry her, did you? Oh, God no. Please tell me you didn't sleep with her. You bastard... Tell me you didn't. Tell me you're not completely lost." Her eyes were wide, her pretty, little mouth twisted with revulsion.

"We were about to marry at St. Nicholas's Church this morning, before you intercepted us. And as for the rest, that is no one's business but our own," Sebastian firmly warned.

"Oh," she breathed, relaxing minutely. "One of you must not have really wanted to marry then since it was so easy for me to "intercept" you. Not to mention the fact that you couldn't have gotten married there anyway. St. Nicholas' hasn't operated as a church in nearly seventy years. It's a museum now."

This was perhaps the most stunning and shocking thing Mags had said, despite all of her many accusations. I knew with a depressing and heart-breaking certainty that it must have been Sebastian who was unsure about marrying me because this morning I had wanted to marry him more than anything else in the world. And now I was uncertain too. My whole world had been turned upside down. Everything I thought I knew, everything I thought I could trust, was wrong.

"I need to know though, Sebastian, if you've already had sex with her," Mags continued bluntly. She flinched slightly as she said the words, obviously not wanting to think about it for too long. Despite myself, a warm glow began spreading across my cheeks.

"I will not answer that question. It's none of your business."

"I'm not asking because I'm curious – I'm asking because I have to know. That's how Caoilinn was able to so thoroughly manipulate you in the first place. To be so physically intimate with her again would mean giving her full control over your mind and your will. Please, please tell me you didn't." Her eyes flickered nervously back and forth between us, the panic slowly and obviously rising in them. Sebastian took a breath to speak, his irritation clear but I interrupted, wanting to end this silliness.

"We didn't," I stated flatly.

"You didn't have to answer her," Sebastian quietly told me.

"I did. After all, she *is* your wife."

I felt sick saying it aloud but it was obviously the truth and there was no denying it. Obviously, they must have been intimate. I had to face this fact and it pierced my heart with stabs of jealous, distrustful pain. Sebastian stiffened, opening his mouth as if to object. I could tell I had hurt him but no matter what the circumstances of our situation, Mags was his wife. How was it right to pretend otherwise? In a way, she did have the right to know.

Mags glanced at me grudgingly. "Thank you," she muttered.

I didn't answer. There was nothing I could say in response. Sebastian turned to me, a deep crease between his brows, his eyes such a dark-gray that they almost appeared to be black.

"Gracelynn... I think we should leave. We need to talk."

"No!" Mags immediately objected. "There's no effin' way I'm letting you walk out that door." Sebastian ignored her and waited patiently for my response. I felt so tired, so worn out, I just wanted to curl up under a blanket and sleep away the rest of this horrible day and hopefully when I awoke tomorrow, it would all have been a bad dream. I knew it wouldn't be that easy.

"I wanted to find someone who could help us, someone who would point us in the right direction, remember?" I reminded him. "I think… I think we might need Mags. She may be our only hope. We have to stay – for now."

"Of course you need me," Mags dismissed with an irritated snort. "It'll take seven of the Others to overpower us now, as long as we stay together – and as long as we all want the same thing."

"Numbers mean nothing. We still don't have a way to stop them," Sebastian pointed out.

"You might not, but I do." This caught both of our attention. Mags smiled, obviously enjoying being in control of the situation once more. "For whatever reason, you may have wanted the Others to remember you, Sebastian, but I certainly didn't and I still don't – they don't even know I exist. I can travel with you, take you to the head temple in Greece and we can ambush them, take 'em down six at a time. They'd have no idea what was coming."

"The head temple?" I asked. Mags ignored me.

"Six at a time? How many are there now?" Sebastian asked warily.

"There are thirteen of the Others – twelve of those you should remember, one more has joined since you and I left them. Altogether, there are sixteen people who possess the Lost Magic, including ourselves."

"The Lost Magic," I found myself whispering the phrase. Caoilinn had referred to our ability that way but this time, the words made more sense to me. It was a magic I had lost, a magic that had been lost itself in time, a magic that I felt I was losing myself and my life to all over again.

"Yes. You were the last one born to it naturally. The secrets and intricacies of it have been lost in time, just like your soul." Mags made the statement an insult. Anger briefly sparked within me.

"And what will we do with the Others once we ambush them?" Sebastian asked.

"We'll kill them," Mags pronounced coldly, her eyes green daggers poised for the kill. In that moment, it was nearly impossible to believe that she was a girl of just seventeen as she had initially appeared. As she spoke, I saw the ancient, dangerous being that she truly was – and I felt afraid.

"No," I immediately objected, despite my fear. "I won't do it again, I can't. I won't kill any of them – I refuse. There has to be another way."

Mags eyed me curiously, a new wariness in her eyes that made her look older still. "Again? You have been busy, Caoilinn."

"Mags," Sebastian warned.

I suddenly hated the familiar way that he spoke to her and jealousy flared up within me, hot and full of bitter fury. My necklace throbbed painfully against my chest as I struggled to get my emotions back under control.

Mags gave him a cheeky smirk as she turned her attention away from me. "We don't have to kill them with magic. We can knock 'em unconscious and then do it the old-fashioned way. It'll be just like old times," she added with a twisted laugh.

Sebastian looked as horrified as I felt. The smile quickly slipped from Mags' face when she noticed the change in his expression.

"Relax, Sebastian. My God! It was just a joke. But really, how else do you expect to deal with them?"

Her question was met with silence once more.

"There has to be another way. We'll think of something," Sebastian assured me. He sounded like he was trying to convince himself.

I forced myself to look at Mags, pushing the words to my lips. "How can we trust you?" I immediately regretted speaking as Mags fixed me with an icy glare. I forced myself to stand my ground though, to meet and hold her eye.

"You're asking *me* that?"

"How can we trust you?" Sebastian repeated for me, his voice as cold as Mags' expression.

"They want to kill you, Sebastian – they will kill you if they catch you. I'd die if they took you from me." Her eyes softened, her words grew hushed. It was another intimate moment that I was intruding upon. Sebastian awkwardly cleared his throat.

"How can I trust you to keep Gracelynn safe?" he rephrased.

She met his gaze levelly, without hesitation.

"The Binding that Caoilinn cast between your souls in the moments before her death was selfish and cruel for so many reasons. One of the many implications was that it intensified the pain of her death for you, ten-fold. In one instant your soul was bound to hers for eternity and then just as suddenly it was ripped away. I know how that pain has tormented you throughout the centuries that followed, and especially since the Binding has now been recast and the connection is now doubly-strong… *I* would never, ever put you through that pain again." Mags spoke with such passionate conviction that it was impossible to doubt her words. I looked down at my hands in shame as I was forced to face up to all the blind mistakes I had made, all the suffering I had caused through those seemingly-innocent acts of speaking Sebastian's true name aloud and then recasting the Binding spell between us. I was overwhelmed by my guilt, it dragged me down to a dark and black place that I wondered if I'd ever escape from. Was I really no better than Caoilinn then?

I rose from the couch; I could take no more. I felt like I was suffocating, like I was drowning with no hope of ever breathing the fresh, sweet air again. Sebastian watched me move, his eyes wide with confusion and fear as I started to walk towards the door.

"Gracelynn, stop! Where are you going?" Sebastian called after me. I could hear the panic rising in his voice. I was afraid to see his expression and lose my strength so I didn't turn around.

"I need to get out of here," I mumbled, my voice thick, my words barely coherent.

"Let her go," I heard Mags' voice say.

Another spark of anger flared that I quickly smothered. She was right. He should just let me go. I picked up my pace, throwing open the apartment door and rushing out into the hall. I made it almost to the stairwell at the hall's end before I collapsed to the floor, my head in my hands as my thoughts and emotions spun wildly around me and

I struggled just to breathe.

I thought I wanted to be alone but I must have really just wanted to get away from *her*. Sebastian found me almost immediately. He sat down beside me and leant against the wall, waiting patiently for me to look up. He didn't reach for me, didn't touch me, he just waited until my breathing steadied and I slowly looked up to let my eyes meet his. We shared a look in silence – pain, regret and suffering dominating both of our expressions.

Sebastian looked away first. He pulled out a cigarette, lit it and offered it to me. I said no with a quick shake of my head.

The hall was eerily silent. Mags hadn't followed us and there were no sounds or signs of any other tenants though the building appeared to be populated and well maintained. All I could hear was my shaky breathing and the crackling of Sebastian's cigarette as the cherry flared brighter and burned up the tobacco and paper with each drag he took.

It was my turn to wait in silence. It wasn't until he butted his cigarette out against the sole of his boot that I turned my head towards him. His expression was painful to see, his eyes burned with regret, his beautiful mouth so sad, the faint lines around his eyes and across his forehead deepened from stress and fear. He met my gaze steadily, allowing his pain to flood through his eyes and out from his soul.

"I'm so sorry, Gracelynn," he whispered and I knew he meant every word.

I nodded, my eyes filling with more tears. In that moment, I hated myself so much. "I'm sorry too." I slowly slid the beautiful, silver engagement ring from my finger. "I can't accept this any more." My voice was barely louder than a whisper but I knew he heard every word. I held the delicate ring out to him with my badly shaking hand.

"I won't take it back. I love you. I still want to be with you, to marry you." He lifted his hand towards my face but I quickly turned away, unable to bear the heartbreak that I was causing him. It hurt me more than he could ever know.

"I don't see how you can anymore," I replied sadly. The tears began to flood my eyes and I didn't even try to stop them. They blurred my vision and choked my throat as I held the ring out to him again. This time I wasn't quite able to meet his eye. "Please, take it."

"No. It's yours. Don't do this Gracelynn, please. Just talk to me—"

"What choice do I have? You're married, Sebastian, to Mags. And your love for me, your love for Caoilinn, it was all based on lies. Everything I've ever done has been wrong…"

"We don't know that. I don't believe that – I can't."

I glanced at him as he shook his head. I never should have looked. The tears that quivered on his lashes and washed through his beautiful eyes tore at my heart and soul. I could see the pain I was causing him and it was unbearable. I stuffed the engagement ring into my pocket and tried to take a slow breath. I needed him to accept the truth. I wanted him to be happy, even if it wasn't with me.

"I'm leaving," I quietly announced. His expression broke at my words, a silent 'no' of horror forming on his lips. I found myself whispering the words to him through the hot, salty tears that began sliding down my cheeks. "I want you to go back and talk to Mags. I want you to let me go. I just want you to have a chance at the happiness I don't think I can ever give you."

"Gracelynn, please," he begged as I rose and began walking away once more. Only this time, I didn't want him to follow me. This time, I knew what I had to do.

"I'm sorry," I repeated before stepping out into the stairwell and rushing down the flights of stairs. With tears streaming down my face, I fled from Sebastian, from Mags, from the past and from the truth as fast and as far as I possibly could.

Chapter Eleven - Lost

I blindly wandered the streets of Berlin all day. I wanted to be ignored, to crawl under a rock and disappear, and so, not a single person looked my way. My moods flickered between numb disbelief, bitter anger and an all-consuming, broken-hearted sorrow. It was one of the worst days of my life and would have easily won the prize if it weren't for the still fresh memory of Sebastian being nearly beaten to death last winter. I clung to that horrible memory, reminding myself that though this was bad, that day had been so much worse. I could survive this, I would survive.

I found myself buying a pack of cigarettes of all things and ended up lighting them one by one but never taking a puff. At some point the scent of cigarette smoke had become impossibly intertwined with my memories of Sebastian. There was something unexpectedly calming about watching a cigarette slowly burn itself out as the twists and curls of thin, gray smoke entwined themselves through the air.

The rain came and went throughout the day. Towards dusk, the raindrops began to fall more heavily, the sky darkening unusually early because of the thick, black clouds. I let myself get drenched, willing the icy drops to wash away my shame and pain, to erase all traces of the past that seemed to cling to me wherever I went. It was almost refreshing to splash through the puddles along the still-bustling, early evening streets. As raindrops soaked through my clothes and ran down my face, I began to feel increasingly at peace. There was turmoil still clawing away at my center and pain gnawing on the edges of my heart but I could accept it, for now. I could push it far enough away from my immediate thoughts that I could function, that I could think, that I could survive. And with this calmer, more rational sense of mind, I could see what I had to do. I had to go back.

I looked up from the puddle-strewn sidewalk before me and examined the building fronts that lined the streets. My subconscious mind must have already come to the conclusion I had only just consciously reached. I immediately recognized the route back to Mags' apartment, I had been slowly making my way in the right direction for some time. I could make it back there now within an hour.

I walked faster, with more purpose having decided what I must do. The rain was starting to truly chill me now and my teeth began to chatter. I felt sick and depressed, and angry and afraid, and I couldn't stop thinking about Sebastian and Mags who I'd left alone together all day. I hated to admit it, but I was jealous. I was so many things in that moment and it was impossible not to feel them all. I was hurt and confused. I was furious at myself for being so weak that I couldn't stay away but at the same time, my heart was rejoicing that I was returning. I couldn't be with Sebastian, not now, not in the same way as before but I allowed myself a small sliver of torturous hope that maybe, just maybe, we could still want to be together enough that fate would eventually find a way. I knew it was wrong to think it, I felt sick to my stomach that I wanted something so selfish and wrong and I couldn't help but think I was behaving like Caoilinn but still… it was what my whole heart and soul wanted to believe.

I knew I had to focus my thoughts on Sebastian, on what was best for him. First and foremost, I had to ensure his safety and that meant staying with him and with Mags, and helping them to destroy the Others. I shuddered at the thought. No matter what, I wouldn't kill one of them again – I couldn't. Not even to save myself, not even to save Sebastian. There was still a dark shadow across my heart that I knew would never see the light again. I had killed a piece of myself when I killed Walter and I would never, ever, be able to want another to die enough that I could make it happen again, despite now knowing the correct design the spell required.

The closer I came to Mags' apartment, the clearer my thoughts became. As far as my heart went however… I was unsure. I loved Sebastian with everything I ever was and ever would be but suddenly, it didn't seem to be enough. How could I trust him when there was so much of his past that I didn't know, that I didn't understand? I had thought it didn't matter but now that the past was catching up to us, how could I pretend that it didn't affect our future? And if his love for Caoilinn had truly all been a result of her magic manipulating his heart's desires, if it were all based on lies, then could I trust that he really loved me now? Was I really what he wanted? I knew he thought he wanted to be with me but could he even trust himself? And then there was Mags… his wife. I could tell she loved him and she had been fighting for him, working to keep him safe for so long but could I really trust her? If she were the better choice for him, shouldn't I step back and allow them their happiness? Shouldn't I want Sebastian's happiness more than my own? I thought I did but the idea of giving him up… it was difficult for me to consider for long.

It was later than I expected when I reached the door to Mags' apartment. My pace had slowed with the complexity of my thoughts weighing down upon my conscience. I was tired, cold and hungry when I reached her door but relieved that it was late enough that there were no noises coming from within. I didn't want to face either of them, not yet. And I was a little afraid of how I might find them, of how much they may have reconciled in my absence though I tried to convince myself that was what I wanted, that was what was best.

I quietly opened the unlocked door and silently closed it behind me. The lights were all off except for the single lamp in the living room that hung over Sebastian's sleeping head. He was curled up on the floor beside the couch, his expression surprisingly peaceful in sleep and Mags was nowhere in sight.

There was an extra pillow and blanket carefully folded on the couch above him. I wondered how much he had hoped I'd return or if he had just known my practicality would eventually win through. He'd left enough space between himself and the couch that I could easily slide my body down beside his and beneath the warm blanket that covered him. It was inviting and tempting in a nearly-irresistible way. I watched him for a minute, admiring how handsome he was, how unconventional and yet undeniably attractive his features were. In the calm of sleep, it was easy to believe him to be nothing more than a peacefully resting, seventeen year-old boy. But he was so much more than that – so very much more.

I wanted so badly to crouch down beside him and to touch his face, to run my fingertips over his smooth cheeks and feel the soft curve of his lips. I wanted to look into his stunning eyes and lose myself, to tangle my fingers through his messy hair and hold myself as close to him as I dared. I wanted to hear his smooth and lilting voice. I wanted to tell him I was sorry, to beg him to run away with me and leave Mags and the past and everything else behind us, to let the Lost Magic remain lost forever. But as much as I wanted it, I knew that I couldn't let any of that happen. For a long time I didn't move, I didn't speak a word.

I eventually slipped off my shoes and quietly tip-toed around him. As silently as possible, I unfolded the blanket left for me on the couch and wrapped myself in it. I didn't bother to turn off the lamp, I was afraid the change in lighting might awaken Sebastian. Trying my best not to disturb him or upset the squeaky springs of the lumpy, old couch, I lowered myself down upon it and immediately closed my eyes.

It was the first time I had slept anywhere other than in Sebastian's arms in months. I was cold, I was hungry and I was miserable. My exhaustion won through though and I felt myself rapidly falling towards sleep in dizzy, disorienting circles. And as I fell towards the black of unconsciousness, I couldn't help but think angrily, Why, Caoilinn? Why would you do this to him? Why would you do this to me? Why?

THERE WAS A tap at my door; I briefly considered not answering it. I never received any visits from friends — I had no friends. There were few of the other Sisters who dared intrude upon my private quarters and the ones who did were never there for a pleasant reason. I was tired and I had wanted to go to sleep early that night while the memories of my afternoon visit with Seamus were still fresh in my mind. I could not ignore my duty though.

I opened the door with a barely suppressed sigh.

"Why are you disturbing me, Padraigin?"

The youthful-appearing Sister stared at me with her dull, brown eyes. She was always so calm, so collected in appearance. She was part of the upper-council that sat just below the High Priestess. She was one of the five whom I had been commanded to share the Lost

Magic with. She was one of the few whom my sisterly-oaths demanded I obey. It irritated me to be bound by those oaths – they had been taken from me before I was old enough to truly understand what they meant.

"That's hardly a proper welcome, Caoilinn," Padraigin chastised with a slight frown. She glided into my room, taking the only seat available – my bed. "I have wanted to speak with you for several days now. It would appear that you want to avoid the council as of late." She spoke in near-monotone, without a trace of emotion to her voice. There was an edge of suspicion to her words though that cut clearly through and pierced me with sudden uneasy fear.

"Appearances can be deceiving." I casually leant against the wall across from her, preferring to stand and look down upon her than to sit on the cool, dirt floor at her feet.

Padraigin arched an eyebrow at me but did not immediately respond. I felt a tiny bead of sweat gathering at the nape of my neck. I deliberately kept my breathing slow and even, not allowing my true emotions to betray me for even a split second.

"Another Sister has been chosen to join us," Padraigin announced after a long pause. I shifted uneasily. "She will be inducted into the temple with the next new moon. Her potential is great. She is a strong candidate to receive the Lost Magic."

"There are already five other Sisters whom I have shared my gift with," I began to object.

"It is not your gift," Padraigin interjected, her voice stern. "The magic belongs to the Gods and you shall do what is required to please them. It is their will that you share their gift with your chosen Sisters."

"Yes, Sister." I bowed my head as I agreed, knowing it was wise to appear submissive. Inwardly, I fumed.

"You have been neglecting your duties as of late," Padraigin continued. I raised my head to meet her gaze and found her large, brown eyes surprisingly sharp and piercing. "You spend too much time outside the temple and in the village. You invite temptation and you walk the lines of your oaths. We do not want you to fall upon the wrong side of those lines, Sister. It could be deadly." She paused, letting the depth of her words sink in. I continued to hold her gaze, refusing to give anything away. "You have been warned. Even you are not above temple law, Caoilinn. The Gods and your Sisters will hold you accountable."

I nodded my head in acquiescence. "I obey the Gods and their wants first and foremost, Sister; they guide my heart and my life. My will is theirs."

I could see the frustration building in Padraigin's eyes no matter how she tried to prevent it from showing on her face. I knew she was warning me to stay away from Seamus; somehow the Sisterhood had discovered the connection between us despite how strongly I wanted it to remain hidden and unobserved. I would admit to nothing though and I adamantly refused to listen, no matter how it might be in my best interests to do so. It was too late for me, there was no turning back no matter how dangerous the road.

"The Gods are always watching, Caoilinn."

I didn't respond. I merely stared back at Padraigin blankly as she rose and slowly exited my chamber, the door quietly closing behind her.

My heart was beating quickly with excitement and fear as she left. For once, I felt the full youth and naivety of my brief eighteen years of life. It was apparent that Seamus and I had run out of time. I had wanted to wait until the new moon to perform our mating ceremony but we now did not have spare time on our hands. The Sisters of the temple were already suspicious; how much they suspected and how much they knew no longer mattered, their suspicion alone was enough. I decided I must take Seamus as my mate that night, before any of the Sisters could try and stop me. I wasn't afraid of them, their powers were no match for my own (that I had made certain of) but Seamus would be vulnerable until he had his own magic to protect him. Once we were mated, both my magic and his would protect us. It would buy us the time I needed to prepare our escape. I still didn't plan on remaining any longer than a few more days.

I felt another rush of excitement as I considered what I was about to do. I had never dared defy the Sisterhood before – I had never truly considered breaking my oaths. I had never indulged my wants when I knew that they were wrong. I had never made such bold and risky moves and it was thrilling and liberating all at once. I couldn't wait to be free from this place and to move forward and onward with Seamus at my side, into a bright and mysterious future that stretched endlessly before us.

The sun was already setting and I didn't want to wait any longer, I couldn't. I summoned Seamus to the clearing with my wants and began to make haste there myself. I slipped out of the temple easily and without attracting any attention or notice. The grounds within and around the temple were practically deserted anyway, most Sisters retreating inside for nighttime prayers, worship and meditation. I didn't even bother to pull up the hood on the light cloak that I wore, I was so confident that the pure strength of my love and my magic would protect me. I was vaguely aware of the vanity of my thoughts but who could deny that I was the most powerful, the most talented and feared of all the Priestesses despite my lower position. And I was so close to having everything that I never even knew I had wanted. Was it so wrong to silently rejoice?

Seamus was already waiting for me in the clearing when I arrived. He sat cross-legged in the center, attempting to appear calm and patient but his true emotions were obvious. He leapt to his feet as he saw me approaching, his face brightening, his eyes intensifying in a way that stole the air from my lungs and left me dizzy and weak. He grinned as he stepped forward to meet me, taking up both of my hands in his.

"I've been sitting here for hours, hoping you might come," he announced, "when suddenly I was struck by the overwhelming certainty that you would be here soon. It was so strange – I knew that I was exactly where you wanted me to be and that you wanted to be here too."

He swept my hair back from my face with one hand as he spoke. For a second I found myself speechless and stunned, struggling to find the correct words as I was overwhelmed by his amazing, gray-blue eyes.

"I'm not sure that my magic works that way," I told him, surprised by the breathless quality to my words.

"It does," he assured me with another heart-stopping smile. I blinked, feeling slightly dazed as I smiled back at him. I forced myself to focus, reminding myself of why I was there and what must be done.

"Some of the Sisters in the temple are growing suspicious. It isn't safe to wait any longer. If you are certain that you want to be my mate, it must be done tonight."

Seamus' eyes widened, his lips parted slightly. I could tell it was a lot for him to take in at once. He squeezed my hands, wetting his lips quickly before speaking.

"I am certain that I want to be your mate. I have never been so certain of anything in my life," he assured me, his eyes steady and intense.

"But?" I waited but he didn't respond, he continued to stare deeply into my eyes. My heart was already reacting to him, the beats rapid and uneven. "But you're uncertain about the magic?" I guessed. "I was never given the choice, so I can't imagine the weight of the decision. To choose to live forever, to have incomprehensible powers that are nearly limitless yet so restrictive to your nature, and to bind yourself to another for eternity… I imagine it's overwhelming."

Seamus gave me a wry smile. He leant forward and slowly kissed me, stealing my breath and thrilling my being with each sweet and subtle movement of his lips. I had to fight not to tremble in his arms. He brought his forehead to rest against mine, our faces so close our breaths intermingled with our words.

"There is no 'but', no hesitation. I am sure of what I want."

"I don't want you to harbor any regrets – they'll be eternal ones," I quietly warned. He smiled and started to kiss me again but I quickly pulled away, aware of the darkening night around us and the rising, silver moon.

"I've meditated on the matter every night since you first proposed that we mate and I think I've found a solution." I slid off the ring that my mother had given to me, the only jewelry I ever wore, the only heirloom I possessed. It was bulky and roughly made, the metal twisted in and around itself to form a simple love knot. It was the design of the knot that had first given me the idea of using patterns to focus my magic and direct its purpose. I had recently made an adaptation to the ring. A small piece of amber was now pressed into its center, a chip from the teardrop shape of my necklace that appeared to form the shape of a tiny heart. It was my gift to him and my promise.

"The ring will be a part of our mating ceremony, both a symbol of our love and commitment and a carrier of an intricate spell. I never want you to regret your decision, I never want you to feel trapped by a choice that I wanted you to make and so this is your reassurance. If ever you come to regret the choices that you have made to be with me, if ever you no longer love me and return this ring to me, the magic I am about to bestow on you tonight will be broken and you shall return to the way you were before we met."

"Caoilinn, this isn't necessary," Seamus objected. I silenced him by lightly placing a finger over his lips.

"If you won't wear it to reassure yourself, wear it to reassure me," I requested. He considered, then slowly took the ring from my hand. He silently slipped it onto his finger. It fit perfectly.

"Thank you," I breathed as he accepted the ring, feeling a sense of calming relief wash over me. The ring helped to ease my guilt. It was a comfort to me to be able to offer him a choice when I had taken so many others away from him. If I ever performed the Binding though… I pushed the thought away. It was unlikely that it would ever come to that and I didn't like to think about the consequences of having to make that decision. As long as he accepted and wore the ring, there would be a way out for him.

"Are you ready to begin?"

He silently nodded, his mood becoming as solemn as my own as the smile faded from his face. His eyes were bright beneath the moonlight, sparkling with anticipation and burning with the same fiery flames I could feel consuming my heart.

I had witnessed the mating ceremony many times. I had spoken the words and performed the rituals before countless young couples. I had never before understood their embarrassment to stand beneath the moon in their own skins, to join in the way that man and woman were designed and as the Gods and tradition demanded — until now. It was necessary though, not only as the central component of the mating ritual but also to provide the intimate connection necessary to share as much of my magic and ability with him as I could possibly allow. The magic within me demanded it, as did every cell in my body. I felt feverish and nearly possessed by my desire.

I fought the flush that was creeping into my cheeks and concentrated on keeping my hands steady and my eyes on the mossy ground as I slipped out of my robes. I heard Seamus' breath catch at the sight of my milky skin glowing under the faint moonlight. I took a deep breath, closed my eyes, tipped my head back and began to chant. The ceremony had begun.

I JOLTED AWAKE as my mind leapt forward two thousand or so years into the present. It took me a while to calm myself, to get both my breathing and my heart rate back under control. For once I wasn't disoriented upon waking from the strange memory-dream; I knew exactly where I was. The instant I opened my eyes, the heavy sadness in my heart returned and all the horrible memories from the past twenty-four hours rushed back to me, slapping me in the face and washing my cheeks with shame.

It was dark in Mags' living room. Someone had turned the lamp off during the night. I hoped it had been Sebastian and I wondered if he had watched me sleep for a while like I had been watching him. There was a very strong likelihood.

It was too dark to see the clock on the mantel but I guessed the time to be close to dawn. I decided to lay as still and silent as possible, to take some time to think and to plan before Sebastian and Mags awoke. I was sorely tempted to wake Sebastian myself so that I might have some time alone with him before Mags was up but I knew that wouldn't be right, it wouldn't be fair. I tried my best to push my selfish wants aside and to focus on the present, or rather how the past affected my present situation.

My dreams of Caoilinn were definitely becoming stronger and clearer as the past and present seemed to be so closely woven together. I was fairly certain this would be the last time I would remember Caoilinn as I had absolutely no desire to ever want to "be her" again. The dreams hadn't just become clearer and more detailed, it wasn't just what I saw and said and heard when I was Caoilinn that affected me. It was what I felt, what I thought and what I knew when I was her, that terrified and sickened me.

Caoilinn was self-possessed, her ego strong and her confidence calm and cool. She was full of ancient wisdom and youthful naivety. She had faced so many hardships in her young life that once she met Seamus and that new, powerful passion had been awakened within her, she threw herself into the heady, passionate affair wholeheartedly and without thought. She quite clearly wanted to lose herself in her love for Seamus forever. She was deadly and dangerous. Caoilinn had loved Seamus, there was no doubt about that, but she had loved him selfishly, possessively, in a limitless way that knew no boundaries or at least she ignored any she encountered. She had felt guilt over her actions, true, but not enough to stop her from doing what she wanted.

A growing sense of dread and unease chewed at the edges of my stomach. The dream had confirmed much of what Mags had said. I had felt Caoilinn's guilt and known her carefully guarded secrecy – even when she was with Seamus. I had shared her darker thoughts and sensed the deadly strength within her. I tried to swallow down the bile that was rising in my throat, bubbling and burning up from my gut.

Was Sebastian's love for me based only on lies and deceit then? Had Caoilinn knowingly manipulated him? Had she taken him as her mate so that she could selfishly use her own magic to ensure he would never truly forget her or move on? Had she wanted him to live forever, constantly searching for her and to never be able to find happiness on his own just because of her own inconsiderate wants? Had she used him to escape from the hardships of her life without truly considering all the consequences of her actions? And then what about me? Was I no better than her? Had I been using my magic all along to bind Sebastian even more tightly to me? And my reluctance to sleep with him before we married; had I subconsciously known that once we were intimate I would be able to fully manipulate him with my magic? Was that why I had kept to my chastity so devoutly? Was I the one who hadn't really wanted to get married that day? Was I afraid of what I might do? Or had I refused to sleep with Sebastian as just another way to control and manipulate him? At our cores, were

Caoilinn and I the same after all?

No. I wouldn't accept that, I couldn't. I would not punish myself for her mistakes nor would I allow myself to make the same mistakes either. My heart was rapidly sinking and I could feel myself falling deeper and deeper into a black and bottomless pit of depression. The only way out, the only way to keep myself alive was to feed the tiny spark of anger within me. I clung to it, I encouraged it, I worked to let it grow and roar within my core.

I was furious. I was angry at Caoilinn and myself, for all the mistakes we had both made. How could I possibly ever think I deserved to be with Sebastian now? My only hope was to make it up to him, to try to right the wrongs that had been done, and to hope that maybe… no. It wasn't fair to hope.

I wanted so badly to blame Mags for it all. I knew it was just jealousy, but a part of me deep down inside was screaming that she was the one to blame. I wanted to hate her. I wanted to lay the blame for all the terrible things that had happened lately at her feet but how could I? It was petty and childish and I knew it was wrong. Her love for Sebastian was undeniable. Her actions were obviously all motivated by her desire to help him, which I had to admire and appreciate even if her methods of helping him meant "protecting" him from me. But what if he did need her protection? The magic that was awakening inside of me was raw and powerful and overwhelming. I was trying my best to understand it, to control it but it scared me still. Even I wasn't certain what I was capable of anymore. It was terrifying but I had to admit, I could no longer truly trust myself.

I tried to focus my rage, to redirect it. I understood all too well how powerful a weapon anger could be – and how unpredictable. I would never kill another human being again, I felt that it would kill me if I did but I would find a way to protect Sebastian and to destroy the Others. I would also help to fix the mistakes Sebastian had made in the past and then once I could give him the freedom to make a fresh start, I would let him follow his heart and hopefully make the choice that he truly wanted, whatever that might be. Until then, I would do nothing to influence, encourage or sway him. It was obvious to me now that we couldn't have any type of relationship until this was all over with and behind us.

The weak morning light was starting to leak into the room around the thin curtain that covered the window. Sebastian's breathing started to lighten, his eyelids fluttered as he began to stir. At almost the same time, I heard the sound of Mags' bare footsteps enter the room.

Her eyes met mine immediately, the anger in them clear even in the low light. She froze, staring at me warily. I tried to push back the ugly, seething, jealousy that just her presence seemed to ignite. It didn't help that all she wore was a skimpy, army green tank-top with no bra and a pair of very short, black, cotton shorts. Her thick, reddish hair was pulled up into a messy pony tail on top of her head, revealing the row of tiny studded earrings that lined the edges of both her ears.

"You're back," she stated, keeping the volume of her voice low. She made it sound like an accusation. She definitely looked annoyed to see me.

I didn't answer, I just glared back at her. It was very difficult to remember that I needed her help to stop the Others. I sat up, the couch springs squeaking loudly.

"Gracelynn?"

We both turned at the sound of Sebastian's sleepy voice. He was pushing himself up off the floor on one elbow, squinting at me in the near-darkness.

"I'm here."

He breathed a sigh of relief. "I was afraid you might not..." he didn't finish, the rest of his fears left hanging silently in the air. It was then that he seemed to sense we were not alone. He turned, peering between the couch and the armchair at Mags' bare legs.

I fought the rising, painful throb of heartache in my chest. So it must have been Mags who had turned off the light then since Sebastian was surprised to see me. It was Mags who might have watched me in my sleep. The thought both angered and unnerved me.

"I need some coffee. Should I make a full pot?" Mags asked, breaking the quiet tension in the room.

"Yes," Sebastian and I simultaneously responded. We started to share a smile and then both seemed to remember what we were doing. We couldn't pretend things were the same anymore, they weren't —

they couldn't be.

"I suppose it's safe to assume you'll be coming with us then?" Mags demanded as she began making the coffee. She didn't bother looking my way as she spoke – I wasn't surprised.

"I think you need me, don't you?" I replied a little snippily.

"Yes," Sebastian answered. "We need you." He said it in a way that might have meant more, it was hard to tell. Mags slammed the lid on the coffee maker, drawing both of our attention back to her.

"Sebastian says you have money. We'll need you to cover our travel costs. I want to be on a train and heading out of Germany by noon."

"Are we going to Greece then?" I guessed.

"That's where the Others will be. They'll be waiting for us there," Mags announced. She smirked as I visibly shivered. "Not feeling so tough this morning?"

"You should fill Grace in on some of the things you told me yesterday," Sebastian announced quietly, ignoring Mags' taunts. It was strange for him to be speaking in such a soft and defeated voice. He appeared unusually quiet and withdrawn this morning but I was too.

"Sure, I'll get her all caught up," Mags agreed. I was surprised by her sudden willingness. "You look like hell, Sebastian. Why don't you go take a shower? You could obviously use one and I'll have coffee and breakfast ready for you when you're done." Her obvious concern for him and her domestic tone irritated me all over again. Seeing hints of the tender side to her personality only made me feel more jealous and bitter. She seemed much happier and more relaxed around Sebastian today. They must have worked out some of their issues while I was gone. My gut twisted painfully at the thought.

"That actually does sound like a good idea. Gracelynn… do you mind?" Sebastian asked hesitantly.

"No, of course not. Maybe I'll help cook," I added. Mags frowned and for a second Sebastian looked like he was about to smile. He knew the chances of me cooking anything even remotely edible were slim-to-none.

He took his bag with him into the bathroom and minutes later we heard the shower turn on. It wasn't until we were both certain he was out of ear-shot that Mags and I began talking.

"How much of Caoilinn's life do you remember?" Mags waited impatiently for my answer, her green eyes hard, her lips pressed together tightly as she tapped one of her chipped, black fingernails against the countertop.

"Not much," I admitted. "But it's slowly coming back to me."

She nodded, her expression turning thoughtful. "Sebastian told me about how you killed one of the Others' latest recruits. Did you know he thinks Caoilinn is still alive inside of you?" She didn't wait for my response. "He thinks it might have been her, not you, who killed Walter."

"He's wrong." My voice came out chillingly cold. I met Mags' piercing gaze with one of my own. She looked away almost immediately.

"He said he spoke to her, after it happened. That she spoke through you…?"

I didn't answer. I felt angry and hurt that Sebastian had shared so much with Mags, that he had described to her that shameful moment that haunted and tormented me still.

"If Caoilinn is still such a strong part of who you are, how can I trust you? I'd have to be as crazy as Sebastian and I assure you, I'm not. If Caoilinn's still alive within you somewhere and able to control your actions, how can we trust anything you do or say?"

"You can't," I stated flatly. She had asked the very question that I had been asking myself constantly since I awoke. How could I be trusted?

"Well, at least we agree on one thing," Mags muttered, shaking her head as she began to take plates and cups out of the cupboards.

"And how do you know so much about the Others? How do we know that we can trust you?" I demanded.

Mags spun back around with a smirk on her face. "Sebastian can always trust me, because I'm his wife. *You* should probably watch your back." There was an undercurrent behind her teasing words that made me defensive.

"And I know about the Others because I thought it would be in the best interest of both Sebastian and myself, if I kept an eye on them while I was looking for my husband and awaiting his return.

Prudent, don't you think?"

I ignored her smug expression and stood up, stretching my sore back and tense shoulders as I did so.

"So tell me what you know." I began folding both mine and Sebastian's blankets while I waited for her to begin. After several long and stubborn minutes, Mags began speaking.

"Sebastian is more powerful than any of the Others, including myself. Still, he needed my help to erase the Others' memories of us. Some of them had been our companions for hundreds of years, they depended upon us for our guidance and for our companionship – we were a family. We could only erase their memories one by one. It was a difficult task but Sebastian's happiness was worth it, only, he wasn't happy. There was something bothering him still, sucking him down into this deep pit of depression and madness."

Mags glared at me accusingly before continuing. "I awoke one morning and he was gone. I wanted to find him but his magic over-powered my own and he remained hidden. I could still remember him and since I knew eventually he'd come back to me, I decided I should make preparations for when he did.

"I kept an eye on the Others and watched their movements with interest. While Sebastian and I had made them forget us, their cre-ators, we hadn't thought to erase their memories of you, Caoilinn. They knew there was a soul out there somewhere who possessed unheard of knowledge and control of the Lost Magic, and they re-membered the legend that this ancient Priestess would be searching for her lost love. They knew it was in their best interests to keep you and "your love" apart - at all costs. I watched as they added another, from the original damned twelve to the current thirteen, and they began searching–"

"Don't you mean twelve?" I interrupted as the image of Walter's lifeless body and glazed-over eyes flashed through my mind.

"No, thirteen. The one you killed had only recently joined their ranks. I had heard rumors but wasn't going to count him in their numbers until I confirmed his existence myself. It was the first time they had increased their numbers over thirteen or initiated one as old as he was rumored to be. It takes a great deal of power to awaken the Lost Magic within another – we had thought only Sebastian and yourself were powerful enough to do so but apparently the Others were able to combine their abilities to add to their numbers after we left them. This Walter must have done something truly valuable for The Order to go to the trouble..."

"He found Sebastian and he nearly killed him. He kept an eye on me and he ensured my mother kept me and Sebastian apart," I told her quietly. I moved closer to the kitchen, taking a seat on one of the stools on the living room side of the counter.

"That would do it." Mags angrily cracked an egg into the frying pan she'd been heating up and then swore loudly as tiny pieces of the shell were mixed in with the runny whites.

I hesitated before asking my next question aloud. "How was Sebastian able to create so many of the Others?" Mags stared back at me blankly, forcing me to continue. I swallowed down my irritation along with my pride – I needed to know. "Caoilinn thought an intimate connection was necessary to give Seamus the ability to control the Lost Magic..."

"The better you know someone, the easier it is to give them access to the Lost Magic. To give as much magic as you gave to Sebastian you would need to know them very 'intimately'." She suddenly smirked. "But don't you worry, he may have had close friendships with all of the Others, but he was never so close to them as he was to me. That's why I'm almost as powerful as Sebastian."

I had guessed as much but to hear her confirm it… I fought the sudden violent urge to hit her in the face. My gut twisted painfully as I struggled to control my emotions. I tried to focus on the facts at hand and quickly changed the subject.

"So what is 'The Order'?"

"It's the society that the Others formed after Sebastian and I left. There are seven hidden temples of The Order set up around the world. They use civilians like Walter and offer them promises of eternal life and limitless powers if they obey and serve them; it's your typical cult organization. They have connections everywhere."

"But… why? Can't they get whatever they want anyway?"

"They couldn't find you, Caoilinn," Mags pointed out. "They had their suspicions about you before they could remember Sebastian but there were other young women they were watching too. Somehow, your magic was still protecting you even before you reawakened it. Then once Sebastian started wanting to know if there were other people like him, the Others' memories began to slowly return. They weren't immediately certain, so they were merely keeping an eye on you and Sebastian. Once you made him remember everything, the mental blocks Sebastian and I had put in place were shattered. The Others remembered everything too and they started coming after you both immediately. I wanted to follow them but something kept redirecting me back to Berlin."

I frowned, distracted. There was something about what Mags had said that just didn't sit right. I couldn't quite put my finger on what it was.

The apartment was suddenly very quiet aside from the sizzling of the eggs cooking in the pan and the steam rising from the coffee maker. The sound of the shower had turned off and an eerie silence hung in the air along with the strong scent of coffee. Mags leaned over the counter towards me, her green eyes flashing suspiciously. She lowered her voice, ensuring that only I would hear what she was about to say.

"The main temple of The Order is in Greece, I know exactly where it is and I will take you there. I'll help to overpower the Others and bring an end to their existence – I'll slit all their throats myself if I have to. But just know, I'll be watching you too and if you so much as make one move that I think threatens Sebastian or I..."

She held my gaze steadily, the threat clear and bright in her eyes. To both of our surprise, I smiled. Mags straightened up, leaning away from me uneasily.

"I will never be a danger to Sebastian - you don't have to worry about that. But *you* should probably watch your back," I added. Mags didn't smile back, she looked pissed off and also, just a little less sure of herself. I didn't know why I was antagonizing her when I knew that I needed her help... it was so hard not to hate her.

The bathroom door opened and Sebastian stepped out, his hair damp and tousled, his clothes fresh and clean. He smiled a little uncertainly, first at me and then at Mags.

"Everything alright?" he asked, looking back and forth between us.

"Fine," we answered together in tight, flat voices.

"I'm going to have a shower now," I announced. I didn't really want to leave Mags and Sebastian alone again but I desperately wanted to escape from the room.

I grabbed some clothes from my own bag and then headed towards the bathroom door. Sebastian hadn't moved and stood blocking my way, watching me with his sad, ancient eyes.

"Did Mags tell you what the plan is?"

I nodded, only briefly meeting his gaze. It was too hard to be standing this close to him but to feel so infinitely far apart. He moved closer, angling his body away from Mags and leaning down towards my ear. I nervously held my breath.

"I know you don't want to talk to me but if you'll just listen... I owe you an explanation. There's so much I wanted to say to you yesterday but you didn't give me the chance. You didn't want to hear me," he said in a low voice, only meant for me.

The urge to escape became even stronger. I wasn't certain I was strong enough to deny him. "We'll talk later," I hurriedly agreed, side-stepping around him. I glanced at him quickly and was surprised to see he looked as relieved to postpone the conversation as I felt. He nodded his agreement. He still looked sad; there was a new heaviness to his eyes.

"Enjoy your shower," he said politely, though it sounded forced.

"Enjoy your breakfast," I answered just as quickly. I made an effort not to slam the door behind me as I rushed into the sanctity of the bathroom and away from the love of my life – of my existence, whom I feared I may have lost forever.

Chapter Twelve – A New Design

Just like Mags had wanted, we were on a train by noon and headed south out of Berlin towards Germany's border. The cost of our passes had been much more expensive than I expected – over $1,500 for the three of us. I was glad my father had provided us with the funds necessary for this trip but I tried not to let my thoughts linger on why he had suddenly become so helpful; the guilt and shame was even worse than before.

We would be passing through six countries and traveling for a total of three and a half days before we reached Thessaloniki, Greece. We all wanted to get to Greece as quickly as possible and this ensured the convenience of direct routes and quick transfers when necessary. I still couldn't understand why we weren't just flying directly to Greece and when I voiced this question aloud, Mags met my curious gaze with a withering glare.

"The Order is meeting in two weeks time to discuss what to do about you and Sebastian – the *whole* of The Order will be there. There will be some discussion but it is obvious that they will primarily convene to combine their wants and their magic to stop you both. The ceremony will be performed on the night of the full moon. There will only be a few members of The Order, six at the very most, who would be near the temple already. They will want to find us before then and will be watching the airports. But our magic should be strong enough to confuse them - as long as we all want the same thing," she added with a brief sneer in my direction.

"Stop it, Mags," Sebastian warned, tiredly. "Gracelynn is with us on this."

I pressed my lips together firmly, biting the words that were fighting to spring to life on my lips. What had he meant by that? Did he doubt I was "with them" on everything then? I immediately felt angry and hurt but Mags allowed me no time to recover.

"There are too many trains in Greece for the Others to watch them all and as long as we don't want them to find us, they shouldn't. We should have just enough time after we arrive to deal with the first five before the rest start trickling in. They're coming from all over the world – some may not arrive until days before the ceremony but others will begin to appear immediately."

"It doesn't give us much time," I pointed out.

"If you have a better plan, Caoilinn, I'm dying to hear it," Mags snapped.

"My name is Grace."

"Whatever."

We glared at each other for several long seconds. I was starting to really, really dislike Mags and it was becoming increasingly difficult to remember why I shouldn't.

Sebastian didn't seem to notice the tension between me and Mags. He stared out the window of our small private compartment on the train, his own inner demons weighing down his handsome face. When we had boarded the train, Mags had immediately (and possessively) taken the seat beside Sebastian. I almost wished she hadn't, as now I would have to sit across from him for the next four and a half hours until we arrived in the Czech Republic. I turned my attention to the window, watching the landscape blur by in a daze as I tried my best not to look his way.

The idea of traveling across Europe with Sebastian would once have seemed like a dream come true but it had turned into such a horrible and twisted nightmare that all I wanted now was to go home. I couldn't enjoy the sights we were passing and so I didn't even try. I desperately missed Vancouver Island's mountains and valleys, the rocky beaches, the tall cedar and fir trees, the farms, the small towns, the beautiful city of Victoria that had become my home. I longed for the cool salty breeze that was always rising off the ocean and the beautiful tapestry of fall colors that would be splashed throughout the leaves in Beacon Hill park by now. I was miserable and afraid and homesick. It was almost a relief to know that one way or another, this nightmare would soon be over with.

I became distracted when Mags began talking to Sebastian in a low and intimate whisper. I tried to ignore them but it was hard not to glance their way as they sat directly across from me in the small and confining space. I became even more jealous when I realized that Mags had successfully pulled Sebastian from his silent, brooding thoughts and he started to smile and answer her in a quiet voice of his own. They were joking around about something in Gaelic and apparently quite enjoying each others' company. I tried my best not to listen and stubbornly closed my eyes, wincing every time I heard Mags' loud, joyful laugh and Sebastian's quiet chuckles. It was a horrible, torturous train ride and was only the first of several in the days to come. I knew I deserved this punishment and heart-wrenching pain but it didn't make it any easier to bear.

The quiet murmur of Sebastian's voice in the background of my thoughts along with the train's gentle bumps and rhythmic sway lulled me towards a strange kind of sleep. I was still aware of where I was and the people around me but I had also sunk so deeply into myself that my pain was numbed and my thoughts were strangely lucid and dreamlike.

I daydreamed in this quiet, gray place, letting my thoughts wander and leaving my pain behind me. It was within this peaceful sanctuary in my mind that a design began to form within my thoughts. The looping, twisting, thick black lines of a pattern gathered and took shape before I was even consciously aware of what was happening. My eyes snapped open.

"I need some paper, and a pen," I announced, looking directly at Sebastian for the first time since we had boarded the train.

Mags and him were both staring at me in surprise. Sebastian looked unexpectedly guilty, suddenly leaning away from her.

"I thought you were sleeping…"

"Here," Mags interrupted. She tossed a pen at me and then began digging through the pockets of her leather jacket. When she didn't find what she was looking for she reached over and into Sebastian's jacket pocket, digging around without hesitation. He looked as if he were about to object but before he could say a word she triumphantly pulled out a wrinkled yet clean-looking napkin.

"Use this."

I snatched it from her hands, desperately trying to ignore them both and to hold the dark pattern in my mind. The pen trembled in my hand for a second as I took a deep, slow breath and worked to collect my thoughts. I then slowly began to draw, the first line of the pattern stretching out and then looping back on itself, my pen moving in a graceful dance across the wrinkled napkin.

"What-?" Sebastian began to ask. I was dimly aware of Mags hushing him. I shut them both out, pushed the world far away and let my mind find that quiet, powerful place waiting within.

It had been a long time since I'd let myself get lost in a drawing like this. It was peaceful and relaxing, and the perfect escape. As the design neared completion and I began to rise out of my trance, I became aware of exactly what it was I had drawn. My pen came to a halting stop. I fought the strong urge to tear up the drawing and throw it away. I immediately knew it was wrong.

"It's part of your tattoo," Mags stated calmly, speaking to Sebastian. There was something hidden deep within the thickly accented tones of her voice, an edge of uncertainty perhaps. "I think it's from the one on your back," she continued. I was surprised when she turned and addressed me. "What does it mean?"

I didn't answer immediately. I frowned down at the drawing I had created, trying to understand it. I felt like I had known just a second ago exactly what it was but the certainty was rapidly fading.

I had been upset when I started drawing. I was angry at Mags and myself, and even Sebastian. I felt tortured and tormented by the present situation and the knowledge of the horrible things that Caoilinn had done. My emotions had summoned the power within me, had brought memories and knowledge from my past life forward to the present and I had created this design, this focal point for a spell that would… I quietly gasped.

"What?" Mags demanded. Sebastian placed a warning hand on her arm. The sight of him touching her made me flinch. He leant towards me, his voice and eyes patient and full of only half-buried pain.

"It's okay, Gracelynn. If you don't know…"

"I know." I dropped my eyes in shame. "It's a focal point, almost like instructions for a spell that… that causes pain, excruciating pain. It's a method of torture that eventually causes death." I spoke quietly, in a chilled voice that barely carried across the small space in our travel compartment.

My pronouncement was met with shocked silence, even Mags seemed stunned. I was so disgusted at this revelation, at this black and twisted spell that Caoilinn had discovered, that Sebastian had protected for hundreds of years having had it encrypted within the beautiful design of his tattoo, that I had to fight the nausea that was rapidly rising within me. I stared at the beige swirls in the dark brown, worn carpet that covered the floor in our compartment and focused on breathing in and out.

"We could use that spell on the Others," Mags suggested.

"No," Sebastian and I objected together. I briefly met his eye, appreciating his support and then dropped my gaze in shame once more. I was horrified by the cold, monstrous, darkness within me.

"Just a suggestion," Mags dismissed, obviously trying to keep her voice light. "They can't all be spells for torture and death though. No matter how twisted Caoilinn was, there must be some spells she knew that we can use."

"I still can't believe…" Sebastian started muttering to himself. I quickly glanced up to see him looking out the window again. He was scowling and squinting out at the sunny day, his forehead creased and his eyes straining. His lips were moving rapidly as he continued talking softly to himself. I met Mags' eye to find a similar expression of alarm on her face as I could feel on my own. She reached over and tugged on his sleeve.

"Sebastian?"

He completely ignored her and closed his eyes. His whole face scrunched up tightly, his teeth clenched together as he muttered in a low and indistinguishable voice. I thought I saw a droplet of dark red blood gathering at the base of his nostril.

"Sebastian, please," Mags coerced, reaching up to gently touch his face. He jerked away from her hand as if stung, his agitation clearly increasing. His voice began to grow louder, his words flowing faster and clearer. It was then that I realized he wasn't speaking English but was rambling away in Gaelic. I had no idea what he was saying but Mags looked horrified. His whole face had drained of its natural color and was now a sickly grayish-white. A drop of blood trickled down from his nose, staining his lips a ghastly red.

I knew I had to do something.

I fell forward onto my knees before him, reaching up and firmly holding his face with both my hands. His mad ravings quieted and slowed at my touch, his pained expression relaxing slightly though not completely. Even in this desperate moment, it still felt so good to touch him, to be close to him once more.

"Stop, Sebastian. Come back to us," I urged in a voice much calmer than I felt. His eyelids flickered at the sound of my voice but didn't open. His muttering abruptly stopped as a low groan began building in his throat. The sound of it made chills run down my spine, the pain and suffering so clear in that one single noise that it terrified me through and through.

"What the hell are you doing to him?" Mags shrieked. She jumped up and grabbed at my arms, roughly pulling them from Sebastian's face. What happened next shocked us both.

With her hands still on my arms, her face suddenly twisted and contorted in pain. She screamed both in anger and fear as she suddenly jerked away from me, shrinking back and sliding as far from me in the small space as she could get. I didn't have time to consider what had happened as Sebastian began moaning again. His body had become rigid, his hands were clenched into fists and his head began to slowly shake back and forth.

I ignored Mags and grabbed his face again, firmly pulling his forehead against mine.

"Please, stop," I begged. I hesitated only for a second before continuing, ignoring Mags as thoroughly as possible. "Seamus... please. Come back to me. Don't leave me. I need you so much." I was terrified and struggling not to panic. I wanted so badly for him to stop, for him to open his eyes and to be okay that I couldn't believe it wasn't happening. I instinctively knew he was lost in the past somewhere, losing himself to the overwhelming memories that swarmed his mind. And there was only one thing I could think to do to pull him back. I crushed my lips against his, kissing him as hard and roughly as I dared. I released all my passion, all my frustration and pain into that one moment, and all my boundless, eternal love for him.

His eyelids flickered again, his muscles began to relax. His cold lips, now warmed by mine, began to soften and yield, and to very slowly kiss me back. And the kiss that had begun with such rough desperation, slowly melted into the sweetest, most tender and heartfelt kiss that we had ever shared. A warm passion was steadily building within me and when he opened his eyes, for a second I could see the same loving warmth radiating out from deep within him. And then his eyes clouded and he was pushing me away.

"Caoilinn? I mean… Gracelynn? What…? Why were we…?" he blinked rapidly, looking around our compartment, desperately searching for something. His eyes fell on Mags, crouched in the corner, looking wary but fierce. She glared at us both accusingly, the pain clear in her eyes. "Mags. Mags, I'm sorry. I never meant to… I mean, we shouldn't have…" he stuttered, more confused and discomposed than I'd ever seen him before. He looked back at me, his eyes begging me for help but I wasn't sure what it was he wanted. I felt like I didn't know anything anymore.

"Relax, Sebastian," Mags snapped, she glared daggers at me as she slowly stood. "It's not *your* effin' fault."

I felt confused myself as I remembered what had happened. How had I made Mags let go of me like that? And why had Sebastian kissed me back so passionately and then suddenly pushed me away? And why was he apologizing to her and not to me? My eyes tried to fill with angry and frustrated tears, a painful sob gathering and sticking deep in my chest. I stubbornly swallowed it back down.

"I'm still so confused… What happened? Was it another episode?" I was surprised when he directed the question at me. I wished I could give him another answer than the truth but I couldn't lie to him. I silently nodded and the crease between his brows deepened. "But I thought… I thought it wouldn't happen anymore. I thought if you and Mags both wanted me to stop remembering…"

"I thought so too," Mags agreed. She dropped down heavily in the seat beside him, her eyes full of fury as she stared at me, vigorously rubbing her arms. "Caoilinn must want you to remember something; she's forcing the memories back up and they're scrambling your mind."

"No, Gracelynn would never want to hurt me," Sebastian automatically denied and for that, at least, I was grateful. He looked at me with questioning eyes though.

"She hurt *me*!" Mags pointed out sulkily. "She burnt my hands just now. She's more powerful and goddamn capable than you know, Sebastian. She's trying to hide her abilities from you but I can see the truth."

"No! That's not true!" I objected angrily, rising to my feet. "I was trying to help him and you were stopping me. I just wanted to make you let go. I didn't mean to hurt you."

"Bullshit. You wanted me to feel pain."

I opened my mouth to deny it but no sound came out as I realized the truth. I had wanted her to let go but I hadn't wanted to be gentle about it. I had wanted her to feel some of the pain that I was feeling, if only for a second. What kind of monster was I?

"I just wanted to help Sebastian," I continued in a quieter voice.

"Can't you see he's had enough of your effin' 'help'?" Mags spat back at me.

"Stop it – both of you!" Sebastian interrupted. He squeezed his eyes tightly shut and began to dig his fingers into his temples. We both immediately fell silent. I was terrified for a moment that another 'episode' was about to begin. Sebastian slowly reopened his eyes though, his fingers sliding from his skull.

"We have nearly three more days left on this train together and we need to all start wanting the same thing if we're going to have any chance of surviving the days after that. Let's just put everything else aside and focus on working together. Please?" He looked back and forth between us, his eyes pleading in a way I suspected Mags was as powerless to deny as I.

Mags rolled her eyes. "Get real Sebastian," she scolded but in a much lighter tone. "What, did you expect your wife and your girlfriend to be instant best friends?"

To my surprise one side of Sebastian's mouth twitched towards a smile. "I suppose not," he agreed. He glanced at me as if inviting me to join in the joke but I couldn't smile, I couldn't find anything funny about our situation. My expression quickly melted his mirth.

"I'm starving," Mags suddenly announced, standing up and stretching. "Want to come with me to get something to eat?" she invited Sebastian.

"Sure," he agreed. He turned towards me. "Let's all go."

"No, you go ahead, I'll wait here. I don't feel well."

Sebastian continued to look at me, trying to catch my eye as if to see the truth behind my words. I had spoken honestly, I had never felt so sick and confused in all my life.

"Maybe I'll stay with Gracelynn…"

"No," Mags and I objected together. Mags smirked at me as she slid open our compartment door. "See, she doesn't want you to stay either. Let's go." And without looking back, Mags stepped out into the narrow corridor that led away from our compartment and down towards the tiny, twisted stairwell at the end of our carriage that led up to the dining area.

Sebastian hesitated in the doorway. "I'll bring you something back, in case you change your mind," he told me quietly before stepping out into the hall and closing the door behind him.

Mags was a better choice for Sebastian than I was – I kept telling myself that anyway. It hurt so much that I couldn't trust myself around him, that he could no longer trust me. I hated seeing him with Mags but if I really loved him, if I truly wanted what was best for him, I knew that I was going to have to stop fighting this and start really wanting the right thing. I was trying but obviously I wasn't trying hard enough. It broke my heart to even think it but I was going to have to want them to be together – to really want them to be together, so he could be happy and safe. It was the right thing to do, impossible as it seemed.

When Sebastian and Mags returned I had calmed and composed myself. I forced myself to watch the way they behaved around one another, to see the obvious bond that hundreds of years in each other's company had created. I had to admit, Mags knew Sebastian almost as well as I. She sensed his moods, she knew how to tease him, she knew what subjects would spark his interest and pull him from his gloomy distractions. She had enough control over her magic that she could offer him protection too - unlike myself. I tried not to wallow in my misery. I tried to be happy that Sebastian would be safe and loved. It was hard.

I spent the rest of the day going back and forth between sketching more mysterious designs and trying my best to be friendly towards Mags. She was suspicious at first and mostly ignored my attempts at conversation. I could tell Sebastian appreciated my effort, smiling at me gratefully and trying to find common ground between Mags and myself - there wasn't much. Mags gradually warmed up to me, mostly because of Sebastian's encouragement. The more I learnt about her, the more I found myself reluctantly admiring her and viewing her with a new, slightly grudging, respect.

Mags was tough in both appearance and attitude. She smoked, she swore, and she had more piercings and tattoos than Sebastian. She spoke too loudly, took offense easily and she knew how to stand up for herself. She was full of spunk and confidence, and had a dry and sarcastic sense of humor that took me a while to understand. And she loved Sebastian, perhaps nearly as much as I did. It was obvious every time that she looked at him, every moment that she was in his presence that she would do absolutely anything for him. At some point, I stopped being angry and just felt very, very sad.

The first night we spent on the train we were somewhere near the border of the Czech Republic. I really wasn't paying too much attention and wouldn't have even realized we were in the Czech Republic if we hadn't had to switch trains. Our new cabin had two fold down beds - a double bed on bottom with a single bunk above. Mags flatly refused to share a bed with me; no matter how friendly we pretended to be towards each other she still didn't want me close enough to touch her. She joked about her and Sebastian sharing the double bed but Sebastian insisted upon sleeping on the floor, leaving the top bunk for me. It took me a long time to fall asleep. My face was barely a foot away from the ceiling and the rocking of the train that had felt so soothing before now seemed to jar and jolt me with every noisy bounce over the tracks. I felt so lonely. The feeling was only intensified when I heard Sebastian and Mags quietly talking and laughing. I fell asleep facing the wall, just in case one of them looked up and saw the tears on my cheeks.

The second day of travel, we journeyed through both Hungary and Croatia on several different trains. I spent most of the day attempting to focus and gain more control over my magic; it was the only useful thing I could think to do. I meditated, I drew more designs for spells (some of which I understood the meanings of, most that I didn't) and I practiced "wanting" things to happen – all with little success. Even though I was now constantly aware of the ancient, raw power within me, actually focusing and harnessing it was beyond me. It felt like the more I tried, the more I failed and the more I failed, the more frustrated and desperate I became. The only thing I seemed to succeed at was wanting Sebastian to forget about me – I rarely noticed him looking my way. Most of the time he seemed absorbed in reestablishing his friendship with Mags. It tore at my heart and destroyed my soul to see them growing closer but I knew it was right and I forced myself to want the right thing for once.

I worked hard to be polite and friendly towards Mags, to keep the peace between us all. The only conflict I initiated was when we returned to our cabin after dinner on the second night and I refused to sleep on the top bunk again.

"I'll sleep on the floor if I have to but there's no way I'm sleeping up there," I stated firmly. I stubbornly folded my arms across my chest and met Mags' glare with one of my own. I couldn't be certain if it was because I wanted it or not but Mags almost immediately backed down, looking uneasy and annoyed at the same time.

"Fine. We'll rotate beds then to make it fair. That means you're sleeping on the floor tonight – then tomorrow I'll take a turn."

"No, she doesn't need to sleep on the floor," Sebastian objected. I felt a twinge of pain as he referred to me as "she". He didn't even look at me when he spoke.

"It's fine," I mumbled, grabbing a pillow and tossing it down onto the ground.

I quickly made up a bed on the hard, thinly carpeted floor with just a pillow and two blankets. I was happy not to be on the top bunk again and I lay down with my back to the others, immediately shutting my eyes and praying that sleep would find me quickly that night. For once, I got what I wanted.

I hadn't expected to dream of Caoilinn again; I knew I didn't want to remember anymore of her life and so it was a surprise when I did. It wasn't like my other dreams where I relived her memories, saw through her eyes and thought her thoughts. This was different. I jolted awake from the strange dream, flashes of images and flickers of sensations all that I could remember. Confused and frightened tears gathered in my eyes as I sat up in the darkness, disoriented and feeling so very alone.

"Gracelynn?" I heard Sebastian whisper from his bed just a few feet away from me. "Gracelynn, what's wrong?" The fear and worry in his voice were obvious and my tears over-flowed because I knew I didn't deserve his concern.

I heard blankets rustling as he moved towards me in the darkness. A second later there was a quiet click and a small overhead light turned on from the underside of Mags' bunk. Thankfully, Mags didn't awake, her soft snores just barely audible over the noise of the train.

I stared at Sebastian and he stared back at me. His eyes looked as sad as I felt; my heart felt as if it were tearing wide open. He was so handsome, so undeniably attractive sitting there under the soft yellowish light, shirtless yet still in his jeans. I couldn't help but notice the contours of his muscles and the perfect shape of his body. My heart pounded as it ripped apart and my mind spun from all the conflicting emotions that threatened to overwhelm me. A quiet sob burst free from my lips.

"Oh, Gracelynn," he whispered, his expression breaking as he quickly slid off the bed and knelt down on the floor beside me. He reached for me with his warm, familiar hands and I was powerless to resist him. He pulled me up into his arms and I leaned gratefully into him. The feel of his arms around me, his warmth and the rhythm of his heart beating and the smell of his skin, it was all so familiar and wonderful and I hated myself for loving him so much and for being too weak to let go.

"What's happening to us?" he murmured into my hair. "I've felt so confused lately."

"Me too," I whispered back. I clung to him tightly, never, ever wanting him to let me go and yet knowing that he should. "I just want you to be happy, even if it's with someone else. I'm trying so hard to want the right thing," I confessed, choking back a sob.

"I…" his voice trailed off into silence. "I don't understand what's happening," he repeated, sounding as confused as I felt. "Why were you crying?"

"I had a bad dream." I felt like a small child as I answered, foolish and afraid. His grip on me loosened and I slowly slid from his arms.

"I know what that's like."

"Haven't your nightmares stopped now that Mags is here?"

"I thought they had," he slowly answered. He frowned, looking puzzled. "They're not the same now anyway. They're certainly not as vivid and I don't remember them when I awake but sometimes I feel like they're still there."

"I'm sorry," I automatically apologized.

"Me too."

He sighed and leant back, the light above him shining down on his chest, highlighting the Celtic knot tattooed over his heart. My eyes were automatically drawn to the simple yet complex design, my attention focusing in on the small, scrolled text that formed the dark, weaving lines. My mouth popped open in surprise as I realized I recognized what I saw.

"Gracelynn?" Sebastian leant forward again, the tattoo disappearing back into the shadows and my mind automatically clearing with its absence.

"Sorry, I'm fine. Just tired," I lied, hating myself as the words sprung to my lips.

"I'll let you rest then, if you're sure you're okay…?"

"I'm fine." Another lie.

Sebastian frowned again, he still looked confused, like he was struggling to say something but wasn't sure exactly what it was that he wanted to say.

"I'm sorry I woke you." I lay back down as I spoke, firmly turning my back to him as my hands began to tremble.

There was a long pause. I could feel his eyes on my back. "Good night," he murmured softly. Seconds later the light clicked off. I waited until I heard Sebastian's breathing slow and deepen before I even dared admit to myself what I had seen, what had scared and shaken me so much.

I knew somehow that it had been the dream that had helped me to remember the ancient, archaic form of Celtic. I felt even more terrified than before. I had read the words in Sebastian's tattoo and I had understood the warning – and it was about me.

She cannot be trusted. Her wants are not your own. Don't let her find you.

It was the final confirmation that I needed – that everything Mags had been saying was true. I was the enemy. I was the biggest threat to Sebastian's happiness and sanity. And I was too much of a coward to admit the truth to Sebastian even now.

I would take the warning for him, I decided. I would stay as far from him as I could and want his happiness above all else. And once the Others had been dealt with, once I was certain that Sebastian was safe, I would leave him forever so that I might never, ever hurt him again.

The pain in my chest was too great for any amount of tears to offer relief. There was absolutely no release for it, no comfort I could possibly find. I lay awake for the rest of the night, letting the pain destroy me.

The next morning, I stayed true to my word. I avoided Sebastian, ignoring him as much as possible. I could tell that I must finally, truly want for him to move on, for him to reestablish his connection with Mags and be happy with her for he didn't look my way once. When they left to go upstairs to the dining cart for breakfast, Mags reached for his hand and he let her take it without hesitating or ever once glancing my way.

Overnight we had passed through Serbia and were now on our way down through Bulgaria, towards the southern border the country shared with Greece. We should arrive in Thessaloniki shortly after lunch. Apparently the head temple of The Order wasn't too far from there, though Mags wanted to "lay low" in Thessaloniki for a while and survey the surrounding area. She wanted to take some time to form a more concrete plan before we laid our "ambush" and it seemed like a good idea.

I didn't comment on her plans, I didn't say much all day. I felt like a zombie, like the core of my being had been removed and destroyed and I was nothing but an empty shell making all the correct motions but with no feeling or emotion.

At lunchtime I went with Sebastian and Mags to the dining car and picked away at a sandwich and a fruit salad. I ate the food without tasting it, my tongue as numb and unresponsive as the rest of me. After just ten minutes, I excused myself and headed back down to our cabin alone. I wasn't certain if either of them really noticed when I left. They were laughing and joking, talking about something that had once happened hundreds of years in the past.

Alone in the cabin, with nothing else to do, I took out the sketch-pad and black calligraphy pens I had purchased from the train's gift shop and began to draw. It was easy to fall into the trance-like state now, I was halfway there already. Time ceased to exist as there was nothing but me and the pen and the dark, looping, weaving lines. This design felt different than the others, the pattern more complex and detailed. I let my instincts take over and formed each precise loop, line, spiral and twist as I knew it was meant to be. And as I drew, I let my mind wander, idly contemplating what exactly this spell might be for. My pen came to an abrupt stop with the last line of my drawing. My trance-like state suddenly shattered as the realization hit me - it was the design for a spell to erase the memories of another person. The design was familiar to me too. It was similar in both pattern and intricacy to the tiny, dime-sized tattoo hidden in Sebastian's hair but not exactly the same. There were a few subtle differences. What did it mean?

I studied the design curiously. Though I was relieved it wasn't a spell for torture or death, I was confused that I had drawn it at all. Obviously all the Others, including Mags and Sebastian, already knew how to erase memories without using a design. This spell was just as useless as all the others I had recalled.

I let out a frustrated sigh, reaching for the page to tear it up but something made me hesitate. The design really was quite complex and beautiful. The symmetry and balance to the pattern was impressive and the way it seemed to all be formed from one line that never ended until it looped back to its own beginning… it was strangely fascinating.

I closed the sketchbook and tucked it away, leaving the drawing unharmed. At least it was proof that I might be able to remember some spells that weren't deadly or torturous. I would keep the drawing as my one and only pathetic symbol of hope.

The train appeared to be slowing down, probably for our last stop in Bulgaria at Kulata before we crossed the border into Greece. I wondered why Sebastian and Mags hadn't returned to our cabin yet. We really needed to sit down together and discuss our plans. As much as I didn't want to be anywhere near the two of them for any extended period of time, it was obviously necessary to make sure that we all wanted the exact same thing before we traveled any closer to the Others.

Just then the door to the cabin burst open and Mags and Sebastian rushed inside, Sebastian's eyes were wide with alarm and Mags' were bright with excitement. Before I could even ask, Sebastian looked right at me, his expression and tone intense.

"The Others are here."

Chapter Thirteen – Ceremony

"We only have two options, to run or to fight," Mags stated flatly as she pushed her way into the cabin. "There are two of 'em and they must have sensed us as soon as we sensed them. They were right here at the station when the train pulled in but they'll be running by now, trying to get far enough away that our magic won't affect them. Then they'll warn The Order that we're here. We have to stop them. We need to all want for them to come back, to face us so that we can take 'em down."

"No," I immediately objected. "We still haven't come up with a plan on how to deal with them and–"

"I'll deal with them," Mags promised darkly.

I swallowed hard, not liking this situation at all. I reluctantly turned to Sebastian. "What do you think?"

He hesitated before answering. "I don't know. I just… I don't know. I don't think we can let them get away."

I shook my head, my mind working fast. If Sebastian and Mags both wanted the Others to come back they would and then who knew what would happen? I couldn't even guess at what Mags had in mind for "dealing" with them, and I didn't want to risk any chance of Sebastian being captured or hurt. I didn't want Mags' violence to bring back any more nightmarish memories from his past either; the way he'd been acting lately, I wasn't certain that he could handle it. I was left with only one option.

"Fine. I'll do it then."

Mags and Sebastian both stared at me disbelievingly. It didn't help my confidence at all when Mags began to laugh.

"You'll do what?" she smirked.

"I'll deal with them. I want them to come back and I want them to talk to me."

The smile slowly disappeared from Mags' face as she realized I was serious. Sebastian just continued to stare at me.

"I can do this, I know I can. And I can't see any other real option."

Mags opened her mouth to object but I immediately cut her off, pushing on before she had the chance to speak.

"If you try and *deal with them* and something goes wrong, they'll know who you are; you'll give away our numbers. Besides, if you do something that stops them from returning to The Order, the rest of the Others will become suspicious. They'll start hunting for us before we have a chance to surprise them," I pointed out.

Mags slowly closed her mouth, glaring at me indignantly.

"And just what the hell is it that you plan on doing? I know you're too much of a coward to use any of Caoilinn's nasty spells."

I took a nervous breath in, slowly exhaling through my nose as I tried to calm and focus myself. I was aware the whole while of Sebastian's eyes on me. I didn't dare look his way but I had a strong suspicion he was barely breathing or blinking.

"I'm going to alter their memories," I announced, a quiet power behind my words.

Sebastian still didn't move or speak.

"That's not possible," Mags denied. I could hear the doubt in her voice.

"It is. I know I can do it," I insisted, trying to sound more confident than I felt.

"Did you remember a spell? Is it a new design?"

Before I could answer her questions, Sebastian suddenly jumped up. Both he and Mags turned expectantly towards the front of the train.

"They're back already," Sebastian quietly announced. "They're so close now… they must be boarding the train."

This was really it, I realized. No going back now. I squeezed my amber pendant in my fist, pulling strength from and through it.

"Stay in the cabin with Sebastian," I instructed Mags, my voice surprisingly level and calm. She scowled at me, obviously not enjoying my new "take-charge" attitude. I had nothing to lose. The only way that the Others could hurt me now was by hurting Sebastian, and there was absolutely no way I was going to let that happen.

Sebastian stepped in front of me slightly, blocking my way to the door. "Gracelynn, I don't think you should do this." He was frowning as he spoke, looking both worried and confused. I automatically took a step back, flinching away from his proximity and the painful swirl of emotions that arose in his presence.

"Don't worry," I tried to reassure him. "We just all have to want this to work."

His forehead creased even more, his eyes looked strained. Then he slowly nodded and stepped aside. "I'll... we'll be right on the other side of the door if—"

"I'll be fine," I told him firmly. There was a new, authoritative power in my voice that made even me want to believe myself. Sebastian's brow relaxed slightly.

I quickly stepped around him and out into the hall. I took another calming breath and then tried to reach out with my mind, searching for an awareness of the approaching Others. There was a definite sense of danger and anticipation hanging in the air but as far as specifically sensing the Others, my efforts came up dry. Even so, as soon as they descended the staircase at the far end of the hall, I instantly knew it was them.

The first to appear was a young, European girl. Her nationality was hard to place as well as her specific age; she could have been anywhere from 15-20, though there was a strong likelihood that she was at least several hundred years old. She had olive-toned skin, dark hair and large dark eyes; there was an exotic quality to her beauty. She was tall and toned, and could easily have been a model despite her casual clothes. She froze the instant she saw me, recognition and awareness flashing through her nearly black eyes. She must know who I was. It took me a second to realize her hesitation was caused by fear. The knowledge added to my courage and gave me strength. I stood up straighter, pushing my shoulders back and staring back at her as steadily and expressionlessly as I was able to.

A young man came down the stairway behind her into the narrow hall. His eyes met mine immediately. It was no surprise to see that he was handsome, I had come to expect it of the Others. He was tall and thin but in a lean, well-proportioned way. His skin was a beautiful, warm tone of brown, his hair shiny black and his eyes were large and almond-shaped. He was older than the Others I had encountered before him, appearing to be in his mid-twenties. I could guess from his appearance that he was from some part of India or Nepal but who knew where he had spent the majority of his unnaturally-long life.

They stood close together at the end of the hall, completely frozen. They had obviously not expected to encounter me like this. I saw my advantage and took it.

"Hello," I greeted in an eerily calm voice. I knew my words carried clearly to their ears though I didn't strain at all to be heard. I wanted them to hear each and every word, and so they did. "Do you know who I am?"

There was a long pause before either of the Others answered. My heart began pounding in my throat, my nerves increasing with each passing second. I forced all my emotions deep down, burying them within me where they couldn't distract or influence my actions. I embraced the cold, numbness that was left behind, finding a new strength and focus there.

"You're the reincarnate of Caoilinn," the man stated, a barely perceivable tremor to his voice. I was surprised by the polite, English accent with which he spoke though I didn't let any of it show.

"I *am* Caoilinn," I stated firmly. My voice sounded deadly, my eyes were ice. I wasn't sure why I said it but it felt right and it inspired the reaction I had hoped for. The Others watched me warily, both their eyes widening and their stances tensing. I found myself slowly smiling. I wasn't sure where this new confidence was coming from but it was thrilling and emboldening. For once in my life, I felt truly powerful and in control. "I'm afraid I don't know your names. Come forward," I commanded in a soft and sweet voice that sounded nothing like my own. It cracked down the hall like a whip, demanding to be obeyed.

The Others immediately began moving towards me, their faces shadowed by fear and uncertainty. The tall man's face was slick with sweat despite the air conditioned interior of the train. They came to a stop just three feet before me. I was surprised when the girl spoke first.

"My name is Angelina," she announced in an unexpectedly low and smooth voice. There was a faint accent to the way she spoke but not one that I could place. "And this is Jai. We are original members of the ancient Order and we have come to summon you, Caoilinn, and your companions to the Head Temple."

I blinked once, watching curiously as a drop of sweat began to form at the girl's forehead. Jai shifted uneasily behind her as the silence stretched out.

"I want you to have no doubt, that you are here because I summoned you and for no other reason," I corrected, a clear edge to my voice. Angelina swallowed visibly, her confidence rapidly fading.

"What do you want with us?" Jai asked in a strained and breathy voice. "You have obviously summoned us back here for a reason."

I locked my eyes with his and waited until he looked away before I spoke.

"I want to know why you are in Kulata? You will tell me the truth – the whole truth."

This time, there wasn't even the slightest pause before Jai answered. "The Order is gathering all of its members. There are five originals at the Head Temple, including ourselves. We wanted all the Others to join us and we wanted you and Sebastian to come so that we could decide what to do with you," Jai stated in near-monotone. I immediately recognized the false quality of a well-rehearsed speech.

"I don't want to hear lies!" I snapped. It wasn't an act either, I was abruptly furious that they would try to deceive me. I reached to brush my long hair back over my shoulder and was vaguely surprised to find the short wavy curls that barely brushed my shoulder tops. I locked eyes with Jai again, letting my anger burn through into his deep, almond orbs. "Tell me the whole truth - *now*."

I was barely aware of Angelina's gasp as Jai's whole body began to tremble. His eyes became unfocused and started to glaze over. His lips slowly began to move.

"We were stationed along the border at the most likely entrance points – The Order knew you were arriving by train. Whoever found you was to capture you and bring you to the Temple. You, Caoilinn, were to be questioned by The Order – the rest of your fate left undecided. Sebastian was to receive punishment for his crimes against us, the severity of which would eventually result in his death. We were lead to believe that you did not have this kind of control over your ability. Another is aiding you; you are obviously drawing strength from him through the Bond…" Jai's eyes slowly shifted as he spoke to the cabin door that stood just a foot behind me at the end of the hall. I reacted to the subtle threat in his eyes instantly.

I reached past Angelina and grabbed Jai by the hair. His eyes bulged as I touched him. Angelina let out a faint squeak of fear and then dropped down onto the floor. I didn't want her to interfere and so she couldn't move.

"You did not see or sense any of us passing through or anywhere near the border. You stayed near the train station all day; it was boring and a waste of time. You will report that to the Others and nothing else. You will never remember anything else of today and you will never question it. The rest did not happen." I spoke slowly and softly, my voice a hypnotic chant. I focused on the small and intricate pattern that had jumped into my mind as I spoke, weaving my words between the complex loops and lines. Jai's eyes were unfocused and staring straight through me, his face sweaty and pale. His lips trembled and then moved, the words barely audible as the train's engine suddenly fired to life.

"It did not happen," he whispered as the train began to vibrate.

I released his head as soon as he spoke the words, letting him collapse heavily to the floor. I thought I heard movement in the cabin behind me but I didn't dare to turn or break my focus for a second. My amber necklace was burning red hot against my chest, fueled by the heat of my anger and the raw wave of power that coursed through me. I reached down and roughly grabbed Angelina by her silky, black hair, dragging her mercilessly to her feet.

"No," she gasped. Her eyes were huge, round saucers with tears sparkling at their edges. Her face was a sickly white. "It isn't possible. You can't do this to us. I don't want to believe you," she denied, obviously panicking. I ignored her.

"What you want doesn't matter." I focused on the pattern again, the design springing to mind easily and clearly. I poured the heat and power of my anger into it. "You did not see or sense any of us passing through or anywhere near the border. You stayed near the train station all day; it was boring and a waste of time. You will report that to the Others and nothing else. You will never remember anything else of today and you will never question it. The rest did not happen."

"It did not happen," Angelina whispered back to me before her eyes rolled back in her head and she collapsed on the floor beside Jai. The silence that followed roared in my ears and left me dizzy and weak.

"How in the hell did you do that?" Mags demanded as she stepped out of the cabin behind me. I ignored her, holding desperately onto the last of my strength as I sensed I was near collapse myself.

"Help me move them, the train is about to leave," I commanded, my voice hard and cold, inviting no more questions. She took a small and nervous step away from me, her eyes carefully studying my face and reevaluating me once more. "Now!"

Mags flinched at my tone and then jumped into action. Between the two of us, we quickly and easily moved the two unconscious bodies off the train and onto a bench on the platform outside. There was no one watching us, not a single person to help or to interfere just as I had wanted. I felt nearly intoxicated by the power and thrill of the moment. Even exhausted as I was, I felt I could take on the world.

We climbed back onto the train only seconds before it starting moving and pulling away from the station. I could already see Jai stirring on the bench as our train car rattled past.

"Your spell left a mark," Mags accused as we walked back down the slowly swaying hallway. "The Others will notice it, however you may have tried to hide it beneath their hair."

I immediately knew what she was talking about. I had noticed it myself, the tiny, dark web of lines that twisted through a small patch of Jai and Angelina's hairlines just above their temples, in a position identical to Sebastian's tattoo.

"They will not notice it, they will not question it. It is part of the spell," I answered without thinking. The response came haughtily and automatically, catching even me by surprise. I was still speaking in that strange, high voice that commanded so much power and respect. Mags noticed immediately, taking another step back from me. The color was rapidly draining from her face and she suddenly looked horrified.

"Caoilinn?" she whispered. It looked like her hands were starting to tremble.

"How could you?"

I spun around at the sound of Sebastian's voice, surprised to find him marching angrily towards me. It was only then that I realized he hadn't come out of the cabin to help deal with the Others and I suddenly realized how strange that was. I was even more shocked and horrified when I noticed the tears shimmering angrily in his dark gray eyes. The cool, calm focus that had possessed me began to waiver.

"How could you?" he repeated, shouting angrily at me as he came to a stop just inches from my face.

"Sebastian, calm down," Mags murmured nervously. We both ignored her this time.

"It was the only way to protect you," I answered him calmly, my voice still not sounding quite like my own. The last of my confidence and strength suddenly left me, dread and unease abruptly sweeping over me like a dark cloud blocking out the sun as I realized what I had done. I had forced the two Others to answer me against their wills and I had brutally and somewhat violently tampered with their memories. It was all to protect Sebastian but still, it was wrong.

"This was the only way to protect me?" he yelled, his whole body shaking. I shrank back from him, confused and afraid. I swayed dizzily on my feet. "Why, Caoilinn? Why? How could you do this to me?"

And that was when I realized that he had been listening on the other side of the cabin door, able to hear my whole conversation with the Others and drawing his own conclusions from it. He had heard me announce that I was Caoilinn and his mind, so confused already from the overwhelming amount of memories both past and present that I had caused him to remember, his mind had finally cracked. He couldn't separate me from her at all anymore.

His face was thunderous, his eyes nearly black and dead of any emotion except for the raw, all-consuming pain that burned up all the light and brightness within him. I began to shake, terrified of what I had done, afraid that he was about to strike me and even worse, afraid that I deserved it. He didn't hit me. He reached up with one hand and swept his hair back from his face, tugging hard against his scalp to reveal the tiny, thin black lines of the small and intricate tattoo above his temple. I gasped, feeling all of the blood drain from my face as I realized what he was thinking. The accusation in his eyes and his wild fury suddenly made sense.

"This isn't a tattoo from a design in your spell book. This is the mark left behind from one of your spells! You have lied to me about everything — *everything*. I can see now that my love for you was only ever a lie that you yourself made me believe. I will never forgive you for this," he pronounced in a voice so chilling and cold, I would never have recognized it as his own if we hadn't been standing face to face. He glared at me with such fierce, hateful eyes that I shrank back and within myself, too shocked and horrified to utter a single word in response.

"Sebastian… please…" I managed to choke out, miserable tears already washing down my face. I could hardly breathe from the pain in my chest, from the fear of him hating me forever. It was like a nightmare playing out before my eyes. I reached out to him desperately and my heart was severed from me in a way that felt excruciatingly permanent as he jerked away from my hand.

"Don't ever touch me again," he warned in a voice so deadly it gave me chills.

I stepped back, my legs going weak and my whole body numb as he moved past me and down the hallway towards the stairs. I let myself slide down to the floor, too stunned to think or speak — I could barely breathe as it was. Mags carefully stepped over me, flashing me one quick, almost pitiful look.

"I'll talk to him, he'll listen to me," she told me over her shoulder as she hurried after him. It didn't sound like much of a reassurance, her voice was too confident, her expression almost smug.

And then I was left alone.

I stared at the wall across from me, looking at the loose threads in the carpet's edge and the scuffs from passengers' shoes near the base of the wall. I sat there in numb silence, tears quietly flowing down my cheeks as I allowed the anguish inside of me to rise up and swallow me whole. I still couldn't quite process what had happened but as I sat there, staring at the wall, I forced myself to relieve events and to see it all from Sebastian's perspective.

Sebastian thought I was Caoilinn or at least, he thought she really was still alive inside of me. And I had just shown him a new, darker side to Caoilinn, confirming all of his recent suspicions. Since Caoilinn and myself were the only ones powerful enough and with the knowledge necessary to complete the memory altering spell, obviously Sebastian had realized that Caoilinn had altered his memories. And there was no way for me to either confirm or deny these suspicions.

I didn't know what the truth was anymore. I knew that I wasn't Caoilinn. I refused to admit that any part of her might be alive inside of me still but... I had been able to embody her somehow, however briefly. When I confronted the Others, I had felt like her – like I did in my dream memories. I had even started to talk like her and think like her but had it been no more than just playing a role? Could she really be alive still, somewhere inside of me? I didn't know what to think. I only knew that Sebastian was furious at Caoilinn, that the faith that he had held in his love for her for thousands of years had now been shattered. And that if he truly believed her to be a part of me, then part of his love for me had been permanently altered too. There was no turning back now, there was no hope for our future. I knew that I had now lost him forever.

At some point, my tears stopped and I dragged myself back into our cabin. I was surprised to find myself there, not completely aware of how or when I'd crawled between the doors and curled up on one of the small bench seats. Kulata was very close to the Greek border and I knew we'd be disembarking the train at Thessaloniki soon. I decided I would start preparing to get off the train. It only took a few minutes to pack up my things but it felt so good to be doing something that I began tidying the small compartment, picking lint up off the chairs and floor, restacking the magazines that had been left for us and ordering our empty pop cans beside the small garbage can – anything to keep my mind off of what had just happened.

There was a light and hesitant tap on the door that made me look up in surprise. I hurried over and slid the door open, unable to guess who might be knocking so timidly.

"May I come in?" Sebastian asked in a quiet yet calm voice. He still didn't quite meet my eye. I was shocked to see him standing there. I had never thought he would speak to me again so quickly, if even at all.

I nodded mutely, stepping far back so he had more than enough room to enter.

He hesitated for a moment before stepping inside, quickly shutting the door behind him. He gestured for me to sit and I immediately did so. He remained standing, shifting uneasily from foot to foot.

"I am furious with Caoilinn," he pronounced darkly, it was strange to see his expression twist so painfully at just the mention of her name. "But I shall try not to take it out on you. It is going to be hard, I can't seem to separate the two of you like I used to… but I don't want to blame you for her mistakes. I know we need to work together still." He finally looked at me, his eyes so clouded and confused, his emotions so complex that it was impossible for me to read them. He frowned, rubbing with his fingers at the headache that I could guess was building in his temple.

"Thank you. I don't want you to hate me. I'm so sorry for… for everything. I don't want you to hate me, no matter how I might deserve it," I whispered miserably, staring down at my hands. My heart still throbbed painfully but it wasn't quite as bad now that he was talking to me again, now that he wasn't yelling and glaring at me with his hate-filled eyes.

"I don't want to hate you," he answered quietly. He sat down beside me, a careful distance left between our bodies. "Gracelynn… I'm so confused. I know Mags loves me and I remember loving her once but I thought you loved me once too and I don't want to… I mean, I just want…"

The door smoothly slid open before he could finish and Mags strode in. She looked vaguely surprised to find us sitting so closely together. Irritation flickered in her emerald eyes.

"Did you apologize to her?" she demanded.

Sebastian blinked, immediately looking confused. He ran his fingers quickly through his hair.

"I think I did, didn't I?" he asked me, the quiet intensity with which he'd been speaking to me moments before having vanished.

I forced myself to smile at him as reassuringly as I was able to. I felt so horribly nauseous though. His obvious confusion and rapidly changing moods scared me and I feared for his sanity.

"You did," I softly assured him.

"And did you tell her?" Mags pushed.

I looked at Sebastian questioningly.

"Tell me what?"

He shifted almost uncomfortably before answering.

"In Thessaloniki, there's a Church not far from the train station – we'll be heading there first." Mags gave Sebastian an encouraging smile as she sat down in the seat across from me. I could tell already that I was not going to like what I was about to hear. "Mags thinks we should renew our marriage vows, that it may help break the bond I share with Caoilinn and reduce her influence over me. I want to know what memories it was that she altered and since there's almost always a loophole left behind by our magic…"

"No," I denied, surprised by the soft and calm quality to my voice despite the emotions raging and raving within me. "Your magic and the magic of the Others leaves loopholes, ways to possibly undo what you want to be done but Caoilinn's magic is different. It is as permanent as the marks on your body - on our bodies." I added, glancing down at the black tattoo of the Binding spell that twisted up and around my arm.

Sebastian hesitated, suddenly looking doubtful. Mags jumped in immediately.

"It's worth a try," she pointed out. "We're already married anyway, what harm could there be in renewing the vows that already bind us?"

She was right. There was no harm in them trying, other than the harm it would secretly and silently do to me. I couldn't object. I knew that Mags wanted to try and help Sebastian and that she also wanted to renew her vows and her commitment to him because of her love. How could I say I loved Sebastian, yet hate anyone who loved him?

If his choice was between her and I, I could no longer deny what the better, healthier choice for him to make would be. And how could I not want that? How could I not want for him to be happy, even if that happiness meant losing him forever?

"I'd like to try," Sebastian agreed.

I nodded. "Do whatever you want."

Mags eyed me strangely. She was probably surprised that I'd given up so easily but I really had given up now. I could see that the only possible future that I could or should want for Sebastian, was for him to be happy with someone else. It would be wrong, immoral even, for me to want anything else.

We gathered our things as the train began to slow and approached the station in Thessaloniki, Greece. I had been looking forward to getting off the train, to ending this horrible, travel nightmare but now that I knew where we were headed… Well, it didn't really matter. Nothing really mattered anymore. I felt utterly destroyed. My heart had been run through the blender too many times to ever rebuild the pieces. All that was left for me now was to keep Sebastian safe and to want the right thing. It was my only possible redemption.

The station at Thessaloniki reminded me of an airport. It was a small but busy place, bustling with travelers and tourists alike. It was fairly obvious that none of us were Greek but we didn't attract any unwanted notice, we wouldn't have even without our abilities. The train station itself was located in downtown Thessaloniki and we waited just outside the large front entrance of the station for a bus that would take us to the church Mags had in mind. As we stood sweating under the hot, midday sun, I stared silently straight ahead, ignoring all the sights and sounds around me and concentrating on holding myself together and fighting the strange sensation of the solid ground swaying beneath me with the same steady rhythm of the train.

"Perfect! This one will do," Mags announced as a large city bus pulled into the pick-up/drop-off zone. She grabbed Sebastian by the hand and pulled him along as the bus came to a slow stop before us – her and Sebastian were the first two to board.

I let the crowds push ahead of me and stumbled onto the bus

last, reluctantly taking the only empty seat left that just happened to be immediately behind Sebastian and Mags. I stared at his messy, black hair that shone under the sun streaming in through the window. I studied the back of his neck, the hint of his tattoo that coiled up and out of the neck of his t-shirt, his broad shoulders and the small, dark earrings that looped through his ears. Every time I saw Mags lean closer to him, each word she whispered into his ear with a flirtatious smile lighting up her beautiful face, every tilt of her head that caused the waves of her red-gold hair to crash against his black locks, every joyful smile and gesture she made before me only increased and deepened my pain, extended my agony. And still I watched. Still I forced myself to look at them, and only them, for the duration of our ride.

It was a short eternity later when the bus came to a stop and Mags stood up. She and Sebastian didn't even check to see if I followed them as they rose from their shared seat and made their way to the front of the bus, Mags' hand firmly clasping Sebastian's once more. I followed them reluctantly. I had no choice.

I hadn't paid much attention to my surroundings since we'd disembarked the train but I forced myself to look around now. The street we found ourselves on in Greece was full of character and life, a unique blend of modern and ancient Greek architecture, frescoes and sculptures.

The street we were now walking down was wide and paved, with sidewalks and buildings that rose up at least two stories high on both sides of the street. There were restaurants and coffee shops mixed in with stores and the occasional pub, hostel and hotel. I guessed that this would be the district we'd be staying in, if we were even going to stay here. Mags still hadn't told me the exact location of The Order's head temple in Greece. I had no idea of what her plans were beyond this "renew our vows" idea.

"There's the church," Mags announced happily. She gestured down the street to a small church that was nestled in between two old buildings just before the street curved away and around the corner. The church itself was a brick building with one small spire rising up from it. There was a set of ten or so concrete steps that led up to the large, wooden front doors. A large cross on the tip of the spire flared gold in the sun and the sign near the street announced the church to be of the Christian Orthodox faith.

"Let's go find the minister," Mags suggested as she began practically skipping towards the stairs. In her joy, she didn't immediately notice that Sebastian hadn't followed. It even took me a second to realize that he had hesitated near me, pausing at the bottom of the stairway and suddenly watching me with his beautiful, ancient eyes.

For a moment I was struck by how intensely sad he looked. I could remember a time when his eyes had always smiled at me, when they had sparkled with such joy and youthful hope that he could literally raise my spirits with just one look. Now I couldn't remember the last time he had looked that way. My sadness sank impossibly deeper within me, combining and intertwining with his own.

"Do you want to wait outside?" Sebastian asked me quietly, a tinge of familiar concern in his eyes. "You don't need to be here for this and it won't take long."

I immediately shook my head.

"I want to hear your vows," I answered honestly, my voice emotionless and yet still bleeding with pain. I wanted to hear him renew his vows to Mags, to sever all ties to me, to know that he was happy and to allow my heart to permanently break. "The only thing I want is for you to be happy, nothing else matters anymore," I added in a hushed and lowered voice, not wanting for Mags to hear.

And I realized it was true. I just wanted Sebastian to be happy — whatever that meant or entailed. I could survive anything, just as long as I knew it was what he honestly and truly wanted. There was nothing with the power to hurt me now that I had given him up. I had no more fears or reservations. I calmly and sadly accepted the truth into my heart and I was no longer afraid of what he may or may not want; I wasn't afraid of the past and what was or wasn't true. I wasn't even afraid of the Others anymore. I was only afraid to see him keep living with that sad and empty look in his eyes.

In that moment, I just wanted him to be happy with my whole heart and soul. It wasn't completely selfless of me either for it was far easier to want him to be happy than to want him to be with Mags, even if it meant the same thing. I knew that my motivations were selfish to some extent and I readily admitted that to myself as I tried to accept my flaws along with everything else. And so that was what I chose to focus on. It was both a burden and a relief to stop making myself want what I thought was the right thing and to just want what I knew was right – Sebastian's happiness.

"Sebastian, come on," Mags urged from the top of the stairs.

The sad and distant moment between us ended. His eyes brightened slightly, refocusing on my face with a sudden intensity that was both familiar and frightening. I could see the emotions boiling deep down within him, the sadness, the confusion, the loneliness, the betrayal and the anger – the pure fury of his rage towards Caoilinn. He nodded to me, his gaze steady and intense, and then turned and began walking up the stairs towards Mags, his back to me - perhaps forever. Despite wanting his happiness so very, very badly, I still dragged my feet as I followed.

The inside of the church was cool and silent. We stepped into a small entranceway with fresh flowers in several large vases spaced about the small room and an open book with a pen for visitors to sign. There was a large, carved cross hanging directly opposite the entrance doors and the entranceway was lit up with a warm, golden light that filtered down through the skylights above. Mags latched herself onto Sebastian's hand again and pulled him through the entranceway and to the double doors that led into the church beyond. I took a deep breath as if preparing to plunge under water, and then followed.

As soon as I stepped into the church, I was overwhelmed by the familiar sense of peace and power that all churches seemed to possess. It made my breath catch and the fine hairs on my arms stand on end. It was similar to the way I had felt at the Giant's Ring in many regards and I struggled to fight back the wonderful and painful memories that stirred in my chest. There was a definite feel to this place that marked it as a holy place, a place for worship, a place to be closer to God, a place where no vow could or would ever be spoken lightly. For a moment, we were all silent and awed.

"May I help you?" a tall, dark-haired man asked as he turned from the holy altar where he had been lighting candles.

"I'll go speak with him," Sebastian murmured to Mags but in a voice just loud enough for me to hear also. "I'd like for him to use specific vows, the same ones that we first spoke to one another so long ago."

Mags beamed as Sebastian strolled down one of the aisles and approached the minister with a smile on his face, already speaking fluently to him in Greek.

I looked about the church with wide eyes, hardly daring to step too far within its holy sanctuary. The interior was larger than it had appeared from the outside. There were at least thirty rows of pews with two aisles dividing them into three sections. The ceiling rose up high above us, a smooth and white arch beyond the curved and exposed beams. At the front of the church was a large and beautifully arranged wooden altar, behind which a massive sculpture seemed to grow out of the wall itself, depicting Jesus crucified on the cross. I felt both awed and slightly afraid by the intensity of this sacred place.

Sebastian turned and gestured to Mags, urging her to come forward. His eyes seemed to take me in too as he beckoned to us both and as always, I was unable to resist. I knew deep down in my heart that I needed to witness this and I would not back down now. And so I followed Mags to the front of the church and slid quietly into the second row pew, reaching for the bible tucked into the back of the row in front of me automatically and squeezing it tightly in my hands.

The minister announced something in Greek, in a deep and resonant voice. He moved to stand before the altar, Mags and Sebastian following him. My heart had begun picking up in pace and was now throbbing painfully in my chest, practically hammering against my ribs as if it were about to explode.

I tried to remind myself why I must want this, why Sebastian's happiness was so important to me. I knew how I didn't deserve him. I hadn't wanted to believe it before but there was no denying it now. I hadn't wanted to admit that Caoilinn was a part of me but she was. I could see Caoilinn in myself; I could feel her in both my weaknesses and my strengths. And I wasn't afraid to see my weaknesses, to admit I had flaws and to accept them as a part of me too. I had been raised to believe I was perfect and that I was somehow better than those around me and it had always felt like a lie, but I think a small part of me had wanted to believe it nonetheless. Part of me had wanted to be perfect, to be good and to be innocent, to live apart and above the flaws of others. I could see now that I wasn't perfect – that I was so far from perfect it was almost laughable. And though I may not deserve Sebastian, he did deserve to be happy.

A calm, acceptance washed over me as the minister began to speak.

"We are here today to remember the sacred vows you spoke before God, within the house of God, that tied you to one another as husband and wife," the minister began, surprising me by speaking in English, his tone serious and somber, his heavily accented voice echoing throughout the silence of the empty church. Mags smiled at Sebastian encouragingly, reaching for his hand but surprisingly, he brushed her aside, giving a small, disapproving shake of his head. "These vows were not to be taken upon lightly and marked a lifetime commitment to one another, a commitment you have not fulfilled."

It took me a second to really hear what the minister had just said. I could see the shock and confusion on Mags' face as the meaning of the words sunk in.

"What are you–" Mags began to ask but Sebastian cut her off firmly.

"I don't want you to speak. Just listen."

It was what I wanted too. I was filled with a sudden desperate and sickening curiosity. And so Mags had no choice but to be quiet and to listen.

I held my breath as the minister continued. Hardly daring to hope, not knowing or understanding what was happening other than the fact that I knew this wasn't my doing, not directly or intentionally at least.

"Under the grace of God, in the name of God, by the authority invested in me by the Orthodox Christian Church of Greece, I disavow the marital vows spoken between Sebastian Mattias Caldwood and Magdalene Bridget Driscoll. With the power invested in me and under the eyes of God, I pronounce your marriage to be annulled. May you never enter into its commitment lightly again," the Minister finished in a stern and disapproving voice.

All of the color had drained from Mags' face. She stood there, absolutely speechless with her mouth hanging open. Sebastian was expressionless still, as calm and collected as if this were a daily occurrence for him. I couldn't believe what had just happened. Was it real? Was it true? In just a few seconds could Sebastian's marriage to Mags really be over?

"Are you satisfied?" the minister asked Sebastian.

"Yes, thank you."

"Remember that your marriage is only annulled in the eyes of God, any legal commitments you may have made to one another still stand."

"Yes, I understand. We made no other commitments. Thank you for your time," Sebastian politely answered. The minister gave a quick nod, looking annoyed still, and then strode away down the aisle.

"What have you done?" Mags demanded, spinning to face me with fury in her eyes. "You bitch! I should never have trusted you! How can you do this to Sebastian? How can you say you ever loved him when you obviously want to destroy any chance of happiness he has?"

"I didn't want this," I objected. There was a steady power behind my words that made Mags pause and listen. "I thought he wanted to renew his vows to you so that was what I wanted too. I want whatever he wants; I only want for him to be happy."

"This was what I wanted," Sebastian pronounced darkly. He glared at Mags and then turned to glare with only slightly less ferocity at me. "You have both been 'wanting' what you think is right for me for too long. You've been pushing me into the wrong decisions and confusing my thoughts, my wants and my desires at every minute. You both stole the decisions from me that were mine and mine alone to make - until now. I think Gracelynn must have finally realized that the only course of action is to want for me to be happy above and beyond all else."

Mags and I both stared at Sebastian in shock. I couldn't believe what I was hearing. Had I done it again? Had I unintentionally manipulated him and forced my own wants upon him? I was both horrified and strangely relieved.

"You, I can forgive." He spoke to me more softly. The anger was still there in his eyes but the outrage was gone. I could see how I'd hurt him, see how I'd confused and betrayed him but I could also see that somehow, impossibly so, he did actually love me still. My heart rejoiced as it came pounding back to life, tearing its way back into my chest and up through the darkness and desolation that had weighed down upon it. My heart ached painfully but it was incomparable to the torment I had been suffering mere moments before. There were still so many mistakes I had made, so many wrongs I had done but I accepted them now and to know that Sebastian saw and accepted my mistakes and flaws too was all I had ever truly wanted but never dared hope for.

"I have wanted the wrong thing for you before too. What we think is best is not always… what we…" he frowned in confusion, still not quite back to his old self. He gave a quick shake of his head, squinting at me slightly as if he had another headache. "There's so much to say Gracelynn and so much for both of us to understand and remember and confess, and hopefully to forgive… But you," he turned to Mags who had now dropped down to her knees. Fear filled her eyes as Sebastian turned to her with a powerful fury in his.

"You tried to make me forget, you tried to trick me again as you did three hundred years ago and I will never – ever, forgive you for it. This time I will never forget who you truly are, Madailein Driscoll," he coldly pronounced.

"No," Mags gasped, her eyes widening in horror as she looked in panic back and forth between Sebastian and myself. The name was oddly familiar, sparking a reaction deep down within my core that flared and twisted angrily in my gut. What did that name mean?

"I remember everything now – *everything*. All the memories that you tried to steal and take away from me, how you betrayed and manipulated me for hundreds of years all in the name of your twisted Sisterhood and their dying wish."

"What are you talking about?" I asked. I was so confused. I struggled to keep up, to understand what was going on.

Sebastian turned to me with an angry fire still burning in his eyes. "Madailein is not and was never the first of the Others to join me.

But she was the last of the Sisterhood to come after you."

Chapter Fourteen – Scars and Fresh Wounds

"What?" I gasped. I could hear Mags breathing quickly – almost panting now, her eyes darting about wildly as if she were looking for a way to escape. She was starting to slowly rise to her knees, her eyes glistening with near madness. "Stop," I commanded in that firm yet sweet voice that demanded to be obeyed. She froze in her tracks. "Ever since Sebastian first told me about my past life, when I was once Caoilinn, I have been afraid of the past, afraid of the magic I possess, afraid of who I really am and afraid of what the truth about me may be. But I'm not afraid anymore. I want to know the truth – the whole truth. You will sit and explain yourself to me now."

There was no doubt in my mind about what I wanted anymore. I wasn't even remotely surprised when Mags sat back down on the step before the altar and sullenly folded her arms across her chest, glaring at me with her tear-filled eyes.

I stood up and moved to the very front pew, sitting just a few feet in front of her. I was both surprised and pleased when Sebastian came and sat beside me, close enough that his shoulder brushed against mine.

"Who are you?"

I watched as Mags fought my will and tried to deny my wants. My magic was far too strong. Her mouth twisted angrily, tears spilled from her eyes but her lips began to move and the truth was slowly dragged from her.

"My name is Madailein Driscoll. I was the last Priestess anointed to the Sisterhood and I was to be the next to receive the Lost Magic from you. You never deigned me worthy enough for your notice though – not until the day we came for you and then the knife in my hand was impossible for you to ignore," she coldly sneered.

My whole body went numb as a vision flashed before my eyes - Mags' face leaning over mine, a cruel smile twisting her pretty features as she wiped away a drop of blood that had splattered against her cheek. The stars and moon were so bright, the world shimmered hazily under their eerie light. The scent of lavender perfumed the air and a drop of silver dew slid slowly down a blade of grass beside my face, a tearful goodbye as my breath shuddered from my lips. The cold world faded away and darkened…

"She was one of the Sisters who murdered Caoilinn," Sebastian growled beside me. His whole body had become so tense that I placed a cautioning hand on his thigh without thinking. He relaxed slightly at my touch but Mags flinched at the sight, her eyes flashing dangerously.

"You deserved to die," Mags spat at me. "You manipulated Seamus, you abused your power, you betrayed your Sisters – your crimes were limitless!"

"Is that the truth, Mags, or is that just what you want to believe?" I asked her quietly and calmly. She didn't answer, instead she glared silently at the floor. "If Caoilinn did not grant you your powers, and Sebastian didn't start creating the Others for several hundred years after Caoilinn's death… how is it that you are here now?" I questioned.

She answered without hesitation. "When we discovered that Seamus had escaped and your body and spell book were missing, we guessed at what you had done. We realized we had been too late and that you had already given the Lost Magic to him. The Sisters did not know how to grant me the same abilities as theirs but they did find a way to give up and combine their abilities. They sacrificed their magic to make me strong enough to hunt Seamus and to hunt your reincarnated soul, to keep you apart and to stop the secrets of the Lost Magic from falling into the wrong hands. The only spell I was strong enough to use, the only one the Sisterhood had understood was the memory-altering spell and even then, I could only make small alterations to the minds of others. I tried so hard to be strong, to be the

perfect Sister and to bring honor to the temple and the Gods but…
I was weak," Mags whispered to the floor. She briefly glanced up at
me, her eyes filled with hate at how I was forcing her to admit her
weaknesses and reveal all her secrets.

"I hunted Seamus for hundreds of years but he always escaped
me. He didn't want to be caught and I'm sure that you, wherever
your soul was in that time between death and rebirth, didn't want for
him to be caught either. There were a few times I came close, close
enough to watch him, to get to know him from his movements, his
actions… and I started to fall in love."

She looked up at Sebastian, tears shining brightly in her eyes. It
was a moving sight, her shining green eyes, her pale, freckled skin,
her trembling full lips all framed by waves of golden-red hair as she
shifted to kneel before him.

"I loved you too much to ever be able to hurt you, Sebastian. I
saw how kind you were, how lonely. I realized how you were just an
innocent pawn in all of this, how Caoilinn had used and betrayed you
as much as she had the Sisterhood. It took me another hundred years
to decide but eventually I knew what I wanted and what I must do."

"You lied to me. You deceived me. You manipulated and brain-
washed me," Sebastian accused in a soft and deadly voice.

Mags flinched away from him, shaking her head in denial.

"I wanted to be your friend, your companion — and I was. I didn't
want to hurt you by letting you discover the truth, so I let you think
that I was normal when we first met. I let you believe what you
wanted, that you loved me enough you had made me like you. And
then once we were close enough, once I had gotten to know you as
intimately as I do now, it was easy for me to make you see the truth."

I could tell she believed every word that she was speaking, no
matter how deranged and distorted the truth. My stomach twisted
and bitter acid burned the back of my throat. I tried not to think too
much about what she had just said but the words and their meaning
echoed through and through my mind, bouncing off my brain and
clashing through my head painfully, intimately…

"What about the Others?" I spoke a little too loudly, my voice
echoing ominously around the large, empty church.

"We created them together," Mags announced, smiling almost timidly at Sebastian. He glared back, his eyes black and unyielding. "Seamus was so unhappy searching for you, he was so lonely that I knew it was the right thing to do. It was what I wanted for him."

"And?" I demanded, sensing that there was more.

Her eyes narrowed at me briefly before she reluctantly continued. "I knew it would be best for him to forget about Caoilinn, he was starting to already but I needed numbers on my side. I needed the Others to help make him forget. It was my idea to create them and mostly my own magic and wants that did so."

Sebastian let out his breath in a sharp hiss. I could tell this was new information to him. I could hardly imagine how he was feeling in that moment but I pushed onwards, needing to hear the whole truth for once and praying that somehow I would understand it.

"We were so happy for a while. We were surrounded by the Others - our friends, our companions who were like family to us, and we had each other. You were finally forgetting Caoilinn and falling in love with me. The world was our playground and we could have whatever we wanted, whenever we wanted. I wanted you to be happy, we all did, so we wanted you to live without fear, without guilt, without being held back by consequences."

Sebastian began trembling beside me, his whole body vibrating from the emotions rising and building within him. "You were the one who manipulated me, who controlled me. You used me and the Others. The things we did... the unconscionable way we all lived..."

"Yes, I encouraged it. Once we had been intimate, I was able to direct your wants so much more easily. I made sure you wanted the right thing, I helped steer you in the right direction. I was only strong enough to alter a few of your memories of Caoilinn, just enough to place doubts in your mind, to make you forget the images from her spell book that were hidden in your tattoos. It was easy to lead you to the truth – you'd already had your doubts about her. We all wanted a better life for you than the one she had trapped you in because we knew you'd never be selfish enough to want it for yourself. It was what you needed. You were so happy once you forgot her – you wanted to forget her. You even asked us yourself to erase the last of your memories of Caoilinn and we did. You married me and took a new name, forgetting and moving forward from your former, miserable self," Mags was half-smiling as she spoke, a wistful expression on her face. It sickened me to my core.

"It was you who altered my memories?" Sebastian questioned in a dangerously quiet voice.

"It was the only spell I knew, the only one the Sisters knew to teach me. You needed to forget your "quest", to let Caoilinn go and move on. And it was too painful for you to remember her the way you did, perfect and innocent and faithful. The memory of her was torturing you on a daily basis. I freed you," Mags replied with a small shrug.

"You lied to me. You stole my memories, you tampered with my mind!"

"No," Mags denied adamantly shaking her head.

"But he started to remember Caoilinn. You made a mistake in the design," I jumped-in, filling in the gaps from her story with the limited knowledge I had. I needed her to keep talking, I needed to hear all of it. Now that I was ready to hear and face the truth, I wanted to understand it all.

"Yes, a small one," Mags answered bitterly. "It was the only design I knew but I could never get it quite right. The memories should have been completed altered but your dreams kept influencing you, and you were suspicious of the truth. And that Binding spell was stronger than I'd ever realized. When Caoilinn was reborn, if Sebastian were even within a few hundred miles of her, he would start to remember and he'd start to draw strength from her through the Bond. The Others realized she must be close and started to question whether we should keep you two apart, whether perhaps we should find Caoilinn and learn more about our magic from her. I was afraid they were starting to want the wrong thing. You had started to question our ways already, Seamus. You had already decided that creating the Others might have been a mistake so when I suggested we block their memories of us and run away, to start our lives anew together, you easily agreed."

"But you underestimated how close David and I had become,"

Sebastian stated in a cold, flat voice. "He was like a brother to me. He wanted me to escape from you – he told me who you were and he willingly let me block his memories so that you would not suspect his betrayal. And now he hates me for it, he blames me for it all even though he was the one who told me how you had manipulated me, how you had encouraged the Others to manipulate me also, how you had confused my thoughts and made me forget Caoilinn and my quest. I should have killed you."

"No," Mags whispered in shock. "No, you would never want that. You couldn't."

"I couldn't go through with it," he agreed, sounding angry and ashamed. "The strength of our abilities were almost perfectly matched. You didn't want me to leave but I wanted to be as far from you as possible. Our conflicting wants cancelled each other out. You'd manipulated me so thoroughly with your magic that the only way I could forget you was to convince myself you were dead. And so I was able to run and run, as far from you as possible, wanting to forget you and the Others and everything else. I was so sickened by what I had become, by what I had done, by how many people I had hurt and betrayed." Sebastian's voice began to tremor. I could virtually feel the pain and darkness radiating out from him as he remembered.

"And so you hibernated," I finished. "That was the horrible thing that happened that you could never remember. It was what made you want to hide from the past and from the world for hundreds of years, buried beneath ice and snow." Mags looked at me strangely, obviously surprised by this revelation. I remembered how shocked I had been when Sebastian had first told me of his hibernation. And now it seemed to make such perfect sense in a crazy and distorted sort of way. "And what about you? What did you do after Sebastian left?"

"I searched for him," Mags calmly replied. "I looked everywhere I could think of. I wanted to find him so badly but I never did. I kept an eye on the Others from a distance and once it was clear that they were starting to remember Sebastian, I approached them."

A quiet gasp of shock escaped my lips before I could stop it. Mags sneered at me before continuing.

"I negotiated a deal with The Order. I would bring you to them,

Caoilinn, and Sebastian could go free. Those two idiots in Kulata nearly ruined it all. The Order must not have trusted I would follow through on my promises. I was to bring you to the ceremony in three nights time where I would assist The Order in attempting to strip you of your powers and your life."

A chill ran down my spine as she spoke.

Sebastian stood, an expression on his face that I had never seen before, an expression that welcomed death and destruction, his fury immeasurable and awesome.

"You were going to hurt Gracelynn?"

He spoke softly but his tone was terrifying. Mags somehow became even paler. She shook her head, her wavy hair bouncing off her shoulders but no words reaching her lips.

"Caoilinn had many secrets but her love for me was pure," Sebastian continued. "But you - you tarnished my memories of her, you stole and manipulated my thoughts and you tore away a piece of who I am. You took everything from me, all in the name of some sick and twisted love. You tricked me into creating the Others and living an unforgivable life that haunts me still. You destroyed me!" he thundered, his voice booming around the room. The candles on the altar flickered, the pews began to tremble. "And you tried to keep me and Gracelynn apart. Despite what Caoilinn may or may not have done – it is Gracelynn who I love now and nothing else matters. That you tried once again to make me doubt her, to make me question my love for her – you would have destroyed any hope of happiness I ever had! And then you planned to kill her? To betray us all? I swear it Madailein, you will pay for this!" he raged.

I wasn't certain what Sebastian was doing, but I knew I needed to step in fast before he wanted something to happen to Mags that he most certainly would regret. It was difficult to think rationally as I was nearly as furious as he. To realize how Mags had lied to and used Sebastian, to see how much pain and darkness she had caused him and how close she had come to leading me to my death – it was unforgivable. I knew in my heart that she deserved to die for all she had done.

I stepped forward, reaching for her with a steady hand. My necklace blazed and burned against my chest as the fury raged in my heart.

And I realized then that it was not just my anger fueling my actions but it was also Caoilinn's and Sebastian's and even the Others' as they had been betrayed not by Sebastian, but by Mags. Mags was the cause of Sebastian's nightmares, of his guilt, she was to blame for everything – even the dire situation that we faced now. Mags had hurt too many people, she had told too many lies and abused her power, and she deserved to pay.

"Please," she whispered as I grabbed her face firmly by the jaw, glaring down upon her. Her smooth, ageless skin was ash-white, her eyes huge and round, tears streaking down her lightly freckled cheeks. "Please."

"Gracelynn," I heard Sebastian say from behind me in a tight but calm voice. I felt him move forward and knew he was reaching to stop me. But he was far too late.

"Goodbye, Madailein Driscoll," I murmured without emotion.

"Stop!" Sebastian cried out as Mags' eyes rolled back into her head and her body slumped to the ground. "NO! Gracelynn, stop! Don't do it!" he yelled, wrapping his arms around me from behind and pulling me back from Mags.

I blinked, confused and disoriented as a wave of exhaustion hit me. I fell weakly back into his arms, allowing him to pull me down onto the pew where I leant against him heavily.

"Oh, Gracelynn no," he whispered into my hair. "No. Why did you do it?"

I couldn't make sense of what he was saying.

"Why did I do what?"

"Mags. Why did you have to kill her?"

"What?" I shook my head, struggling to find the strength to sit up. I turned to him in confusion, glad that his warm and firm arms were around me still.

"She may have deserved to die but how could you do it? You know the toll it took on you when you had to kill Walter but to do it again… there must have been another way," he quietly murmured, his blue-gray eyes sad and heavy with regret. He kept glancing at me with a strange expression on his face, like he didn't really know who I was.

I pushed away from him, sitting up on my own and scowling in annoyance. "I didn't kill her."

His eyes widened in surprise and disbelief.

"I didn't – check for yourself if you want to. She'll be awake again soon. Her mind was just too shocked to remain conscious," I explained. I swallowed down the hurt feelings that were rising within me. How could he think I killed her? I had told him I would never, ever use that spell again – hadn't I? Did he no longer trust me at all?

"Her mind was too shocked by what?"

He was definitely looking at me strangely now. My eyelids were growing heavier and the church was starting to spin around me. I could feel myself slipping away from the conscious world and struggled to speak, to answer him.

"By the loss of her memories – she won't remember much beyond her name now. She can cause no more harm," I tiredly assured him. I started to slip out of my seat, my body sliding weakly downwards as if I were melting. Sebastian grabbed me before I hit the floor, gently pulling me up and into his arms. I had forgotten how wonderful, how truly amazing just his embrace could be and I relaxed, closing my eyes and resting my heavy head against his chest.

"How long for?"

"Hmm?" I asked sleepily. My thoughts were thickening, my brain slowing down as I fell towards the silent darkness. Sebastian's voice carried to me, chasing me into that quiet, peaceful place and as always, demanding to be heard.

"How long will she forget for?"

I sighed, mumbling out the answer as I let myself fall deeper into the darkness, deep enough that he wouldn't find me, at least for a while. "Forever."

I AWOKE SLOWLY, opening my eyes a fraction of an inch at a time. I was aware that I had awoken in an unfamiliar place, the scent of wood polish and fresh flowers just barely present in the air. I automatically sensed that this was a safe place, one of healing and peace. I could feel the calmness of this place sinking into my bones and soothing my torn and aching heart.

It was so quiet and peaceful, that at first I thought I was alone but then I realized even though my body was lying along a hard, unyielding surface, my head was supported by the firm warmth of someone's leg. My heart skipped a beat as my mind caught up to the present and I realized where I was and who I was with. In that same instant, I remembered everything that had just happened. My eyes flew open.

I was lying along a pew with my head in Sebastian's lap and looking straight up at the high, arched, bright white ceiling above me. The memories came back to me like a flash of light, momentarily blinding my eyes and piercing my mind. My lips parted in a nearly-silent gasp.

"You're awake," Sebastian quietly commented. He was looking down at me now, his eyes a hazy shade of gray. He looked exhausted and sad and somehow, happy to see me. "You collapsed. Are you feeling alright now?" He gently smoothed my hair back from my face as he carefully studied my expression.

"I think I'm fine. Is Mags…?" I whispered, my voice sounding far too loud still within the church's peaceful sanctuary.

"She's still sleeping."

"Oh." I pushed myself up and off Sebastian's lap so that I sat on the pew beside him. For several long seconds we both stared straight ahead, the daunting image of Jesus on the cross rising up behind the altar before us. I managed to get my emotions somewhat under control before I spoke again. "Sebastian, I'm not sure what Mags will be like when she wakes up. I was so angry and I acted instinctively – I'm not even sure what exactly I did. I just know she won't remember much of the past… probably nothing. She might not even know who she is."

He didn't immediately answer. I glanced at him sideways to read his expression but was distracted by the sight of Mags, laid out along the pew just a few feet away from him. She slept so peacefully, so innocently… I could hardly believe what I had done to her.

"I don't know how you did it either. There aren't any markings on her."

"No," I agreed, already knowing that there wouldn't be. "This spell didn't require a design because I wasn't changing anything or twisting the way fate is meant to play out. I was removing her memories, severing her from her past. There is a permanent mark that has been left on her mind but we won't see it or know the full extent of the damage I've done until she wakes up."

Sebastian flinched at my harsh words but even though I was ashamed and uncertain about what I had done, I refused to lie or downplay the details to him. From now on, I wanted nothing but the whole and all-encompassing truth between us.

"It's no less than she deserved but still…"

We sat in silence a while longer, Sebastian's words hanging in the air and haunting my thoughts. There was barely an inch of space left between us on the pew but right now, it felt like that gap were a mile wide.

"Everything that's happened – it's hard to believe," I commented, thinking of Mags and the shocking truths she had shared.

"Yes," Sebastian agreed. "I never realized how confusing it could be to have someone else's wants influencing your own so powerfully. It's daunting to feel so powerless and to have those choices taken away from you… I'm sorry I ever did that to you, when I once tried to make you forget me. It's still so hard for me to understand how you could do it to me." There was no accusation in his voice, just an intense hurt that throbbed with each word he spoke.

He stared straight ahead, refusing to look my way but I sat and waited patiently until he finally met my teary eyes.

"I was so afraid of what the truth might be, I didn't want to know it," I tried to explain. "I thought you just loved me because Caoilinn's magic was making you feel that way and I didn't want that. It felt like every time I tried to help, every choice I made was hurting you somehow and I was so afraid I was using you just like I thought she had. I didn't want you to love me – I didn't love myself anymore. I thought Mags could make you happy, that she would be better for you. I thought you wanted to be with her so that's what I tried to want to."

"And that's exactly what she wanted," he agreed, a slight bitter twist to his words. "There was just enough hesitation in you though that I had moments of clarity – and periods of intense confusion. I never stopped loving you but I could feel you pushing me away. I thought you didn't want to be with me anymore because of my past, because of the mistakes I had made – because of Mags. However misguided, I did love her, once upon a time and she wanted me to remember that. There must have been a small enough part of me that wanted to be happy with her again that she was able to push me towards the wrong decision – with your help. It never felt right though. Life doesn't make sense without you. How could it?"

"I thought I was doing the right thing. I thought it was what you wanted," I whispered.

"You were wrong. How could you ever doubt my love for you?"

"But with everything Mags had revealed about Caoilinn, combined with what I'd experienced in my dreams when I was remembering her life…"

"This has nothing to do with Caoilinn," he stated firmly and quietly. He reached over the invisible barrier between us and took up my left hand. Somehow, the beautiful, silver engagement ring that had been hidden in the bottom of my bag had reappeared in his hand. "And it has everything to do with us. How many times must I tell you that I love *you*, Gracelynn Stevenson? I love you more than life, more than death, more than love itself. I love absolutely everything about you, how innocent and naïve and wise and stupid you can be. And I can never, ever, live without you. So please, don't ever try to make me again." And with that, he slipped the small, silver ring back onto my ring finger, squeezing my hand tightly in his. "I am not asking you again – I am telling you. I will marry you, whether you want to marry me anymore or not," he added with a small smile that twisted up the corner of his mouth.

"How can you still love me, after everything I've done?" I wondered aloud as I gazed down at the beautiful ring on my finger and the beautiful hands encircling mine.

"I don't know but somehow I still do. It's impossible for me not to. Don't think I've forgiven you though," he warned, semi-sternly. His eyes darkened as he gazed into mine.

"I won't," I promised quite seriously. I would never let myself forget what I had done, what terrible mistakes I had made. And I would spend eternity, if necessary, regaining his trust and making it up to him.

"About that spell though," he continued on in a lighter tone, "how are you certain that Mags' memory loss will be permanent? The magic has never worked that way before."

"You told me once yourself that Caoilinn's magic is different than yours and the Others'– and you were right. My spells are permanent, there are no loopholes left to be undone unless I choose for there to be."

Sebastian cocked his head at me, his expression puzzled.

"Like your ring," I explained, my fingers twisting around in his to stroke the warm metal of the thick ring that encircled his finger. "Caoilinn created it so that there was a way out for you, should you ever want to leave her and be 'normal' again. Of course, there was no turning back after she cast the Binding spell," I admitted guiltily. It still bothered me that she had knowingly bound him to her at the moment of her death, increasing his pain and his loneliness for centuries to come.

"I wonder though… if there are loopholes in the magic of the Others, including yours, then shouldn't there be a way to undo what you and Mags have done?" I continued my train of thoughts aloud.

Sebastian frowned, not following me for once. "What do you mean?"

"The magic of the Others was all a result of yours and Mags' wants – so their ability can't be permanent. You were the only one who was granted powers by Caoilinn herself but the rest… there should be a way to strip them of their abilities," I concluded.

Sebastian considered this, his expression thoughtful.

"It's possible," he conceded.

I was certain I was right. I could feel the truth behind my words as I spoke them. There had to be a way to undo the magic of the Others… but how?

"I can try to summon Caoilinn's memories in my dreams somehow. If there was a way, she must have known," I suggested nervously. Sebastian immediately shook his head.

"She didn't know how to take back the magic. She said it was permanent and I know she was speaking the truth."

"The magic that she had granted you may have been," I objected. "But not the magic that you and Mags gave to the Others."

"But Mags' magic was from Caoilinn. It was the magic Caoilinn had given to the Sisters, passed on to Mags," Sebastian argued.

"Perhaps that changed it?"

"Perhaps." He sounded doubtful.

My brows twitched downwards but I kept my expression light. I didn't want to argue just then, especially when I knew I was right.

"How's Mags?" I asked, changing the subject.

Sebastian smiled, a little ruefully perhaps, and turned to examine the girl.

"She's awakening."

I peered around him and saw that it was true. Her eyelids were just starting to flutter, her head slowly turning from side to side. I found myself holding my breath as she opened her eyes, relieved to see that they were clear and focused. She looked first at Sebastian, then at me, and then she frowned.

"Sebastian? Grace?" she asked uncertainly. Neither of us spoke. I was both shocked and relieved that she knew our names. She struggled to sit up, looking around completely puzzled. "Why the hell am I sleeping in a church?" she demanded, looking at us for answers.

"How much do you remember?" I asked, avoiding her question. She scowled down at the floor.

"Well… we were traveling together on a train and we were on our way to Greece, weren't we? Are we here now? Weren't we supposed to meet up with someone? Friends of yours or… something?"

"Sort of," Sebastian hedged. He glanced to me incredulously.

"How did we meet?" I demanded. I wanted her to answer immediately and she did.

"We met in Berlin, right? I think… I think you guys needed a place to stay and came to my apartment. Yeah, that's right. Then we decided to go to Greece together, didn't we? It's so hard to remember… My head is effin' killing me!" She grimaced, reaching up to massage at her temple.

"Where were you born?"

"I… well, I'm from Ireland. Is that how we know each other?" she asked, looking at Sebastian questioningly.

"How did you get to Berlin? Who are your parents? Who are you?" I drilled.

"My name… is Magdalene Driscoll and I… Damn it! I don't know how I… I just don't know!" she snapped in frustration, squeezing both of her eyes tightly shut.

"That's enough," Sebastian murmured, placing his hand lightly on my arm.

"I just need to make sure–"

"I know," he assured me. "But she doesn't remember."

"Why can't I remember?" Mags demanded, a touch of anger to her voice as she glared up at us.

"Because I made you forget," I responded honestly.

"Why?"

"Because you wanted to forget," Sebastian jumped in. I appreciated him telling the lie for me, my guilt was already difficult enough to bear. "There are people chasing us – chasing you and it was too dangerous to continue on with you knowing what you did, so we erased your memory." Again, I felt a wash of gratitude at his use of the word 'we'.

"Oh." Mags seemed to believe Sebastian but she obviously didn't understand still. "But how did you erase my memory? Did I hit my head?" She began raking her fingers through her hair, searching her scalp for bumps or lacerations.

"We'll explain it all to you tonight – we need to find a place to stay and figure out a plan," I told her.

"Are we meeting your friends tonight?" she asked, her scowl suddenly brightening. "Wasn't there some kind of party or celebration that we were coming here for?"

Sebastian shook his head. "No, not tonight but soon."

"Oh, okay." Mags stood up, obviously disappointed. "Can we go outside? I could really use a smoke – and a drink."

"Sure, oh – wait. There's one more thing." A thought had suddenly occurred to me and I needed to ask now, while the memory might still be fresh enough in her mind. "The people we came here to Greece to meet up with, the… party that we were supposed to attend, do you remember where it is?"

"Nope," Mags answered with a shrug. "Why should I? It's your lame party, isn't it?"

My spirits were rapidly fading, my stomach sinking down to the ground as a pit of hopelessness opened up in my chest. I turned to Sebastian but I could already see the answer in his eyes.

"Did Mags ever tell you where the head temple of The Order is hidden?"

His eyes were wide, his expression grim as he slowly shook his head and whispered, "No."

We were doomed.

Chapter Fifteen – The Hunt

There was a hostel not far from the church and close to the train station. We decided to stay there overnight while we figured out our next move. It was early evening by the time we had eaten and settled into our room. Mags had been unusually silent since we left the church. She sat down now on the bunk across from me and Sebastian and stared us both down with accusing eyes.

"Are you going to explain to me what's going on now?" she demanded. "Who are the people that you said are 'after us'? And why does no one ever seem to question or even notice the strange things that you two do? And why *are* all these strange things happening – that apple you gave me that had no seeds, or the birds that seemed to follow us down the street, swooping and dancing across the sky, or how every time I tried to ask one of you what was going on, something else weird would distract or interrupt me."

Sebastian sighed and sat down on the bed beside me. I decided to take the lead on this one and answered Mags before Sebastian could even open his mouth.

"We're not exactly like other people," I began to explain.

Mags rolled her eyes. "No kidding."

"The *three* of us, we all have this kind of special ability to make whatever we want happen. It's more powerful when we all want the same thing and strange things often happen around us as a result of our… abilities," I tried to explain. "The people who are after us call themselves The Order and they want to stop us."

Mags stared at me doubtfully. "You're saying I have some kind of magical powers too? And this *Order*, they want to stop us from doing what?"

I hesitated, still not sure how much we could trust her.

"They have the same abilities that we do," Sebastian explained.

"But The Order is dangerous – none of them can be trusted. We're going to try to take their powers away, or at least, Gracelynn will, and they will do anything to stop us – even kill us."

I wanted to trust that Sebastian knew what he was doing but I wasn't certain if it was such a good idea to tell Mags this much. Still, I forced myself to relax and trust that we both wanted the same thing and so everything would be okay.

"Okay, fine. Say I believe you, why is my memory so patchy? I still don't understand how or why or even what you made me forget?"

"We made you forget because there were things that you knew that were too dangerous. We had to make you forget, there was no other choice. I'm sorry but I can't explain anymore," Sebastian apologized and he did sound genuinely sorry. I could see part of my own guilt clouding his eyes.

"Ugh!" Mags complained pressing both of her hands against her head. "And this freakin' headache is killing me! I'm just so confused!"

"Sorry," I murmured and I was surprised to have meant it too. I was definitely feeling guilty now but not regretful – there really had been no other choice.

Mags lay down on her bunk, draping an arm dramatically over her eyes. "So what now?" she muttered.

Sebastian didn't answer, I could tell he didn't know what to say. It was a good question after all. I took a deep breath and decided to tackle the answer, speaking my thoughts aloud.

"The Order will be meeting in three nights' time. They'll come looking for us, guaranteed, and there will be enough of them that if they all want to find us, they easily will." I turned to Sebastian, feeling a small jolt of energy pass through my body as my knee brushed against his. "I think we're going to have to abandon our original plan – there's no way it would work now that we don't know where we're going. We're too close to escape them. I think our only option is to wait for them to come to us, and in the meantime, search for the loophole."

"If there is one," Sebastian quietly pointed out.

"There is."

"But where would we even start to look?"

"I don't know," I admitted, thinking hard.

"Are you guys trying to talk in code?" Mags demanded without opening her eyes. She rolled away, turning her back to us and pulling a pillow over her head. "I'm going to sleep. Maybe this bizarre nightmare will be over when I wake up."

"I doubt it," I answered softly.

I didn't know if she heard me or not but within minutes she was quietly snoring. It was barely eight o'clock but I felt exhausted too. The spell I had cast to erase Mags' memory had really wiped me out, not to mention the heavy emotional toll the day had taken on me.

"Tired?" Sebastian asked as I tried to stifle a yawn. I nodded.

"Are you?"

"I could sleep."

We both stood and then hesitated awkwardly. I suddenly felt shy and stupid and completely unsure of what to do. Our relationship definitely wasn't the same as it had been before we met Mags… I just wasn't sure where I stood with him now. I desperately wanted him to come and sleep in the lower bunk with me, to hold me in his arms and make me forget all my fears but I wasn't sure if he was really ready to do that. I hoped he'd forgiven me enough but...

"This is ridiculous," Sebastian muttered as he took a quick step towards me and pulled me into his arms. He dropped backwards as he caught me, smoothly pulling me down and onto the bed on top of him. I managed to hold in my surprised giggle but found myself smiling anyway as I wrestled my way free, sliding off him and over to his side.

Our faces were so close together that I could taste his breath and smell his skin. I stared into his eyes, momentarily hypnotized by their dark, bluish-gray swirls and the long, black lashes that framed them. He stared back at me solemnly, the barest hint of a smile on his lips.

"I'm so sorry," I whispered after some time.

"I know. I am too."

We continued to stare at each other silently, reading all the thoughts and emotions hidden within one another's eyes.

"It's so strange to have missed you so much, when you were here all along," he commented sadly.

"I know exactly what you mean," I agreed. I hesitated, and then forced myself to ask the question that had been hanging on my lips all day. "So where does that leave us now?"

Sebastian half-smiled. "Engaged, sharing a room with my ex-wife who's had her memory erased, and hunted by powerful, ancient beings who will probably kill us once they find us," he listed.

"That's not what I meant."

"I know." There was another long pause before he eventually pulled away, rolling onto his back to stare at the underside of the bunk above us. "I love you, Gracelynn, I don't think I could ever, ever stop but… I don't think you can understand how much your lack of faith has hurt me. I want to trust you, I want things to be like they were but…"

Tears prickled at my eyes and my throat grew tight. But I still wanted to hear the truth.

"But it can't be the same – it's not," I finished for him.

His silence was agreement enough. I rolled onto my back and stared up at the bunk above us too, listening to the sound of Mags' soft snores as my heart teetered on the edge of breaking, yet again.

"I don't want to lose you," he confessed. Without looking, he felt around with his hand for mine, linking our fingers together. "I want to be with you, I love you and I want to marry you still, it just may take some time to figure out what our new relationship is going to be like."

I felt a hot tear trickle down my face. I didn't attempt to wipe it away.

"I love you too. I'll earn your forgiveness somehow," I promised, squeezing his hand.

He pushed himself up on one elbow and leaned over me, meeting my tear-filled eyes with his own steady, dark ones. He hesitated for only the briefest of seconds before he lightly and sweetly pressed his lips against mine.

"You have my forgiveness – you had it instantly. It's my trust that was questioned."

It was fair enough for him to say but I thought about how I had doubted him, how he had been with Mags, how many secrets he might still have in his past and how many ways I knew he could hurt me now, and I realized he was going to have to re-earn my trust also.

"Let's learn to trust in one another again then, and in ourselves."

He nodded his agreement, then bent his head to gently kiss my cheek where that single tear had fallen.

"I'm sorry I hurt you," he whispered against my cheek. "But it was your fault, you know," he continued in a lighter, teasing tone.

I threw a playful elbow into his ribs and he laughed. The silence slowly stretched out between us again though and a heavy sadness weighed down on my heart. Things weren't the same, how could they be?

"Good night, sweetheart," Sebastian whispered, squeezing my hand and then rolling onto his side with his back to me.

I bit my lip, trying to remind myself that at least we were together, at least we were talking and working things out – it could be so much worse. I forced myself to be strong, knowing that no matter how much Sebastian had been joking, I really had brought this all on myself. I swallowed my sadness and pushed aside my pride and rolled towards him, shuffling right up against his back and curling into it, my forehead pushed up between his shoulder blades and my heart praying he wouldn't reject me.

He immediately reacted to my touch, some of the tension melting from him as I felt his muscles relax and soften. I heard him sigh again but this time it sounded peaceful and relieved. I allowed myself a small smile.

"Good night," I whispered and closed my eyes, finally feeling like I might be able to find sleep.

In the morning, I awoke in Sebastian's arms. At some time in the night, he had rolled over and pulled me up against him, holding me tightly and protectively against his chest. I'd barely awoken when he did so but remembered my sleepy relief to find myself enclosed in his solid embrace.

He lay behind me, his arm tightly around my waist and a small smile on my face. I opened my eyes and was surprised to see Mags, lying on the bunk across from us, staring right back at me. She wrinkled up her nose in distaste.

"You two make me sick," she accused as she sat up and fluffed at her wild, wavy hair. The sound of her loud voice and the squeak of her mattress as she sat up roused Sebastian. Aware of Mags still watching, I tried to hide my disappointment as Sebastian rolled away from me and sat up.

"Disgusting lovebirds," Mags grumbled as she stood up and stretched. "Were you this bad the whole way here? Is that why I wanted my memories erased, because you two made me so nauseous?" she joked sarcastically.

I sat up and slipped out of bed, eyeing her warily. Even though it was my doing, it still seemed strange for her not to remember anything. I still couldn't quite get past the feeling that she wasn't to be trusted.

"Ha-ha," Sebastian mumbled sleepily as he stood up beside me. "What time is it?"

"Six am," Mags answered cheerily. She flashed me a wicked grin. "Grace's snoring has kept me awake since five though."

I blinked at her in surprise – not because of the snoring jibe but because it was the first time I had ever heard her use my name and not call me Caoilinn.

"What?" she demanded.

Now Mags was staring at me strangely. I shrugged, trying to be casual.

"Nothing. I don't snore."

"Of course not. You're obviously far too perfect."

"Mags," Sebastian sighed.

Mags shrugged, flashing him a smile. "Sorry, I'm a bit of a bitch before my morning smoke and coffee. Speaking of which, I'm going to need more cigarettes and coffee."

Sebastian shook his head and surprisingly, I found myself fighting an amused smile.

"She's right. We might as well get up and get going – we've got a lot to do today. Primarily, avoiding The Others and searching for clues," I agreed.

"Clues to what?" Mags demanded. She turned her back to us and then abruptly tugged her t-shirt up and over her head.

"Geez, Mags," Sebastian muttered in annoyance as he turned his back.

She ignored him, keeping her own back turned as she continued to change into a fresh shirt.

"Don't be such a prude Sebastian. Clues to what?" she repeated.

Again, I wasn't certain how much we could trust her but it would be a lot easier to just tell her the truth – I wanted to be able to tell her the truth, I realized. I wanted to trust her, a little, so I did.

"Clues of how to stop the Others and take away their magic."

She spun around, her expression incredulous.

"Wait, you don't even know what you're doing?"

"I have an idea."

"Do you?" She fixed me with a hard stare but I refused to back down, matching her emerald glare with an ice-blue one of my own. "I think you're playing a dangerous game and it looks like somehow you've dragged me into it. It's safe to turn around now, Sebastian."

He slowly complied, his expression one of aggravation.

"Let's go get breakfast, then we can try to figure out where to start."

"And smokes!" Mags chimed in.

"I already know where to start," I calmly announced. They both turned to stare at me, Mags skeptical and Sebastian surprised. "The tattoo along your ribs – the hieroglyphics. It's the only clue left that we haven't deciphered. It's got to mean something."

Sebastian slowly nodded, looking thoughtful.

"There's also the text that forms the tattoo over my heart…" his hand drifted to his chest as he spoke.

"I know what that means," I quietly answered. Mags raised an eyebrow, Sebastian looked at me sharply but didn't say anything. My tone had made it obvious I didn't want to discuss it just then. "Breakfast?" I reminded him.

"And smokes," Mags added as we picked up our bags and left our room.

There was a small store downstairs in the hostel that thankfully sold cigarettes. Sebastian also purchased a map of the city, confessing that he hadn't been to Greece in quite some time and hadn't seen much locally that was familiar.

It was nice to see Thessaloniki in the daytime and to start to get a real feel for the country. Yesterday was such a blur, I felt like I was just arriving in Greece today.

The city rose up and away from the Mediterranean Ocean, the clean, white-washed buildings crowded in close together in rising rows. The city was exactly how I would have imagined it. The traditional Greek architecture of pillars and arches marked the city streets with a distinctive European flare and blended with a touch of modernity like wi-fi in the cafes and neon signs in windows.

It was early but there were already quite a few people out and about on the streets. I liked a city that woke up with the sun. It was refreshing and invigorating, it gave me hope. Even Mags' spirits seemed lifted as she happily puffed on a cigarette, striding along just behind us.

We stopped to eat breakfast at a small café not too far from the hostel we had stayed at. It was the perfect time to sit down and discuss our plans and to pore over the map Sebastian had purchased. There wasn't a lot to say; we really didn't have a lot to go on and I had the definite feeling that we were grasping at straws.

"There's a library not too far from here. Should we try that first?" I suggested, taking a sip of water.

"We might as well," Sebastian agreed.

"Ugh! You want to go to a library? But it's such a beautiful day and we're in Greece! Can't we go to a beach or something?" Mags somehow managed to grumble around the cigarette she was lighting.

"Mags, this concerns you just as much as it does us," Sebastian reminded her. "We're not here on vacation – this is serious. We need to focus all our wants on the same things here; we must find a way to stop the Others and keep them from finding us for as long as possible."

Mags frowned at Sebastian. "Too serious," she said to him then turned to me. "Too boring," she labeled me. "What the hell am I doing with you two again?"

I tried to keep my jaw relaxed and stop myself from grinding my teeth in irritation. A smile twitched at the corner of Sebastian's mouth. I tried to give him a disapproving look but he was careful not to meet my eye.

We decided to walk to the library since it was close to where we'd stopped and Mags insisted that we experience a little more of Greece first-hand. It turned out to be a surprisingly good idea and it was nice to relax just for a little while, to stroll under the hot morning sun and watch the city awaken, to take in all the sights and smells and sounds. It was even nicer when after Sebastian's hand awkwardly brushed against mine several times, he suddenly linked his fingers through mine. He flexed his fingers, squeezing my hand and rubbing his thumb gently against the base of my own. My heart skipped a beat and for a little while, the tension between us eased and things almost felt normal again although our relationship had never truly been 'normal' by any standard definition.

We found the library easily. Thessaloniki was a surprisingly easy city to find our way around in, even though Mags couldn't remember ever being there anymore and we were largely dependent upon our map.

The library was located in a more modern-looking area of town. It was a fairly large building that was open early on weekdays. The doors were just being unlocked as we arrived, a comforting reassurance that our wants were still influencing events around us. The building was air-conditioned too – another blessing on this hot summer day.

We split up upon entering – I was going to search the computer systems, Mags was going to start searching the shelves and Sebastian was going to talk to the librarians. It was a disappointment when Sebastian let go of my hand and started walking up the stairs to the second floor but I knew I had to focus, I knew we had work to do.

"Wait," Mags called after him, surprising both of us. He slowly turned and walked back down to where we stood. "I'm going to need to see it."

"See what?" Sebastian asked.

"Your tattoo."

"Oh. Yes, I suppose that would help," he hesitantly agreed. A sudden flare of jealousy caught me off-guard but I quickly swallowed it back down, reminding myself that I wanted to trust Sebastian and that he deserved my trust.

He glanced around before reluctantly lifting up the bottom of his t-shirt, exposing his flat stomach and the four hieroglyphics that were tattooed down the left side of his rib cage. Without hesitation, Mags stepped forward and ran her fingers over the markings. She started to smile a little to herself as she began tracing each symbol with her finger. That was when Sebastian abruptly pulled back and I found myself quietly exhaling. It sounded almost like a hiss.

"Thanks, I think I should remember that," she commented cheekily, flashing him a devilish grin.

"Uh, right," he agreed, looking oddly flustered. Mags turned to smile at me, inviting me to join in her joke. "I'll be upstairs," Sebastian announced, glancing at me quickly before turning and heading back toward the stairs.

"Yes, let's get started," I agreed, attempting to keep my voice light and friendly. I remembered once when I would never have dreamed of doing anything remotely violent and now here I was, struggling not to slap Mags. I knew it was all just bravado even in my thoughts though – Mags was obviously tough and I was fairly certain she wouldn't hesitate to hit me back and twice as hard. Not that I was ever really considering hitting her, of course.

Mags was still smirking as I walked away, heading towards the row of computers up against the library's far wall. I tried to focus and concentrate on what I needed to do and not on what had just happened. It was like Mags was just trying to get under my skin. Apparently, even when she couldn't remember all that had happened in the past, irritating me and flirting with Sebastian were just natural parts of who she was.

Over the next several hours my frustration and irritation only continued to increase. It seemed like nothing was going the way we wanted anymore and I was starting to get worried. Sebastian had spoken to all the librarians working that day and none of them could give us any useful tips or information so he had ended up joining Mags in her search. Neither of them could find anything that resembled the hieroglyphics of Sebastian's tattoos in any of the books on the shelves, no clues, no hints – nothing.

"How are you making out?" Sebastian asked, taking the empty computer seat beside me. Mags stood directly behind me, tapping her fingers impatiently against the back of my chair.

"This system is infuriating!" I complained, struggling to keep my voice at a library-appropriate volume. "Every time I think I've found something useful, I click on the link and it doesn't work or it redirects me back to the library's main page. And there's so much Greek and English mixed together that half the time I don't even know what I'm looking at! I'm starting to wonder if the Others aren't closer than we thought because it feels like someone definitely doesn't want us to discover what those symbols mean."

"We would have sensed the Others if they were that close," Sebastian argued. "And they don't know any more about my tattoos than we do. At least, I don't think they do."

"Are you sure you're even doing it right?" Mags questioned, her fingers still tapping irritatingly behind me.

I clenched my teeth together and breathed through my nose, forcing myself to answer Mags calmly.

"Yes, I'm sure."

"Well, it doesn't look like you're actually searching the Internet. I think you're just searching the library's internal database but if you click on here…" she reached right over my shoulder as she spoke, taking the mouse from my hand and clicking on a small box in the corner of the screen.

I leant away from her and she immediately moved in closer. I found myself rolling my chair up against Sebastian's, reluctantly making room for her as she pushed her way forward.

"There!" she said triumphantly, gesturing to the screen.

"What did you do?" I asked, forgetting to be annoyed and just feeling relieved that we might have actually gotten somewhere.

"I extended the parameters of your search to include all the libraries across Greece and the world wide web. This is what came up under 'rare Egyptian symbols and definitions'."

I watched in amazement as she scrolled down the page. This website showed hundreds of different hieroglyphics and all you had to do was click on one to reveal its meaning. Within seconds Mags had found one of the symbols from Sebastian's tattoo and decoded it.

"This symbol represents fertility or motherhood or family… there's multiple interpretations. And this symbol looks like it could be a variation of the backbone of Osiris which represents strength and inner power. And this one looks sort of similar to the symbol for sacrifice or it could represent a violent death or destruction… and that's it. I can't find anything even close to the last symbol."

"Okay. Well, that gives us a start at least. Mags, why don't you keep looking on the computer? Gracelynn and I can have another go at the shelves now that we have a little more direction as to what to look for."

"Sure," Mags agreed with a shrug. "I'm taking a smoke break first though. Ugh, this is so boring!"

She stood up and walked away from us, her curved hips swaying the whole while and her reddish hair flaring out behind her.

"She's something else," I muttered with a little shake of my head.

Sebastian wisely chose not to comment.

We spent the rest of the day in the library with limited success. I hated to admit it but Mags did a lot better with the library's computer system than I did. She found several titles of books, research papers and journal articles that might help us discover the meanings of the rest of Sebastian's hieroglyphics or provide more information on those already uncovered. Unfortunately, only one of these titles was available in the Thessaloniki library – the others were all spread out across Greece and unavailable for request within the next few days. We did find one book, *Mesopotamian Art*, that showed a hieroglyphic that might be a variation of the fourth symbol of Sebastian's tattoo. It was a symbol that represented worship and faith in the Gods, often used on the tombs of particularly zealous priests and royalty. There were so many possible meanings for each symbol and it was hard to find hieroglyphics that were identical to Sebastian's, the best we could do was to find ones that were as similar as possible. I wasn't even certain if we were looking in the right place anymore. The possible interpretations that we had discovered so far made little sense.

When the library closed that evening, we returned to the same hostel we had stayed at the night before feeling dejected and tense. The Others would surely be coming for us by now, they could arrive at any moment to take us to the ceremony that would be happening in only two nights' time and we were no closer to discovering a way to stop them. I was starting to panic. I could tell Sebastian was still doubtful that there were any useful answers hidden in his last tattoo and Mags obviously thought my idea was a complete waste of time. But, it was all we had to go on and I was determined to use anything we had.

The only positive I could find from the day was that Sebastian and I were slowly growing closer again. I had almost enjoyed my time in the library with him, stealing glances at one another, our hands and bodies occasionally brushing together, speaking with our heads close and our voices soft, sharing our ideas and discussing possibilities. He had held my hand on the walk back to the hostel and it had felt almost as natural as before we met Mags – almost. It was hard to forget and move on from what had happened when Mags' presence was a constant reminder of my guilt, my lack of faith, my mistakes and his indiscretions. And it was so hard to be patient with Mags too. I was still very angry with her and wanting to blame her for the situation we were in. I knew that wasn't really fair. And I was also feeling guilty, very guilty. Because mixed in with her jokes and complaints and loud, somewhat obnoxious attitude, there was also fear and confusion and uncertainty, for which only I was to blame. She was trying to accept things as they were and not question too much about why her memory had been erased (because this was what both Sebastian and I wanted) but I could see her doubts. I'd catch her with a dazed, disoriented expression on her face or a confused frown, or with her eyes clenched tightly shut and her fingers digging into her temples as she fought the headaches her memory loss had left behind. The guilt ate away at me.

Mags was delighted that night when after eating dinner, Sebastian and I agreed to go for a walk with her down to the waterfront. It was just starting to get dark and the city was lighting up all around us. The air was warm and muggy still and I wiped sweat from my forehead as we set out and down the street, admiring the slow transition from day to night life. Thessaloniki really was a beautiful city and I wished I was able to enjoy it more. Even now, as I was trying to relax and take in the night, it was impossible to fully appreciate the beautiful scenery around me.

We lost Mags just as we approached the waterfront. There had been a loud and busy club we passed that she couldn't resist. I had wanted to object when she said she was going dancing but Sebastian shrugged, stating, "What's the worst she can get up to? Just let her go." And even though I worried it was a mistake, it was too tempting to escape from her presence after spending almost every minute of the past week or so in her company. And so suddenly, we were alone.

We continued to head down towards the water, walking slowly but barely talking. I could tell there was a lot on Sebastian's mind, as well as on my own. When we finally crossed the busy street that ran along the waterfront, and came to look out at the ocean's edge, the twilight hour was darkening into night. Stars were starting to come out one by one, and their silvery brilliance was reflected upon the surface of the sparkling, black waves. There were several boats in the harbor too, their lights shining back brightly at the city that was lit up and sprawled across the rising hill. It was a beautiful sight but I still couldn't appreciate it, I was far too focused on the person by my side.

Sebastian was staring straight ahead at the ocean, his eyes looking like they could see for miles and miles. A cooler breeze was rising off the water and ruffling his hair, cooling us both down. I studied him with hungry eyes, feeling like it had been years since I'd really been able to look at him. I admired his stunning features; his large, mysterious eyes, his long lashes, his straight nose and soft, curved lips. I noticed the faint lines around his eyes and brows that had never been there before, and the sadness and exhaustion that seemed to be ever-present in his expression now, no matter how he attempted to hide it. Without thought or pause, I reached out to touch his cheek, my fingers itching to connect with him and break down the barriers that I felt building between us.

He turned to me as soon as my fingertips brushed his skin and a question hung in his eyes. I immediately pulled my hand away, almost guiltily, though I wasn't certain why. He kept looking at me, kept waiting and I forced myself to stare back. The moment stretched between us, my heart heavy, my hopes bright.

The warm air was going to my head, the breeze was teasing at my heart and the stars and lights began spinning around us as I looked into his eyes. A shooting star suddenly arched high across the sky, its path perfectly reflected in the inky black waters below. And just as suddenly, the realization hit me. I heard the words Sebastian's silence had spoken so clearly to my heart.

I had released Sebastian from my wants when I had come to the realization that all I wanted, all I truly needed or desired, was his happiness. But as I looked into his eyes, I realized then, in that moment, that all he had ever needed to be happy was my trust, my faith, my love.

It was so simple, so obvious, I couldn't say why I hadn't realized it sooner. And almost as if he saw my thoughts in my eyes, a smile started to slowly spread across his face, a warm, gentle, loving and thrilling smile that made my body tingle all over.

I reached out to him again just as naturally and impulsively as before but now with no doubts or hesitation. My hands slid around his neck, my fingers twisted tightly into his hair and I pulled his mouth down to mine, inhaling his breath as our lips crushed together. I became lost in the moment, in the night, in my love and fiery passion for him. Suddenly, the world made sense again.

Chapter Sixteen – An Invitation

Mags was out clubbing until the early hours of the morning. Sebastian and I had only just fallen asleep when she returned to our small hostel room, reeking of cigarette smoke and vodka. We had stayed up most of the night ourselves, talking, laughing, just being together and reconnecting. There was still some sadness left between us, still some hurtful memories. I knew that time would help the pain to fade but would never entirely erase it. And perhaps that was a good thing. Either way, we were now both ready to move on. The walls between us had been broken down and we were as close physically, mentally and emotionally than we had ever been before. I finally felt whole and at peace with the world, like everything was starting to make sense again and falling back under my control. I knew what mistakes I had made and how to fix them. I finally understood what I wanted, I knew what I needed and I wasn't going to let anyone or anything stop me from getting it.

I awoke just after eight o'clock, knowing the library would be opening soon. The moment I first stirred, Sebastian's eyes opened, a smile already on his face and his arms automatically tightening around me.

"Good morning," he murmured, gently kissing the tip of my nose.

I smiled back at him, my heart light and happy for the first time in weeks.

"Perfect morning," I corrected, wriggling forward on the mattress to kiss him back on the lips. It was a slow and lingering kiss and it took several minutes before we were both ready to speak again. "The library's opening soon. We should get moving."

"The library – again? Gracelynn, just because you want to find answers there – if they don't exist, even you can't create them," Sebastian patiently pointed out.

I sat up and stretched, covering my mouth as I yawned. "The answers are there. I figured it out while we were sleeping last night and woke up with the realization."

"What realization?"

"That we were looking at the problem the wrong way — we were wanting to find the wrong answer." Sebastian stared back at me blankly and I smiled, pleased to be confusing him for once. "The hieroglyphics are clues to stop the Others, I'm certain of it. We had assumed that you encoded the answer within them but I remembered the designs last night in a dream — Caoilinn knew those symbols, Sebastian. They were in her spell book."

He sat up and frowned, rubbing the sleep from his eyes.

"It's possible… I remember having them tattooed over my ribs, and I remember thinking I would preserve the symbols for you but I can't remember what they meant or why I should save them." He squinted up at me, the strain of trying to remember obviously causing him pain and frustration. "I wonder if it's one of my memories that Mags tampered with?"

"Relax." I lightly ran my fingers through his messy hair, combing it back and attempting to smooth it down unsuccessfully. "It's not important. I know those symbols were in the spell book, Sebastian — I remember them. Caoilinn must have traveled to Egypt or somehow encountered an Egyptian, or she found an artifact from there but somehow, she knew those symbols and she used them to hide vital information."

Sebastian opened his eyes and peered up at me, taking in my steady expression and my firm, confident voice. He nodded, accepting the truth of my words and easily placing his trust in me.

"Alright," he agreed. "But what difference does it make if Caoilinn knew of the symbols or not?"

"Because, we were assuming that their meaning was connected to Egypt somehow, because they're hieroglyphics. But I think, no - I know that she would never have done something so obvious. She used an Egyptian code to hide an Irish secret. That's why we need to go back to the library — we were searching in the wrong section."

Sebastian bent down to pick his shirt up off the floor. He gave it a quick shake before pulling it on over his head and then standing up beside me.

"If you think this is what we need to do… let's go then."

I smiled, appreciating his easy trust more than ever.

I was certain this time that I'd figured things out. Everything just made so much more sense today than it had yesterday. With this new-found clarity I had awoken with, I felt like there was nothing that I couldn't do. I knew we were going to find the answers we needed today and I hoped, that it would be in time.

"Should we wake Mags?" Sebastian asked, glancing at her, fully clothed and sprawled out over the top of her blankets, her hair a wild mess, her makeup smudged and her snores soft and steady.

"No, let her rest. We don't need her for this and if everything goes the way we want it to, we should be back here by noon anyway."

"And she'll probably still be asleep," Sebastian commented with a half-smile. I found myself smiling too and shaking my head.

"I'm just glad she came back. It makes me nervous leaving her alone but…"

"We want her to stay with us, so she will. We're all she has, now that she can't remember anyone else," Sebastian pointed out. I shifted uncomfortably as I was struck by another wave of guilt. He was right, she was our responsibility now.

"We won't be long," I repeated as I led the way from our room.

It was another hot and beautiful day outside. I set a fast pace to the library, working up a sweat. The day seemed brighter and more beautiful to me, full of hope and possibilities. The sky was a hot, summer's blue, the buildings bright and white, the air full of excitement and noises as the city awoke and came to life.

We found the library easily, without ever consulting the map. The doors had just opened as we approached and the library staff greeted us with familiar and curious smiles. I took Sebastian straight to the computers, gesturing for him to sit down in front of the screen.

"I'm useless with the computer system here," I admitted. He grinned at my slightly sour tone.

"You're not useless at anything," he argued, he was still smiling though as he sat down and logged on.

"Alright, so what are we searching for?"

"Start with the broadest search parameters possible. Search for mother, fertility, strength, power, sacrifice, death, destruction and add 'Irish history'," I instructed. Sebastian obliged and so our search began.

We spent the morning searching for different variations of the symbol meanings and definitions that we knew. It wasn't until just before noon when Sebastian typed in "mother, child, sacrifice, power, death, Irish, myths and legends" that we finally found what we were looking for – a perfect match of 8/8 words.

"Ireland's Earth Mother," Sebastian murmured, letting the mouse arrow hover over the title on the screen. It was a link to an article posted online, written by a graduate student studying Irish symbolism and lore as part of a thesis. I leant down over Sebastian, resting my chin on his shoulder as he clicked on the link. We read together, our breaths held.

The article began by describing the importance of the female figure in ancient Celtic societies and lore. Women were powerful, fertility was celebrated and considered a gift to be shared. The legend of the Earth Goddess or the Earth Mother was often told through paintings, sculptures and other artifacts from that time.

The Earth Mother was the Goddess who created Ireland, pulling the island up from the ocean's floor and blessing it with fertile green lands and life. She loved the land and gave it to the children of the Earth, often walking among them in disguise so that she might rejoice alongside them.

The Earth Mother loved Ireland so much that she fell in love with a mortal man and joined with him in celebration of all the life around them. A new life was created within the Earth Mother and a child was born who was half-God, half-man.

The Gods did not approve of the Earth Mother walking alongside the mortals who worshipped them. They were angered when they realized that she had born a child of man. As a warning to her, the Gods killed her lover and threatened to end the life of her half-God son if she did not separate herself from the mortals.

The Gods had not anticipated the strength of the Earth Mother's love for her child. Mad with pain from the loss of her lover and overwhelmed by fear for her child, the Earth Mother did the only thing she could think to save her son from the Gods' wrath, she turned her powers on herself. She sacrificed all she knew to protect her child and pass on to him her powers so that he might rise up and join the Gods as their equal – and he did.

The Earth Mother's body joined her mortal lover's in the earth and her fierce spirit flowed freely into the people of the land. The mothers learned to protect their children above all else and the people of Ireland were forever known for their passionate and faithful ways.

I knew Sebastian had finished reading at the same time I had, but neither of us spoke or moved. It was clear to me that this was the legend that Caoilinn had wanted to remember, this was the answer to the problem that we faced. The Goddess had sacrificed herself to save her child. She had sacrificed herself to save the one she loved.

"Well…" Sebastian took a slow breath in through his nose. "I guess we'll keep looking then."

"What do you mean?" I asked. "This is it – I know it is. This is the legend that Caoilinn wanted to remember, this is the only way to fix her mistakes."

"What do *you* mean?" Sebastian turned around in his chair, staring straight at me with hard, demanding eyes.

"The only way to stop the Others, to take away their powers, is for me to sacrifice myself. There must be a way for me to take the Lost Magic from them through my death."

"No." Sebastian's voice was flat, his eyes black and piercing. "Absolutely not. That is not what this means. We don't even know if this is even the right legend that the symbols were meant to point us towards – they might not have been pointing us towards anything at all! This is just a story that's been told and altered millions of times over the past few thousand years – it might not even be the same legend that Caoilinn knew. Sacrificing yourself would do nothing!" His voice was steadily rising, echoing around the library and bouncing back at us off the shelves of books.

I sighed, feeling strangely calm and centered. "I know this is the answer, Sebastian. I'm certain. Really, it's okay," I tried to reassure him. And it was okay; I was afraid but I was willing to do whatever it took to save him.

He jumped to his feet, grabbing me roughly by the shoulders and shaking me slightly as he spoke.

"Stop it, Gracelynn! You want to find a solution so badly that you're grasping at anything that might be even remotely possible. What good would sacrificing yourself do? Caoilinn died before, remember? And the magic lived on without her."

"Yes, but she didn't want it to die with her, she wanted the magic to live on inside of you so that you might find her again. But this time... this time I know what I must do."

"Stop talking like that," Sebastian insisted, his fingers digging into my shoulders almost painfully. "This is ridiculous! Promise me you won't do anything stupid – promise me you won't try to sacrifice yourself."

I stared back into his intense eyes, a peaceful calm settling over me and into my very soul. There was absolutely no doubt in my mind that this was what I was supposed to do. I guessed that Sebastian knew it too and that was why it was hurting him so much. There were no other answers, there was no other way. But I loved him too much to cause him any pain if it were within my power to stop it.

"I promise," I lied while looking him levelly in the eye. I wanted him to believe me, and he did. The worst part was, I didn't even feel ashamed.

Sebastian pulled me tightly against his chest, hugging me and whispering in my ear.

"You don't know how it scares me to hear you talking like that."

"I'm sorry," I whispered back, meaning it with my whole heart. "It's getting close to noon, we should go check on Mags."

"I suppose we should. And then do you want to come back and keep searching?"

"No," I answered a little too quickly. Sebastian pulled away from me to eye me suspiciously. "You're right – we don't even know what we're looking for here and the Others will be coming for us soon, probably tonight or tomorrow... maybe we should run?"

Sebastian considered, raking his fingers through his hair.

"We could try. Perhaps if the three of us wanted to escape them, and they only send five or six after us… We could go to Egypt and try to finish deciphering the hieroglyphics, discover the real meaning behind these symbols."

I nodded, carefully not reacting to his words.

"Let's run then," I agreed, knowing the whole while that we had absolutely no chance of escaping the Others but it was better than sitting around waiting for them to catch us.

"We'll go get Mags and leave today, this afternoon in fact. No more buses or trains – we'll head straight to the airport."

Sebastian seemed happier now, focused and ready with a course of action decided upon. He seemed to have completely forgotten about the Irish legend; I wondered if he had just pushed it out of his mind or if it was because I had wanted him to forget?

We hurried back to our hostel, Sebastian's calm confidence fading with every step and being replaced by a frenzied sort of panic. The day that had begun with such warmth and optimism now felt harsh and overwhelming. The brightness of the sky hurt my eyes, the heat of the day was choking me, the air smothering and hot, the sun burning and blistering above us. The noise of the traffic and streets hurt my ears and the stunning white buildings blazed their reflected light into my eyes. There was a sense of dread and unease in the air that was undeniable. Our pace increased as we rushed back towards the hostel, we were nearly running by the time we reached its doors.

Sebastian froze as soon as we entered, his whole body tensed as he lurched to a stop, his hand on my arm in an iron grip that effectively held me still beside him.

"What's wrong?" I asked, but in my heart I already knew.

"The Others," he whispered. His eyes were wide as he turned to me. "They're already here."

"How many?" I calmly responded. Strangely, I wasn't afraid or even that worried. I felt I knew exactly what to do.

"Just two I think, three at the most."

"It'll be safe for us to talk to them then."

"I suppose so…" he frowned, his grip slowly relaxing on my arm. "This doesn't feel right; I should have sensed them before now. There must be more, hiding nearby. Perhaps I should go up alone."

"No." My voice was firm yet soft. I spoke with an inner confidence and strength that I found myself calling upon more often these days and growing ever more familiar with. I knew he would be unable to deny me. "Let's go together."

I gently pulled my arm out of his grip and boldly stepped forward, leading the way to the stairs.

Despite my confidence and strength, I began to worry as we made our way up to the third floor. The Others were obviously waiting for us in our room – with Mags. I wondered how long they had been alone with her and what exactly they had been doing. I could only hope that Sebastian and I had wanted to keep her safe enough that it would be so, despite being separated all morning.

When we stepped out of the stairwell and entered the hall, we could clearly hear Mags' voice floating towards us. Her words weren't clear but her tone was; she sounded angry – and afraid. The sound spurred both of us into action.

We rushed down the hall together, not caring that our loud, pounding footsteps gave us away. The Others would be able to sense Sebastian's approach anyway. Sebastian reached the doorknob barely a second before me and threw the door open. He was half a step ahead of me as we entered the room, our eyes met by an unexpected and disturbing scene.

There were two of the Others waiting for us. They were both familiar to me, their names springing to my lips instantly like familiar friends.

"Darius, Jai," I greeted them, immediately and automatically taking control. My voice was calm and soft yet still rang with authority.

"Caoilinn," Jai stated in his gently accented voice. He bowed his head slightly in greeting before he seemed to realize what he was doing. A faint shade of pink flushed his brown cheeks. He seemed awed to be in my presence but of course he didn't remember meeting me before – it was strange to have to remind myself that.

Darius sneered back at me, his dark eyes narrowing. He gave a small nod of acknowledgment before taking a slow, deliberate drag of the cigarette he held between his large fingers and then he turned his beady gaze onto Mags - poor Mags. My eyes widened in shock and my mouth popped open as I took in the horrifying sight of her.

Mags' wrists had been tied to the rail of the top bunk. Though the bunk was low enough that she should have been able to stand, she hung lifelessly by her wrists, the rope bindings clearly cutting into and breaking her skin. Her head was slumped down on her chest, her thick reddish hair obscuring her face. I could clearly see the cigarette burns that marked up and down both her arms, the fresh blisters an angry, puffy red. Sebastian sharply inhaled his breath, noticing the burn marks at the same time I did. Darius's smirk deepened while Jai just watched us both curiously with his large, almond eyes.

"Mags?" Sebastian called out softly. There was a barely detectable tone to his voice that made me look at him twice. I suddenly felt uneasy, aware he was about to do something incredibly dangerous if she did not answer. I wasn't certain if I wanted to stop him or not, I was furious myself.

Mags slowly lifted her head, briefly meeting my eyes and then Sebastian's. Her lip was swollen and a bruise was already darkening her puffy jaw, her eyes were bleary and slightly unfocused yet the anger in them, the pure and uninhibited outrage was obvious. And unexpectedly, her fury was directed at us. Her fiery gaze shifted to me.

"This is all your fault," she spat at me, her accusation bitter and harsh. "They told me everything. I know who you are now, how dangerous you are, why you must be stopped. You deserve to die for what you've done to me!"

"Mags, no," Sebastian denied. "No, you've got it all wrong. They've brainwashed you, tortured you into believing–"

"We've told her no lies, I assure you," Jai politely interjected.

Darius grinned. "We're not like you, Caoilinn."

"Apparently," I murmured in a cool and detached tone. I turned my attention away from Mags, hiding my unease as she continued to glare at me. It was important right now for me to play the part. "What did you do to her?"

"We just wanted to talk to her before you returned, find out how things were going with you three," Darius explained innocently with a twisted, sinister smile. "But she kept insisting she couldn't remember anything."

"They didn't believe that I couldn't effin' remember. They didn't think it was possible for you to erase my memories like that," Mags accused. "The things he did to try to make me talk… I swear I'm going to kill you myself, Caoilinn. I'm going to rip you apart with my own hands - and I'm going to enjoy it." I tried my best to ignore her.

"We didn't think you would be so cruel as to wipe out her mind," Jai pointed out.

"We did everything within our powers to trigger her memory," Darius continued, dropping his cigarette on the floor as he spoke and emphatically grinding it into the carpet. The smell of ash and burnt fabric drifted to my nose, a nauseating combination on the hot breeze coming in through the window. "By the time we realized she really couldn't remember, well, she was a little worse for wear. We then explained the truth to her, filled in some of those large, gaping holes that you left in her pretty little head."

"You lied to me," Mags growled. She was speaking to me again, her eyes burning flames of fire. "You stole my memories, you destroyed my life! And you left me here, to be tortured and tormented without your protection so that you could have Sebastian all to yourself. I should never have trusted either of you!"

"You should have been protected by our wants still. There must be more of them nearby," Sebastian quietly explained. I could see that Mags' anger was hurting him, making him lose focus.

"There are at least five of the Others in the city," I stated, trying to keep my voice level and in control. "These two would never have come alone." I had suspected this from the moment Sebastian said he sensed the Others.

"True," Jai agreed with another nod of his head.

"Why have you come?" Sebastian demanded, though in truth, we already knew the answer.

"You've been invited to attend a sacred ceremony of The Order," Darius drawled. He stood lazily as he spoke, stretching his arms and cracking his neck. "We've come to escort you."

"You will stand trial for the crimes you have committed against us," Jai pronounced to Sebastian. His eyes shifted to mine briefly before he glanced down to look at the floor. "Caoilinn's fate has yet to have been decided."

"Kill her!" Mags demanded, her eyes wild as she strained against the ropes that held her. "She deserves death! Let me kill her! Let me taste her blood!"

I was taken aback by this vicious pronouncement, though no one else seemed to notice. All attention was on Darius as he smoothly stepped forward and struck Mags across the jaw, her head whipping violently to one side and her body sagging against her bindings once more. Blood dripped from her mouth to the floor with a sickening 'splat' sound. A quiet moan escaped her lips.

Sebastian was practically trembling with rage beside me. I still didn't want him to move though, didn't want him to react. I needed for him to let me stay in control of the situation.

"That was unnecessary," I scolded. It was a struggle to keep my voice mild. Darius held my disapproving stare for a second before sharply looking away. My necklace throbbed against my chest, the heat inside of it slowly building.

"On the contrary," Jai disagreed, his voice as soft and polite as ever. "We are also here to exact punishment from the traitor. She was to bring you both to us in payment for her crimes against The Order, though she thought it was just Caoilinn we wanted."

"What crimes?" Sebastian demanded.

"Erasing our memories of you both, assisting you in your escape, turning her back on us for nearly three hundred years. She was to be shown more mercy because she was only your accomplice. But she has obviously failed in the task assigned to her, and failure is not accepted by The Order. We get what we want, when we want it."

"Or else?" I asked.

"Or else we destroy whatever stands in our way. Darius?"

Darius stepped forward again, an anticipatory smile on his face that made my stomach turn. He stepped right up to Mags, lifting her chin with one of his large, wide fingers until her foggy eyes met his.

"I want you to die," he whispered to her. Her eyes widened, her bloodstained lips parted in surprise.

"No!" Sebastian called out as Darius huge hand abruptly crushed against Mags' throat.

It happened so fast, there was no way we could have stopped it. There was a sickening crunching sound as Mags' windpipe collapsed beneath Darius's iron grip. Her eyes bulged, her lips turned purple, her hand weakly rose up to claw at her throat. Before Sebastian or myself could even take a step forward, Darius grabbed Mags' head with his other hand and abruptly and violently twisted her neck, the loud cracking sound seeming to echo through the sudden silence in the room. He released her and she hung as limply and lifelessly as a rag doll.

"No!" Sebastian screamed again. He started to step forward, charging towards Darius but I grabbed his arm, struggling with all my might to restrain him.

"It's too late," I urged him, speaking as calmly as I was able. I was shocked and nauseated, struggling to hold onto my sanity while this nightmare played out in front of my eyes. "He'll only do worse if you provoke him." We were obviously outnumbered, no longer protected by our own wants. We had no choice but to do as they asked and to follow along with their plans. Besides, this was, in a way, what we had wanted too. The Others were the only ones who could take us to the head temple and we needed the whole of The Order to be gathered together at the same time for me to be able to remove all their magic… if my plan would even work. I had never wanted Mags to die; I truly didn't want anyone else to die. I felt so frightened and afraid that I couldn't even summon any tears.

I avoided looking at Mags' body, the horror and shock of it all making my stomach queasy and my knees weak. I needed to focus, to appear to be in control still. It was a struggle. I stood up straighter as I faced Jai and Darius. Sebastian's hand found mine and I silently drew strength from him, praying that somehow, someway, we would both survive the next twenty-four hours. I held onto the hope, no matter how desperate or unlikely. I had spent enough time cowering in fear, being complacent and accepting my fate and I'd had enough. This time, I was going to take action. This time, I wasn't going down without a fight.

"I didn't want her to die." I spoke in Caoilinn's voice, my words sweet and clear in a chilling way that made my disapproval obvious. Sebastian shifted beside me.

"Well, you can't always get what you want, can you?" Darius smirked back at me.

"We'll see about that," I quietly answered, a discrete threat to my words that wiped the snide smile from Darius's face. It felt surprisingly good.

"I've had enough of this. Let's get going." Darius spoke to Jai, gesturing with his chin to Mags' body. "Take care of this, will ya?"

We didn't have to ask what he meant as Jai stood and immediately produced an old, silver, butane lighter, flicking it open with his thumb. He approached Mags with an expression that was almost bored. I swallowed hard, fighting the urge to throw up as I realized what was about to happen.

"You two, let's go," Darius commanded.

I didn't move immediately, taking my time to slowly pick up my bag and Sebastian's from the end of the nearby bed. I didn't want to appear hurried. The sound of flames beginning to crackle and the scent of the burning sheets spurred my actions though. I said a quick, silent prayer for Mags then turned and quickly led us out of the room and into the hallway, almost running to the stairwell with Sebastian right by my side and Darius close behind us.

"Come on, let's move," Darius barked. I could hear Jai running after us now, the fire set and the flames spreading quickly.

I held Sebastian's hand tightly as we raced down the stairs, bursting out the bottom of the stairwell and nearly crashing into a small group waiting just outside the doors.

"Caoilinn, Seamus, how good of you to join us. The car's waiting outside," David greeted us as if we were friends he was merely picking up at the airport.

I quickly examined each of their faces. David, Charlie and a young, dark haired, Greek man who I hadn't yet met stood before us, all of them except for David eyeing me warily.

"We're in somewhat of a rush. If you wouldn't mind?" David gestured politely for me to lead the way. I could already see the large, black SUV parked outside the hostel's doors. Cries of alarm were just starting to be heard on the floors above us. Any second now the fire alarm would sound.

"I do mind," I replied sharply. I held my head high though as I walked past him, deliberately stepping in close as I passed. I was pleased when he took a small, barely perceptible step back. Perhaps my plan might work after all.

The fire alarm began ringing just as we stepped outside. Heads were turning our way as other tourists began to flow out of the building behind us; chaos ensued. The thickening crowd bumped and jostled me, the sudden noise and commotion in the street overwhelming. I spun around in panic as I lost my grip on Sebastian's hand.

"Gracelynn!" he called out. Darius and Charlie were each holding one of his arms and dragging him away from me towards another black SUV parked just two cars behind the one I stood before now.

"We'll be taking separate vehicles," David politely explained, holding the front passenger door open for me.

I stole one last fleeting glance at Sebastian before taking David's proffered hand, knowing I couldn't afford to allow any hesitation or possible weakness to show.

"Of course," I agreed as I allowed him to help me into the car. My heart was pounding in my throat, my stomach tied up in a knot and my fear was just barely held back. I didn't speak again as Nathaniel and Jai climbed into the back of the SUV and David took the driver's seat. We pulled away from the curb, leaving Mags' corpse, the burning building and Sebastian all somewhere behind us. I tried to feel confident, I tried to feel brave but I was trembling down to my very core.

"Where are we going?" I asked, my fear making my tone sound haughty and cold.

"To Hades," David answered with a cold laugh. "We're taking you to the Underworld, Caoilinn, where few souls escape."

Chapter Seventeen – The Necromanteion

I could tell we were driving south-west out of the city. I fought the constant urge to check over my shoulder to see if the vehicle that Sebastian was in was still behind us. I wanted to appear calm and in control - and so I did. I felt like I was still in shock over Mags' death too and the numb, empty feeling inside of me was easy to take hold of. I'd spent most of my teenaged years suppressing my true emotions and it came back to me with a sad and natural ease. I knew I needed to project confidence but on the inside, somewhere deep down beneath it all, I was terrified.

"Where exactly is this little meeting going to be held?" I coolly asked after we'd been driving west for about an hour. David had turned the radio on and old rock tunes were playing softly in the background. The familiar, catchy tunes were drastically at odds with the mood in the vehicle. Other than the music, there was no noise inside the car except for the occasional uncomfortable shuffle from one of the Others in the back.

No one answered me, so I decided to try again. I squeezed the pendant of my necklace, drawing as much strength from its familiar shape and warmth as I could.

"I want to know where we're going." I spoke softly and sweetly but somehow, the sound of my voice filled the small space, demanding an answer.

"The Necromanteion," Jai answered quietly.

David made an irritated "tsk"ing sound in the back of his throat.

"Patience, patience, Caoilinn. All will be revealed to you soon enough," he chastised. He glanced at my hand upon my amber necklace with obvious annoyance. I was surprised no one had tried to take it from me. They would have discovered just how unwilling I was to give it up.

I glared at the side of his handsome face but he refused to acknowledge me again, his dark brown eyes staring steadily ahead. I shifted in my seat, half-turning my body towards Jai and Nathaniel who sat in the back. Neither of them could quite meet my gaze. I spoke slowly and gently, with a chilling calm of my own.

"What and where is the Necromanteion?"

Jai hesitated, his eyes darting forwards to the back of David's head. It was Nathaniel who answered this time, shrugging his thin shoulders uncomfortably.

"The Necromanteion is near Parga, about four hours from here. It is known as the Oracle of the Dead and the chosen meeting place for The Order," he told me softly, his polite, British tones almost apologetic. He only met my eyes briefly and reluctantly before gazing back out the window with a frown. Just from that brief glance, I could tell he spoke the truth and I could also tell that he didn't entirely want this to be happening... whatever *this* was. I filed the knowledge away, hoping it was something I could use later.

"Well, that clarifies everything," I muttered, adding a touch of annoyance to my tone. A smile twisted David's lips that actually took away from his good looks; there was something very wrong about that smile.

"Speaking of clarification, how rude of you it was, Caoilinn, to erase and confuse our memories at The Giant's Causeway — it took us some time to recall exactly what had gone on there. And that's not to mention what you did to poor Walter. That was certainly... unexpected."

"It was deserved," I lied. I swallowed hard, hoping he wouldn't notice. It was a struggle more than ever to maintain the façade of being Caoilinn. I took a slow and silent breath in, focusing on my dream memories of her, of how it felt to be her — her power, her strength, her confidence. I tried my best to embody it all.

"Perhaps I should thank you though. He wasn't a good fit to The Order and it was becoming quite the dilemma as to what we would do with him."

I thought I heard Nathaniel shuffle behind me.

"You should choose your companions with more discrimination,"

I commented dryly. "I can't say I care much for any of them – especially Darius."

David let out a soft laugh. It was a disturbing sound that sent chills down my spine.

"Be careful, Caoilinn. With the current situation as it is, you wouldn't want to offend anyone," he warned. "Darius has his strengths and weaknesses, like most others."

"He tortured and murdered Mags," I stated flatly, not quite able to hide the quivering anger in my voice. I blinked quickly, banishing the image that was building behind my eyes of Mags' tortured and battered body with her head hanging lifelessly at such an unnatural angle.

"You murdered Walter because of the crimes you felt he had committed against you," David shot back calmly. "Tell me, what is the difference?"

I paused before answering, taking a quick moment to consider my response.

"I wonder… how close is the other vehicle to us David? Are you certain that there are enough of you to out-number me right now?" I asked innocently. His eyes flickered to the rear view mirror while his lips compressed into a thin line.

"You don't want to play games with me." His voice was deadly but unexpectedly, I didn't feel that afraid anymore; I didn't feel much of anything.

"Who's playing games?"

There was an uncomfortable silence in the car, one that I quite enjoyed being the cause of.

"Jai, send a message to Krystos. Tell him to stay close," David quietly snapped. "And tell him to be on standby for the signal." He glared at the road ahead, his irritation clear.

"The signal?" I echoed, trying not to sound too curious.

"Yes. If you try anything, Seamus will be killed instantly."

I opened my mouth to respond but no sound came out. Fear struck my heart, momentarily paralyzing my body and stealing my breath. I had no response this time.

"How did you kill Walter?" Nathaniel suddenly asked from the back seat in his soft, accented voice. I turned slowly to face him. He hesitated briefly before dropping his eyes.

"Did you see the mark on his body?"

"Of course," he murmured back.

"That's how."

I turned back around without saying anymore.

"And you did a thorough job of erasing Mags' memories," David commented, his eyes on the road ahead. "A permanent effect, if I'm not mistaken?"

He waited for me to nod before continuing.

"Seamus and Mags had quite clearly given us the impression that such things were not possible. It would appear that either they deceived us or you have deceived them."

"It would appear that way to you," I agreed coldly.

David's black eyes narrowed, his displeasure clear.

"It would benefit you to be more forthcoming, Caoilinn." There was a new dangerous edge to his voice.

"Perhaps," I agreed ambiguously. "But I don't care to discuss any of this with you." I sighed, feigning boredom as I turned to stare out my window, my heart racing. Thankfully, the conversation ended then and there.

I had only the faintest idea of where we were going and what would happen once we arrived. I was terrified about what was happening to Sebastian in his vehicle and could only hope that we would be reunited soon and I would find him unharmed. I knew within a few hours I would be entering a dragon's lair where I'd be badly outnumbered and fighting for both mine and Sebastian's lives. The only weapons I had were my wits, my patchy memories from a life lived two thousand years ago and a premonition about an obscure Irish legend that was possibly referenced by one of Sebastian's tattoos. I tried to hold on to my feelings of confidence and unwavering, emotionless, calm but it was hard. I had a few more hours before we arrived at the Necromanteion and I had to figure out exactly what my plan was before Sebastian and I were at the mercy of the thirteen Others.

David drove straight for the next three and a half hours without stopping for food, drinks or any other reason. I supposed that the

Others in the vehicle didn't want to feel hungry so they weren't but whether it was because I was unable to focus or because they wanted me to be as uncomfortable as possible, I felt half-starved. My throat was parched, my head was pounding and my legs were cramping up from sitting so long. Despite it all, I projected an image of calm, cold, composure, spending most of the drive staring out the window with my head tipped back against the seat and my eyes closed. I tried my best to focus, to meditate, to relax and to plan but it was all to no avail. Ice cold panic was slowly creeping into my bones and freezing my heart as I realized I had no idea what I was doing and that there was a very good chance that Sebastian and I were both about to die.

It was Jai's voice that attracted my attention and broke me from my silent fretting.

"Parga," he murmured from behind me. I lifted my head from where I'd been resting it against the window's glass and blinked my eyes, looking around.

We were just coming into what would appear to be the center of a beautiful, seaside town. The city was built up on a hill, the clean, bright buildings piled up on top of one another as the hill climbed away from the sparkling, blue ocean. Low, rocky mountains covered in green grass and trees surrounded the city, rolling and flowing into the distance beyond. The closer we drove to the ocean, the more tourists there appeared to be. People flocked to the sandy beaches that stretched out alongside the warm, Mediterranean ocean and were dotted with bright white beach umbrellas and towels. Numerous sailboats were in the large bay, their white sails contrasting against the ocean's deep, turquoise-blue. It was a beautiful sight but there was no way I could possibly enjoy it.

We slowed down as we approached the harbor and David pulled into the large parking lot near the docks. There just happened to be two parking spaces available, side-by-side. The other black SUV pulled in beside us seconds after we had parked and I could already recognize Sebastian's profile through the dark, tinted glass of the front passenger seat. I tried not to appear too relieved, I tried not to feel too much of anything. I had to remain focused and in control – it was the only chance we had.

David, Jai, Nathaniel and myself got out of our SUV first and moved around to wait by the vehicle's rear. David tapped his foot impatiently while we waited for the others to join us. The short and stocky, Greek boy who I'd briefly glimpsed before we left Thessaloniki (who must be Krystos) hopped out of the driver's seat. He had dark brown hair, a mischievous smile and surprisingly warm and friendly eyes. Darius climbed out the back seat of the vehicle on the passenger side while red-headed Charlie climbed out of the other rear seat. Another attractive young man who I hadn't yet met followed Charlie out. He had blond hair, bright blue eyes, chiseled features and muscular arms, that appeared to be almost as powerful as Darius'. That left only Sebastian who didn't appear to be moving.

"Get him out," David instructed, gesturing impatiently.

I watched silently and without outwardly displaying any emotion. I still had to fight my apprehension as Darius leant forward and reached for the door with a purely evil smile. Just before his hand touched the handle the door flew open with unnecessary force and unpredictable speed, slamming into Darius's large form and knocking him back into the side of our SUV. The door had somehow caught him in the face and a trickle of blood ran from the side of his mouth.

Sebastian smoothly slid out of the car, a tight, bitter smile twisting his mouth. I immediately noticed his swollen lower lip and the dark bruise along his cheekbone. He stood slightly hunched over as if it hurt him to straighten up and he was obviously favoring his weight on one side.

"You bastard," Darius growled, wiping the blood from his mouth and glaring at Sebastian with enraged eyes. He took a menacing step forward. Sebastian stood his ground, watching Darius with a dangerous look of his own.

"Leave him," David snapped, his sharp tone immediately halting Darius's advance.

"He owes me blood."

"Leave him," David repeated. "I wanted him out of the vehicle and he's out. I warned you not to become complacent with either of them."

"That would certainly be a mistake," Sebastian agreed, boldly limping past Darius and coming right up to my side. He ignored all of the Others as if they didn't exist, an impressive feat considering we were closely surrounded by the seven of them.

"They didn't hurt you, did they?" he asked me quietly, his eyes intense, his tone urgent. I could feel his eyes scanning me over, taking inventory and looking for any possible signs of harm or discomfort as I had just done with him.

"Who would dare?" I murmured back, speaking just loudly enough that some of the Others might overhear. Sebastian relaxed slightly and even looked like he might smile for a second. "What did they do to you?" I raised my voice slightly more this time, ensuring the Others heard my sweet and disapproving tone. Several of them shifted uncomfortably, causing Sebastian to arch a questioning brow.

"I didn't want him to attack me!" Darius half-yelled, cutting off Sebastian's response as he punched the SUV door closed with his fist. A large dent was left in the metal but Darius didn't even flinch. His face was flushed bright red and beads of sweat were forming against his forehead, clinging to his spiky, dirty-blonde hair.

"You just didn't think he'd dare try it again, not after what you put him through," Krystos commented with a laugh. "You probably actually wanted a reason to hit him." I wasn't quite sure what to think of him, even his low voice was friendly. He looked like the kind of guy who would always keep the mood light and be ready for a good laugh. He was the complete opposite of the image I'd conjured of the Others in my mind. There was absolutely nothing dangerous or threatening about him. I tried to keep David's warning about complacency in mind.

"We had a fun ride," Charlie commented with a half-smile. He appeared to be addressing his comment towards either David or myself, it was difficult to tell as he didn't entirely meet either of our eyes.

"Let's just get down to the boat," Jai cut-in. He was definitely nervous, his eyes constantly shifting and small beads of sweat forming on his forehead also. I wasn't sure exactly what was shaking them but I could only hope it had something to do with me.

"Where are you taking us?" Sebastian demanded, slipping his hand into mine as he spoke.

"The Necromanteion," I answered. Sebastian turned to look at me sharply, the name obviously meaning more to him than it did to me. The Others who had been riding in the other vehicle also looked surprised that I had been kept so well-informed.

The blonde beefcake who had been silent until then, stepped forward. "Come on, let's go."

"Lead the way, Francois," David replied, gesturing to the side of the parking area where a long ramp led down to the dock.

The blonde nodded his agreement and then marched ahead, leading our small group, with Sebastian, David and I in the center, down towards the dock.

I hadn't spent much time on sailboats growing up. My father didn't sail, my mother wasn't the outdoorsy type and I was rarely allowed to go out unaccompanied. The few times I had been out on the ocean was with Clarke and his family and despite the company, my memories of sailing were surprisingly pleasant. I enjoyed the feel of the wind on my face and in my hair, the smell of the sea and the sound of the boat cutting through the splashing waves and bouncing gently on the water. I felt almost disappointed when Francois, the platinum blonde leading the way, brought our group to a stop in front of a completely ordinary-looking motorboat with no sails. The paint was peeling in places and barnacles were growing just below the water line. It was fair-sized but there would only just be enough room for the nine of us.

"Krystos, Darius, take them into the cabin," David instructed as we climbed aboard. I idly wondered why the others deferred to him so easily and if it had something to do with his previous friendship with Sebastian? It wasn't a topic I was about to bring up.

Sebastian boarded ahead of me and then gallantly offered his hand. That he could still be so considerate and such a gentleman despite the dire circumstances and his obvious injuries was endearing in the most deep and painful way. He looked at me strangely as I took his hand, reading the powerful emotions I thought I had hidden in my eyes. It made my heart and soul ache, knowing that in such a short time, I would have no choice but to say goodbye to him.

"This way," Krystos said with a smile. He had hopped aboard just after me and was now gesturing towards the open cabin door. I eyed the small space with distaste.

"I'd rather remain above deck."

"So would I," he agreed, glancing up quickly to look longingly at the warm, summer sky stretching out above us. "But this is the way it must be."

"Move it!" Darius barked from behind us. I felt him step on board as the boat shifted under his heavy weight. I slowly turned to come face-to-face with him.

"Do not speak to me in such a tone," I commanded in my sweetest and deadliest voice. In that moment, I could feel Caoilinn's spirit alive within me and I wasn't afraid at all. I met his gaze with my own piercing, sapphire eyes and wasn't surprised when he looked away.

"I'll do what I want to," he growled, though he still didn't meet my eye.

I continued to glare at him. I was vaguely aware of the others watching – some with curiosity, others with open wariness and apprehension. I took a step closer to him, ignoring Sebastian's sudden hand on my arm. I waited until Darius finally looked up and met my eye, and then I lowered my voice to a soft and seductive caress.

"If you think what you want still matters, you're even stupider than you look," I warned, the words springing to my lips automatically and without thought. "And once you understand what I want, you will regret the choices you have made today with every aspect of your minuscule existence and be begging for my forgiveness."

Darius's eyes narrowed and his lips pressed together tightly. I thought some of the redness might have been washed from his pallor.

"Caoilinn!" David's voice snapped from the dock. He pushed his way forward and boarded the ship with one smooth stride. "Do I need to watch you at all times myself?"

"Whatever you want," I replied innocently. I carefully slid my hand into Sebastian's and then led him past Krystos and the Others and into the awaiting cabin, gliding gracefully forward with my head held high. I had never felt so alive. It was empowering to face danger so boldly with such unwavering confidence, and suddenly, I wondered if my wants might just be powerful enough, if I dared to risk it all?

After a sharp gesture from David, Krystos and Darius followed us into the cabin. It was a small and dismal space with just enough room for the four of us to sit around the square table, Sebastian and I on one side and our guards on the other. There were two small windows letting in a bit of natural light but it was still dark and gloomy within. The cabin entrance was narrow and the dark cupboards and clutter-filled shelves only added to the feeling of claustrophobia. I sighed impertinently.

"I hope we won't be going too far," I commented to the air. Darius ignored me but Krystos met my questioning glance with a ready smile.

"Just upriver a little ways, it won't take too long," he assured me, almost cheerfully. It was strange to have to fight the urge to smile back.

"How does The Order use the Necromanteion as their temple? Isn't it a tourist site?" Sebastian asked.

"We only meet there occasionally; we aren't disturbed if we don't want to be," Krystos explained.

"Shut up!" Darius snapped, slamming his hand against the table in irritation. "David said no talking."

I arched a cool eyebrow at him. "Did he?"

"Yes," Darius hissed back but again, without meeting my eye.

"This is going to be a boring boat ride," I commented.

"It can't be any worse than the trip here," Sebastian pointed out, copying my dry, sarcastic tone. Krystos grinned at us but didn't say anything else. Darius glowered.

"Tell me more about the Necromanteion?" I politely requested, speaking only to Sebastian but including Krystos in my gaze.

"I'm afraid it'll have to wait," Krystos cut-in apologetically.

Just then the boat's motor started up, the noise filled the small cabin and drowned out all chances of continuing our conversation. The objects on the shelves began to rattle and vibrate as the boat slowly pulled away from the dock, the gentle rocking motion increasing as we moved further out into the waves and open sea.

I sighed, leaning into Sebastian's side and trying to appear relaxed. Inside, I was nauseous, exhausted and growing more apprehensive by the second. I closed my eyes, shutting out the world so that I might focus on defining my vague plan and fully committing myself to my chosen course of action. I knew that the only way my plan could possibly work was if I wanted this with one hundred percent certainty.

As we traveled out of the harbor and around the narrow point of land, I caught the occasional glimpse out the window of pristine, turquoise waters and high cliffs and coves along the shore. Our speed increased and the waters gradually grew choppier, the gentle lurch of our boat becoming more of a rough, tossing bounce through the wild waves that jarred my bones and eventually broke my concentration.

The boat slowed down again as we began navigating the rougher waters. I could see out the small window that we were passing quite closely to large, jagged rock formations that rose out of the water like deadly fangs, ready to crush and consume our vessel.

"We're entering the Acheron delta now," Krystos shouted out over the noise of the boat's motor. Darius glared at him but Krystos just shrugged and grinned. I looked to Sebastian questioningly and he bent his head to speak directly in my ear. He still had to yell to be heard.

"We'll be traveling up the Acheron River – known in mythology as the River Styx."

I frowned and he turned his head, offering his ear to my lips.

"I don't like the sound of that."

He met my eyes and his own were full of worry and fear. He squeezed my hand tightly beneath the table.

"I'll save you somehow," he promised, lowering his voice so I could barely hear him despite his lips and breath brushing against my ear as he spoke.

I smiled, and sadly kissed his cheek before he pulled away. I didn't dare say what I was thinking aloud, not even to him. I was beyond saving – we all were.

As our boat slowly putted upstream, the door to our cabin opened and Francois gestured for us to come above deck. I was more than happy to oblige but rose slowly, following Sebastian out of the cabin with a steady and dignified grace.

There was little room for us above deck. We were forced to stand, crowded in amongst the Others. I guessed that we were nearing our destination now and looked around with a mix of anticipation and dread.

I could see why the Acheron River was thought to be the mythological River Styx – the river that the Ancient Greeks believed one must travel to enter the Underworld, the world of the dead. The trees that lined each side of the river rose up thickly and blocked out much of the day's bright sun, their boughs dipped into the dark and muddy waters. Flies buzzed in the air and there was a disturbing scent of rot and decay that clung to the humid breeze. Despite our boat's loud motor, there was a strange and heavy silence that weighed down upon us along with the stifling heat. No matter how calm and composed I was trying to appear, I couldn't push aside the creeping sense of unease that was shadowing my heart and chilling my soul. I could see it affecting the Others too, their expressions growing even more solemn, their eyes darting around uneasily, their stances shifting and their confidence wavering. Only David appeared to be unaffected. He was as cold and calm as ever.

David cut the motor and let the boat drift up to a small dock that had appeared on the side of the river, nearly hidden amongst the shadows and tall reeds. Nathaniel and Charlie easily leapt from the boat and onto the wooden dock, tying the ropes and securing the motorboat with a practiced ease.

The flies buzzed around us and the water quietly lapped at the boat's sides. Every now and again the boat would bump noisily against the dock, making us all flinch at the loud, knocking sound. A sickly, warm breeze stirred the air and sent chills down my spine. I clutched onto Sebastian's hand tightly.

"Let's go." David's voice cut through the eerie silence.

He stepped up onto the rail of the boat and stood balanced with one foot on the dock. He turned around, holding his hand out towards me just as gallantly as Sebastian had done. There was nothing warm about his expression or the look in his eyes, he seemed to be taunting me, daring me to take him up on his challenge.

"Caoilinn?"

I hesitated only a second longer before releasing Sebastian's hand

and gliding forward to accept David's firm yet cold grip.

"Thank you." I spoke coolly, my head held high as I managed with surprising grace to climb out of the boat and onto the dock, coming to a smooth stop by Nathaniel's side. He took a small step back from me.

Once we were all off the boat, David led the way up a small path leading away from the river and winding up the steep hill. It felt more like we were in the jungle than in Greece with the thick grasses and trees around us and the steamy, humid air that seemed to be suffocating us all.

We walked in silence, the Others occasionally muttering comments back and forth but never loud enough or long enough for either Sebastian or myself to overhear. We had all worked up quite a sweat when we finally approached a hillside village several kilometers away from the river. I was surprised when David took a fork in the path that led us away from the village and around to the hill that rose up behind it.

"The Necromanteion is an underground temple, hidden within the hill," Sebastian whispered to me as we walked. No one tried to stop us from talking so he continued in a low and soft voice. "In ancient times, people would come here in hopes of conversing with the dead. They would stay underground in the tunnels for days, fasting and given nothing to eat or drink except for hallucinogens from the priests. Then they were brought to the main chamber, into the Underworld itself to gain knowledge and wisdom from the dead. Many did not survive the trial or were half-mad by the end of it."

Someone cleared their throat loudly behind us and we fell into silence once more. Sebastian's whispered words of this place's dark history echoed through my mind and haunted my thoughts as we continued hiking up the trail.

The trees grew more sparse, the grasses taller and drier, the earth rockier and bare. Up above us, not even a quarter of the way up the hill, rose an arched entrance of large, squarish-shaped stones, marking the entrance to the Necromanteion and the Underworld.

David marched ahead and through the entrance. We had no choice but to follow.

"This is just one of the many entrances," Sebastian whispered in my ear as we approached the intimidating archway. "This hillside is full of caves and tunnels, many of which lead to the Necromanteion temple and its chambers within. I don't imagine tourists typically enter by this route or travel too far into the tunnels. One could easily become lost for days."

I didn't respond. I told myself it was because I was out of breath from the heat and the steady hike, and that it wasn't fear that was choking the words in my throat and sucking away my breath.

I found myself following David through the archway and into the shadows beyond. The air immediately felt cooler than outside and goosebumps arose all over my body while my eyes adjusted to the darkness. The Others took out flashlights and lanterns as they entered behind us, the beams of light weakly fighting against the heavy, consuming darkness. We shuffled forward in single file, approaching a steep and narrow staircase that disappeared down into the depths of the Earth.

"Watch your step," David cautioned as he began descending the stairs.

My breath was loud in my ears as I followed him, my heart pounding in my throat. I used one hand to feel along the rough, jagged stone walls as I slowly took the stairs one at a time and with the other hand I tightly gripped onto my necklace as if holding onto life itself. Its warmth was an invaluable comfort in this cold and dark place.

The staircase seemed to go down forever. I had no idea how deep we were when we finally reached the bottom. It abruptly ended and we came out into a narrow and low tunnel that had been carved into the rock itself. David marched straight ahead, barely waiting for us to keep up as he navigated the many twists and turns and led our group ever deeper into the bowels of the Earth.

After some time, I thought I saw the soft, flickering glow of firelight ahead. After spending so much time in the thick, impenetrable darkness I thought at first I might be imagining it, but sure enough, as we rounded the next bend in the tunnel we found ourselves approaching a large cavern that was filled with the flickering light of many pitchy torches.

"David, welcome." A beautiful Asian woman stepped forward to block our entrance, her surprisingly tall figure and striking beauty imposing. She had beautiful, jet black hair that flowed to her waist and small, perfect features with large, dark eyes that dominated her face.

"Lily," David answered with a slight nod of his head.

She smiled in response and lifted a navy-blue cloak over his shoulders, fastening it with a large, golden clasp. It was similar to the thin gray cloak she wore but hers had a smaller, silver clasp.

"Please, join the other Originals," she gestured with her head to the far side of the large, shadowed cavern where three other cloaked figures stood waiting. Even from this distance, I recognized Angelina's slighter figure amongst their midst.

Sebastian and I were ignored as the Others slowly stepped forward. Jai was also given a navy blue cloak and was instructed to stand with "the Originals". Nathaniel, Darius and Charlie were given gray cloaks and moved to stand at one side of the large chamber. The remaining two from our group (Francois and Krystos) greeted Lily with polite nods and then moved to take their places on the opposite side of the chamber where a girl with dark-skin and short, black curly hair stood with a stout-looking young man who had longish, sandy blonde hair – none of them wore cloaks.

I glanced around the huge chamber, fighting the fear clawing at my stomach and the panic that was threatening to overtake my tentative focus and wavering calm. The Others had formed a half circle, the Originals in their blue cloaks in the middle, the gray cloaks to the left and the plain-clothed ones to the right. Their faces were all expressionless as they watched Sebastian and I with cold, accusing eyes, the torches causing shadows to flicker across their frighteningly beautiful faces. Despite the torchlight, the cavern was filled with darkness and shifting shadows, the archways carved into the rock above us disappeared into mysterious blackness as if we really were standing upon the boundary of the living and the dead. I could almost believe the spirits of the dead were gathering here; I felt Mags' presence in the torches' flickering flames, and I imagined Walter's accusing eyes peering down from the thick blackness above me. I tried to push these thoughts away but was still acutely aware of them. The air was colder down here and there was a musty scent in the cold, damp air that made me want to gag – it was the smell of death. I was terrified but I tried to embrace my fear and accept it. I would use it somehow, I promised myself.

"Seamus, Caoilinn," Lily murmured our names softly. The ice in her voice was challenging, despite her gentle tone. Her quiet words echoed unnaturally around the chamber, bouncing back upon our ears in a harsh clash of noise. "Step forward."

We had no choice but to obey as the Others wanted us to. Sebastian took my hand and escorted me forward into the center of the half-circle that the Others had formed. We held hands with a grip that was tighter than usual. My fingers dug into Sebastian's hand in a way that was both desperate and intense. I wished that I would never have to let him go but I knew our time together was ticking away on its final countdown.

Lily stepped around us to take her place with the other four Originals. Once she had joined them, one of the two men I didn't recognize stepped forward, his dark brown hair cut close to his skull, his square jaw and rigid stance all gave him a military appearance. He fixed his narrowed dark eyes on Sebastian, completely ignoring me.

"Seamus Maitiu Coghlan, you have been summoned here today to stand trial and bear punishment for your crimes against The Order," he intoned in a loud and booming voice. I steeled myself against the sound, refusing to shrink back from him.

Sebastian smiled wryly. "It's nice to see you too, Oscar."

"You created The Order and then you attempted to destroy it," the other man I didn't know spoke up, his words bitter and his contempt clear. He wasn't as handsome as the rest of the Others, though he was still attractive in his own way with his wavy blonde hair, hooked nose and wide-set, blue eyes.

"The Order was never meant to be," Sebastian calmly agreed. "Surely you can see that, Jonathon. Haven't you all questioned your existence at some point throughout the years? Haven't you all wondered who you really are and why you are here? Haven't you felt how unnatural, how immoral your powers are and questioned whether it was right for them to have ever been granted to you?"

"You attempted to erase the memories of your fellow brothers and sisters. You manipulated us and used us to fulfill your own wants and then abandoned us when we no longer met your needs. You hid the truth of our abilities and potential from us, and you broke your sacred vows to The Order – the vows that you swore upon with your life." David spoke slowly and calmly, his eyes holding Sebastian's steadily. There was an emotion hinted at behind his cold, hard accusations that I thought might be betrayal and pain. I wondered if I were merely imagining it.

"You manipulated and confused my thoughts. You aided Magdalene in keeping Caoilinn and I apart. You erased my memories, distorted my perceptions of the truth and took from me a vow that would never have been willingly given," Sebastian answered just as evenly. I could see the anger rising in his eyes and I sensed his sudden fear.

It was a tense moment. David and Sebastian's eyes were locked together, the Others all waited in silence. The only sound was the occasional crackle from one of the torches and my own breathing that sounded unnaturally loud in my ears. I couldn't stand it any longer.

"What vow?" I asked. My tone demanded an answer, my words echoing ominously around the chamber that more and more, was feeling like my tomb.

All eyes turned to me except for Sebastian's. He continued to glare steadily at the five Originals before us – his accusers, judge and jury.

"Seamus made a vow before both the five Originals and the four members of the Second Order." Oscar indicated the four others standing to our side in their gray cloaks. "He vowed that he would never reunite with Caoilinn. He swore that he would never combine his powers with hers and share in her strength and secrets. He promised that he would never abandon The Order for her and if he were ever to do so, he vowed to gladly pay with his life."

A chill ran down my spine, paralyzing my whole body with fear. The sudden look in David's eyes made my blood run cold.

"It is time to live up to your grand words," David murmured to Sebastian. His expression was strange, a mixture of regret and cruel anticipation. I watched in horror as Darius stepped forward from the side of the circle, reaching for Sebastian. What was even more terrifying, was that Sebastian made absolutely no move to run or to fight. A silent scream tore through me, shaking my whole body and ripping up and out of my throat to meet my silent and motionless lips. But I couldn't move or make a sound either – I could barely breathe. And abruptly I knew, that Sebastian was about to die.

Chapter Eighteen – Silence and Darkness

I didn't notice Lily come up beside me until she placed her small hand delicately on my arm. She seemed to be particularly wary not to touch my skin, her touch so light on my shirt sleeve that her fingers seemed to almost float above it.

"You must step aside now, Caoilinn," she instructed me. She only had to apply the slightest pressure on my arm to get me to do what she wanted. I was both terrified and infuriated to be manipulated with such ease. I had spent far too long feeling powerless and afraid. For years I had let my parents and my peers dictate my life and make decisions for me. And for months now I had been running non-stop, constantly afraid for my life and Sebastian's, never able to relax or to go home. I was done with being frightened, I was finished with quietly standing by and letting others control my life. A power was steadily growing inside of me along with my righteous rage, the silent flames of which were both familiar and long-forgotten.

Lily led me to the side of the half-circle. I let the fire continue to build within me, my eyes blazing down on Darius and Charlie who had now joined David. I watched in horror and outrage as they each took one of Sebastian's arms and threw him to the ground. Sebastian didn't resist. His skull met the hard, rock floor with a loud and sickening crack. Images flashed before my eyes at the sound, the nightmarish memories of last winter when he had been attacked and had nearly died cutting through my mind and severing the last of my doubt. My necklace blazed against my chest, my anger grew to consume my remaining fear and yet still I was unable to move, unable to speak, absolutely powerless still to resist the Others or to aid Sebastian in any possible way. I could do nothing but watch.

Darius and Charlie each knelt on one of Sebastian's arms while Krystos stepped forward to hold Sebastian's legs. There was no humor in his dark eyes now, only the solemn shadows of death.

I watched in mute horror, hardly able to believe what was happening as the five Originals moved forward, each pulling a large ornamental knife from their robes with curved blades that were obviously sharp and more than ready to be used. There was something strikingly familiar about those knives. Something stirred deep within me at the sight of them, my stomach clenching, my breath catching in my chest. My mind flashed backwards in the blink of an eye and the knowledge struck me with terrifying certainty – those were the same knives that the Sisterhood had used to murder Caoilinn with. I had no doubt in my mind that those weapons had been provided by Mags, probably to carry out my own murder. I could imagine her outrage at learning they had been turned against Sebastian, though it would be but a pitiful spark against my own fury that raged barely within my control.

My mind worked rapidly and calmly as I watched the five Originals surround Sebastian. The torches flickered and dancing shadows stretched about the cavern like demons creeping through the dark boundary between the world of the living and the world of the dead. I knew I had to do something. I could feel that Sebastian was hanging on the cusp of life and death right now. Time slowed down and weighed heavily upon the air. I could almost count the seconds he had left to live. I was the only one who could possibly save him but what was I supposed to do? There had to be an answer, there had to be a way. But how? I was certain Caoilinn had left me a clue; that the myth of Ireland's Earth Mother was meant to save him somehow. I knew that I should have learnt something from the tale, that she had meant for me to come to some kind of realization… that I could end this all… by somehow sacrificing myself or…

I gasped. Only Lily who stood the closest to me heard the soft sound, her eyes flickering my way suspiciously. The realization hit me and with it came a cold and powerful control. The fire in my heart turned to ice. There was absolutely no doubt in my mind anymore – I knew exactly what had to be done.

"Stop." I spoke clearly and calmly, my voice commanding more attention than it ever would have if I yelled. Whether it was because

I wanted them to or not, the Originals stopped their advance on Sebastian and all eyes were suddenly on me. Their faces betrayed little emotion but I could sense their surprise. I took two steps towards them, not yet close enough to interfere but near enough that they knew I was no longer bound by their control, not entirely at least.

"How is she…?" I heard Nathaniel whisper.

"Silence! Focus!" Oscar yelled, his loud, drill-sergeant's voice echoing around the chamber and into the darkness above.

"Calm yourself, Oscar," I chastised, frowning in disapproval. "You have no need to be alarmed. Your wants no longer prevent me from aiding Seamus as I no longer wish to save him," I calmly explained.

The Originals stared at me with disbelieving eyes, the others watched in astonishment and disbelief. Sebastian lay on his back with his eyes tightly shut and his lips moving rapidly as if he were speaking to himself. I was worried for a second that my nearly perfect imitation of Caoilinn had once again confused his mind, but I abolished the thought almost the instant it occurred; I didn't have the energy to spare to worry over it. At this point, it was much more important to save Sebastian's life now and worry about his sanity later. And besides, it would be better if he were confused, if he didn't truly understand what was going on until it was too late for him to stop me.

"I don't believe you," Jonathon stated flatly, narrowing his eyes as he stared down his bent nose at me.

I shrugged, indifferent.

"She lies!" Angelina chimed in. The others remained silent and expressionless.

"He has made too many mistakes, done too many wrongs and committed too many crimes against us all. For that, there is a price he must pay and I want him to be punished," I coldly pronounced. Sebastian's eyes opened as my words seemed to have finally broken through his mad mutterings. He arched his back slightly and tilted his head back, staring up at me with confused and disbelieving eyes. It would be hard for any of them, including Sebastian, to doubt my conviction, my absolute honesty because I wasn't lying. I would speak no words but the truth – this couldn't possibly work otherwise.

The five Originals slowly lowered their knives but they did not put them away or step back. David watched me with suspicious eyes, the shrewd intelligence within them shining brightly.

"What kind of trick is this?" he demanded.

"I speak to you nothing but the truth. I no longer want Seamus to be my eternal companion – it was a mistake right from the start. I never truly wanted him this way. I needed friendship, companionship – I wanted to find another like myself, so I created one."

"No, stop! Don't do this Gracelynn!" Sebastian called out as he suddenly seemed to guess at what I might be doing. Before he could say anymore, Darius ruthlessly kicked him in the side of his head, leaving his head rolling from side to side and his eyelids flickering as he struggled to remain conscious.

"What do you want, Caoilinn?" Jai asked softly, speaking for the first time since we'd entered the chamber. His gentle brown eyes probed into mine, willing me to speak the truth.

"I want to join with The Order, to lead you into a glorious new era," I pronounced with a small and tempting smile. "I will teach you the true nature of your magic and share with you the truths that I know. I will give you the lives and the potential that you have long been promised and that you deserve. I will give to you powers that rival my own and I will share with you my knowledge," I promised, my voice soft and hypnotic, enticing. I could see the glow of anticipation in some of the Others' eyes and I knew that they wanted to believe me. It was all I needed.

"And why would you do that? What's in it for you?" Jonathon demanded.

"No matter what you may or may not have to offer us, Seamus' life will not be spared," Angelina joined in. Her beautifully arched brows were pulling down as she watched me.

"I know."

Sebastian began tossing and turning restlessly again, his eyes had reopened though they were still unfocused, his expression wild.

"Stop, Caoilinn. Please," he begged. I thought I saw tears sparkling in the corners of his eyes. "Please don't do this."

I steeled my heart against his words, against the sound of pain and betrayal that cracked his voice. I slowly began moving towards him and was pleased when none of the Others stopped me. They all just watched, their faces blank except for their hesitant suspicion. I came to a stop just two feet away from Sebastian's side. It was with great effort that I didn't let out a sigh of relief as I had reached my goal. I couldn't give myself away now though.

"You are weak," I told Sebastian softly and sadly, my voice heavy with regret. My words weren't truly for him, I only needed the Others to hear them. I truly regretted that he was conscious at that moment for I knew the pain that I was about to cause him would be unforgivable. And yet still, I pressed on. "You are not the same man that I fell in love with two thousand years ago. You are not the same person who I bonded myself to, who I gave powers and promises to that have connected us through the hundreds of years we spent apart."

"No," he denied, his eyes wide with horror. He thrashed against the Others now who held him just as tightly. Tears openly fell from his eyes, his expression half-crazed.

I turned my attention back to the Originals, unable to look upon Sebastian any longer lest my conviction waiver.

"Let me join you. Let me lead you," I whispered, my words full of promises and laced with forbidden secrets and possibilities unknown. "I want for us all to be equals – that's all and everything I want now, I promise you. I will lead you all to your true destinies."

The five Originals considered me with flat and emotionless eyes. I could feel the others holding their breaths, hardly daring to move let alone speak up to their leaders. I knew how badly they wanted to believe me. I could feel their desire in the air. They hungered for more power and I was the only one who could offer it to them. I knew there was no way they would resist. I could sense how close I was to victory and I was both joyful and horrified at the prospect.

"Please, don't do this," Sebastian cried out again, his voice desperate and agonized. The sound of it echoing around the chamber nearly broke me, his pain bouncing off the walls and battering at my ears from every direction. Another kick in the head from Darius silenced him and he abruptly lay silent and still. I barely turned my attention his way, sensing that he still lived and having to be satisfied with that. I focused my entire being on the five people before me. This was my moment of truth.

"You will stand by and observe without hindering our actions while we end his life?" David asked, arching a questioning brow at me. I nodded my agreement.

"He must pay the price for the wrongs he has done."

"Why should we believe you?" Angelina demanded.

I shrugged. "His death is irrelevant. He will be reborn in the future and then perhaps he might meet the potential I once saw in him. But he is not the same person now that I made so many promises to years ago and regardless, he has broken most of his vows to me in the years that have separated us. You have kept us apart before with the aide of Magdalene; didn't I give him up easily enough then? Didn't you say yourself it was like I no longer wished to find him?"

I let the Others consider this in silence, allowing time for my words to sink in. I was almost grateful that Sebastian appeared to be unconscious now, noting out of the corner of my eye that his breathing was shallow and his pallor white. I tried not to let my thoughts linger on him for too long.

"I only ask that you grant me one favor before his death - let me break the Binding that I share with him first? Otherwise I will share in the pain of his death. It would not only be excruciating in ways that you can't imagine but it would also debilitate me for some time. Grant me this one mercy, and I shall ensure that all of your powers meet the full magnitude of my own."

"Perhaps we should allow the Binding to remain in tact," Jonathon suggested, his bright blue eyes looking thoughtful. "It would make a fitting punishment for rejoining with Seamus and for the murder you have committed of one of our own."

"No," Jai immediately objected. He shifted uncomfortably as the attention of the group was turned on him. "If the Binding remains intact his soul will be drawn to Caoilinn's again in his next life. Though he would be born without access to the Lost Magic, he could share some of Caoilinn's ability through the bond once he was close enough to her."

"This is true," I confirmed, giving Jai a slight nod of my head. He met my eyes for the briefest of moments and I could have sworn I saw something there. A silent understanding passed between us. I suddenly wondered if there could be others present who might have guessed what I planned, who might even want for me to succeed.

"Fine," David agreed. "Strip him of the Binding and be quick about it. My knife yearns to spill the blood of this traitor whom I once called brother."

Another chill ran down my spine as the words "spill his blood" seemed to echo eerily around the chamber. I nodded my agreement and stepped forward, gesturing for the Others to move back. The three holding Sebastian down hesitated, looking to David for approval.

"You don't want to be touching him when I remove the Binding," I warned them. "I'm not sure exactly what it would do to you but I can promise, if you feel even an ounce of his pain it will be nearly too much for you to bear."

David slowly nodded to the others that they should move back. The three rose together, slowly stepping away from Sebastian's still form on the floor. Sebastian and I were once again left alone in the center of the half-circle, the Others having all backed up now by several feet. I prayed that it were distance enough.

Sebastian lay with his eyes closed, his face pale and gray. A trickle of blood had run from his ear. His breathing was shallow and fast, a sheen of sweat glistening on his forehead despite the cold, damp air. I took a deep breath and then began speaking to him softly, my words just loud enough to carry to the Others' ears.

"You are no longer Seamus Maitiu Coghlan," I pronounced slowly and carefully. "You are not the same man who I fell in love with two thousand years ago. You are not the same person who I made promises and vows to that should have lasted an eternity. And so, I feel justified as I break those vows now."

Sebastian's eyes flickered, my words reaching down into his subconscious and dragging him back up to the present.

"I abolish all vows and commitments made between us. I am sorry, but your life must now run its natural course. You will die and you will be reborn without the magic I once granted to you — it will be lost to you from here on and into forever."

Sebastian's eyes fluttered open, his vision slowly focusing on my face as I reached for his left hand.

"Caoilinn?" he murmured, his words thick and sluggish as if he had just awakened from a deep sleep. "What are you doing?"

"I am breaking the Binding between us. The magic that has linked our souls for two thousand years, the bond that we have shared through so many lifetimes – I'm afraid it must be destroyed." My voice caught a little at the end as I stared down into his frightened and bewildered eyes. He shook his head slightly in denial.

"I don't understand. Why are you doing this? Please…" he begged.

"It is what I must do," I told him, speaking with a soft intensity that I directed solely at him. More than anything, I wanted him to understand what I was about to do – I needed for him to trust me. He blinked, his eyes suddenly focusing and clearing, his expression became one of calm acceptance.

"I trust you," he whispered, his lips barely moving as he spoke. I doubted that any of the Others had heard him, but still I spoke quickly, hoping to cover up the sudden change in both his expression and tone.

"I hereby break all vows and promises that commit us to one another. I strip from you the magic that we once shared," I intoned in a loud and clear voice. My words fell about the chamber flatly, without echoing as they should have. I was dimly aware of the Others stirring uneasily as some heard the discrepancy in my words. "I am sorry," I whispered, my voice finally breaking. My hands trembled as I pulled from his finger the ring inlaid with a piece of amber from my necklace and I focused my wants on breaking all Caoilinn's vows and promises to him. With the removal of the ring, I took away from him all the magic Caoilinn had bestowed upon him, once upon a time, and I used the loophole that she had left for both him and herself.

I had done the unthinkable. I had taken away my commitment to him and with it, I had stripped him of all his magic and all the magic connected to his – the magic of the Others. With my whole heart, all I wanted was for Sebastian to live and the only way for him to survive was for him to lose his abilities, for his magic to truly be lost and for him to lose the Binding to me. And the only way I could take away his magic was to give up my own as I had wanted to with every tiny fiber of my being. Through my dream memories of Caoilinn, I had gotten to know and understand her. I had come to the realization that she had only said it was impossible to remove the powers she had granted because she never thought it possible that she would be able to give up Sebastian or to give up her own ability. But although I had come to accept that Caoilinn was a part of me – I had also realized that she wasn't me. This was perhaps the one thing that she would never have been powerful enough to do, but I could do it and I had.

There was silence in the chamber but I could immediately sense the difference. The darkness that had hung overhead suddenly seemed thinner, more permeable. The torches seemed to burn brighter and the danger and fear that had filled the space was abruptly abolished with the shadows. I could tell the Others sensed the difference too, though they obviously didn't immediately understand what I had done. I felt an emptiness deep down inside where my magic had always been, even when I hadn't truly been aware that it was there. I felt like a piece of me were missing now and I was surprised by the sudden sense of loss and abandonment that was rising up within me. I had stripped the Lost Magic from us all but I reminded myself that I was not powerless yet – no, I would never be that again.

Sebastian slowly sat up as I slid his ring onto my finger, though in truth it was my ring, it had always been mine.

He turned to stare at me wonderingly, his eyes slightly wider than usual with fear. He was still pale but his eyes were bright and focused, his injuries healed and diminished by the last of my wants.

"It's gone," he whispered.

"It was never meant to be," I agreed.

He nodded thoughtfully, knowing the truth of my words.

"But how did you…?"

"They never expected me to give up my ability – Caoilinn never would have, so they didn't think to stop me. It was simple really and it was the only way to take away your powers and to take away theirs. That was the sacrifice that Caoilinn knew must be made but couldn't bear to ever make herself. The magic was always meant to be lost, it should have died with her and now I have finally righted the last of her wrongs," I softly explained.

"What have you done?" Oscar barked, an unexpected edge of panic to his loud, commanding voice.

I ignored him and pulled my necklace from around my neck, the leather thong that held it breaking as I did so. The amber glowed with an unnatural light, throbbing and sparkling like a firefly in my hand. It held all of the Lost Magic now – it had been the only outlet I could think of to contain the vast amount of ancient power and secrets. As long as I held it, I could still direct the magic to fulfill my wants but the same would be true for whoever held the necklace now. It was dangerous and I knew it must be destroyed. I took a slow, deep breath and focused my wants, directing the magic into a complicated design that would hold the thirteen Others in place and prevent them from interfering. It was difficult to control the actions of so many people at once, especially when I was drawing upon the magic through my necklace instead of directly from myself. I felt my control wavering as the Others slowly began to move forwards.

"I have to destroy it," I told Sebastian quietly, though it didn't truly matter anymore if the Others overheard. My voice came out low and strained as I struggled to focus on the spell and to speak at the same time. "It's going to be dangerous. If we survive, and we may not, most of our memories will be obliterated and the Binding between us will forever be broken; the spell still remains in tact for now but it must be broken in order for this to work."

The Others inched closer. My hands began to shake as I struggled to focus and form the complicated design in my mind that would complete my last spell. I needed to make sure Sebastian understood before I did this. I wasn't certain that I could "want" it enough unless I knew that he accepted my decision.

"Are you sure this is the right thing to do?" he asked. "If you erase the Binding and the past history between us… what if we don't know each other anymore? What if our love doesn't exist without the magic?"

"Then what kind of love is that?"

He considered, dropping his eyes to the ground.

"The necklace!" one of the men yelled. "Get it from her!"

The Others struggled to move closer, fighting against the magic that I was desperately trying to hold them back with.

"We'll know once and for all if our love is based on a magic that bound us together two thousand years ago or if it's something more," I pointed out. Sweat was beading on my brow as I struggled to concentrate, as I tried to be strong enough to hold them back.

Sebastian's frown brightened and he slowly smiled, the warmth and love in his eyes momentarily overwhelming.

"I already know the answer to that."

"Then what is there to fear?"

We shared one last smile before I closed my eyes, committing myself to what must be done and finally wanting it with my whole and complete heart.

"I'll protect you until the end," I heard Sebastian whisper.

I placed my faith in him and tried my best to ignore everything around me and to focus on the complicated design that twisted through my mind, heart and soul. The dark lines twisted and turned, looped and knotted and braided together in a pattern so complex I began to tremble and sweat as I willed the magic to submit into the correct form and laced it through the air, filling the chamber with its power.

As my concentration shifted to completing the design, my control over the Others weakened even more. I was dimly aware of Sebastian rising to his feet and moving protectively in front of me, ready to defend me as the Others slowly closed in.

I was aware of movement around me. I heard the definite sounds of a struggle and the loud crack of a bone breaking. Someone cried out in pain – or rage, it was difficult to tell. I pushed it all away, ignoring what was going on outside of me as thoroughly as possible as I focused with all my might on completing this complex and deadly design. The pattern had to twist in and on itself, starting and ending as one unbreakable line so that there was no clear beginning and no end. It was the most complicated spell I'd ever attempted and required more focus and magic than I'd ever imagined possible.

Sebastian suddenly cried out and at the same time, someone slammed into me. My concentration briefly wavered as I fell down hard on my back. The wind was knocked out of me but I didn't dare open my eyes or even try to move. I was only dimly aware of the sound of my own panting as I struggled to regain my breath. The back of my skull throbbed with a dull pain where it had connected with the cold, hard ground. I imagined if my eyes were open, my vision would be spinning as I teetered on the edge of consciousness. My mind pulled backwards, sliding further into the quiet place deep within me where the powerful dark design was being formed. I held onto my necklace while I fought to remain conscious. And I slowly drew more and more of the Lost Magic from the necklace, allowing the magic to find a home within me and to fill my mind, heart and soul with its powerful, ancient magic.

"No!" Sebastian yelled, his voice coming from just a few feet to the side of where I lay. The fear and panic in his voice seemed intensified as it echoed around the vast chamber. My heart was abruptly chilled, an icy calm taking over me as I realized one of us was about to die. There was no way I could ignore Sebastian's cry. My whole body responded to the sound, praying that there might be some way to help him. My eyes automatically flew open, desperately searching him out as I pushed myself upright. My head spun from my sudden movement and I barely managed to hold onto the image of the nearly-completed design in my mind.

A scream caught in my throat as I saw David lunging towards me, the wickedly curved blade of his knife extended and coming straight for my throat. Sebastian was only a half-step behind him but I could tell he wasn't going to make it in time. I knew this was the end, sadly, it had to be. The scream that had begun building in my throat changed to a sigh of relief as I realized, at least, that Sebastian was still alive.

Time stopped and my thoughts suddenly became crystal clear. I saw every detail of the scene before me, I saw every moment of my life behind me and it all abruptly made perfect sense. In the blink of an eye, I completed the pattern that I had been weaving in my mind. The lines fell together in perfect harmony and I knew that this was the way it was meant to be. Time started again.

David took the last step towards me, his dark eyes glowing victoriously, his hunger for revenge and violence twisting his handsome face into that of a murderous monster. And just as the tip of his knife made the first cut into the soft, unprotected flesh of my throat, I thrust my amber necklace against the ancient ring on my finger, reuniting the small, heart-shaped chip with the teardrop pendant it had come from so long ago. As soon as the two were rejoined I released the magic into the air, filling the chamber with its pattern of destruction and hope, and letting it braid and twist into the amazing and endless design I had created to contain it.

The last thing I saw was Sebastian's face, the cold terror in his eyes and the silent scream on his lips. The last thing I felt was the icy steel of David's knife, biting into my neck and burning pain down my throat. And then the world exploded in a flash of light that blinded my eyes, blasted my ears, drowned out my heart and my soul, and blazed through my entire being. Pain ripped through me, tearing up my arm that held the necklace and searing down my whole right side. I was consumed by the light that flared from my necklace as hot and bright as the sun. It burned through me in an endless torrent of heat and pain, wave upon endless wave. I feared that there would be nothing of me left behind when it was finally extinguished. And I accepted it.

Slowly, silently, the heat cooled, the light faded and I fell into a world of silence and darkness.

Epilogue

I opened my eyes and found myself in a strange place. The lights were bright here, the walls sterile and white. The air smelt strange, a mixture of antiseptic and stale-smelling laundry that immediately offended my nose. I blinked my eyes, trying to focus my vision and figure out what and where this place was.

I was in a hospital. I was in a private room with just the narrow bed I lay upon and a small bedside table beside me. The sun peeked in at the tiny window between the drawn blinds and reflected off the glass of a small television set, mounted in the upper corner of the room. I looked down at my body, trying to figure out what was wrong with me and struggling to remember why I was there.

An IV was inserted into the back of my left hand and I was hooked up to a drip that hung beside my bed. Bandages covered my whole right arm, completely obscuring my skin from palm to shoulder. I shifted tentatively beneath the rough, starched sheets that covered me and immediately gasped in pain. I wanted to throw up and scream at the same time, and ended up just panting in shocked silence. It wasn't just my arm that there was something wrong with – it was the whole right side of my torso, I realized. I lay as still as possible after that, fighting the waves of fiery pain and nausea that my slight movement had caused. It was while I lay there, quietly panting between my clenched teeth, that the door to my room cracked open and a familiar face peaked inside.

"Sweetheart, you're awake." My father spoke in an unexpectedly hushed voice as he stepped into my room and quietly closed the door behind him.

I was surprised to see his eyes were filling with tears, the mixture of joy and relief obvious on his face. I tried to smile back at him, happy to see him but still not fully understanding what was going on.

I was also still wrestling with the overwhelming pain that was crashing down upon me in steady waves. A blinding headache was steadily creeping through my temples, throbbing through my skull with each beat of my heart.

"Dad… what happened?"

"Let's not worry about that right now. The nurses thought you might awaken soon but still, you need to rest," he gruffly instructed, brushing the tears from his eyes as he came to take a seat beside my bed.

I nodded my agreement, still feeling bewildered.

"But I don't even know where I am," I said in a quiet and scared voice.

My father reached for my left hand, holding it between his two large and steady ones and patting the back of mine gently while carefully avoiding the IV.

"We're in Athens, at the hospital," he slowly explained.

I watched his face eagerly, distracted from my pain by this new information. He sighed and reluctantly continued.

"You were on a tour of some old caves just outside of Parga with a group of tourists and there was… an explosion of some kind."

I struggled to remember the events he was describing but my mind came up perfectly blank. I winced as the dull ache of pain between my temples increased to a piercing throb. It took me a second before I could speak – it was so hard to remember, to focus on anything.

"There was an explosion? Do you mean like a bomb? Please… I can't remember anything. Tell me what happened?"

My father hesitated, looking torn. He roughly cleared his throat.

"The authorities are still investigating it – there has been speculation of the explosion being some kind of terrorist attack. You were with a group of fourteen other tourists and had traveled deeper into the temple ruins of the Necromanteion than most tour groups allow. There was an explosion in the central chamber, it blew out part of the wall and half the ceiling collapsed in on you. All fifteen in your group were injured to varying degrees and knocked unconscious – all with significant memory loss. No one seems to remember exactly what happened. The doctors can't quite explain it…"

"Oh." I frowned, trying so hard to remember but no matter how deep I dug through my mind, my hands came up empty. I didn't even have the sense that I should remember; it was like there was nothing there where the memory might have been. "What happened to my arm and my side?"

"You were one of the three who was closest to the centre of the explosion," my father informed me, his eyes both angry and sad at the same time. "Nearly the whole right side of your body has been badly burned. You nearly bled to death also — a piece of shrapnel had cut through your throat, only just missing your windpipe and your carotid artery. If the rescuers had found you even a few minutes later…" My father abruptly looked away, rubbing at his eyes again and noisily clearing his throat. I watched and listened with near sick fascination. It felt like he were telling me a story about someone else, despite the matching pain that coursed through my body and burned at my throat.

"I was so afraid I'd lost you, Gracelynn. You don't know what a relief it is to see you open your eyes, to hear you voice — we've been waiting weeks. You both would have awoken sooner but the doctors thought it best to keep you in chemically-induced comas until the worst of the pain had subsided."

"Both of us?"

My father's expression soured, his displeasure obvious now.

"Yes, you and the boy you were traveling with — Sebastian. He has sustained almost identical injuries to yours and awoke just a few hours ago himself."

"Sebastian," I repeated, wondering over the familiarity of the name on my lips. A face flashed through my mind — black, unruly hair, color-shifting, gray-blue eyes, long lashes, perfect lips, piercings and mysterious tattoos. Unexpectedly, my mind focused on the details of his lips, their perfect shape, their softness and their warmth, the taste of them… "He's my boyfriend," I realized, speaking aloud.

I hadn't been asking but my father nodded his confirmation.

"Yes, something like that."

"And we were traveling together… we took a train through Europe and… there was a girl who traveled with us for a little while, I didn't really like her though but… what happened…?" I spoke my confusing thoughts out loud, trying to make sense of the bizarre and disjointed memories that were suddenly darting through my mind. I had only glimpses of images and brief flashes of knowledge of our trip through Europe. I could barely remember Sebastian at all, to tell the truth, let alone the places we had been or the people we had met. I wished I could remember why we had been so deep in those caves too and what had caused the explosion but I couldn't even remember traveling to the caves in the first place. All I remembered of Greece was a library I thought I might have visited and a flash of walking through a Greek city with someone, perhaps Sebastian, at night time.

"I wish I could remember," I whispered, my eyes filling with frustrated tears. It was frightening to have so many holes in my memory. My father instantly comforted me.

"It's not important, darling. The memories may come back to you but they may not. You may well never regain them – you should accept the fact that they are most likely permanently gone. All that matters now is that you are alive and you are safe. And in just a couple more weeks, we should be able to take you home."

"Home?" I echoed, struggling to remember where that was.

"Yes, you'll come back to Toronto with Dahlia and I – she's here too, you know. Your mother has even made arrangements to stay in Toronto for a while until you've recovered more – she's also in Greece, by the way."

"She is?"

"She's quite concerned about you, dear. I know your mother hasn't always been the most maternal but she does love you, in her own way. We're going to take good care of you, sweetheart, don't you worry. I've already lined up the best physiotherapists and plastic surgeons to work with you upon our return home," he informed me. I could tell he was trying to be reassuring in his gruff, take-control type of way but all of this information was overwhelming. The room starting spinning and a fresh stabbing pain drilled into my skull.

"Ah!" I gasped, squeezing my eyes shut and automatically reaching for my temple – with my right hand. The movement of my badly burned and injured arm sent even more agonizing pain coursing through my body. I was vaguely aware of my father calling for help as I slid, with silent relief, into the quiet, still darkness that beckoned to me.

Over the next week or so, my condition slowly continued to improve. The pain lessened and I was slowly weaned off the drugs I hadn't realized I was on (strong pain-killers including morphine and several others whose names I couldn't pronounce). My thoughts became clearer, my hazy memories of the past few months sharpened, but still – I remembered no new information about the explosion or the events leading up to it than I had the first day I awoke.

As my condition improved, I had several visitors whom I was able to tolerate for longer and longer periods of time as my mind cleared and my pain lessened. My mother came twice a day, her thin face drawn and lined. I was surprised to see her even though my father had told me she was there - and I was even more shocked by her genuine concern for me. She told me I looked awful, she criticized the hospital staff and the small size and plainness of my private room and she chastised me constantly, telling me that this was what I got for running away from home with an "obviously troubled youth" like Sebastian. But she also painted my nails for me, and brushed and braided my hair, and brought me magazines and books to read. She confided that she had been very lonely since Walter, a member of our household staff and close companion of hers whom I couldn't quite remember, had quit her service and disappeared. I almost believed it when she said she had missed me. There were definite moments when I even enjoyed her company – it was strange.

The police also came to visit me several times during my hospital stay. They always asked the same questions, wanting more details about what our tour group was doing in those ancient ruins and pressing me for more information about the explosion. I could tell them nothing new. It was both frustrating and terrifying to have such large, gaping holes in my memory though I was definitely starting to grow used to it. It was reassuring at least, to hear from my father, that none of the other tourists could remember anything either. At least I knew that I wasn't entirely alone.

But I was alone. Because though my mother visited me twice a day and my father and Dahlia spent most of the remaining daylight hours with me in my hospital room, I never once saw Sebastian. I knew he was awake and that he was in the hospital still. I even learnt from my father that his foster parents, the Jensons (whom I vaguely remembered), were also in Greece and staying in a hotel across the street from my father's. Apparently, they would be taking Sebastian home on the same day that we were to depart as his injuries were healing at a remarkable pace, almost identical to my own. But still, Sebastian never came to my room.

I felt so confused about my relationship with Sebastian. I couldn't remember much of the past year that we had known each other, there were only patchy glimpses of strange, foggy memories. Some information was there, and some wasn't. I knew he was my boyfriend, I knew I had been very much in love with him but… I couldn't remember exactly why. It was strange, remembering that you loved someone but feeling almost as if it were someone else's memories, someone else's thoughts and emotions that you were remembering. It was all so confusing, and disorienting, and frustrating. And it made it even worse that he was staying away from me. It made me feel both afraid and relieved in a sad type of way, that he might be feeling the same way as I did.

It was just two days before we were both scheduled to be discharged from the hospital in Athens that Sebastian finally came to my room. I was doing a lot better by then, wearing my own clothes instead of the plain, thin hospital gown and moving around a bit on my own. My burns were healing quickly and some of the bandages had already been removed, exposing the fresh, red scars and melted skin around my right wrist and forearm. My mother was horrified by these marks so I tried to cover them up when she came to visit to avoid upsetting her. I found them strangely fascinating though, often staring at my scars in bewilderment as I tried to recall how exactly I had gotten them.

It was late at night, long after visiting hours when Sebastian knocked softly on my door. He didn't wait for me to answer, just quietly slipped inside with a small and uncertain smile. He paused just inside the doorway, staring at me and suddenly looking confused, like he wasn't certain exactly what he was doing there or if he were making a mistake. I wasn't sure either.

I studied him in silence, noting the differences between the boy who stood before me and the one of my memories. He was a little thinner and paler than I remembered. His hair was slightly longer but just as messy as I recalled. He wore loose sweat pants and a t-shirt that showed his bandaged right arm with almost identical scars to mine peeking out from beneath the white, linen wrap. He was even more attractive than I remembered, I realized. His pink lips pursed together thoughtfully, his dark eyes were deep and intense above the faint marks that shadowed them. I suddenly felt intimidated, and unexpectedly shy.

"Hi," I greeted him softly.

"Hi," he answered. He hesitated again and then stepped forward. "Do you mind if I sit down?"

"Not at all."

He took the empty chair closest to where I sat in my bed. I slowly shifted my body upright more, wincing slightly from the twinge of pain in my side as I moved. I ran a quick hand through my shoulder-length, curly hair, feeling a little self-conscious. I was glad, more than ever, that my mother had helped me to bathe and wash my hair that morning.

"Do you remember me?" Sebastian asked. He definitely looked nervous, like he was holding his breath. The sight relaxed me a little.

"Yes. Well… mostly," I clarified. He smiled and I relaxed even more, automatically responding with a smile of my own.

"It's strange, isn't it? To remember but to not really remember at the same time."

"It's confusing," I agreed. I watched him curiously, trying not to stare too much at his attractive and compelling features. "How much do *you* remember, exactly?"

"Not much," he admitted. "I remember our school – Craigflower Academy. I remember spending time with you there, sort of. I can't remember many specific conversations or details but I remember you. I remember… your ex-boyfriend, Clarke, and his friends beating me up. And then I remember that we broke up for a few months but

I can't remember why exactly… and I don't remember getting back together but I'm sure that we did."

"Yes, we did." We shared another smile that made me blush and lower my eyes. I couldn't remember anyone making me blush in a long time. It was strange the reaction this boy was causing within me. "I can't remember why we broke up either – or how we got back together. I was mad at you about something, I guess it wasn't that important."

"And then, I'm told, we ran away together just before graduation."

"My dad told me that too. He wasn't impressed," I added with a smile.

"I don't know what we were thinking – literally," Sebastian agreed with a teasing grin. "I can remember riding my motorbike across Canada with you. We camped… I think. I actually can't remember that much of it to tell the truth."

"Neither can I."

"I know we visited your father in Toronto briefly but I can't remember what we did there…?" He looked at me questioningly, leaning forward expectantly in his chair. I looked into his eyes and for a moment, I found myself lost within their gray swirling depths, searching for that faint and familiar hint of blue. My heart skipped a beat and butterflies fluttered in my stomach. I looked away, trying to focus and calm myself as I prepared my answer. My father had told me about Sebastian and I visiting him in Toronto and it was one subject that I felt quite awkward about. Still, Sebastian deserved to know the truth or as much of it as I had been told, anyway.

"Well…" I paused trying to gather my thoughts. It was hard when Sebastian was staring at me like that. I couldn't believe how intense his eyes were. "My father told me we dropped in on him unannounced. I don't remember any of it really but he said it was obvious we were in some kind of trouble. He suspected we might be involved in some kind of criminal activity – maybe even with a gang or something. He said we both looked a little "strung out". Apparently, we convinced him that people were after us and that we needed to get out of the country fast. He bought us tickets to Europe and made travel arrangements for us, he had been planning on doing so for me as a graduation present anyway. He wasn't even quite sure why he helped us out – he told me he's regretted it every day since we disappeared but I guess we were quite convincing…"

"Oh." Sebastian frowned down at the floor. He looked as confused as I felt. "I don't remember any of that."

"Neither do I. I don't remember ever doing drugs or being involved in any gangs – or even any kind of trouble… Dahlia, my father's new wife, tells the exact same story though."

"Bizarre," Sebastian muttered. He winced, rubbing his forehead with one hand.

"Do the headaches still bother you much?" I blurted out.

He opened his eyes, looking at me strangely.

"Did I have headaches before?"

"No… I don't think so. I just meant… are you feeling better? They said our injuries were almost the same and I've been having headaches since I woke up," I struggled to explain. It was hard when I wasn't entirely sure what I meant.

"The headaches are slowly improving. David's been having them too – he was also standing close to the explosion. We were put in the same room so we've been chatting. I can't really remember him but at the same time… I'm certain we were friends. Everything about him is so familiar almost as if I know him as well as you – well, not quite." He shrugged with an almost embarrassed smile.

"My burns are healing fast," he continued. "It's strange, David was found even closer to you than I was but he doesn't have a single burn on his body – only bruises, a broken arm and the memory loss. A nurse told me that my burns are identical to yours on my arm, hand and side but my back was also badly burnt and so was the left side of my rib cage and part of my chest."

"Oh, I'm sorry. I didn't realize." I immediately felt guilty. My father had never mentioned that he had been even more badly burned than I.

"I didn't lose any blood though. I heard you nearly bled to death." His eyes flickered to the stitched wound still healing at my throat. He winced as if in pain himself but whether it was from imagining me bleeding to death or imagining the pain of my injury, was hard to tell.

"I survived. My throat doesn't bother me nearly as much as the burns do. I can't imagine how it must be to have them on your back and both sides… I'm sorry," I repeated, somehow feeling as if it were all my fault.

He shrugged. "Don't worry about it," he dismissed. He sounded like he really meant it too. "How are you feeling?"

"Better each day, but still very confused." I paused, trying to remember what we had been talking about. My short term memory seemed to have been affected from the explosion too and I often found myself struggling to focus and recall recent events. Each day got a little easier though. "Do you remember much of our trip in Europe?" I asked as I recalled where we had left off.

"Very little. We spent a few days in Ireland, and then I remember taking a train through South-Eastern Europe. My memories of Greece are patchy at best," he admitted.

"That's pretty much the same as me."

Our eyes met again and once more I felt that same, strange, electric spark between us. We both quickly looked away, my heart was still beating a little too fast.

"Do you remember…" Sebastian paused, taking a deep breath. I looked up curiously, aware that he suddenly appeared quite nervous. He met my gaze, smiling almost shyly as he slowly reached forward and took my left hand. His touch was soft and gentle, his fingertips smooth and warm as he gently stroked around the bruise from where my IV had been inserted. The familiarity of his touch and the new excitement he was causing me was both disorienting and thrilling. My lips parted slightly as he gently stroked my hand, his fingers lightly twisting at the small, silver ring wrapped around my finger. "Do you remember when I gave this to you?" he asked quietly, raising his eyes to mine as he spoke.

My breath caught in my chest.

"Yes," I whispered back. It was one of my few clear memories from the past year. I remembered every time I looked at it - how he had proposed, how I was engaged to a boy I felt I barely knew. But this time, with his warm hand gently holding mine, and his intense eyes right in front of me, I remembered even more. The magic of

The Giants Ring came back to me, that strange and ancient place we had camped out at where an inexplicable and exciting energy had hung in the very air. I remembered how we had stayed up all night talking and then how we had eventually slept in one another's arms, wrapped in blankets upon the sweet, dewy grass. I remembered the brilliant starlit dome that had filled my sight, arching from horizon to horizon above us and the silvery light of the moon that had made the whole world sparkle and glow under its magical light. I remembered the look in his eyes, the quiver to his voice as he had given me the ring and asked me to marry him. And suddenly, the memories no longer felt like someone else's but they felt like my own – they were my own. I nearly gasped from the wonder of it.

"I'm glad you remember," he confessed with a half-smile. "It's my clearest memory. I've been thinking about you almost nonstop since I awoke but I was so scared to come and see you. I was afraid that you might not remember, that you might not..." he didn't finish his sentence, he didn't have to.

"I do," I assured him.

He squeezed my hand in such a familiar and reassuring way that my heart instantly lightened and was filled with a new, bright optimistic hope that I knew I had forgotten.

"So what now?" I asked him.

His expression became more serious, his eyes even more intense as he considered. He really was quite handsome, my heart skipped a beat as our eyes met.

"I can't remember our plans beyond that we wanted to get married," he admitted. "And in light of recent events, it makes sense to postpone things, to take some time to..."

"Remember one another?" I suggested.

He shook his head with an amused smile. "No, that's not what I meant. There's a lot I can't remember but even still, I feel like I've known you my whole life." I felt another pleased blush threatening to creep into my cheeks as he spoke. I was starting to feel the exact same way, I realized. I wished he'd come to visit me sooner – this was the most sense anything had made since I'd woken up. It was the most calm and relaxed I'd felt in weeks. "I was going to say, maybe we should take some time to make some new memories together," he hesitantly suggested.

I smiled. "I love that idea."

"The Jensons, my foster parents, told me that you're going home with your father – to Toronto?"

"That's what he's arranged," I confirmed.

"Is that what you want?" he asked, taking me by surprise.

I took a moment to consider. Strangely enough, it was question I hadn't yet asked myself. What did I want?

"I don't want to disappoint him but… my only other option is moving back in with my mother." And no matter how hard she was trying right now, I still couldn't bear the idea of moving back in with her. Even if I couldn't remember the past few months clearly, I had a definite sense of freedom and independence that I knew I had recently gained and I didn't want to lose that.

"That's not your only option."

I looked at Sebastian curiously, feeling butterflies rise in my stomach once more.

"You could come home with me," he continued. "I've already discussed it with the Jensons and they'd be more than happy to have you. They have a guest room in their house – you've stayed with us before. Your mother would be close by and your father would be welcome to visit anytime." He watched me hopefully. I could tell he was holding his breath again as I considered. "I think David might come to Victoria too. He can't remember his family and no one's come looking for him. I'm the only friend he has right now... The Jensons would like you both to come back with us. And of course, I would too…" he babbled. He smiled, appearing to laugh at his own awkwardness as a familiar dimple appeared in his cheek.

I could faintly remember the Jensons, a quiet, kind and unassuming couple. I remembered their generosity, how they had taken me in before when I'd had no where to go. I remembered their warm and welcoming old home, and their cozy guest room, and I suddenly remembered how little time I had spent in it and how familiar Sebastian's bedroom had become during my stay there. I didn't even try to fight the blush this time.

"My father will be upset at the change in plans – especially with such short notice. My mother's going to be quite angry too but… it's nothing I can't handle."

A slow smile spread across Sebastian's face that warmed me through. I became lost in his eyes again and for a second, I felt certain that he was about to kiss me and my heart pounded hard in anticipation. But he pulled away, reaching into his pocket for something.

"I almost forgot, I have something for you." I watched curiously as he pulled something small and metal out of his pocket and held it out for me to examine.

It was an old, tarnished ring that was crushed and bent out of shape so badly it couldn't possibly be worn. There was something oddly familiar about it, especially the small piece of amber pressed into it that appeared to be in the shape of a tiny heart. I took it from him gingerly, turning it in my hand and wondering over the strange warmth that radiated from it and the captivating way the small bubbles in the amber stone sparkled and held the light. It felt almost as if it had a life of its own.

"One of the rescuers found it in the rubble near us. He came to the hospital to visit us both, to see how we were doing and he left it with one of the nurses, thinking it might belong to one of us. I've been saving it for you… it feels like it should be yours. I know it's too bent to wear but I thought you might want to put it on a necklace or something, a memento of a day neither of us can remember," he added with a wry smile.

"Thank you." I squeezed the ring tightly in my hand, overcome by the sudden certainty that everything was going to be okay. For the first time since I awoke, I felt amazingly confident and empowered. I didn't feel like a victim anymore – I felt like a survivor. "It'll be my lucky ring," I pronounced with a smile.

"I'm glad you like it. I've been wanting to give it to you since you woke up. And -" he paused, reaching out to lightly and hesitantly brush back my lose hair from my face. "And there's something else that I've been wanting to do."

My heart was steadily beating faster, my breath coming light and fast. I hoped I knew exactly what he wanted, but I played along anyway.

"Oh, and what's that?"

He heard the teasing tone in my voice and leant forward with a smile.

"This."

And his lips met mine in the most magical kiss I could ever remember experiencing. A passion was slowly building between us that stole my breath away and captured my heart. And even though I had lost so many of my memories, and I was left scarred and injured and confused, I was overwhelmed by the abrupt certainty that I had somehow ended up with absolutely everything I had ever wanted.

Acknowledgments

There are so many people to thank who have helped make this book come to life. Thank you first and foremost to all the fans of Amber Frost. Your support and enthusiasm helped me to write each and every word of this story. This book would not exist without you.

And I could never have written this book without the support of my friends – most especially, my Mommy-friends who remind me that I'm not really a crazy person, my life and kids are just crazy sometimes. Special thanks to Paul for being my Ireland-consultant; I really wish I could have fit in a pub scene with two old men and a Gaelic football game. And I'd also like to thank my friend Camille, who promptly answers any and all text messages no matter how random they are or how busy her own life is. You keep my website running, give great, dependable advice, and you don't judge or laugh too hard at some of my, er… "less-inspired" ideas. You're a true friend.

My family has been so amazing through out this process – what would I do without you? My noisy, messy, loud boys make me laugh and remind me what life is really all about. My sweet husband is so supportive and always knows how to make me laugh (by the way, you're not funny). My sister is absolutely always there for me. My family in England have loved and supported me from all the way across the Atlantic (and North America) and of course, there's my Mum. If I listed everything my Mum has done for me, I'd honestly have to write another book. So let's just sum it up with - thanks for being my Mum and being the best one imaginable. It wouldn't be so bad to turn into my mother… but I'll probably still try to avoid it!

And finally, I'd like to thank Michelle from Central Avenue Publishing. Thanks for being so easy to work with, and for believing in me and my work. All your hard work is appreciated so much! I write stories, you create books – I think we done good!

Thank you.

ABOUT THE AUTHOR

Suzi Davis is a British-born Canadian writer and artist and has been writing stories and poetry for as long as she can remember. Her current focus is on writing young adult novels whose genre allows her to explore the relationships between families, friends and young lovers. Interested in the paranormal, there is always an added element of magical fantasy to whatever tale she spins. Suzi lives on British Columbia's Vancouver Island with her husband and young sons.

SILVER DEW is her second novel and the sequel to the bestselling *AMBER FROST*.

Find out more about her at authorsuzidavis.com